Dangerous Reach

Forbidden Series ~ Four

Cynthia B. Ainsworthe

Other Works by Author

Cooking with Passion

Forbidden Footsteps

Remember?

Front Row Center's Passion in the Kitchen

Front Row Center

<u>*When Midnight Comes*</u> and <u>*Characters*</u>
Two short stories in the horror anthology *The Speed of Dark,*

Copyright © 2018 Cynthia B. Ainsworthe
All rights reserved. 2018 Copyright Words and Passion Publishing, first edition, 6590 49th Way, Pinellas Park, Florida 33781, United States
Printed in United States of America.
Cover design: Trish Jackson
London, England, street map: Baedeker's
ISBN 13: 978-0-9971253-5-1 Paperback
ISBN 13: 978-0-9971253-6-8 EBook EPub

IN DEDICATION ...

To Cindy, my loving daughter. You are always there offering support and love, eager to see me succeed. You're a true blessing in my life.

To Mitch, my husband. These years seem to fly by. I look at you and still see the loving man who is, and has been there from the very beginning, never faltering in your immense love and confidence in me.

To Mark and Adrienne. From the time when my wanting to write a novel was a mere item on my bucket list, your love and encouragement spurred me on and never wavered. Thank you so much.

To all my fan readers. Your loyalty is priceless. If it wasn't for you, my stories would remain in the dark.

WHAT OTHERS ARE SAYING ...

5 Stars! "Cynthia Ainsworthe's writing is fun, sexy and exciting. She uses her creativity and femaleness and turns it into pure sex with heart-stopping suspense. They are well-written reads. Once you start to read one, you won't want to put it down because you know you're in for a juicy ride." ~~ Terri Garber, renowned actress of screen and television. Quote by Terri Garber used with her permission.

Ms. Garber portrayed feisty *Ashton Main* opposite *Patrick Swayze* in the television miniseries adapted from John Jakes' novels *North and South, Book 1, 2, and 3,* as well her role as *Leslie Carrington* in *Dynasty;* roles in *As the Word Turns; Sporting Chance; Law and Order; Cold Case,* and innumerable other credits.

5 Stars! "I have read thousands of works from amateurs to Bestsellers that are looking to be adapted to film. Cynthia's writing is a perfect example of the quality that I look for in such a novel. The elegance of dialog and titillating description fits in nicely with those of the Bestsellers and transitions beautifully to the screen." ~~ Scott C. Brown, renowned Hollywood Screenwriter & Producer of screen and television.

Mr. Scott C. Brown is known for Andre Norton: The Grand Dame of Science Fiction & Fantasy (2016), Temecula Uncorked and Superman vs Doomsday (2017).

5 Stars! "Original and Riveting ... Front Row Center is a superbly crafted, riveting and original ... face-paced narrative ... confidently recommended for readings who prefer their romance literature to be sophisticated, complex, thoughtful, thought-provoking, and thoroughly entertaining ..." ~~ Midwest Book Review on novel *Front Row Center,* review at Amazon.com.

5 Stars! "This romance has it all ... lust, love, suspense, danger ... Great job!" ~~ Huffington Reviews on novel *Remember?,* review at Barnes & Noble.com.

5 Stars! "Cynthia Ainsworthe is one of those talented new writers that rewards readers to move past the NYT bestseller lists. Glad I discovered her book." ~~ T. R. Heinan, on *Front Row Center* review at Amazon.

IN ACKNOWLEDGMENT ...

To Trish Jackson, my wonderful editor. You are a jewel in my life, always ready to help and listen. No question is too trivial for your complete and unending attention. You are forever eager to investigate one more issue.

My gratitude to John B. Rosenman, a talented author and generous person on so many levels. Your encouragement has spurred me on to push myself to higher levels, forever striving to find that perfect word or elegant prose.

My heartfelt thanks to those who assisted me in the creation of *Dangerous Reach*. Sincere advice is a treasured gift.

"Reaching for more …
can be dangerous …"

~~ CB Ainsworthe

Dangerous Reach

Victoria Embankment, London

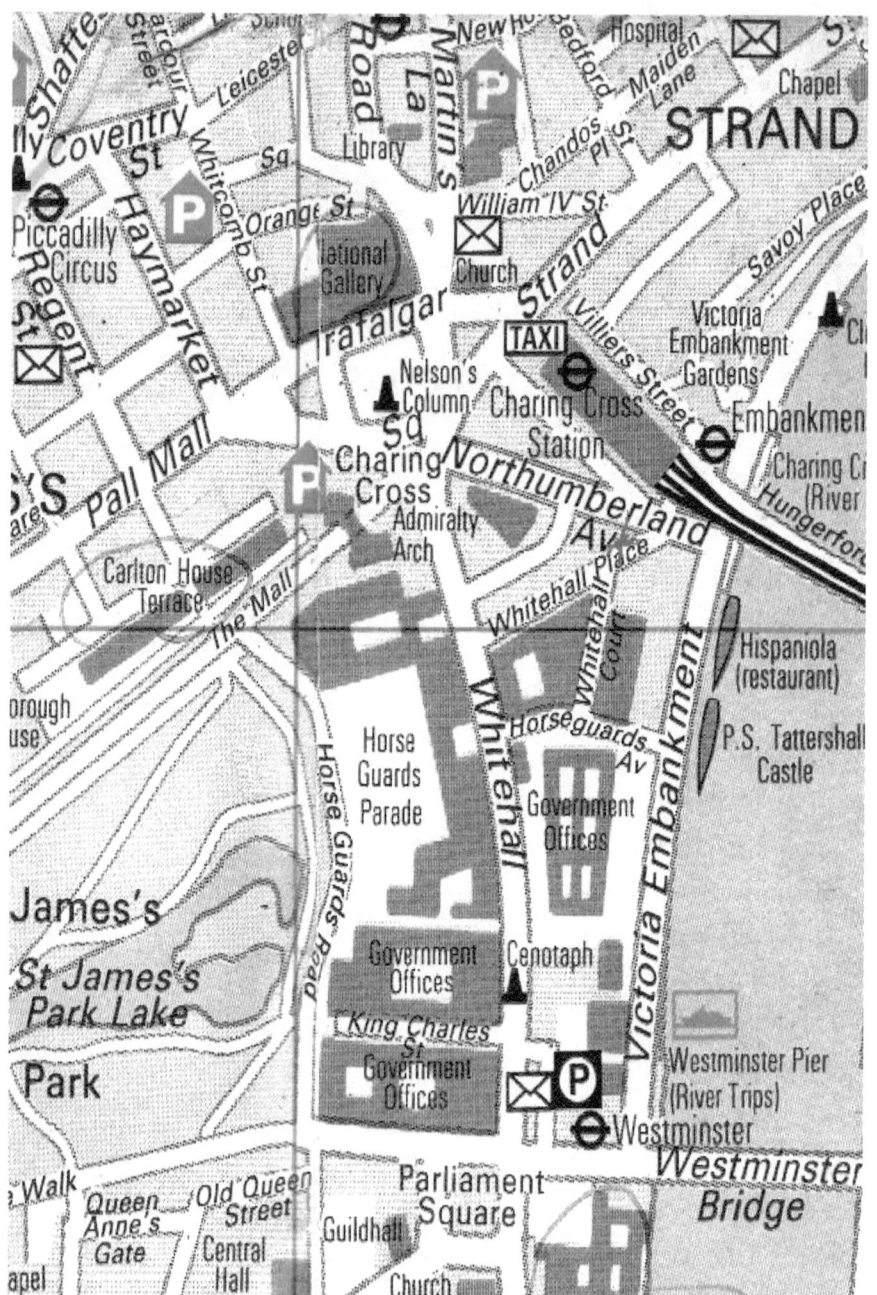

Location of Corinthia on Whitehall Place across from Whitehall Court.

One

"DON'T GO NEAR that hellcat, Trenton," David Carson advised his American friend with a smooth English accent. "She'll have you for dinner and will expect you to thank her for the privilege of being devoured." His twinkling brown eyes let his American friend know he knew secrets of London's who's who. A chiseled jaw and striking features caused the female members of the crew to give this Londoner a second glance on more than one occasion.

Trenton Lowe's mouth dried. He swallowed a couple of times. *I hope she's single. What a knock out!* He fought the beginnings of his arousal as he scrutinized the shapely redhead flitting around the cocktail area filled with royal and prestigious wedding guests. A few young men circled around her like sharks closing in on their next meal.

A slight fragrance from rose displays mixed with subdued conversation filled the room. He stood next to David, his new British friend and co-producer outside the ballroom at Claridge's in Mayfair, London, enjoying the champagne and delicacies served on silver trays by white-gloved waiters. Soft silver sounds from a string quartet elevated the ambiance to refined gentility.

Trenton didn't know many of the guests and sized up this gathering as being similar to the insincere Hollywood parties his profession demanded he attend. The only difference was this English beauty sashaying about the room, playing the sublime hostess role to the hilt. *Is she truly this audacious or overacting?*

He nudged David's elbow. "I have no idea why I'm invited. I have no connection to these people."

"This April wedding fete is meant to impress. Word is, the infamous duchess orchestrated the entire event eclipsing much input from the bride's mother." His friend spoke in a low tone, careful not to be overheard. "You are here to meet the groom, Amelia's cousin—Stuart Dumont-Bradford, ol' chap. He's written a novel or has nearly completed it and she most likely hopes that you will produce the blasted thing, making it the next blockbuster on the big screen." David's cynical chuckle erupted, running his hand through his medium brown hair. "The groom is a new marquess and viscount. He's not properly royal."

"How's that?" *British doubletalk drives me crazy.*

"He doesn't require to be *addressed* as a royal." He took a hefty swallow of champagne from his glass. "Prefers to be addressed as 'mister', of all things—ruddy damn improper if you ask me—damn improper."

"Who placed me on the guest list? Stuart?" Trenton sipped from the slender flute. He couldn't pull his eyes from her image. It was as if she were a phantasm drawing him in.

"No. He's too polite for such an obvious overture." David lifted his glass slightly in her direction. "That vivacious redheaded lovely over there—the one in the bright green dress—a spitfire and devil-may-care vixen—Amelia Hollingsworth, the Duchess of Steffen-fordshire." He chuckled, then smirked. "You're in bloody good company. Mostly nobles and royals here, save for the bride and her relatives. Though, the bride's stepfather is the renowned Larry Davis—Yank singer and composer extraordinaire. When you meet her, address her as 'Your Grace'. If you yourself were royal, then you would call her 'duchess'. I was invited for the same purpose—networking and PR to elevate the groom's endeavors."

"I had no idea." He chewed on a shrimp canapé from the rounding waiter while sizing up the beauty with the massive head of hair. "Tell me more about the duchess. She free?"

"Only if you're young." He eyed his friend's face. "Though you look youthful for your age, you don't fit into that category and neither do I. She's more than a challenge for any stout-hearted bloke."

"I've never walked away from a challenge—too pigheaded for that." Trenton continued to study her from across the room. "She married?"

"Oh yes, to the duke." David seemed delighted in relating the gossip about her. "Alistair doesn't care for her. He has ... other interests."

He licked his lips. A force made him want to taste her kiss, feel her warmth pressing against him. "If I had a wife like Amelia, I wouldn't leave her alone. I'd have her in the bed, on the sofa, wherever I could find privacy."

David stared at his friend. "Feeling a bit randy? She's more than a handful—too much for me."

"Sounds like my kind of woman." Trenton gazed at her, contemplating his new quest.

"You haven't been divorced that long. You're ready to jump back into those same old brambles?" David laughed. "What are you, masochistic?" He elbowed his friend's arm. "Try out the waters of beauties before settling on one—get your sea legs back."

"It's not my sea legs I'm concerned with." He wet his lips again and ran his finger between his neck and shirt collar. "There's a mystique about her."

"Yes. She does have that—in spades." David finished his drink in one swallow. "It's well-known she pays for her young lovers."

Amelia smiled beguilingly at one of the waiters. Trenton watched her slip a card from her purse onto the tray. The young man smiled and tucked it into his uniform jacket pocket.

She's smooth. Doesn't she realize that most in this room know what she's up to? Doesn't she care about negative gossip?

"How about an introduction?" Trenton's eyes remained fixed on her, Amelia's every nuance burned into his memory.

"That's easy." David placed his empty glass on the waiter's passing tray. "Follow me."

The two men squeezed through the milling guests, making apologies as they approached her. David lightly tapped Amelia's shoulder. She turned to him and flashed an electrifying smile at Trenton. Her eyes gave him a silent invitation. Or was that what he hoped the message was from her?

The English co-producer sported a broad smile. "Your Grace, may I introduce you to a dear American friend of mine?"

She smiled with an arched eyebrow, giving him an up and down appraisal. "By all means."

He continued, "I'm pleased to introduce Mr. Trenton Lowe, Hollywood producer and a fine connoisseur of all things beautiful and creative, and—"

She spoke before David could complete the introduction. "Very pleased to meet you, Mr. Lowe. I'm Amelia Hollingsworth, the Duchess of Steffenfordshire, and a connoisseur of all things pleasurable and tasty. Please call me Amelia. I find titles such a bore, as well as those who have them, equally so. Of course there are exceptions—my cousin Stuart Dumont-Bradford, for one. He's an extremely talented author."

She's certainly direct. "I'm very happy to meet you." He knew her melodious voice would haunt him night and day. Her green eyes with blue borders gleamed with mischief and would be difficult to forget, the color of pine with patches of sunlight. Bedroom eyes. He could stare into them all night and well into dawn and beyond.

Amelia cleared her throat, breaking his intense thoughts. She flashed him a sassy smirk and cocked her head, obviously sensing what was in his mind.

She extended her hand. Trenton took it gently in his, not certain if he should leave a kiss on her glove. Her middle finger gently stroked his palm. He got her message—loud and clear. His mouth grew dry again causing him to swallow hard.

"So you make movies?" She stepped past the two men and gestured for them to follow her to the side of the room. "I find that utterly fascinating."

"Your Grace, a few movies have my name attached to them." The words scratched past his raspy throat. He took a glass of champagne from the waiter's tray. *Any minute she'll serve me the pitch on a silver platter.*

David left to socialize with the other wedding guests.

"Please, call me Amelia. Remember, I *already* told you that. Titles and royal protocol are tiring and meant for stuffy snobs." She edged closer. "I've never had a Hollywood producer before." She sipped her drink and looked up at him beneath her long false eyelashes. "Are you tasty?"

Trenton coughed loudly and nearly choked on the effervescent liquid. He took a napkin to his mouth. "No one has evaluated me in those terms. You are very frank in a refreshing sort of way." He glanced at her cleavage. *She does have nice tits.* She grinned while her eyes followed his, clearly enjoying him appraising her assets. "Back to your question. I haven't had any complaints."

Amelia inclined her head and raised an eyebrow. "You haven't been evaluated by me. I have very high standards."

Trenton stepped back to the point where he felt a chair against his legs. "You are assuming that I would want your critique."

Amelia smiled and ran her tongue along the upper edge of her teeth. "You like the chase? A bit of a challenge induces or strengthens a rising?"

His brows arched. "A 'rising'? I don't understand."

She chuckled and fingered his jacket lapel. "That's British talk for an erection ... I assume you still have them?"

Trenton's face warmed. "Yes. But, that isn't something I normally discuss, especially at a wedding reception."

What will she do? Pitch Stuart's novel through the back door? Trying to keep me off balance?

"I never go for soporific party talk." She winked. "Too much time can be wasted with the superficiality of niceties, only to be left wanting when the meat is separated from the bone." She touched her décolletage, drawing in his focus. "The bone is what counts.

Don't you agree, Trent?"

He cleared his throat. "It depends on which perspective. By the way … my name is Trenton."

"To me," her tongue slowly ran across her lips, "you are known as Trent. That is the name I've chosen."

"You have, have you?" He glanced briefly around the room. "What if I don't like being called Trent?"

"After one night with me, you would like any name I call you." She sipped her champagne. "Yet, it doesn't have to be at night. Mornings and afternoons are good, too."

"Amelia, how can you be so blatant?" *Is her husband near?* "Aren't you worried about gossip?" He shot a brief glance to the wedding guests and then back to her eyes, captivating eyes he couldn't escape.

"I swim in gossip—especially if it's about me." She took her calling card from her purse and slipped it into his inside jacket pocket. Her fingers lingered on his chest. He enjoyed the warmth of her touch. It raised his core temperature a few degrees.

"I was told you're married." He took another swallow. "What makes you think I'm interested in a married woman?"

"If you weren't, you would have left after the first introductions." She moved a step closer. "Alistair has his diversions, too. We have an understanding. He doesn't mind in the least."

I can nearly feel her breasts against my chest. Her fragrance enveloped him—another detail that would haunt him. His pulse quickened even more.

A young man approached and whispered in her ear. Without a word she turned and flicked him off like an annoying mosquito.

"Am I keeping you from something, or someone?" *I bet he's one of her diversions.*

"Oh, him?" She turned and watched the man walk away. "They're a penny a dozen. Like Alistair, he understands. He'll be replaced when I tire of him." She returned her attention to Trenton, inclining her head in an enticing fashion. Her finger tapped his chest. "I might have found his replacement already."

"I'm at the backside of thirty and don't intend on being a plaything for a bored woman who has nothing better to do than to pay young men to entertain her." *She is totally off-the-wall and extremely spoiled.*

"I never said I paid anyone!" The seductiveness in her face faded as her eyes pierced his, and she spoke with steely softness. "Before you listen to gossip, Mr. Lowe, you had better verify your sources. I *don't* need to pay. Men clamor for my attention."

I hit a hot button there. "I apologize. I was way out of line."

"Quite right." She pouted as her fingertip drifted to her cleavage. Desire clouded Trenton's eyes and drove his actions. "Maybe we could meet for a, a cup of tea?"

I can't believe I'm asking her out. She's a married woman, and a royal at that, not to mention a spoiled brat.

"After insulting me, you plan to make up for that verbal assault with tea?" A small smile curled the corners of her mouth.

"I'm in London for a while, working on a movie deal, I mean filming a movie." Flustered, he rubbed his forehead. "Lunch? Maybe dinner would be better for you?"

"Your proposal is sounding better by leaps and bounds … almost as good as what it takes to rumple the sheets." As she talked, he watched her breasts rise and fall with each deep breath. "I prefer dinner. My afternoons have been rather booked with one charity or another, not to mention the boys."

Trenton pulled out his phone and checked his schedule. "Next Thursday is open. Where should I pick you up—at your place?"

"Where are you staying?" Amelia took a swallow of champagne, her eyes boring into his.

"The Corinthia. You know where it is?" *That was dumb. Of course she knows where it is. She lives in London.*

Her smile held a trace of a smirk. "I think I can find it." She slowly stroked the stem of the flute. "Shall we say seven for Thursday next?"

"Seven it is. Unless you want to come sooner." He leaned down, feeling a surge of confidence.

"'Come sooner'?" She chuckled. "I like your choice of words. I had better come first, if you get my drift." The tip of her tongue slipped between her lips.

"You may be disappointed." He moved closer and whispered, his head all but touching hers, "I have no intention of bedding you."

"That's your lack of intention—not mine." Her fingers traced his jaw slowly. "The duchess always gets her target … and the target is *always* grateful for it."

"I'm only taking you out to dinner as an apology—nothing more." *Why am I so attracted to her?*

Amelia patted his chest. "Yes. That's the premise to fit with social convention."

"As I mentioned before," *How am I going to make her understand?* "you are *married*. I'm not comfortable getting involved when a husband is in the picture." *Her lips are like raspberry jam dropped into a bowl of cream. I could watch her mouth move all day not to mention those tits.*

I wonder if they're real and how they'd feel.

"You'll have to do better than that." Her free hand grazed his thigh. *Is she gonna grab my dick next? No one seems to notice her, or if they do, they don't care.*

"Seriously, maybe dinner was a bad idea." *I want her. Why? She's forward and obvious.*

"Ridiculous! We can have a nice friendly dinner." Her seductive smile intrigued him and spawned lewd images of them together. "Besides, I might have only been playing with you. I love games of all sorts. If I merely suggest something, it doesn't mean I'm serious."

"I-I have never met anyone as free-spoken as you." *Her body is driving me insane. Damn! I want her!*

"Yes. I'm a rare breed." She looked about the room. "I must go and mingle. Time to check up on the bride and groom." As she left, she called back to him, clearly not caring if guests overheard. "Thursday at seven. Don't keep me waiting, nor wanting. Bring the condoms."

Trenton nodded. He glanced at eavesdroppers and smiled, trying to hide his embarrassment. A few eyed him and smirked, obviously recognizing Amelia's new target.

Her temper is as fiery as her hair—that makes me hot! Is she just one big tease wrapped in a gorgeous British package? Will I give in to her? Oh man, I want to. No woman has ever gotten the better of me, except for my bitch of an ex.

CLIVE BRADFORD NOTICED Alistair Hollingsworth, his cousin-in-law, motion to him. Compliments bounced off his ears as he made his way through the wedding guests and walked to the fringes of the room during the cocktail hour. "Such a lovely wedding you've given your son", "This is the wedding of the year," as well as "What a smashing event! Tomorrow's newspapers will be all abuzz."

"Jolly good hosting." Alistair jutted his chin to the bride and groom enjoying the reception. "They make a pretty couple. Seem right happy."

"I would've preferred he married a girl of social standing instead of a liberal-thinking Yank." Clive took a large swallow of scotch from his glass. "She has the social graces of a gutter snipe."

"All the same, he looks happy." Alistair arched a brow. "How did you and Stuart reconnect? No one ever knew you had a son. You've been rather mysterious on that point—almost as if you're hiding a cloak and dagger scheme." He chuckled and sized up his cousin. "You're so silent—one would think your son is an operative for MI6."

"Not nearly as dark as all that." He shifted his weight and tightened his grip around his drink. "Instead of inquiring about my son, what about your wife, Amelia?" He eyed her with more than a modicum of suspicion.

"Nothing unusual on that front." Alistair looked over in her direction as she flirted with a group of male admirers. "She's merely looking for her next replacement. She has her extracurricular activities and I have mine. The royals accept her behavior—even joke about it." An amused smile flashed. "She revels in that type of adulation."

"Indeed. Aren't you concerned that she might find someone who would steal her away from you?" *Alistair is a fool.*

He raised his brows and smiled broadly. "Are you serious, ol' man? Not after all these years. We have an understanding. She has a ruddy grand title, and I have her money."

Clive stiffened. With glass in hand, he pointed with his index finger, emphasizing his words. "You have her money until she divorces you." *How can he be so blind to the possibilities?* "Don't forget her late father's—my first cousin's entail—that can't be broken. He had made a point of mentioning that very fact to me."

"Why are you digging all this up?" Alistair's eyes narrowed. "I know nothing more than what I see. Apparently, you and I are looking at the same woman and arriving at different conclusions. Your displeasure with your new daughter-in-law has soured your perspective. Have another drink and celebrate your new rightful heir."

I'm sick of his ramblings. He's stupid and will remain so with his dying breath. "Not that this will interest you a twit, but I've been invited to speak at Harvard in the States to impart my vast knowledge to young medical students."

"Good show, ol' chap. How did you pull that one off?" Alistair eyed a young waiter as he wet his lips.

"No effort on my part. The Harvard Board recognized my expertise and accomplishments." He watched Cindy thank guests across the room for coming to the wedding.

Damn that Amelia for ruining my life. She even insisted the bride's gown be designed by the same establishment that Lady Diana had. What did she care—it wasn't coming out of her coffers.

Clive looked at his cousin. "We better make our way to the ballroom. The announcement will be made soon for the new *lord* and *lady* to make their official appearance."

Alistair nodded, put down his drink on a server's tray, and followed his friend.

~~***~~

All white décor with rose centerpieces on tall pedestals at each table added an understated refinement in the ballroom. Claridge's held the prestigious reputation as the most fashionable hotel in London society. Mirrors and opposing windows presented a sophisticated elegance.

After the required dancing of bride and groom, and family members had joined in, Stuart took a break by sitting next to his bride at the wedding table.

Clive strode over to his son with cool confidence and a determined look. "We need to speak." He silently cursed his rotten luck and wished for the umpteenth time that the boy had never been able to trace his roots and verify their relationship as father and son.

Stuart looked up, kissed Cindy's cheek, and followed his father to the quieter cocktail area in the outer room.

"Are you going to give me a lecture about not squandering the family fortune?" He looked directly at Clive.

"No. You seem levelheaded. I want to ensure that you know the family rules." Deep lines furrowed in his forehead as his eyes grew cold.

"What are those, father dear?" Stuart stood with a quiet arrogance that drove Clive mad.

"Family confidences are to be kept strictly in the family," he barked, then poked his son's chest for emphasis. "Don't get any ideas of putting what you suspect in your next novel. That could ruin both of us."

He should thank me for all I've given him, even if it was the result of a blackmail scheme by Amelia.

"My, my, threatening your son on his wedding day." His chuckle smacked of sarcasm. "You are as melodramatic as your pompous life, filled with protocol and insincerity with one goal in mind—how to keep your world whole with no fraying edges caused by those whom you deem as unworthy."

"I'm impressed. You can link more than two words together." Clive shot a sideways glance. Amelia and a man stood not far from them, apparently in their own private conversation. He returned his attention to Stuart. "Just keep your mouth shut—that includes your writings. People of quality don't air their laundry in public—dirty or otherwise." He scowled and threw a final threat at his son as he started back to the ballroom. "Remember, you take me down, and you will fall first. The family shares in not only the good, but the bad also." *He's so bloody cheeky after all I've done for him. I hope to hell he behaves. He hasn't been properly brought up—way too common.*

He glanced contemptuously at Amelia. *She is the one to watch out for, though. Always mixing things up. She's out to get me—I can smell her intent from here.*

~~***~~

Amelia watched Clive leave his son and return to the festivities in the ballroom. She hurried over to Stuart, stopping him before he had a chance to leave. She touched his arm lightly. Trenton waited a few feet behind them.

"Stuart, what the bloody hell was that all about?" Her eyes darted back and forth across his face. "Did he threaten you?"

"Not exactly." He adjusted his tie as if Clive's words still made him uncomfortable. "Warned me to keep quiet about the family skeletons and such. Something to the fact that if he falls, so will I."

Will Clive ever stop with his threats? "Leave Clive to me. He may have all those fancy degrees, but my cunning is sharper than his scalpel." She looked back at Trenton, then returned her attention to Stuart.

"Return to Cindy. You two will be on your honeymoon in a few hours. Forget about the source of your birthright—he's not worth the effort."

She watched Stuart leave to rejoin the others. *I'll have to look after him. He has the Bradford cockiness, but I bet he's never dealt with someone like his father.*

Trenton touched her shoulder. Kindness colored his eyes. "Is there a problem?"

"Nothing that I can't handle." She licked her lips and tilted her head. "The only real problem is first—I don't have a drink, and the second—I'm not in your arms."

He cocked an eyebrow and flashed a smug smile. "I can accommodate both instances."

"It's what comes next that is the true test." She slid her tongue along the edge of her upper teeth.

"A test?" His fingers danced down Amelia's back, making her shiver beneath the silk fabric. "I do very well at tests of all varieties."

"You haven't had me as your teacher." She chuckled as his hot breath caressed her ear. "I'm a strong proponent of a student repeating his lessons over and over until he gets it right."

"Staying after school can be most enjoyable." He kissed the tip of her ear and breathed heavily, causing her to stifle a gasp. "I sincerely doubt the teacher will be dissatisfied with my studies. I've always been an apt pupil. Isn't repeating the same task a hundred times the usual punishment for a bad boy?" His smile broadened. "You're such a tease."

"I like the way you think ... bad boy. I am not a tease. I am just a reminder of what you can't have. It's like a 'do not enter' sign—it begs you to walk through the door." She glanced at the other guests. "We had better join the others. I'm fond of Stuart and Cindy." She smirked. "I don't want them to think I absconded with you ...." Though I detest being proper, I want their day to be special. Besides, I must keep a wary eye on Clive."

"Really? He seemed okay, in a stiff kind of way." He placed his hand at the small of her back as they entered the room. She garnered her control and resisted the joy his touch could bring. It was too soon in their relationship to relinquish her trump cards and find pleasure in him.

She looked up at Trenton. "He's stiff and unscrupulous at the same time, if you get my meaning—nothing that I can share. Maybe one day I'll find the courage ...."

I've never had an older man before. He's so handsome. I hope he doesn't want an emotional connection—that would ruin everything. Should I bed him after dinner or before this coming Thursday?

Hmm, I might not bed him at all—that question is delightful to ponder.

Three

AMELIA SAT IN a comfortable chair in the Corinthia's lobby lounge, where she had a clear view of the reception desk and front door. She checked her watch.

Quarter past seven. He should be waiting for me and not me for him. She tried not to focus on the elevator doors. A rumble of butterflies sought haven in her stomach and the fabric of her gloves stuck at the palms from perspiration.

Why am I so nervous? It's not like he's the first man I had dinner with—not the first at anything for that matter.

She took a small sterling compact from her purse and looked in the mirror. *I have to admit, I look good for thirty-three. He's lucky to be seen with me …. Hmm, I don't know if I'll let him have me. Trent had better not want Greek—that's a deal breaker.* The low hum of conversation provided ambient noise and, oddly, irritated her.

Various guests walked past her or milled in a corner admiring the enormous half-spherical crystal chandelier hanging from the room's center. Others enjoyed a drink while seated in the plush beige upholstered chairs.

She angled her position as to avoid appearing anxious—needing to maintain her aloof façade. Concierge personnel, dressed in dark charcoal gray suits, busied themselves filling requests of prestigious guests. A doorman, complete with black top hat, created a slight breeze when he opened the main door and walked to his post on the sidewalk.

Again, she checked her watch. Twenty minutes past. She pushed to her feet. *I've had enough of this. No man stands me up!*

She left the chair, entered the lobby, and headed to the entrance. A cluster of family tourists blocked her way as they loudly discussed where they wanted to eat.

A gentle tap on her shoulder and a man's voice startled her. "Don't try to stand me up. You're not getting off that easy."

Amelia spun around and flashed her glaring eyes. "Stand *you* up! That comment does not fit this situation. I'm not the one who is twenty, no …" She inspected her watch, "… twenty-two minutes late. In any culture, that behavior is considered rude."

"Ah, but you weren't here at seven. I was." He flashed a charming, yet authoritative smile. "A last minute detail occurred that I had to attend to, then I returned back to the lobby." He started to usher her to the brass and glass doors on Norththumberland Avenue. "You now owe *me* an apology for your wrong assumption."

He's not so easily controlled. Such great fun—a true battle of wills. "The night will reveal who is entitled and to what."

~~***~~

The roomy black cab pulled up to The Lanesborough, considered the most sumptuous and expensive hotel in the city, on Hyde Park Corner in London's Knightsbridge section. The tall Regency architecture made an imposing site with two massive white columns. None of this opulence impressed Amelia. After all, such grandness was commonplace in her world.

A gloved doorman wearing a bowler hat opened the door. Amelia stepped out first while Trenton paid the driver. She waited politely, all the while eyeing her prey with subdued aplomb.

We're not far from my home. He plans on checking in, have room service provide dinner, then dropping me off as some paid tart? Not so fast, Mr. Lowe. I'm not a strumpet—common or otherwise. Very clever of him not taking me to his hotel.

Trenton placed his hand on her waist as they entered. He strode directly to the concierge's desk and spoke a few words to the distinguished man.

What is Trent doing? Checking in? He has to do better than this.

A hotel employee appeared and led them to Aspley's Italian restaurant on the same floor. Entering the spacious room, Trenton approached the maître d' and gave his name. The man checked his list at the podium, then promptly escorted them to their table.

Amelia took in the romantic Italian surroundings of glass ceilings and extravagant crystal chandeliers. Soft music surrounded them. *He is trying to seriously impress me. This has a Venetian ballroom feel. Does it represent his true standard of living?*

She slid onto the upholstered loveseat, while Trenton occupied the opposite one. The waiter stood at hand, waiting for their orders.

Trenton didn't look at the server. "We'll enjoy the seven course dinner with appropriate wine parings. Her grace will order first."

My, my. He wants to prolong the dining experience. Why? Does he think this will be a heavy meal and hamper bedroom activities? This table is far from hidden. Is he planning on being a good boy, or merely putting me off guard?

Amelia placed her order, opting for the Yorkshire lamb for her main course, while Trenton chose the Mediterranean selections.

How can he remain so trim eating heavy foods? Does he work out? I wouldn't mind being the mat for his pushups.

"I see that you ordered a very rich meal? One can barely move after a repast of that sort ..." She sipped her champagne. "... unless you plan on returning to your bed alone for a nice sleep. Personally, I prefer a bit of exercise to induce my slumber—very satisfying *exercise.*"

"A full meal could mean a person building up for a work-out marathon." Trenton took a spoonful of his fish soup. "Besides, the portions are rather small for each course—no chance of feeling weighed down."

"Do you have any after-dinner plans?" She ran her finger around the rim of the glass while looking intently in his eyes. "A walk perhaps, or ... other things?"

"That all depends on the lovely lady I'm with." His eyes caught her gaze and wouldn't let go. "I'm open for suggestions." The attentive waiter refilled their water glasses.

"Suggestions can hold delightful possibilities." She paused as the server placed their entrées before them and removed their fish plates. "Some suggestions can be more satisfying than others."

"You do enjoy this wordplay, don't you?" He reached for her hand. "But when the gloves come off, will all parties be equal?"

"I never disappoint, Mr. Lowe. Rarely is there energy left for a repeat performance." She took a forkful of meat and chewed with seductive relish as if capturing a scene from *Tom Jones.*

"I have never been with a woman who required a second helping." His slow and confident smile taunted her.

"Such a high opinion of yourself." Amelia's tongue moistened her lips with a lingering stroke. "One always looks best in their own mirrors. It's others' opinion of that reflection that cuts the muster."

"Touché." He chuckled, then touched her hand. "There is truly only one way to settle this."

She tilted her head and arched an eyebrow. "Your hotel, or here at The Lanesborough?"

"I haven't asked." He leaned into her. "Are you proposing to me? Is that how it works here in England? Sounds a bit American for a woman to make the first move." He squeezed her hand and inhaled deeply. "Always willful and wistful—makes for a dangerous combination."

"You should be so lucky." She sat straighter and pulled her hand from his. "I was merely verbalizing *your* thoughts. That is your real intention—exploring our relationship on a physical level."

He laced his fingers and spoke with a soft and yet a commanding air. "*If* and when I make love to you," he gently stroked the top of her hand as if caressing her naked body, "I plan on taking my time— all night as I discover what you enjoy most, my tongue circling clockwise on your nipples or soft bites, and what pushes you over the edge—from panting to agonizing moaning." He gritted his teeth as if already enjoying her body and breathed in slowly. "And make no mistake, I *will* get you there—more than once."

The image he painted brought her body to brisk attention—every nerve in her body waving and begging frantically for more. Had she met her match?

After dessert, Trenton gestured to a waiter for the check, then spoke softly to him requesting a car be sent.

He asked for a taxi. I guess we won't be staying here. I'm looking forward to seducing him in his hotel room.

The black taxi crept through the typical London traffic congestion. Amelia didn't notice the address that Trenton gave the driver. *We're not headed in the correct direction for the Corinthia. What does he have planned? A new nightspot or some place more dangerous and thrilling? I love not knowing what will be next.*

Her townhouse came into view as the car pulled to the curb. Trenton turned and looked at her with undisguised lust.

His lips brushed against hers and then went to her ear. "I suppose you expect me to request a nightcap?"

"Are you asking me to invite you to my home?" Her hand squeezed his thigh. His firm muscle made her want to feel his skin beneath the fabric. She wanted him to say yes—to seek her on her terms.

Trenton paused, as if in thought. "No. This dinner was my apology to you. I had thought it was your expectation—that we continue the evening in more private surroundings." He grinned. "I have to admit, I have no such intentions." He left a kiss on her neck.

"For that privilege, you need to be nearly twenty years younger." Amelia stiffened, then removed her hand and grabbed the inside latch, opening the door. "I don't appreciate refusals, nor do I provide an opportunity for another such insult." *Of all the bloody nerve. He thinks he's that irresistible? Damn it! He is—I want him more than ever.*

She took her keys from her purse, then rose to leave the backseat. He briefly palmed her buttock. A thrill racked through her. She wanted more of his touch. *Damn him for making me feel this way!*

He spoke through the rolled down window, "I hope we'll have

another opportunity to share a lovely evening—even an afternoon. Soaking up English culture is fascinating. I enjoy your company—your scintillating personality."

Amelia smiled briefly then climbed the few steps to the front door.

He didn't even have the courtesy to walk me to my door! How dare he not try to take me to bed—and deny me the pleasure of refusing him! I need to forget about Trent and move on. Yet, I still feel his touch on my bum burning through me.

~~***~~

The bright lights and the excitement of London's streets pulsed with the same energy as New York City, but Trenton hardly noticed. His mind was too unsettled. Amelia's refusal of a second meeting gnawed at his gut.

Talk about being an enigma! She's the purest definition of that word. She wants to go to bed with me and then refuses. What's with that? She doesn't think twice about jumping a toy boy's bones. Can she relate to a man closer to her age? I thought I had a chance. Now, I'm not so sure. I want her. There must be a way.

Four

TRENTON STROLLED THE meandering paths of Whitehall Garden, sandwiched between Whitehall Court and Victoria Embankment on the Thames, only a few blocks from the Corintha. He paid no attention to the colorful spring flowers, statuary, and others enjoying this park—one of London's green lungs. The noisy city traffic couldn't intrude on his thoughts. He had finished yet another production meeting with his English colleagues, but that wasn't what was troubling him.

He sat on a green bench and gazed at the river, watching boats and ships steaming pass each other. Restlessness grabbed him and wouldn't let go. An old memory filled him he had long forgotten—feeling smitten, as a teenage boy with a girl sitting at the back of the classroom, his gut quivering in waves of excitement.

What is it about Amelia that has such a hold on me? It's more than her striking good looks and voluptuous tits. The Hollywood beauties have no effect on me—not like this, and they're much younger, too. She's hinted that she's happy with her status quo. Am I merely something different for her, or is it that—she's my something different?

Trenton's cell phone chimed the melody from one of his blockbuster movies. There was no identification on the display, and he supposed the caller needed a detail regarding his London movie project.

"Just how long are you going to be dining the London bigwigs?" He held the phone away from his ear, cringing at his ex-wife's shrill voice. "I need an advance on the alimony. Carl and Jennifer invited me to spend time with them in Seattle."

"Naomi, we've been through this before. I'm tapped out until I get paid. You forget I work for a studio and they issue the checks." *She must be using someone else's phone.*

"You're not tapped out. You have an expense account. I doubt you're living on cheese and ale." He heard an exasperated sigh escape.

"My expenses are watched." He stood up and started walking. The crunch of gravel stressed his irritation with every step. "If I lose my job, there is no money for me ... and no money for you—can't get blood from a stone."

"What do you suggest I do? Turn tricks on Hollywood Boulevard?" He did his best to ignore her snicker.

Trenton stopped in his tracks. The blood pounded in his jugular. "I suggest you live within your means. Twenty grand each month is a fortune to most people. Make it work for you. Cut down on the designer clothes, expensive champagne, and exclusive restaurants."

"You want me to turn into a bag lady." Her voice rose an octave.

"What you turn into or not turn into is none of my concern." He flopped down on another bench and looked at his Rolex. "We are divorced. Get on with your life. I have with mine."

"What about Jason? When he hears how you're mistreating me, he won't be happy." He envisioned her thin lips and narrowing hate-filled eyes he had seen so many times during their numerous arguments.

"Your son by your first marriage? He's not my blood. How he feels or not feels is no concern of mine." *She's not going to let go of this. I won't give in to her anymore.*

"He could make trouble for you at the studio." Her voice cut with an icy edge.

"No threats. They don't work on me." He stood and turned back toward the hotel. "I'm done with this. Goodbye."

Trenton slipped his phone inside his jacket. Hands in pockets, he strode in determined quiet strides with his eyes straight ahead, hardly noticing the other people around him.

What hell is Naomi up to? Is she all talk? Jason? Nah, he's an upstart. No one would listen to two words out of his mouth. Could he maneuver himself to talk with the head of the studio? Krantz wouldn't give him the time of day, would he?

~~***~~

Amelia stirred her Oolong tea with a faraway stare at the delicate finger morsels and scones arranged on the three-tier display. A half-eaten cucumber sandwich lay on her plate. She saw tourists and loving couples in her periphery, but took no notice. The pleasing peach brocade décor of the Dorchester's Promenade Room did little to soothe her restlessness. Trenton's alluring aloofness frustrated her and yet compelled her thoughts.

Why is he resisting me? And, more importantly, why does his quiet resistance make me want him? He's not young as my other boys. True, Trent's more suited to my age—that's unnerving. I don't feel in control— another thing that upsets me.

She brought the cup to her mouth and took a sip, leaving a trace of lipstick. Amelia ignored the hushed voices and glances of other royals seated at tables as they obviously found it curious that she was without a toy boy escort.

What is Trent's angle? Am I merely a diversion for him? The same as Reggie and all the others were for me? I have to find out his true intention. But, how? What is the trick to get him off guard?

Her cell phone rang, jarring her thoughts. She made a face.

"I haven't heard from you." It was Reggie. "I thought you had forgotten me."

"Other things have occupied my time." *Damn and blast! He's getting possessive.*

"Other things? Or, another man?" He sounded hurt and dejected.

"Would another man matter to you all that much?" *If he keeps pestering me, I'll dump him before I find a replacement.*

"Yes. I've grown very attached to you." His sincerity seemed forced.

"Attached to my money is more like." *He lies well.* "I told you from the beginning. No attachments—just fun. More fool you for letting yourself believe our arrangement has any resemblance of substance."

There was a long pause. "I thought that since it's been nearly a year, that there was more depth to what we share. I'd be tremendously upset if you send me on my way."

"Stop your sniveling." *Now he's pathetic.* "I need to get back to my tea."

"Are you alone? I hear voices in the background." His tone of a hurt and humble child repulsed her.

"Goodbye, Reggie. I'll call you when in need." Amelia promptly ended the call, not allowing him to say another word.

Her brows drew together as she slathered a scone with Devonshire clotted cream and then dropped a dollop of raspberry jam on top.

I need to isolate Trent. Get him away from outside influences. Have him on my turf and level out the cricket field, or better yet, tip the field in my favor. I'll have to act soon. I don't know how long he'll remain in London before Hollywood will whisk him away and out of my grasp.

Amelia grabbed her phone from the table and tapped the screen. The ringing tone sounded harsh while she waited for the answer, urgency mounting. Her stomach tightened. She noticed her fingers trembling slightly as she fingered the napkin in her lap. Ring-ring, ring-ring continued in her ears.

Why won't he answer? A business meeting? Another woman?

"Hello, Amelia." His voice held a smile. "What delightful idea has crossed your mind?"

He keyed my number in his contacts. "I want to steal you from all those worrisome movie-making details." Her finger traced a line around the rim of the cup. "A well-deserved break can nourish the creative juices."

"I have this weekend free. A mid-afternoon meeting for Monday is my next obligation." She heard faint male voices in the background. "A change of scenery might be just the thing."

"I thought a quiet jaunt to Hollingsworth Manor might be to your liking." Her lips curled to a smile. "I'll have my driver pick you up at the Corinthia—say this Friday at two?"

"I was going to meet David at a pub that day at three, but he won't mind if I back out. It wasn't anything to do with the movie—merely guy talk."

"Splendid." She let out a satisfied sigh. "I'll already be there, making everything ready for you. We'll have a lovely relaxing time ... getting to know each other better."

"Sounds like a plan." He chuckled. "There is much I want to know about you."

"Careful, Trent." Her tongue ran along the top edge of her teeth as if he was sitting next to her within kissing distance. "No one has discovered all of me—and the best of the lot have tried and failed."

"That poses a delicious challenge ..." he lowered his voice, "... one I long to win."

"Game on, Mr. Lowe." She envisioned him in her countryside lair, craving her body. "The winner takes all and then some."

"I'd love to continue this wordplay, but another meeting is calling," his voice faded, "discussing possible locations to scope out."

"I understand. Pack country-casual. It will be just us two." A small giggle escaped. "I'll be waiting."

Hmm, he thinks he'll have me. He won't unless it's on my terms. If I give in, will I still want him? I've been with the "boys" for all these years, nearly since the beginning with Alistair. Can I be satisfied with only one man for any length of time? What makes Trent so extraordinary? Under different circumstances, I'd know my next move. Now, I'm not so sure. God knows I want his body. But, he must want me more—the scales need to be in my favor.

Five

CLIVE AND ALISTAIR enjoyed gin and tonics in the club's smoking lounge. Members in three-piece suits talked in softened voices about financial trends or political situations while seated in comfortable leather wingback chairs. Pipe smoke drifted from one conversation to another. As a former smoker, Clive savored the rich aroma.

A long silence ensued between the two men, each in his own private thoughts.

"Alistair, what is your wife up to these days?" Clive swirled the ice cubes in his drink before taking a swallow. "Misbehaving as usual?"

"What a curious thing to ask, ol' man." He let out a disgusted chuckle. "I imagine the same as always—some eighteen or nineteen-year-old lad. She never likes them older than twenty-two." His brow furrowed. "Why do you ask?"

"There've been photos in the news of her and that Yank movie producer." He looked directly at his cousin-in-law. "Doesn't that concern you?"

"Not in the least." Alistair finished his drink in one last gulp, and motioned to the roving server for a refill. "I doubt she is genuinely interested. Amelia likes the idea of being seen with him—adds shock value to the royals—wants to keep them off-balance, you see. After all, he *is* in the entertainment business—no better than any entertainer as far as social rank goes—my tailor is his betters any day."

"Don't forget the entail." Clive arched his eyebrow and tapped his knee with a pointed finger. "If I were you, I'd keep a closer eye on her."

Alistair let out a laugh. "Well, you're not, so I won't. She'll never leave me. Amelia likes embarrassing the royals too much. As I mentioned before, that Yank is far too old for her liking."

Clive fingered a napkin. "Don't ever say I didn't warn you."

"You like to mix things up for her. You've always had it in for Amelia." He took a few nuts from the nearby bowl and popped them in his mouth, clearly observing his friend's reaction.

"Yes." His jaw tensed as he shifted his gaze to the Persian carpet. "She's never been proper—never lived up to the royal blood in her veins."

"She is that." Alistair eyed a young man cleaning up spent napkins on coffee tables. "You don't wish her harm, do you?"

Could it be Alistair has more than a half dozen brain cells? Clive didn't answer directly. He finished his drink in one large gulp and stood up. "I need to get back to the laboratory."

Whatever I decide for her, it will need to be done with finesse.

~~***~~

Trenton sat on the comfortable plush leather backseat of the Hollingsworth town car, following the long winding driveway flanked by full green oak trees. He wondered how much farther they had to go before the manor house would come into view. Plush emerald fields with lush evergreen forests beyond hinted at what must be a sumptuous country residence.

He leaned forward as the mansion came into view. Tall Georgian columns, bordered by enormous floor-to-ceiling windows could never be described as understated.

If the inside is anything like the exterior, I see why Amelia is so spoiled. She's surrounded by luxury—here and in London.

The car came to a stop under the porte-cochere in front of two massive carved wooden doors. A gray-haired distinguished looking man, dressed in a black coat and gray striped pants approached. Trenton chuckled to himself. He had to be a butler. The driver left the car, hurried around the back, and opened the passenger's door.

"I'm Mr. Charles Beddingfield, the butler to their grace, Lord and Lady Hollingsworth." His smile was curious and manufactured according to protocol.

Trenton extended his hand. Beddingfield reluctantly gave a brief handshake, as if such familiarity was unacceptable between a guest and a person of service.

"I'm Trenton Lowe." He smiled and looked briefly at the door. "Her grace invited me to spend a few days in the country."

"Very good, sir." The footman appeared and promptly took the single suitcase from the driver standing by the open trunk. "Oliver, here—the footman," Charles angled his chin toward the young male servant, "will take your luggage to your room. Her grace is awaiting you in the main drawing room. If you will kindly follow me, Mr. Lowe."

The gravel crunched underfoot as Trenton made his way to the front landing. Entering the large foyer, he looked upward at the vast staircase and the balcony gallery, the height almost dizzying him as his eyes took in the tall walls sporting various coats of arms among portraits of what must be long-dead ancestors of the Hollingsworth bloodline. The echo of their footsteps on the white and black marbled tiled floor bounced off the stone walls.

Turning to the left, Mr. Beddingfield led the way to a sumptuous room of pale blue and gold with antique French furnishings. Amelia stood at the far window with her back to the room as she looked out at the classic English garden.

The butler cleared his throat. "Your grace. Mr. Trenton Lowe." Beddingfield stepped backward a few steps, then turned and left, closing the door quietly.

Amelia approached him, extending her hand. "I trust you had a nice trip. I hope my driver didn't bore you with his chatter."

"He barely said two words." He took her hand while she led him to the silk damask settee where they sat down. "Though, I did find the quiet comforting. Gave me time to think." A silver service with finger sandwiches on a tray rested on the coffee table between them. The formal brocade drapes and décor were far from the cozy English atmosphere he had enjoyed in the London pubs.

"Thinking about movies, or something else?" Amelia poured coffee from a sterling pot into a fine porcelain cup. He nodded when she lifted the creamer. Her fragrance of spices and pheromones hit him sharply, and he liked it.

"A myriad of things … mostly of the female kind." He took the cup from her. Their fingers touched and lingered a bit too long. He studied her downward gaze. *She seems pensive. Is something troubling her?*

"Other females?" She chuckled while reaching for a watercress sandwich. "I don't like the sound of that. Very few have achieved the level of captivation as I."

"You certainly are self-assured." Trenton leaned back resting his arm across the top of the sofa within caressing distance of her shoulder. Her eyes went to his lips as if reading them, making him want to kiss her at that moment. "Most can't carry off such egocentricity—you do so with aplomb, and I have to admit, that's part of your charm."

"I'm merely a beast in the jungle, surviving all the hidden dangers." She looked directly at him. "Some dangers are more deadly than others."

"Are you playing with me? Setting up a mystique that you are in peril and need me to be your knight and save you?" His eyes searched her face, eager to discover the real Amelia.

"We don't know each other well enough to delve into such a complicated subject." She heaved a ragged sigh while stirring her coffee. "No more serious talk. Our time in the country is for fun things. When people get serious, then truths have to be faced—that could ruin everything."

"I didn't mean to pry." He played a lazy design on her shoulder with his fingers, fighting the desire to lay her down on the sofa and ravage her body with kisses and so much more. "You're my hostess and acquaintance—and I hope … in time, my friend."

"Friends?" Her light laugh escaped. "I thought we already crossed that bridge."

"Friends can always become more—lovers." *She's teasing me again.*

"Lovers—that's a very good situation for us." Her fingers glided along the top of his hand as she licked her lips with a languishing stroke. "But, arriving to that definition is such fun. That path should never be rushed."

"I'm all for a slow path, provided there is an endpoint." He leaned toward her, his hot breath at her ear. "A dangling carrot with no reward is unkind and extremely frustrating. I don't do well with frustration. I make certain satisfaction is the choice prize for all concerned, and always … ladies first." The more he was with her, the more he wanted her. He moved his hand to her hair and ran his fingers through it, relishing the silky feel.

"Your brush stroke of words paints a delightful picture in my mind." Amelia leaned into him and grazed her lips seductively against his. "Reality can fall short of one's imaginings. Veracity is such a disappointment when that happens."

"There's only one way to find out." He glanced at the door and then back at her. His fingers played lingering light strokes on her neck. "I believe the bedrooms have been prepared?"

"Why don't you go and make yourself ready." She glanced at her diamond-studded watch. "We dine at eight in the dining room. Oliver will show you the way."

"That's over an hour away." Trenton drew her closer and left a gentle kiss—a kiss that spoke of tenderness and not the lustful thoughts that consumed him. His hand shook before making a fist to control his burning impulse.

Amelia pulled away and took a deep breath. "Dinner is best before any activity." She stood and went a few steps across the room to a tapestry pull cord, and gave a gentle tug. "The journey is to be savored, like a fine wine."

Trenton smiled slowly. "There is more than fine wine I wish to taste."

Oliver appeared quietly. "Yes, your grace."

She turned to the young man. "Please show Mr. Lowe to his room and make certain he has all that he requires. Have Agnes come to my suite and assist me with dressing for dinner."

"Certainly, Milady." He turned to Trenton. "If you will, please follow me, sir."

Amelia swayed past him and into the foyer, presumably to her own room.

I'd rather follow her instead of Oliver. Amelia's games never stop. What hell has she devised? Is this one big sojourn of teasing to fill her ego? I sure as hell want to fill more than her ego!

She won't control me!

Six

AFTER DINNER, AMELIA and Trenton took their Cognac in the library. The floor-to-ceiling mahogany bookcases, filled with priceless signed editions lent an understated elegance to the room. They sat on the settee watching Oliver tend to the fire. The dancing flames reflected the heat of attraction Amelia felt watching Trenton sip his drink. He cocked his head while his eyes seemed to penetrate her soul as if wanting to know her deepest secrets.

"Does your gaze signify you want to explore this house or me?" She tasted the warm, amber liquid while never taking her eyes off him.

"What do you think?" He chuckled. "Drafty rooms and hallways hold little interest—especially when compared to your allure."

"I must say, Trent, you'll have to do better than that to turn my head." Her temperature rose while taking in his strong and commanding features, thick head of hair, chiseled jaw, intense dark eyes, full lips, broad shoulders, and strong muscular hands. She fantasized how his hands and mouth would feel on her body. She let out a long deep breath.

Amelia watched his eyes follow her finger trailing from the base of her throat to her cleavage peeking from the neckline of her golden dress.

"I've only begun." He inched closer, extending his arm across her shoulders. "As I've mentioned before, I've suffered no complaints." His thumb stroked the back of her neck. His hot breath caressed her ear. "This evening can end in a burst of fireworks. A slow burning fuse is the most enjoyable."

She leaned her head back as his lips grazed the perimeter of her ear and then nuzzled in her red curls, sending ripples of pleasure down her spine. She wanted to give in, but not yet. He wasn't nearly panting enough—claiming her prize would have to wait. Amelia took a deep breath as her eyes half closed. Deep down, she had lived this moment since their first meeting.

Trenton placed their drinks on the table. His hand firmly cupped the back of her neck, bringing her lips close to his. His kiss taunted her as he brushed against her mouth and then pulled back. She let out a ragged breath. He gently bit her bottom lip—teasing her as she had done to him since their first encounter. Her heart pounded as she parted her lips to receive his kiss. He kissed her with tenderness and not the passion she anticipated. Disappointment stabbed at her. She inclined her head. "Trent, are you purposely restraining your feelings? Don't you want to go to bed with me?"

"All is not what it appears on the surface. I'm more complex than the men you associate with—in or out of the boudoir." He reached for his Cognac and took a large swallow.

"My past, in particular, my marriage to Alistair is far from what it seems." She stared into space, hoping he wouldn't hear how fast she was breathing. She wanted him now and her need grew more urgent with every passing minute.

"Would you like to share?" His hand stroked up and down her back as she leaned forward.

Her brows rose as she turned to face him more directly. "What is this? A playground game of I'll show mine if you will show yours?"

A languid smile curled the corners of his mouth. "I want to know more about you. I feel there is a story about you. You seem to use your frivolous façade as a smoke screen—keeping your truth stashed safely away—free from any potential harm."

"You see all that, do you? Aren't you being clever." Amelia rubbed her upper arms, an inner chill racing through her. "You've been reading too many scripts, Mr. Lowe."

She took an unladylike swallow of her drink. Her eyes grew serious as she gazed at the crackling fire, her passion instantly deflated.

"You might as well know what all of London and the British aristocracy has known all these years." Tears welled up in her eyes.

"If it's too painful, then don't go on." He hugged her shoulder. "I didn't mean to pry. I felt compelled to know you beyond the laughter and flirtations."

"Why is that, Trent?" Amelia looked at him with tear-rimmed eyes and quivering lips. "No one has ever cared about my feelings or what is important to me. Why you?"

"I don't know. I guess I care on some level and want to make a difference if I can." He gently stroked the top of her hand, his fingers soothing and yet encouraging.

"I'll tell you if you promise not to pity me. If you do, you'll be back to London in the morning." She winked and forced a smile.

"No pity from me." He crossed his heart. "Promise. Boy Scout's honor."

"Good enough, then." She took a deep breath for courage. "It was the custom of titled families, for the father to arrange a marriage for his daughter. That's what my father did for me. I was seventeen at the time. His title was rather low on the hierarchy ladder and dear old daddy wanted more for his daughter than the mere title of 'lady'."

"That sounds reasonable, though not considerate of your wishes." He squeezed her hand. His eyes pleaded that she unburden her torment.

"Yes. But, my father didn't really care if liked this man, never mind loving him. He never looked beyond Alistair's title of duke." She bit her bottom lip and sighed. "I went to his bed as a virgin and remained as such until I took my first lover." *I can't reveal the whole truth. It's just too bloody humiliating.* She huffed. "From a girls' boarding school to a union with a eunuch. Alistair probably swayed his guilt by not making a fuss when I went to university in London. At least I was able to get out and speak to others besides the servants."

"Why? How could he not want to make love to you?" Trenton leaned his chest against her shoulder, nudging her chin with his finger so she would look at him. "You are beautiful and fascinating."

"Alistair had my money and I had his title—being a duchess was my father's goal for me. He thought it would result in me being well-placed in London society." A tear fell to her cheek. Trenton wiped it away with his fingers.

"I can see this is too painful for you." He handed a cocktail napkin from the table to her. She dabbed her eyes. "I was merely curious. I didn't mean to make you cry."

"It's all right. Maybe after all these years, I need for this to come out—to say the words, in some way release the pain." She took a deep breath as her hands balled into fists. "Alistair never loved me as a husband. It's more like a brother and sister relationship. I know I hinted to that when we first met."

"Yes. I recall that. I thought you were joking." He looked intently in her eyes, his arm embracing her.

"The guile of laughter tends to neutralize the sting and pain of truth." Amelia took another deep breath. "Alistair is one hundred percent gay. The stable boys or young men at the club fill his bed. I never have."

"Did your father offer you refuge from his mistake in arranging your loveless marriage?" He stroked her hand as if to give her courage. "Couldn't he see how unhappy you were? Didn't he care?"

"My father was dying of cancer. He never sensed my sorrow— never told me of his illness before the marriage. I only found out about his grave condition after we returned from our honeymoon."

She turned to Trenton, then swallowed hard, finding the words difficult to utter. "Daddy died … died six months after I married. I never told him the truth. Even on his deathbed, he thought I was happy." Her bottom lip trembled. "I wanted him to have a peaceful passing."

Tears ran hot paths down her cheeks. He held her close as her chest heaved and she stifled a sob.

She continued, "My father thought he was doing his best by me— making certain my life would be settled and right, before he died. He probably thought it would be his last gift to me."

"What about your mother? Surely she must've known you weren't happy?" He patted tears from her cheeks.

"Mummy died when I was six. Various nannies filled in the gaps." She paused as a new pain gripped her heart. "A kind nanny is a poor replacement for a loving mother."

Trenton finished his drink in one swallow. "Any brothers or sisters?"

"None. Had Mummy lived, I'm sure they would have tried for a son to inherit. After my father's death, the estate and title went to some closest male cousin somewhere up country." She took a fresh napkin to her eyes again. "My dowry was immense enough to maintain my lifestyle and save the Hollingsworth social standing— mainly to pay off Alistair's estate debts so it wouldn't need to be turned over to a government trust. There is still a whopping sum left over to maintain his inheritance long after he's dead and buried." She jerked her head in disgust. "His bloodline is so old that there is even a town bearing the family name along with this home— Hollingsworth Manor. I don't know why the family didn't christen this place Steffenfordshire Manor. Now you understand why he is so desperate to maintain the estate—bloody family pride."

"I'm so very sorry." Trenton gently kissed her temple and pulled her close to his chest, she relishing the sound of his heartbeat. "I see all the pain you've dredged up."

"In an odd way, it feels as if an enormous weight has been lifted." She looked up in his eyes. Her fingers traced the outline of his lips. "It's as if you have set me free."

"I'm glad my questions have resulted in some good for you." He took her glass, walked over to the Cognac decanter and poured two fingers worth, then handed the fresh drink to her. "Drink up. This will help."

"Sex has always been the cure for me, and not alcohol." Amelia caressed his hand before accepting the drink. Tossing her hair back, she stared up at him, knowing her eyes must be red, and feeling a childlike helplessness.

Did I expose too much to him? Will he bolt away?

"I think sex, at any rate for now, should be when you have had time to grieve what you just revealed to me—your marriage, or lack of one." He placed a gentle kiss on her cheek.

Her emotions were so conflicted. On one hand, she wanted to rekindle the passion and delicious anticipation of minutes ago, and yet his kind eyes and encouraging smile kindled her heart and made her want more from him than sex.

He eased down on the settee. His embrace provided a cloak of protection from the painful reality she forced herself to face.

"That will feel very odd for me." She kissed his lips softly. "I've never had a man interested in me for more than what I could provide—be it sex or expensive gifts." She leaned against his chest.

"Well, you've met one in me." His fingers glided through her hair and settled on her neck in delicate strokes. "You are so much more than a fleeting afternoon passion or an expensive watch."

"Thank you, Trent." Amelia kissed the back of his hand resting by her throat. "I thought I knew myself—knew what I wanted—but that's the nicest gift anyone has given me." She looked up at him. "You're the first to see me cry since childhood. I've never let anyone see me cry."

He kissed her temple. "There is nothing you need to hide from me—tears or otherwise."

The warmth of his arms and the feel of his chest rising with each breath reminded her of when she was a little girl; sitting on her father's knee, safe from all cares, and believing all things were possible. Tears welled in her eyes again and she blinked them away. This secure feeling hadn't been in her grasp for so many years.

"DID YOU SLEEP well?" Trenton inquired as he buttered his morning toast. He couldn't resist glancing at Amelia sitting across from him at the dining room table. She had bared her soul last night and he needed to know if she regretted exposing her tormented heart to him.

"Surprisingly, yes." Her smile hinted devilish thoughts. "I feel refreshed and full of energy. Our little nighttime chat did wonders for my spirits."

"Glad to hear it." He cut into the fried eggs, watching the yellow liquid flow to his sausages. "The conclusion might've been less than anticipated."

"Anticipated by whom, Trent?" The mischievous glint in her eye suggested the beginning of wordplay. Her mouth lifted at one side. "Perhaps you were the one disappointed that the evening didn't end on a more physical note."

"Perish the thought." *I love her flirtatious nature.* "I have no expectations—other than spending a lovely day getting to know the most mysterious and fascinating woman in all of London."

Pouring cream in her coffee from the silver pitcher, her eyes sent him a message of what might await them later that day. He took a deep breath and envisioned his lips meeting hers.

"It's not that I haven't heard those same words before ..." The tip of her tongue peeked out for a brief moment. "But, I love the way you say them."

Amelia returning to her bubbly self lifted his spirits and erased his concerns that he had probed too deeply into her psyche.

"I'm merely being truthful. When I see someone with your unique qualities, I speak my mind." Never averting his gaze from her, he sipped his coffee—his eyes burning with his unspoken lust.

"Well, after my tearful display last night, you know my secrets—no mystery there." Amelia stabbed a piece of sausage with her fork. "What about you? Any deep, dark stories in your past? I hardly know anything about you—other than you're in London involved with a movie project."

"I'm not complicated. Hollywood only sounds glamorous to those who don't work in that city." He put his fork down and interlaced his fingers. "A lot of unwritten rules. Either you learn them or you're out on the sidewalk looking in."

"Care to share?" She took the cup to her lips.

Trenton noticed Oliver still stood quietly in the room. "Why don't we discuss this during a walk around the grounds? The weather is perfect—sun's out, birds chirping, seems warmer than the cool of last night."

"Fine by me." She put the napkin to her lips, and started to rise. Oliver immediately assisted with her chair.

"You knowing your own mind is ... is ..." Trenton stood from the table and walked to her, inches separating them. "... well, is damn intoxicating. Don't ever change."

"No fear, Mister Producer." She tapped her finger on his chest as an impish grin curled her lips. "I have no intention of it."

~~***~~

Amelia and Trenton strolled the back English garden of the Hollingsworth Manor. He gazed out to the vast horizon. She glanced at his face, trying to read his thoughts by his serious expression. This silence he imposed gnawed at her and heightened her curious nature. Even the sound of gravel beneath their steps irritated her. She wanted to know more about him. After all, didn't she bare her soul to him the night before? Why couldn't he do the same?

"By your silence, I assume that business is plaguing your thoughts?" She reached for his hand.

Her heart sank when he avoided her touch by placing his hand in his corduroy jacket pocket.

"Other things more troubling than a movie deal are consuming my gray matter." He flashed a smile then returned his focus to the landscape. "My past is always there—ready to pounce."

"A past?" *How bad could his history be? Alcohol? Drugs?*

"We all have a past." His steps slowed to a stop. He looked in her eyes a long moment. "Some pasts are good—others, not so much, and can be damn hellish."

"Want to share?" She touched his arm warmly, wanting him to open up to her. "A willing ear will often pare things down to a manageable size."

"Sounds as if you're giving me back my own advice I served to you." A light chuckle escaped with a raised brow. "Whether I tell you or not, nothing will change for me."

"Humor me, then." She interlaced her arm into his elbow. "Of course, if it's too personal, I understand."

Trenton turned his attention to the path at his feet, and resumed walking. "It's a rather sad story with a troubling ongoing future."

"Stop teasing me. I see the pain on your face, and I'm the last one to judge you or anyone else—not after the reputation I've cultivated all these years." *His sensitivity is a magnet—one I can't seem to resist.*

"I was a fool to marry Naomi all those years ago. I saw what I wanted to see and not what was there." His tone held heavy remorse—his eyes spoke of torment.

"Go on." She slipped her hand from Trenton's elbow into his pocket, finding his hand clenched tightly. He opened it and intertwined his fingers with hers. "I'm interested in what you have to say." *The warmth of his hand feels so right. Why is that? He hasn't bedded me yet. Still, I feel this connection.*

"I don't think she ever really loved me—not as I loved her." He glanced sideways to Amelia. "She was a divorcée and had a twelve-year-old son, Jason—such a spoiled brat. I had never married before. At the time, Naomi seemed down-to-earth and not part and parcel as most women in the Hollywood biz."

Her thumb rubbed his index finger to comfort and encourage him. "A wrong love is never a pleasant memory—though I don't speak from experience—never truly being in love."

"It was wrong on so many levels. I guess the big turning point was the accident." He sucked in air between gritted teeth. His lips thinned as if to hold back a hurt.

"A car accident?" *Was he at fault? Is Naomi disfigured?*

"No. Not a car wreck." He took a deep breath as if the words he was about to utter took all the strength he could muster. "She was pregnant at the time—only three months. We had a terrible argument over some imagined affair she thought I was having with a young starlet. I've never cheated on her—never, not once, not even thought about it."

Did he strike her? Amelia ignored the tickling flower at her bare leg below her skirt. *Does he have a violent side to his nature?* "What happened next?"

"The argument started in our upstairs bedroom, and continued down the hall to the top of the stairs. She was ranting and raving in her usual style. I went to grab her upper arm to get her to listen to me and ..." Tears rimmed his eyes. His hand trembled before tightening into a fist.

"And?" *This is so difficult for him. Did he push Naomi in some sort of rage?*

"And ... she lost her balance and fell down the stairs." He released her hand from his pocket, then reached for a handkerchief, and wiped his eyes. "She still blames me for losing the baby—swears I pushed her." His eyes grew round. "—which I *didn't.*"

He's been wounded—same as I. "Did she not want more children?"

"That wasn't an option. It was a miracle that she was pregnant by me." He let out a heavy sigh and looked directly at her. "She had used one of those intra-uterine devices for birth control for years before I ever came in on the scene. Apparently, she left it in place for too many years—wouldn't take the advice of the doctors, developed an infection and had a history of ovarian cysts. After the D&C was performed because of the miscarriage, the docs discovered that another pregnancy wasn't in our future." He bit his bottom lip and looked intently in Amelia's eyes as he gripped her shoulders. "I felt that loss as much as Naomi—maybe more."

She took his hands in hers, giving a gentle squeeze, and kissed them gently. "Trent, I'm so very terribly sorry. You would have been a wonderful father. I can sense that about you. What you've been through is too horrid for words."

His weak smile clawed at her brittle defenses.

He is more complex than any other man I've ever known.

"I seriously doubt fatherhood will be in my future. I'm certainly no father to my stepson—Jason. He's as cold as Naomi, and I think more treacherous." His eyes took on a soft vulnerability. "Don't look so serious. I'm not in any danger—merely venting my frustrations."

If you're not fearful, then why use the word "treacherous"? I don't like the sound of this.

Is Naomi another Clive? With the same intentions just as vulpine—deadly cunning as a fox?

TRENTON LIFTED THE glass to his lips, paused, and took a sip of the dark ale. The bustle of Grumps Restaurant upstairs, did not reach this downstairs dining area. His business associate, David sat across from him and chatted as he busied himself with cutting a medium rare lamb chop.

As David spoke, his eyes bored into Trenton and made him feel ill at ease. "You've been going on and on about the movie project, which is showing no large issues that would halt filming. I've yet to hear about your weekend with the infamous Amelia." By David's sly smile, he knew his friend wanted to know every dirty little detail.

"Nothing to tell." Trenton took a large swallow of ale.

A smug glint danced in David's eyes and a sly smile emerged. "I find that hard to believe—not with her reputation." His chuckle held a disbelieving ring. "I would've thought she'd have gotten it off with you in every single room and in the stable as well."

"It wasn't that type of visit." He looked past his friend at the rough honed walls. "She's more complex than the surface façade."

A server refilled their water glasses.

"Really?" David halted mid-chew. "Care to share?"

Trenton leaned forward with his wrists on the table edge. "No. I don't betray a confidence."

"Why did you pick this restaurant for our meeting? Amelia suggested this place?" His friend stabbed a petite roasted potato.

"Why, yes. How did you know?" *How does David know about her? Bed partners?*

"Grumps? A favorite hangout for her. One of her hunting grounds. Here," he pointed with his knife toward his plate for emphasis, "and the Dorch—many attractive young men lurk there—the type she can fill her time with."

"Dorch?" He shook his head.

"The Dorchester." David put a forkful of food to his lips.

Trenton's mouth screwed for a moment. "I really don't like hearing this." *Did the studio put him up to spying on me? Did Naomi or Jason call my boss?*

"Ouch! I dare say, she's gotten to you and you haven't even bedded her yet." David sipped his wine. "Or, haven't admitted to me that you *know* the lady in the biblical sense of the word."

"I never said it was my intention to 'bed her' as you put it." David's questions became uncomfortably close. He wanted to be anywhere but here, enduring this conversation.

"It may not be *your* intention, but I'm certain Amelia has already penciled you in on her dance card. She's not one for any kind of serious relationship. You'll only get hurt while she's off on to the next young bloke." His smug and authoritative expression irritated Trenton. People with that cool assertiveness dug under his skin like a sandspur.

"If that's Amelia's intention," he gazed past David's shoulder at a young couple being seated at a table, "it certainly isn't mine."

"You've been warned, dear friend ... you've been warned." His colleague smirked as if he knew it all—he suffered that reaction many times from Krantz.

~~***~~

Amelia and Trenton strolled the halls of Madame Tussauds' Wax Museum on Marylebone Road—a minute's walk from famed Baker Street of Sherlock Holmes notoriety. She had hoped that this excursion would divert the restlessness that brewed from bubbling depths every time she was in his company.

He stopped in front of the royal family tableau, and stroked his chin. "They all look so lifelike, as if you expect to see their chests rise and fall with each breath."

She eyed them a moment. "The royals in wax have more life in them than the ones with pumping blood in their veins." She started toward the next display. "You'd have to know them to understand."

"Understanding them isn't my goal." He reached for her hand. "There is only one royal I'm attracted to ... standing here before me."

"Careful." She smiled to hide her deep buried sadness. "I'm the one who makes advances—my rules, dear Mister Producer. Control is in my blood—that's the order of things."

"Control is my mantra, as well." His intense eyes made her breath catch in her throat, and she nearly forgot they were in a public tourist attraction.

"Ah, but I play it better than you." *I can't give in to him. If I do, my life will not be the same. He's the unknown. Reaching for him could be dangerous.*

"I'll give you points for confidence, Amelia." His mere smile softened her more than any amorous kiss from another man.

She led the way to the next exhibit. "After here, where should we go next?"

Trenton smiled, leaned closer to her, then softly said, "Bed." The heat of his breath warming more than her ears.

"Not yet—if ever." She looked down at the floor, avoiding his eyes. "That subject requires a lot of thought on my part."

Trenton's inquisitive glint and wrinkled brow saddened her. Amelia knew she couldn't let him know how much she wanted to succumb to his touch. To become emotionally involved with Trenton could mean their breakup in the future. The possibility of that pain terrified her. Love for one man was a game she had never played.

~~***~~

Alistair waited for Clive's arrival at the club. He tapped the leather-covered arm of the chair with his fingers as he checked his watch against the clock on the wall above the bar opposite from where he sat. He crossed his legs, uncrossed, and crossed them again. Even the young handsome gay bartender couldn't divert his worry. He stared at the glass of rum in his hand. The low hum of conversation only served to irritate him. Yet, realizing that others were occupied in their own concerns lessened the worry that they would be eager to learn of his.

At last, his cousin-in-law entered and scanned the room for a familiar face. Alistair motioned discreetly with his hand. Clive slid onto the butter-soft chair opposite him, the leather creaking as it took up his weight.

A male server promptly came to his elbow ready to fulfill any request. Clive looked up at the youthful face. "G and T," he said, ordering a gin and tonic.

The young man took two steps back before turning to leave.

Alistair inched forward as if he were about to reveal the deepest of government secrets. "Things aren't right with Amelia."

"Indeed. Things have never been right with Amelia." Clive looked annoyed. "Is that why you summoned me here today—to discuss common knowledge about your wife? I was perfectly happy working in the laboratory. Yet, I must admit, I was confounded with a dead-end issue on my recent formula."

"Hear me out on this one, ol' man." Alistair briefly looked over his shoulder for eavesdroppers.

The waiter cushioned Clive's drink on an absorbent coaster, and placed it on the low table between them.

Alistair continued after the server was out of earshot. "Amelia has been out with Trenton Lowe numerous times—seen in public situations. All appears to be on the up-and-up. It's not as if she's carrying on with a married man."

"So what?" His friend's chuckle reeked of self-satisfaction. "She has a new target. What's this big cloak and dagger issue? Amelia is being Amelia—nothing more than that."

"Her other chaps don't come around anymore." He took a swallow of rum. "She's gone off them, you see. If she becomes serious—and I mean serious with Trenton Lowe—my world will come crumbling down, and those mammoth boulders are beyond my control—I could be out on the street." Terrifying visions of a middle-class existence flashed in his mind.

With the glass to his lips, Clive paused a moment as if in thought. "Aren't you exaggerating this whole situation? You're anticipating events that haven't occurred with no evidence. You'd be better off using that imagination in the laboratory for MI6."

"Clive," his voice pressured in low tones as exasperation rose to the surface, "I'm not some ninny in this." Alistair's free hand formed a tight fist and then relaxed. "If she runs away with him, or God forbid, wants to marry this bloke, I'm done for. You even taunted me with that idea at your son's wedding. Though, at the time I considered such a thing a folly and not a serious concern."

"Yes, yes." He took a large swallow of his gin drink. "But if there's one thing I know about Amelia, it's this—she's not about to leave the lifestyle she has now. With all her ranting, she still loves to have the opportunity to attend royal functions and to shock the blucbloods. Running off with Mr. Lowe would eliminate that little bit of fun she relishes."

"It's still a very real possibility, ol' man." He leaned forward and lowered his voice to a near whisper. His lips drew thin as he spoke through clenched teeth, "The entail her father set up is very tight. It *can't* be broken. I've been to three solicitors, and they all gave me the same answer."

"What collective conclusion did they come to?" Clive inched forward as if he finally understood the seriousness his colleague felt.

"Since there were no natural children or 'issues' as they termed it between us, if there is a divorce brought by myself or her, all financial resources revert back to Amelia." *He must understand the grave nature of my situation.* "If the money reverts back to her, then all is lost—the manor house, my membership here at the club, the entire Hollingsworth estate. I'll be left to living on my wits and only the income from my work—not nearly enough to run the estate. I'd have to turn it over to the National Trust because I wouldn't be able to pay for the taxes." He squeezed the arm of the chair as if that would lessen his stress, his knuckles turning white.

"Steady on." Clive leaned over and patted his hand. "I truly doubt that Amelia would consider putting you into such a social devastation. She hasn't hinted that she wanted to move out?"

He shook his head. "No. Not yet at any rate."

"Look. If Amelia does leave, you can always charge admission to the hordes of tourists—rent out the closed-up ballroom for functions—weddings, conferences, and such—turn it into a B and B for all those wealthy Americans who want to pretend they have British class and standing for a fortnight."

"That would be a social slap in my face!" Alistair stared down at the Persian carpet, seeing his life turning into worthless flotsam. "I'd be just another who fell into the fray of mismanagement. I can hear the hushed comments now, 'Poor ol' Hollingsworth—couldn't keep it afloat'. I shudder at the thought of strangers in my home ... snooping about ... videotaping, and taking horrendous selfies. It's more than one could endure."

"Even if she does take up with that Yank, there's no guarantee that she'd ask for a divorce." Clive finished his drink and gestured to the waiter for a refill. "Spending time with him is not an indication she would make any life changes—one does not necessarily include the other."

"I hope to God you're right." *Would she really have the nerve to ruin my life and her own, as well?*

AMELIA STROLLED THE halls of the National Gallery, on Trafalgar Square, but it didn't ease her tension and confusion about her tangled emotions. She glanced at Trenton frequently and paid no attention to the Londoners who recognized her and mumbled in soft tones. If anything, the absence of such attention would cause her concern and make her wonder if her popularity had taken a step backwards.

Flipping through the museum's brochure, Trenton read the bold text of the points of interest. She rested her gloved hand in the crook of his elbow. His silence allowed her thoughts to deepen and she wondered if he found her coy banter to be more of an irritant instead of an alluring ploy. *There will come a time when he'll have to go. What then?*

They turned the corner and came to one of the museum's common areas. Trenton noticed the various signage pointing to an assortment of exhibits.

"Where to next?" He tilted his head boyishly.

"Well, considering the time, I should be returning home ... unless you have a reason why I shouldn't." *Why do I tease him? I have no intention of having him in my bed—not yet anyway.* An inward shudder ran through her, driving her insecurities. *Falling in love frightens me. Deep down, I'm such a child pretending to be a woman.*

"Well, since you rejected me for more intimate situations, we could see a play." He patted her hand and left a gentle squeeze. "Dinner either before or after the performance?"

"I doubt I'm dressed properly for a night at the theater." She brushed her hand along her skirt for emphasis. "I enjoy performances of many different varieties."

"You're the mistress of nonconformity, why not extend that rebellious nature to another realm? Start a new fashion trend and raise some eyebrows in the process." His chuckle chipped away at her defenses. "As to performances—you're teasing with no promise of a satisfying conclusion."

"I agree to the play only if you do the same, and not dress better that you are now." *I've never noticed this side of him before. There's a hint of an edge.*

"You ignored my comment about teasing me." His finger gently traced the curve of her neck, sending delightful sensations that warmed her and caused her to take a deep breath.

"Maybe. But, I heard it all the same." *Can I resist him? If he has me, will I be able to say goodbye? Aren't there always goodbyes?* "Where can you locate tickets on such short notice?"

"As in Hollywood, I have my connections." His wink and confidence made Amelia want him now more than ever. Wherever he was, power flowed from his pores and with every step.

~~***~~

The London night air had cooled considerably from the warmth of the spring day. Theatergoers milled about in the lobby and on the sidewalk during intermission. Amelia and Trenton enjoyed glasses of Chablis. She relished the stares and waves of whispers that focused on her and yet felt unnerved at the same time.

I don't like these gossipmongers dragging Trent into a sordid tale. He's too good a man to share in my infamous dossier. She looked at him with deep intent. *How I wish I knew in the past what would be my future and who would be in it—meeting Trent.*

"You're so quiet," Trenton began. "What devilish thought is occupying that wistful brain of yours?"

"Nothing that matters." She looked up to the coal sky. "The fat has been in the fire for years, and there is no going back."

"You sound as if the world is on your shoulders." His finger glided along the strap of her designer green dress. "Want to share?"

"Hindsight is always twenty-twenty, isn't it?" Her eyes pleaded for compassion. "Choices—wise or not, live with us forever." A deep sigh escaped. "No sense crying over spilt cream."

"Why so serious?" His fingers lifted her downcast chin, forcing her to look at him. "You have a life any woman would envy—money, a title, social fame."

"All that weighs very little against a shallow existence." She sipped her wine and avoided looking at him, fearing he would see her moist eyes. "Don't mind me. I'm having a weepy introspection moment— a condition females are predisposed to." She shot a glance at the others in the area. "The lights will begin flashing any moment. Let's return to our seats."

They placed their drinks on a nearby table.

As they left the lobby, the warmth of his hand at the small of her back felt good and right. To her surprise, physical desire wasn't the force that drove her to him. It was something more, something that ran deeper in her core. She brushed those feelings aside—fearing to discover a new truth that had always been lurking beneath the surface for so many years.

~~***~~

Trenton and Amelia stood near the building's wall on the expansive sidewalk, as far away as they could get from the hoards seeking a taxi after the play ended. He wanted to explore her deeper feelings but feared her reaction would be to end the evening sooner and squelch any chance of a sexual encounter. No normal hot-blooded man could spend time with her and not be aroused. *What happened to her outrageous devil-may-care nature? Did Alistair say something to her about seeing me? Is his understanding nature overrated?*

"Well, Mister Producer, do you think that play has a chance on Broadway?" She let out a light chuckle. "We Londoners have seen plenty smash hits from the US. Are Americans ready for a British production?"

"Yes. I think it will do very well. Still, it's the critics job to always find fault—flows in their veins. No matter how superb the performance of all involved, there will be a backhanded compliment." He lifted his chin, eyeing the taxis lining up for the next fare.

"It's the same here. Many fine plays and musicals have been shut down by a grouchy reviewer." She squeezed his hand. "Where to next?"

"Since we already dined before the show, how about a nightcap?" He donned his most little-boy pleading expression, hoping she would say yes.

"Splendid. A nightcap doesn't have to end the evening ... unless you have to be up early for some ghastly meeting or other." Her tongue ran along her upper lip.

She seems back to her old self—playful and seductive. "How about the Bassoon Bar at my hotel? I hear the piano bar is quite good and getting to my suite is an easy matter." *Was I too obvious?*

"The Corinthia?" Her smile always enticed him. "I've never been one to hide in the shadows. No reason to start now." She clasped his hand. "On to the Bassoon for a new adventure and delicious possibilities."

Trenton took a firm hold of her waist as he hailed the next taxi pulling up to the curb.

~~***~~

Conversations muted a moment when Amelia and Trenton entered the Corinthia's bar, followed by hushed whispers, fixated stares, and sly smiles. Normally this attention pleased her, but not now. Trenton was worth more than the cheap comments that were lavished on her previous and ever-changing male companions.

He mentioned something to the maître d'. They were escorted to what served as the most secluded table in the rather large room. She slid onto the comfortable black cushion. He sat opposite her on the camel-colored leather chair. A waiter appeared as the host left. Amelia ordered a chocolate martini, while Trenton favored scotch rocks. She placed the green purse that matched her outfit on the glossy table. The pianist played an old torch standard that enhanced her thoughts of a brimming with night hot love.

"So, this is the forefront to your lair." She glanced at the modern art hanging on the walls. "A bit of libation to loosen the inhibitions? Though, I've never needed such lubrication."

"I thought a drink would be nice ... along with more stimulating conversation." He reached for her hand across the table. "How the evening ends is lady's choice."

"My choice, is it?" She touched his finger in seductive strokes. "That could be interesting ... very interesting ... and creative."

"With your allure, and unspoken invitation, do we even need any drinks?" He turned his hand and ran his finger teasingly along her palm.

"You might not desire a nightcap, but I do," she said with a smile. It was her game and her rules.

The server delivered their drinks, placing them on cocktail napkins decorated with the hotel's logo.

"Don't drink too much. Performance issues could be a problem. I hope you don't need alcohol for courage." Confidence welled up from her core. "Did I intimidate you in some way?"

"I've had no complaints." He released her hand, and took a large swallow of scotch. "I always put the lady first."

"Then the little blue pill isn't in your arsenal?" *He's nearly twenty years older than the boys I've had.* "Some pushing forty rely on those little enhancements."

"I've never had the need. For the record, I'm thirty-seven." His intense gaze bored into her soul, searching her depths. "Being near forty isn't the end of the pleasure road—it can be the beginning—and most lasting control." His deep voice slipped into her like smooth seductive satin sheets.

"I like what the man is saying, but talk is cheap. Action racks up the points." Amelia took a hefty sip, closed her eyes and let out a yum after swallowing. "That is what I call a perfect chocolate martini—smooth and tasty on the tongue and delightfully warming to the throat."

"My goal for you is to savor more than that drink before the sun rises." He bit his lip as he inhaled deeply, illustrating his mounting desire.

"A sunrise isn't the object at the moment." She took another swallow of her drink while watching Trenton enjoying his scotch. "Rising of a personal nature is on my agenda—celestial heavens are not."

He reached out his hand to her. "Shall we forego our time here and resume this stimulating conversation in my room?"

Amelia grabbed her purse and slid off her seat. "Why not? The confines of privacy can lead to the utmost stimulating conversations—not to mention the stimulating activities."

He swiftly left cash on the table for their drinks.

They headed toward the hotel's bank of elevators.

Ten

AMELIA HAD NEVER been to the Hamilton Penthouse suite of the Corinthia before—not even with her many clandestine liaisons. Such an extravagance seemed unnecessary to feed her libido for only a few hours. The cream-colored décor and balcony offering an expansive view of the Thames pleased her visual senses. London, all aglow, sparkled against the velvet black sky, the traffic sounds muted by distance. Tantalizing aromas from the many restaurants that lined the streets floated upwards. She stroked the sofa's satin upholstery, walking about the room, taking in the sumptuous surroundings.

"Are all the movie producers afforded such luxury when traveling abroad? You must be more important to the studio than I imagined. Especially for such a lengthy stay, they must value your talents very much." She walked to the patio and peeked out.

"I work for a very good studio. Star Dream Studios didn't get to top status by doing things halfway." He walked to the fully stocked bar and lifted a bottle. "Brandy?"

Amelia turned with a smile. "I'd love one." She sat down on the yielding cushion in the center of the sofa. "A brandy is always a good ending or start to an evening."

"I'm hoping it will be a continuation." Trenton turned on soft music from a control at the bar, then handed her the warming liquid.

She took the snifter. Her eyes traveled up Trenton and gave him a look few men could resist. "Back to your work .... What exactly do you do? Yes, I know you're on set, but what else occupies your time in your profession?"

"I watch out for excess expenses—making certain all is on budget, if not under it, reading scripts that might be of interest for the studio's next project." He eased down beside her and extended his arm on the back of the sofa. "It's a real coup for me if we can wrap early."

"You're describing a climb to Mount Everest. Your position must be demanding and yet powerful. Do you make uncomfortable decisions?" Her hand fell to his knee. She knew exactly what she was doing—and doing it well.

"On occasion, I hate to have to close down a production or lay people off because of not getting the job done right. One glitch can cost the studio millions. There are times when the movie isn't worth the money invested and it has to be shelved." His fingers traced a pattern on her shoulder. "It's tough to shut down a movie—people are put out of work."

"I had no idea that you had such responsibility—it seems very daunting to me." *I love the sensation of his touch.* "You must feel weighed down at times." She fought the overwhelming urge to undress him right then and there, and feel all of him inside her.

"Yes. I do." He let out a heavy sigh. "Knowing I can affect someone's livelihood can put a real guilt trip on me."

"I've never been in such a situation and hope one never presents itself in my future." She paused in thought. "No. I'm wrong. Once I did have to let a servant go, and that really bothered me. I had no choice but to 'toss her out the window' as we English say. She had more than crossed the mark." Amelia remembered the downcast expression of that maid. "I noticed things missing from my bedroom—a scarf here, a blouse there. That's when I hired Elizabeth and I never have regretted that decision."

"Absolute loyalty is required with servants and employees in my business." His lips came close to her ear. His hot breath churned her yearning. "Enough talk about the plight of the possible unemployed. Physical diversions are far more interesting, not to mention more ... pleasurable."

She turned her head to his, their lips only a breath apart. "You're speaking my language, Mr. Lowe. The communication of touch can be most rewarding."

Trenton's hungry stare raked over her body. Amelia held his gaze with her own. His intense desire was obvious and she relished every drop of it.

His lips grazed hers and traveled to her ear, leaving teasing kisses on her lobe. She could smell that woodsy aftershave that she had noticed before. Heat flooded her body all the way to her center. Trenton stood up and clasped her hand. "The sofa is for amateurs. The bed is for making love and where commitments are formed."

Commitments? Is he feeling more than lust?

A small smile curled the corners of her mouth. "Commitment or not, I'm ready for a new adventure." Her heat surged as her panties became wetter. She wanted him now and they hadn't even gone beyond kissing—she went back in time and felt like a young teenage girl on the brink of losing her virginity to her first serious boyfriend.

Trenton grasped her hand and led the way to his bedroom.

The appointments were just as lavish as his living room suite.

Opulent bed linen, drapes, furnishings, and another breathtaking London view provided the utmost in enhancing seduction. With the door ajar, music filtered in from the other room.

The tables had turned. No longer was Amelia stalking her target, she had become his prey and she relished this newfound susceptibility. She walked to the balcony and sank onto a chair, angling her body to face him, and fighting to control her heartbeats.

"Are you playing the coy virgin?" He moved closer to the patio doorway. "I like games. I'm not so old not to remember how to disarm a wary seductress."

Trenton's commanding stance and set jaw sent shivers through her as her stomach tightened. His eyes spoke of more than the typical night of amour. This man meant business and knew he was in control, setting the time and place. There was no going back and she savored this thought.

"What if I want to gaze at the Thames?" *It's been quite a while since I played the innocent maiden.*

"You can gaze all you want." He came closer to her. "The balcony is as good as a place as any, though the hotel personnel might object."

"I've never let objections of others guide my actions." She knew that could get him into trouble, and she pushed herself up as he ambled to her in a cool and confident stride. He stood so close Amelia swore she could feel his heat and his chest fall and rise with each breath and they hadn't even embraced yet. His arm encircled her waist and pulled her to him in one forceful movement, crushing her breasts against his chest and causing her to gasp. She felt his arousal growing firm against her abdomen, enhancing the uncontrollable desire surging through her thighs and pelvis. His strength thrilled her.

Trenton looked into her eyes as he gritted his teeth and inhaled deeply. "The choice is yours, Duchess—here or in the bedroom." He buried his face in her neck sending delightful shivers with his kisses. "You've been teasing me with this body since I met you," he whispered in a low growl, his hot breath in her ear. "And now I'm ready to collect. There will be no frenzied tearing off of clothes— that's what you want." His eyes grew dark and serious. "Torturous foreplay is what you need."

"Time will tell on the frenzied bit." *His commanding strength is wilting my resolve to have my way.* She flashed a glance at the neighboring hotel balconies. "Though I've never given a thought as to who might observe my escapades, I don't think Hollywood would look kindly on their famous movie producer putting on a show for the Corinthia's elite guests." She angled her head to the left, where a couple stood on their landing sipping a drink and staring at them. "They've already had enough of a show to write home about."

"Point taken." He took her hand as they returned to his bedroom.

Amelia sat on the bed, her breath coming in panting gasps as she watched him undress, first loosening his tie and tossing it onto a writing table, then unbuttoning his shirt with swift determination, all the while boring his eyes into her soul with a strong and silent desire. He left his expensive shirt on the chair. A new thrill surged through her when he exposed his bare chiseled chest, feeding her uncontainable yearning.

Trenton sat down on the bed beside her. "You're still dressed."

His lips came close to her neck as his fingers slid the back zipper of her dress downward in a slow movement, denying her urgent need to rip their clothes off and feel him fucking her brains out.

He continued taunting her desire. "You must be feeling quite warm with all those clothes."

"I don't think my undressing will make me any cooler." He mouthed her neck in teasing soft kisses, and she wanted—needed his tongue to explore her body everywhere. "In fact, the more clothes I remove, the steamier my temperature will rise." Could he hear the tremor in her voice?

He guided her hand to his firm erection through the fabric of his slacks.

"There's more than my temperature rising. You have reached the point of no return," she breathed.

"You've been seducing me with that body and those luminous eyes from the first time we met—as I said before—now it's time to pay up." His kisses along her shoulders drove shivers down her back, making her nearly scream with desire, stifling her squeals into gentle oohs and ahs.

Trenton manipulated the back of her bra, unfastening the hook, and releasing her full breasts, his hands cupping them, his fingers teasing her nipples. God she wanted him. He slipped her dress with the loosened bra down to her waist. She fell back on the bed and scooted to the pillows. His eyes held hers while he unzipped his pants, held the waistband a moment, then let them fall together with his underwear, kicking them off in one movement. She shimmied out of her dress, and then forced herself to teasingly slide her panties slowly to her ankles.

She stared at his erection the entire time, licked her lips, and reached out to him. "You haven't even kissed me yet," she purred.

"I kissed your ear, neck, and throat." He removed her flimsy undies legs, sending new shivers down her spine.

"Yes, but not properly—not a proper kiss." *His power is intoxicating.*

Annoyingly, Trenton walked around to his side of the bed and pulled back the covers, delaying what she wanted again. She got up and quickly assisted him with the bedspread and top sheet, then slipped onto the pillow's cooling fabric. He lay beside her. His hand at the back of her neck firmly drew her mouth to his. His lips teased her, partially opening and then just brushing her cheek. *When is he going to kiss me? I can't take much more of this.* His tongue lightly traced the perimeter of her ear and then down her neck. Her hands ran through the hair at his neck, guiding his mouth to hers. He paused a moment, looking into her eyes. His mouth barely opened, as he leaned closer to her lips, the tip of his tongue luring hers with teasing caresses. He kissed her fully, his tongue mingling with hers in the deep recesses, making her moan. Their heat melded into one.

She luxuriated in the feel of his sinuous chest, her fingers gliding over each rippling muscle.

His hand traveled down to her breast and teased her nipples again with gentle squeezes. Her breath came in shuddering gasps as she ran her hand down his back, enjoying the curve of his buttocks under her palm. His engorged manhood rested on her thigh and pressed ever so slightly as he moved closer. He was so close and yet not one with her. Trenton trailed kisses from her mouth, down her neck and to the sensuous hollow of her throat. She arched her back, begging for more of his touch. His hot breath traveled down her body with lingering strokes closer and closer to her seat of desire. Amelia parted her legs, inviting him to enter her. A moan escaped him when her hands found his manhood and caressed him to further arousal, wanting him—desperately needing him to make her his. Trenton's fingers grazed her ever so lightly between her legs. She knew he could feel her dripping juices. "Yes," she moaned again. "Yes, there, please don't stop, firmer."

He replaced his taunting caress with teasing kisses while his fingers explored her soft and wet interior. Amelia gripped the sheet into tight fists. "That feels so good. Trent, I need to feel you ... all of you." Her eyes shut tight, her concentration razor sharp, focusing on the pleasure surging through her.

He slid his body on top of her. The pinnacle of his heated erection just touched her velvet folds. She raised her hips to receive him. He pulled back and only allowed the slightest bit of himself to enter her.

"Stop teasing me. I need you now!" she nearly screamed. He eased into her, inch by inch, filling her deliciously. Her thighs shook with desire until her entire center surrounded him and pleasure shot through her. He moved in a slow rhythm, prolonging the glorious sensation.

She grabbed his buttocks, pulling him to a faster pace. The intensity on his face and his heavy breaths showed he was at the same level of sublime delight as herself. Faster panting, sweat trickling from their hairlines, they both embraced the rapture. She climaxed and shook with uncontrollable spasms. With his last forceful thrusts, his manhood quivered within her as he found his own release.

He rolled off her as they both fought to slow their breathing. The hair on his chest glistened with their mingled perspiration. Amelia turned her head to see Trenton gazing at her with a satisfied smile.

"What are you smiling about?" Her fingertips ran up and down his chest, enjoying the feel of his hair.

"I'm the luckiest man in the world." His hand went to hers on his chest, his fingers stroking her knuckles. "Did I fulfill your expectations?"

"Wonderfully so." She panted and looked in his eyes. "Why did you ask if you pleased me? You assume I'm less than satisfied?"

"No. When I felt you spasm around me, I knew you had climaxed. But not all orgasms are equal." He kissed her fingertips.

"I like your frank talk—expressing yourself directly." She toyed with the hair at his temple. "The English are always so proper, never saying what they mean or what is what."

"There are many times in Hollywood that I have to hold my tongue." He looked up at the ceiling. "But in the bedroom, no need for propriety if both parties are in agreement."

"Exactly! Men have cocks and women have pussies. Call a spade a spade." She chuckled lightly. "You are what my soul needs. I've never known that until now."

His lips caressed her neck. "This is a whole new ballgame—something I'm not familiar with." His eyes held more feeling for her than a one-night stand.

She put her fingers to his lips. "Don't. Don't say something you might regret. Though, at this moment, I would love to hear those words and repeat them back to you. This is not the time. I need to sort my feelings and heart out."

"You will let me know when to say those words, won't you?" His eyes narrowed with sadness. "Just don't wait too long. Life can be shorter than we plan."

"No. Not as long as that ... just long enough for me to know what I want for the rest of my life." Her eyes traced his face.

Sex is more with him than the toy boys. Why? After my first time with him, why does this feel so different?

There's something deep about him—I can feel it. What do I really feel? Is this confusion due to Trent being near my age? A mere infatuation with a slightly older man? I want to be with him again, still ...

Eleven

"YOU SEEM TO have slept well." Amelia turned at the sound of Trenton's voice behind her. He stood bare-chested in the doorway. Only his pajama bottoms kept him decent. What was it about him? Feelings she had never experienced before swirled in her mind and she wasn't sure if she liked them. She had always been totally in control before.

"You can take credit for that." She buttered her breakfast scone as she sat at the table on his suite's balcony.

His easy stride stirred her yearnings as he pulled out a chair. "That was the goal—to take you to a new level of pleasure." He looked at her with a curious expression. "Your eyes were green last night, now they look blue. Contacts?"

"My eyes change color—always have." She studied him a moment. "You needn't look like the cat who swallowed the canary." *His smugness would normally outrage me. But it doesn't. Why?* "I didn't say there has never been anyone like you before."

"Then that's my goal—to win over the lofty and exacting Duchess of Steffenfordshire." He poured himself a cup of black coffee. Amelia slid the cream and sugar toward him. "Your pleasure, and more importantly, your heart is my purpose."

"My heart?" Amelia's jaw set as her lips thinned. "Be careful where you tread. I *am* married, and to a duke at that. No man has controlled me, except for my father, and I'm not about to allow such freedom now ... certainly not to a mere Hollywood movie producer."

"Whoa! Back up." Trenton's strained smile showed fine lines at his eyes. "I must've misspoken myself. I have no desire to control you, or anyone else for that matter." He scratched his forehead with his thumb. "It's just that you've made a big impact on me—a home run. After only one night, I want to know more about you—your likes, passions, hobbies, favorite colors—all of it."

"You ask too much of me, Mister Producer." She looked out to the Thames. "My life has a set path—one my father devised. There can be no going back for me." A deep breath escaped her lips. "I'm trapped in a world of meaningless social engagements and empty sexual encounters."

"I hope you don't consider our lovemaking last night as an 'empty sexual encounter'."

He gave her shoulder a gentle squeeze. She turned her head back to him and knew he could see the tears welling up in her eyes. *What's going on with me?* This flood of emotion was so unusual for her. Why did she feel this way? It was only one night—similar to all the rest.

A light breeze kicked up and blew her hair across her face.

Trenton grabbed both her hands on the table, enclosing them in his warmth. "Amelia, nothing is written in stone. You don't have to feel trapped in a loveless marriage."

He makes everything seem so simple. It's not. "The situation is far more complex than you realize."

"Explain it to me." His eyes begged her to unburden her fears.

"Not now." *He wants more than I can give—more than I dare to give.* "If that time ever comes to be, then maybe you'll know my feelings and all the hell that goes with it." She forced a grin. "You know most from what I told you at the Manor."

~~***~~

Naomi Lowe reclined on the chaise lounge's designer cushion on her balcony. Soft footsteps behind her caused no alarm. She knew who it was by the cadence. Her eyes remained focused on the blue Pacific from her lavish Manhattan Beach home. His shadow fell across her legs. Faint cheers and yells from beachgoers playing volleyball sounded in the background.

Looking upward to his looming stature, she put her manicured hand to her forehead to shield out the sun's glare. "What brings my long-lost son to grace me with his presence? Out of money?" Her agitation had not mellowed since their last terse encounter weeks ago.

"You know me so well, dear mother." He chuckled lightly, his eyes and blond hair enticing to most females. "Grease my palm with some of your alimony loot, and I'll call you mom."

She moved her feet to the side as Jason sat down on the foot of the chaise. She studied him. His father's long legs, muscular shoulders, sun-kissed hair, and her own icy cold blue eyes revealed more about his nature than words could express. Nothing was beyond his consideration—legal or not. She wasn't sure if that was good or bad.

Naomi reached for her Long Island iced tea from the side table. "Why couldn't you be more like your father and less like me? Then I wouldn't have to fight you all the time?"

"What fun is that?" He pulled off a grape from the cluster in the bowl on the table. "It's the best way to communicate—the only way we communicate—everything out in the open."

"Your stepfather is a royal thorn in my side. Only his money eases the discomfort." She pulled her sunhat forward and removed her sunglasses.

"Nothing new there. You've always had it in for him since the accident." He shifted his weight on the cushion and tapped his foot as if eager to leave.

"Yes. That's true, but now that thorn has become sharper with royal barbs." Naomi leaned forward, her arms hugging her drawn-up knees. "In case you haven't noticed, his face is in all the rag media. Trenton has been seen out and about with none other than Amelia Hollingsworth, the Duchess of Steffenfordshire and married to the duke. I don't like that."

"Why?" His nonchalant demeanor irritated her. "He was bound to start back swimming in the pool of females—available or not."

"I don't relish in one-upmanship of his choice of love interests. Not one bit." *Jason could care less about my concerns. Why did I indulge him so?* "There must be a way to get back at him." She studied her son's face. "Any ideas?"

"It will cost. I don't play for free—not even for mommy dearest." He popped another grape in his mouth.

"You're so conniving. Maybe trouble with his boss would divert his attention from that Brit whore." A devilish smile curled the corners of her mouth.

"Careful," he tilted his head and took the tone of a parent, "if he loses his job, you lose your alimony."

Neither Jason nor Trent know how much money I have stashed away. "Let me worry about my own money matters."

"All well and good for you to say." He looked at her in earnest. "What affects your income affects mine."

"You always have your hand out. I thought your modeling gigs were getting you by." Never taking her eyes from him, she sipped her drink and scrutinized his face for any telltale signs of his lying.

"Those gigs are not as frequent as I'd like, and don't pay enough for my lifestyle." He brushed back falling hair from his forehead.

"Lower your standards." She ignored his unspoken pleas.

"I do ..." He leaned in and kissed her cheek. "... every time I come to visit you."

"You expect me to give you money after that kind of talk?" *Damn it! I need his help.*

"It's the symbiosis that cements us—not love between mother and son." He adjusted himself to look directly at her. "So what is this great plan that's churning between your ears?"

"If I know anything about my ex, it's the unnatural value he places on trust." She stroked her son's upper arm and gave a firm squeeze. "Once his trust in the duchess is shattered, he'll drop her so fast she won't feel the wind rushing in her ears before she falls."

"How might this be accomplished?" Interest showed in his narrowing eyes. "We're here in L.A. They're in London."

Naomi swung her legs over the side of the chaise. "He's bound to return to the west coast after the film wraps. If she," she tapped Jason's nose with her finger, "comes here with him, all the better—makes for easier access."

"And where do I come into this little plot of yours?" His tanned cheeks lifted in a smile, exposing artificially bright teeth—he looked like someone from a toothpaste commercial. "Abduct the duchess, drug her, then a drive up PCH, and drop her off a cliff?"

I paid for those pearly whites, and he's not one bit grateful.

Naomi tilted her head as her grin appeared. "My, my, I did spawn a delightful, devious, and utterly ruthless little boy." She took a deep breath. "Let's not get ahead of ourselves. This will take time and planning, but not too much time—not as much as that. I'm not certain you'll need to take Amelia on a tour of the Pacific Coast Highway—we don't know if she'll follow him back to Hollywood yet."

"While you're figuring out how to ruin Trenton's life, how about a little play cash?" He held his hand out, palm upward.

She reached in the pocket of her beach robe and handed him the wad of money. Jason took it and fanned the bills, counting quietly.

"Five hundred? That's it?" His eyes widened. "I spend this much in two hours at the clubs."

"Then, don't go to the clubs." Her eyes followed him as he stood to leave. "Now you'll have a reason to return—to fill your pockets again. By then I might have a plan to get that wretch Amelia out of Trenton's life." She gritted her teeth. "I will remain the only woman in his life—even if we *are* divorced."

Twelve

TRENTON DONNED HIS navy jacket before leaving his hotel suite, and headed to the opening elevator doors. Only one more week of shooting, then a few free days left before he would have to fly back to L.A. for post-production.

The project was under budget, but not as much as he would like. More than a few rainy days had put off the outdoor shoots to the end of the filming schedule. Plus, one of the main characters halted proceedings for a few days after coming down with a cold. Minor scenes without the box-office actor, had to be shot during her recuperation. He took this all in stride, but it still irked him when things didn't go according to plan—his plan.

Tourists and businesspersons loading on at nearly every stop slowed the ride down to the lobby forcing him to the rear where he hoped he wouldn't gag from obnoxious ladies' perfume. Even with so many banks of elevators, he wondered if the entire hotel was emptying out to attend some all-important conference. He was eager to be with someone special and her name was Amelia.

The doors opened. He stood there a moment, his eyes scanning for her in the lobby. All he saw were busy doormen all dressed in formal attire complete with top hats. Trenton went to the Crystal Moon Lounge, where the spherical crystal chandelier provided a sumptuous understated ambiance. Still no Amelia. He checked his watch. His heartbeat quickened. *What is keeping her? Problems with Clive or Alistair?*

He walked to the Northall Bar. His eyes moved rapidly, searching for that luminous face and vibrant red hair. There she was, sitting on a high light blue chair, casually resting her delicate wrist on the white marble island bar. *She didn't stand me up!* He took a few moments to admire her reflection in the facing wall of mirrored tiles, which seemed to magnify her beauty.

She turned in her seat to face him as he strode towards her. He pecked her on the cheek and wrapped his arms around her as if it were a year since last seeing her and not a few days.

"That's an energetic greeting." She looked intently in his eyes. "What has caused this jubilance?"

"You're in my arms." He paused a moment, taking her in. "Nothing is better than that." He eyed the half-consumed cocktail on the bar by her purse. "Do you want to finish your drink? Should I have one with you?"

"I can have a drink any time. Let's go and make some more memories." Her wicked glint had an instant heating effect on him, and he was glad the blazer was covering his pants.

"It's a short elevator ride to my suite." *I don't know why she does that to me.*

"Plenty of time for that." Her light chuckle escaped. "I want to take you to a typical tourist attraction. Seeing you hold the written word in high esteem, you might enjoy this bit of literary fiction."

"What do you have in mind?" *Darn it. Is she avoiding going to bed with me? Didn't I measure up?*

"That's a secret until we get there." She licked her lips.

"Then lead on, McDuff." He assisted her off the chair.

"Ah, you quoted Shakespeare. Now I know I chose the right diversion." She nestled her hand in the crook of his arm as they walked out to the lobby and then through the exit.

~~***~~

The big black taxi pulled up at the famed and fictitious 221-B Baker Street location, actually located between 237 and 239.

Trenton's eyes widened. "The Sherlock Holmes Museum. I didn't even know one existed." He left the taxi after Amelia, then stood on the sidewalk, taking in the façade. "I read all of Doyle's books as a boy." He looked down at her. "You chose a perfect excursion." He kissed her cheek and resisted the temptation to kiss her ear. He couldn't do that. Not here. Not in public.

He cocked his head. "We can always amuse ourselves in other ways before dinner ... in my room." *Will she reject me? Or is she teasing? I just want to feel her delicious body all over.*

"Not yet. Let's enjoy the tribute to Sir Arthur Conan Doyle first, then we'll see about other activities." She took his hand and led the way through the door. "This is a nice way to create new memories ... for us."

Yup ... she's avoiding being alone with me. What's up with that? Yet, she did say "for us". Am I reading too much into her words?

Amelia insisted on paying the entrance fee, stating it was her treat. She explained that the Sherlock Holmes Society established this museum in 1990 and all the furnishings were an accurate representation taken from Doyle's books. They toured all three floors, climbing the narrow staircase, and visiting the carefully staged fake world.

"This is remarkable," he said. "They have everything down to the last detail—his desk, books, whistle, violin, magnifying glass, and his trademark—a deerstalker hat." He surveyed Dr. Watson's bedroom.

"There's even a diary, and extracts from the 'Hound of the Baskervilles'. A movie set designer couldn't have done better."

"I'm glad that I pleased you." She gave his hand a squeeze. "I wanted to show you that there is more to me than the pleasures in the bedroom."

"I never doubted that for one minute. As I said during our first breakfast together, and still our *only* breakfast together, I want to know everything about you." *Is that it? She thinks I see her as a sex toy? Or is she missing younger men and is trying to let me down easy?*

She wedged through the throngs of tourists toward the exit. Some must have recognized her, as they held their phones up for a photo opportunity. Trenton followed as close behind as he could, dodging souvenir shoppers.

On the sidewalk, he brushed his hair from his forehead. "Where to next?"

"I think your hotel would round out the day nicely." Her lips curled into a mischievous grin.

"Really?" *Maybe my fears are groundless.* "I thought you were trying to give me the old heave-ho."

"'Heave-ho'?" She wrinkled her nose in a cute way as if not understanding.

"Giving me the old strike out or brush off." He started to speak when a taxi pulled up.

"I haven't gone off you, if that's what you mean." She got into the backseat, and Trenton slid in next to her. He gave directions to the driver. "That means the same thing as 'heave-ho'." She patted his knee. "You're expanding my knowledge of American English. That's a good thing."

"I want all good things for you." He kissed her lips lightly, still uncertain as to where her heart truly lay—with him or all the boys in her life.

~~***~~

Thirty minutes later, they sat at a table in the Corinthia's The Northall restaurant, waiting for their order. As before, Trenton noticed subtle whispers and head nods in their direction. Amelia sipped her wine as if his choice was exquisite and seemed to take no notice of others in the room.

"Thank you for a very nice day." He chuckled and reached for her hand across the table. "You showed me an interesting site, but none as interesting as the woman I'm with."

"Flattery will get you everywhere with me ... well, almost everywhere." He stroked the top of her hand, but stopped when touching her wedding band. She glanced at his hand. "Right. Yes. Old Alistair looms in the shadows. I only wear that for his sake—so *The Daily Mail* won't print that he and I are on the outs. They don't know the real Alistair as I do. Oh they have their suspicions, but nothing concrete—no compromising photos of him and his boys."

A stylish and well-dressed handsome young man in his twenties came to their table. He slipped her a folded note. She read it briefly and crumpled it up in her fist before tucking it into her purse.

"Anything serious?" *Who was he and what was in that note? Is he one of her toys?*

"Nothing more than an annoying little midge." She gave a strained smile. "And quite disposable."

"Midge?" *Was that a note to remind her of their meeting? A meeting after dinner with me?*

"Midges are tiny bugs, smaller than gnats, and quite a bother." She pulled her hand away to sip her champagne.

"Amelia, I was going to wait until after dinner to say this, but I feel sooner is better than later." He took a couple of deep breaths. Insecurity around women was rarely in his ballpark. "Lord knows I have never met anyone like you. During this relatively short period of time, I feel closer to you than anyone else—my ex included. I probably shouldn't ask this or even suggest it, but I'm leaving for the States after next week ... I want you to come with me. Even if you only stay for a couple of weeks."

She opened her mouth to speak. He motioned his hand for her to stop. "No. Let me finish. There are no strings. I accept that you are married and the reason for your marriage. Any changes you make in the future on that score are all yours and I won't try to influence you. All I know is ... I need to have you in my life on whatever terms you set." He extended his hand to hers. "I need to know how you feel. Please tell me if I'm making a fool of myself."

"That was a very pretty speech, Trent. I know it came from your heart." She placed her hand on top of his. "I will give your proposal serious thought, very serious thought." Her light laugh eased the moment. "For an instant, I thought you were about to ask me to divorce Alistair and marry you."

"Would that have been so bad if I did?" *She's thinking about divorcing Alistair?*

"It would have changed things from the way they are now, and created a very difficult situation for me." She glanced about the room. "I'm famished. What's keeping that waiter?"

"It shouldn't be long before he's here." *I wish I could read her thoughts.* "After dinner, we could have a drink at one of the bars here, or a nightcap in my room?"

"Let's make it an early night." Her warm smile didn't remove the chill she inflicted on his heart. "I need to deal with a few things tomorrow, and I want to be well-rested for that."

Trenton couldn't figure out what was going on with Amelia. One minute she could hardly leave his side, jumping his bones, and the next she acted as if his presence was as vile as poison.

I blew it. Moved too fast and was too obvious. I should have remembered she likes mystique, and I gave her plain old dependability.

Will she be with me in L.A.?

I can always hope.

Thirteen

TAYLOR DAVIS' CELL phone rang at eight in the morning. Glancing at the caller ID, she picked it up from the kitchen counter with one hand while holding a cup of dark brew in the other. The aroma of freshly dripped coffee in the heated carafe filled the room.

"Hi, Amelia. What's the news? Anything to do with Cindy and Stuart?" She looked at Larry as he entered, giving an expansive yawn.

"No. They are fine to the best of my knowledge ..." She noticed the duchess' serious tone. "My carefree life has become very complicated."

"Go on. What's the problem?" Larry shot her a curious look. She placed her hand over the mouthpiece and whispered, "Amelia. Something's up."

He poured coffee in his cup from the counter, then sat opposite his wife.

"Do you recall meeting Trenton Lowe at Cindy's wedding?" Her tone sounded somber.

"Yes. We only exchanged a few words during the reception." Taylor leaned her elbows on the counter as her brow furrowed. "I remember you requested that I invite him and his friend David what's-his-name to the wedding. I have to confess I looked him up on Google, though, just to find out a little more about who he is and what he's achieved."

"He's the one—that gorgeous specimen of male sexuality, producing all those Hollywood movies." A long pause ensued. "Well, my relationship with Trent is more involved than the toy boys I've enjoyed in the past."

"You've always had the attitude of 'love 'em and leave 'em' with the others," she pointed out to her dear friend. Larry watched Taylor's reaction.

"That's just it." Amelia's voice held a hint of tremor. "I have feelings for him that go beyond anything I've felt before. Now, he wants me to return with him to his home in Malibu. He seems to be feeling what we have is far more than a fling with a duchess."

Taylor let out a sigh. "Has he said he loves you?"

Larry's eyes popped as he raised his brows. He whispered as Taylor put her fingers over the mouthpiece, "Trouble on the home front?"

She put her finger to her lips for him to be quiet.

Amelia's deep sigh expressed her grave feelings. "No. But Trent mentioned he wanted me in his life on whatever terms I put forth." Her voice lowered a decimal. "What if he wants more than I can give—be a permanent person in his life?"

"Hold on a minute." Taylor noticed Larry had picked up a copy of *Variety* from the counter and proceeded to read. *Typical man. No longer interested in what Amelia has to say.* "Traveling with him to his home does not require a lifelong commitment on your part. Enjoy the experience and go from there."

"But it could be in the future—a lifelong commitment." She heard Amelia take a swallow of something. "I have some sort of feelings for him. I knew that when we were having dinner and one of my boys pushed a note in my hand. I think deep down, I realized that from our first night together and more so on the morning after. I don't know exactly what these feelings are, mind."

Taylor left the stool and went to the coffeemaker to pour another cup of the decaf brew. "What did the note say? What was Trenton's reaction?"

"He seemed to ignore the note Reggie shoved at me. I only glanced at it and didn't read the message until later—a veiled attempt to expose his liaison with me if I didn't call him. Stupid fool! The entire social set knows of my boys. His threat was of no consequence. After Trent opened his heart to me, it threw me off my pins. I left early and thus declined any further advances for the evening. I hope he didn't take my ending our dinner right after coffee as my rejection of him."

"Has he contacted you since that dinner?" Taylor ambled to the living room and sat on the sofa. "If he doesn't call or email you, then you have your answer of his true intentions."

"The dinner was last night. I guess I'm too eager to hear back from him." She took a sip of something again. "I'm not accustomed to being in the position of hoping a man will call. I'm in the habit of being the one in control."

"If you and Trenton become more involved, then giving up control might be the role you'll need to adjust to." Larry entered and sat down on a leather-upholstered chair opposite her. "Since he's a movie producer, the only boss I'm aware of who Trenton answers to, is the head of the movie studio. I think you're jumping the gun. Take him up on his offer to visit his place and as I said, see where it goes from there. He hasn't been divorced that long and might be just getting back to the dating scene."

"I appreciate you listening to my concerns." Amelia chuckled. "This is all rather new to me. I'm not used to being pursued by a man near my own age." Her voice lowered again. "If I fall in love with him—*really* fall in love—then that would mean me leaving Alistair—a *divorce*. That would upset his world while freeing mine."

"A divorce? That's a bit premature." She flashed a glance with wide eyes at Larry. "All your fears could fizzle out to nothing. When he calls, try not to read too much into what he says or how he acts."

Amelia let out a long sigh. "*If* he calls at all, that's the big question. Reggie could have ended any prospects with Trent because of his bloody note. Maybe Trent only wants me in his life for a limited period of time."

"Try not to get your hopes up." She bit her bottom lip as concern creased her forehead.

"I'll be a mess until he does call, or messages me." Her strained laugh pierced Taylor's ears. "We need to clear the air so I know where I stand .... Look I need to ring off. I'll keep in touch. You've been a dear for listening to my ramblings."

Taylor placed her phone on the coffee table and then stared out towards the patio.

"Well," Larry broke her train of thought. "What was that all about? Amelia having love issues?"

"I think she's fallen for Trenton Lowe." She grabbed a fashion magazine from the cushion beside her.

"Did she say as much?" He put down the copy of *Variety*.

"No. But she did mention that he stated his feelings for her." Taylor flipped the pages as she talked, not focusing on any particular photo. "Plus, she's concerned as to whether he will contact her again. Seems to me that the duchess has fallen in love and doesn't know what to do with this new feeling—as if she's a teenager with a crush on the football star."

"Don't get involved. Let her figure it out." He pointed his finger. "Remember, she's Clive's cousin and you don't want to get mixed up in that can of worms."

"You're right, of course." She paused a moment, then looked directly at him. "How much do you know about Trenton Lowe?"

"Not much. He's into movies and I'm in music. He's a straightforward guy. No gossip in the rags." His eyes narrowed. "Why all this curiosity about Amelia and Trenton?"

"Well, if she does travel out here with him, then she won't be able to keep on top of what mess Clive could create for Cindy and Stu." Taylor's lips thinned. "She's always had the knack of keeping his evil ways from Cindy—a buffer of sorts. Without Amelia, Clive's path to them is clear."

"Stop worrying." He smiled knowingly. "Though, worry is your mainstay where your daughter is concerned."

"This could all be moot, since Trenton hasn't called Amelia since their dinner last night." She took a sip of coffee and studied her husband's expression.

He stood to leave. "I'm back to writing that movie score."

"What movie is that?" *Business secrets again!*

"I don't want to jinx it. I'll tell you if I get the deal." Larry headed to the studio. "Don't borrow trouble where there is none."

Taylor nodded. "You're right."

If she falls hard for Trenton, Clive will side with Alistair. Will Clive try for retribution against Amelia? Target Cindy or Stuart?

Fourteen

AMELIA FELL INTO deep yet troubling thoughts as she held Trenton's hand while they strolled along the hushed galleries of the British Museum on Great Russell Street in London. The silence that had evolved comforted her and at the same time was a source of concern. *Is he quiet because he doesn't want to say hurtful words to me?* The warmth of his clasp provided little reassurance. She glanced up at him hoping to find kindness in his eyes and a reason for her to believe that the insecurities in her heart were groundless. His banal expression offered no clues. *Is Trent sorry he said he wanted me in his life? Is he trying to think of a tactful way to take it all back?*

"I'm glad you called me, even though it was brief and only to set up our outing here." She gave his hand a squeeze.

"I want to make the most of what time I have left in London with you." He smiled wistfully. "Even if that means I return to Malibu alone."

"Then you still want me as your traveling companion?" *I wish I could read his heart.* "Are you giving me a way out?"

"Not at all." He walked to the enormous statue of a pharaoh, sizing up the antiquity. "Your decision should be yours alone with no pressure from me. I realize that there might be complications for you regarding Alistair."

"I rarely give him a second thought—though I'm not heartless, despite what the tabloids say." Her eyes searched his to see if his polite words covered deeper feelings. "There is one exhibit you need to see before we leave—the Rosetta stone is a must."

"A rose by any other name." His light chuckle charmed her.

"I had no idea I was in the company of a Shakespeare scholar." *There's so much I don't know about him.*

"That and 'Lead on McDuff' is about the limit of my Shakespeare quotes." He gave her a sly wink. "Lady Steffenfordshire isn't the only one who has secrets. I'd love to discover every single one of them."

"Single one of what?" She stifled a sigh of relief, feeling her fears might be groundless.

"Your secrets." He placed his hand at the small of her back. "You are one enticing and mysterious woman."

"Some things are best left unknown." *How much of my past does he know?*

With the aid of a tourist pamphlet, Amelia led the way to the famous artifact. She expounded on the facts she could recall from her schooling, hoping that Trenton would realize that her knowledge of the world extended far beyond the bedroom. He appeared enthralled with her telling of the discovery of this significant archeological find. However, she realized his focus was mostly on her moving lips and then her eyes.

Is he listening to a word I've said or remembering our night of love?

After wandering the halls, Amelia and Trenton ended up at the museum's Court Café at the north end of the Great Court. The high ceiling of arches and indirect lighting provided an enormous airy feel to the surroundings.

Having seated themselves on bar chairs at a high table and placed their orders, Amelia wondered if she should bring up the subject of her accompanying him on his return to the States. She hadn't yet decided, and this troubled her as decisions usually came easily and swiftly to her.

"I feel we've been avoiding the elephant in the room." He stroked her hand across the table.

"What elephant is that?" She nearly cooed her words.

"The fact that you haven't told me if you'll fly with me back to Malibu." The server brought their order, placing the tea for her, coffee for him, and scones before them on the table. "For some reason, I get the feeling that you're having trouble telling me of your decision, or if you've even made a decision."

Amelia poured milk in her cup as she talked. "It's not that simple for me."

His kind eyes looked intently into hers, as if his emotions hung by a silvery thread. "It's not like I suggested you leave your husband."

"But you said you wanted me in your life." She felt tears welling up, then took a deep breath. "Has that changed? Were those words spoken during the heat of passion—saying what you thought would fit the situation with no substance behind them?"

"I meant them then, and I mean them now." He squeezed her hand. "I don't want you to feel there were any strings. After a failed marriage, I'm not in the position to offer 'forever' to anyone—least of all to a royal duchess."

"This is all new to me." She took a delicate bite of a blueberry scone, chewed, and swallowed quickly. "I have never had a man want anything more from me than my body and money."

"Your money and title is not the allure for me." He paused and bit his bottom lip to the side. "Your body? Well, I am a man. But, seriously, I enjoy your company and the way you see things—your spontaneous approach to life. That is so refreshing to me, especially since my world deals with the make-believe and subterfuge. Both abound in the movie industry. Careers have been lost for not saying the proper thing at the right time—no matter what the truth is." He chuckled. "Diplomacy is taken to a new height in Hollywood and could teach our government a thing or two on how to make deals."

"Sounds a bit like the royals I contend with—all the pomp and protocol—two aspects that I've always rebelled from. My reputation attests to that." *We have more in common than I thought. I've never really exchanged ideas with a man that didn't involve more than the wordplay of sex.*

"I'm immune to the gossip, whether printed or spoken." He inclined his head boyishly. "Are you ready for a new adventure? Ready to take Hollywood by storm on the arm of a famous movie producer?"

"I like your modesty, Mister Producer." She took the napkin to her lips. "Contrary to your beliefs, my past might be a liability to your career. Am I worthy enough for you to take that risk?"

"Like I said, none of that concerns me." He stroked the ridge on top of her hand. "Won't you say yes so I can show you my world?"

She loved the way he touched her. "How soon do you need an answer?"

"Well, the wrap party is next Friday evening at my hotel, and then I fly out the next day." His eyes softened her concerns. "Would you have your answer by Thursday?"

"Today is Saturday. That means we have less than a week and you'll be gone. I don't know if Alistair would pose any problems." The pressure of knowing she had to make an immediate decision unsettled her. Amelia had hoped there was more time.

Trenton stroked his chin as worry set in his eyes. "You're thinking of turning me down."

"I don't want to give that impression." *I can't stand looking at his pleading eyes ... as if he's a little boy who lost his puppy.*

"Well ... hedging with your answer or lack of one isn't very reassuring." He stared at her hand and then looked squarely at her. "Is it a matter of you not wanting to leave what you have here—the social life with the young male admirers? I'm far from twenty. What I lack in youth I make up for in experience."

"It's none of those things, Trent. I haven't had any clandestine engagements since we met. I don't know why I avoided those boys, but the thrill is tarnished for me—as if I want more from my life." Those words made her cringe inwardly, as if someone else were revealing her truth.

"You have been giving more serious thought than I realized." His eyes brightened with a wide smile. "I was fearful I bored you in some way. Though, had you continued your diversions that wouldn't change my feelings towards you."

"What are those feelings?" *I want to believe him.*

"As I mentioned before, I want to get to know you better. Have you in my life for as long as you want." He traced her lips with his fingertip.

"I'll give you my decision in a few days, or sooner." The heat of his hand traveled up her arm and made her stifle a gasp.

"Sooner would be best." His eyes continued to plead. "Though I'd rather wait for the correct answer than to press you and then get the wrong one." He took a sip of coffee. "It goes without saying that I want you to be my guest at the wrap party at eight o'clock in the evening."

"Does that invitation hold, even if I don't fly to Malibu?" *I don't want to hurt him, but I need to be honest with Trent.*

"Yes. I'm a man of my word. Though I hope the wrap party will celebrate a new chapter in my life with you." He gave her a gentle kiss on the lips—not of passion, but closer to one of love.

She studied every nuance that flickered across his face, searching for any hint of insincerity. There was none.

I want to go with him. Should I follow Taylor's advice and throw caution to the wind?

AMELIA FRANTICALLY HAULED out two large suitcases from the back of her bedroom closet and flung them on the bed. Young Elizabeth, the housemaid looked on with a rutted brow and wide eyes. The duchess shot her a glance and then sharpened her focus to pulling out dresser drawers and then combing through her vast wardrobe of hanging clothes, selecting what she thought might be suitable.

Elizabeth took a step towards the bed. "Milady, are you planning a long trip? Will you need me to travel with you?"

"I haven't decided yet. I want to be ready if I do go." She glanced at the young servant. "I don't think I'll need you for a short trip of only a fortnight or so."

"If it's not too bold of me to ask, Milady ... where might you be traveling to?" She interlaced her fingers and rubbed her thumbs as if worry crept at the back of her mind.

"Not too bold at all, Elizabeth." Amelia went to her jewelry case and rummaged the treasure-trove. "I might be going to Wonderland—like Alice stepping through the looking glass." She placed her precious gems in a velvet roll and secured them with a satin ribbon.

"Am I to mention your possible trip to the others—Milord and his houseman?" She assisted Amelia in folding the clothes and placing them in the cases.

"This is only between us, Elizabeth." She took a half dozen outfits from their hangers and carefully arranged them in the suitcase. "I'll notify Lord Steffenfordshire when and *if* the time arrives."

"As you wish, Milady." Elizabeth cleared her throat while retrieving a small envelope from her pocket and handed it to her mistress. "This came for you today in the post."

Amelia took the message, and read the address. "It's from Reggie. No need to open it. I can guess what he wants—money as usual." She tore the unopened envelope into pieces and placed them in Elizabeth's hands. "When you get a chance, burn that post."

"Certainly, Milady." The young girl started to leave.

"Elizabeth, when is Lord Steffenfordshire expected?" Amelia placed the last garments on top of the others folded in her cases before shutting the lids and latching the locks. Satisfaction showed in her smug grin.

"Milord rang earlier today, and said he would be dining here instead of going to the club." She paused a moment at the doorway as if expecting further instructions.

"Right." Amelia lowered her voice as if speaking to herself. "Better get right to this one and come out with it."

"Excuse me, Milady?" Elizabeth's eyes held mild confusion. "What did you say?"

"What?" The duchess turned and faced the servant. "Oh, that. Nothing. Just mumbling to myself. Carry on with whatever you need to tend to. I'm fine. I'd like to be alone for awhile."

Elizabeth quietly closed the door.

I dread talking with Alistair. Why is that? I've taken vacations before without him.

~~***~~

She found Alistair seated in the library of their London townhouse, swirling his brandy as he pensively looked into space. He didn't raise his head until he felt her body sit next to his on the loveseat.

"Amelia, you must have something important to say. Why else would you be sitting next to me?" He crossed his legs away from her, and took a swallow of his drink.

"Nothing of great import—merely notifying you that I may be traveling to the States for a fortnight." She touched his hand lightly. "I thought you would appreciate me giving you the courtesy of a notice. I haven't properly decided yet."

He nodded. "Well noted." She felt his eyes scrutinizing her with no hint of brotherly kindness she took for granted. "Traveling with Mr. Lowe?"

"Why do you ask? What makes you bring up Trenton Lowe?" *He has no room to criticize me.*

"It's not a difficult deduction with all the photos of you and him in the papers." His sarcastic laugh made her blood simmer just below a boil. "Even my subordinates want me to get autographs of the famous film stars in that blasted movie he's producing." He gazed at her a moment, his determined eyes unnerving her. "You aren't becoming emotionally involved with him, are you?"

"Would you care?" She huffed, then walked over to the bar and poured herself a sherry. "After all these years with you and your boys and me with my male companions?"

"I never heard you complain." He inched forward in his seat with his elbows on his knees. "Not one word—ever."

"Between you and my late father, I didn't have the right." Amelia's disgusted laugh pierced the air. "My wedding night was far from perfect—far from anything I expected."

"You never said anything—not even the next morning." Alistair looked confused. "I thought young Hans would treat you quite well in the amorous department, even if I couldn't."

"No bride expects her marriage to be consummated by an understudy—your best man." Long buried pain burned in her gut. "I was only seventeen and had never been with a man. I'm certain my father didn't think that my new husband would function as a eunuch."

"What is the purpose of all this?" He watched her sit in the chair opposite him. "I have never interfered with your clandestine affairs, and you've been understanding about my private associations."

"Maybe it's time you know that I'm tired of being chattel—chattel that my father's money allows you to keep that drafty old estate up country." She hated the tears welling up in her eyes, blinked several times and looked upwards to the ceiling to prevent them from falling. "If only once in my life, I would like a man to love me for myself and not for what my inheritance could provide. I deserve that. Maybe I would like to have a child some day."

"You are talking pure folly!" He raked his hand through his iron-gray hair. "What we have works very well for us."

"Works for you!" She crossed her arms across her chest, frustration rising. "Not me. I merely adapted to what I was in—sentenced to a loveless marriage."

"Hold on there a minute." He stood up and started pacing the floor. "You were a mere lady—daughter of an earl. Marrying me made you a duchess with access to the upper royal society."

"That was my father's goal for me." She tapped her foot at a rapid pace. "No one, and I mean absolutely no one asked what my hopes and dreams were."

"Is all this discontent because of you going thought a life review of some kind?" His eyes opened wide as his jaw slackened. "Bloody hell! Have you started the change of life prematurely? I've heard of women going off the rails when the hormones go awry."

"Stop it!" Amelia jumped out of her seat to meet him head on. "You're bloody insulting! Don't try to reduce my concerns to that of a simple-headed woman unable to control her emotions. I've been talking to you from my heart, hoping you would care and understand—obviously I was wrong on both counts."

"Steady on." He put his glass down on the coffee table and went to embrace her. She shrugged him off. "I think you'll see things better in the light of day. A good steak will set you right."

"It will take more than a steak and a good night's sleep to set anything right with me." She sighed, pursing her lips. "I'm glad we've had this talk and cleared the air. Now I understand just how little you care. All these years I thought you loved me as a sister. I was so very wrong."

"Don't make rash decisions, Amelia." She started to walk toward the door. "You might regret the choices you make and if you're thinking of traveling with that Yank, you won't have my sanction."

"I've been regretting the choices my father made. It can't be any worse than that." Her eyes flared. "As to your approval—that's never been my concern. My self-esteem can't sink any lower because of you—have been since our wedding night. A young girl so repulsive that her groom couldn't touch her—had to have someone else do the deed. Now it's time to set it right!" She left, slamming the door and stood in the hallway a moment trying to calm the tremors claiming her body.

I didn't want to hurt Alistair. Why did I blow up like that? I haven't yet decided if I'll fly with Trent to his home. Should I? Still ....

Sixteen

THE DOOR OPENED with a miniscule noise and clearly didn't break Clive's concentration as he peered into the microscope while seated on a stool in the laboratory. Alistair stood in the entry for a moment before shutting the door. His rubber-soled shoes didn't seem to be noticed by his colleague and friend. Neatly stacked piles of papers rested on the long soapstone topped table with open boxes of latex gloves and unused slides within reach for a new specimen. Clive appeared to be alone. Alistair pulled up a seat beside him. He wrinkled his nose at the urine smell of the small primates that peered at them from their cages opposite. Tall racks of files and binders from floor to ceiling comprised two walls, while expansive windows made up the fourth. Bright lights shone over the table.

"What now, Alistair?" His voice filled with amused aggravation. He didn't look up and continued focusing the scope. "Stuck on your part of the project?"

"I'm stuck, but nothing to do with the project, ol' man." After a moment of Clive's irritating silence, he cleared his throat. "I need to speak with you." He came closer and leaned against the table.

His friend scribbled notes on a nearby pad. "What is it? I don't need a longwinded dissertation."

"Amelia." He ran his hand through his hair. "It seems she wants to take a trip to the States with that Lowe chap—the American movie producer."

"I'm guessing that her young male companions will be financially hurting upon her departure." Clive let out a chuckle and sneered. "They'll have to find another female benefactor for their allowance."

"This isn't a joking matter." *He never takes my concerns seriously.* "If she leaves with Trenton Lowe, she might not return. My life would suffer very drastic changes—changes I'm not certain I would take kindly to."

"That's easily solved." Clive pulled away from the scope and placed his hands on his knees as he looked at his friend. His sneer screamed that the answer should be obvious. "Tell her she's forbidden to leave."

"She won't have any of it, you see. For all I know, Amelia could be at home packing right now."

"Bad for you, but bloody right for me." Clive returned to his microscope, talking as he squinted. "She would be out of my hair for a while and no longer watching me like a hawk—ever protective of her precious cousin—my son, Stuart, and that dimwitted wife of his."

"You're missing the crux of my situation." He took an expansive breath before continuing, "If Amelia falls in love with this bloke, then she could ask for a divorce. Access to her inheritance would be cut off! I'd be near penniless save for the townhouse in Mayfair. I told you all this before."

"Steady on, old chap." Clive pulled back again from peering at the specimens on the slide and looked into space, his conniving wheels churning. "Has she said anything about divorce?"

"No. But she did mention how she felt her life was empty without love in it." He wrung his hands. "It could only be a matter of weeks, maybe days."

"That would shed a different light on the situation." His forehead knitted in deep creases. "If she divorces you, the entail not only affects you, but has a horrid impact for me, as well."

"How is that?" Alistair raised his brows, leaning his shoulders closer.

"As part of the entail, I have control—supervising her private financial accounts—accrued interest and such. If she divorces you, I lose that control in addition to you losing the dowry from your marriage." He seized Alistair's forearm for emphasis. "The entail is very firm and cannot be smashed!" His eyes widened. "Believe me, I've had the best solicitors examine that blasted document."

"Then I'm done for." He hung his head. "Clive, I've been stressing these very facts to you all along. You're just now realizing the impact?"

He set his jaw. Clearly, he did not like being called out, and contempt poured from his eyes. "I recollect that I was *first*—briefly mentioning this to you at Stuart's wedding reception." His smug smile irritated Alistair.

Pompous arse wallows in being right.

"You needn't look so satisfied with yourself, ol' man." He took a handkerchief from his jacket pocket and wiped the beads of perspiration from his brow. "I don't like the idea of giving up my membership at the club."

"You're making way too much of the situation—letting your fears run wild." Clive laughed snidely. "Don't jump to the end of the book without reading the beginning. Knowing my cousin, she'll soon tire of his company and will be back to her usual clandestine routine."

"I hope you're correct on that one. But my fears seem very real to me. If you had been there when she went on and on about her life, you'd understand why I'm so troubled." He saw no real recognition of the facts in Clive's eyes. "At one point she was on the verge of tears."

"Tears? Amelia?" His eyes grew wide. "That ice-cold bitch?"

"Now, do you understand what I've been getting at?" He pleaded with upturned palms.

"Still, I feel you are being a bit premature." He returned to his microscope.

Clive doesn't appreciate my situation—not one bit. My whole life could crumble and all he cares about is he losing control of her private funds. If she goes, will Amelia remain in the States? What of me? Can I survive?

~~***~~

In Clairidge's private reception room, a joyous din hummed with laughter, and compliments were exchanged between crew and actors at the famous wrap party. Holding glasses of champagne, Trenton and Amelia weaved among the guests. His world enticed her almost as much as his handsome persona. This wasn't a gathering where protocol and strict manners were the code de rigueur for the evening, but a place where people welcomed pats on the back, warm handshakes, and kisses on the cheeks, even if the kisses merely landed mid-air. They found a secluded table in one corner, away from the loudspeaker blaring piped-in music.

"Are you enjoying yourself?" Trenton asked as he reached for Amelia's hand resting in her lap.

"Delightfully so." She glanced about the room as she talked. "Everyone seems so very happy with everyone they meet."

"Don't be taken in by surface appearance." He took a sip from his flute. "It's all fake—expected behavior."

"Really?" Her eyes narrowed as her brows drew together. "They all seem so genuine."

"It's the biz I work in." He chuckled. "The royal muckety-mucks aren't the only ones with rules—Hollywood has rules too. The trick is to know what rules need to be followed and which ones to ignore." He paused a moment, latching onto her eyes with his. His lowered voice hinted of despondence. "I've guessed that you won't be flying out with me tomorrow. You never gave me your answer yesterday, even though I left you at least six voice messages and texted you, too."

"All good things come to those who wait." A small smile curled the corners of her lips. "I haven't said no yet."

"As long as you don't say no at all—now or in the future." He kissed her neck, tingling sensations surged through her, making her want him at that moment.

"You'll have to wait and see." Her eyes lit with devilish intrigue. It was her game and she played it to the hilt.

"Breaking my heart might be fun for you, but it's cruel on the receiving end." He squeezed her hand. "Let's continue this conversation in my suite."

Taking her by the hand, he stood up and led her out of the room to the impressive bank of elevators. *He likes to be in control—I could almost get to enjoy that!*

The ride up to his suite was swift and smooth. More than once, Trenton cast a lustful glance that caused her breath to quicken.

In his suite, Amelia noticed his suitcases lined up by the door like obedient soldiers waiting for a command. She kicked off her toe-pinching heels and surveyed the room.

There's no champagne chilling, no glasses? I guess he's ready to leave at a moment's notice.

She nodded her head towards the luggage. "Are you leaving tonight?"

"First thing in the morning." He embraced her tightly, so tight that she could feel his desire firm against her. "Let's go to the bedroom and see if I forgot to pack something."

She followed him and noticed the turned-down linen. A second set of luggage stood in the corner, nearly hidden by the pooling drapes near the balcony doors.

Trenton flung off his jacket, and practically ripped off his shirt—the clothing falling in a heap on the carpeted floor. He embraced her and smoothly slid down the zipper at the back of her dress, allowing it to fall to the floor. All that covered her body was a flimsy pair of sheer panties. As his lips crushed hers and his tongue explored her mouth, his hand caressed her breast, gently at first and then firmer. Amelia fumbled with his belt and then his zipper. She reached inside, caressing and teasing him to full arousal. She wanted him at that moment and at the same time wanted to prolong the luscious sensation of wanton desire. The rest of his clothing fell to the floor. He frantically pulled off his socks as she placed herself on the bed. The delicious view of his erection drove her mad and made her moist. She didn't wait for him to remove her panties and took them off in one teasing movement, dropping them to the floor.

"I need you." Her breath came in heavy pants. "Don't make me beg."

"Waiting can sharpen the senses." His knee spread her thighs apart with a force she hadn't dreamed of before.

She grabbed his shoulders, bringing him on top of her, feeling his muscular chest press against her breasts, and his beating heart quickening her desire. She wanted him now. He was so close and yet miles away. His fingers explored her velvet recesses, driving her wild to the point she thought she would scream from frustration.

Trenton positioned himself to tease her to near madness with his kisses at her opening. With each glorious sensation, she wanted more. Yes, that was what she loved, and she wanted him to enter her. His kisses brought her to the next level of pleasure. With his manhood in her reach, her mouth caressed him and teased him as his hips began to move with each stroke of her tongue.

Trenton knelt between her welcoming thighs, and eased himself into her, slowly, inch by inch. *Why is he teasing me like this? I want him in me now!* She grabbed his buttocks, forcing all of him into her. Every stroke heightened her desire to where she thought she couldn't breathe. Her rhythm guided his movement. Sweat trickled down their chests. Her ecstasy was at hand when her fingers dug into his back and her arching forced him to keep pace with her passion. A loud moan escaped from her lips. She felt his spasms inside her as her orgasm exploded around him.

He raised his head from her shoulder and looked in her eyes while smoothing the damp hair from her temples.

"You are so beautiful—beautiful in every way." He kissed her lips gently. "How I wish you would fly with me to Malibu in the morning. But, I guess what we just shared was our special goodbye."

"Or, it could be a hello to a new experience ... a new chapter." *I can't walk away from him.*

Curiosity colored his eyes. "What? You mean you will fly on my jet to my home?"

"For a producer, you're not very observant." She giggled like a mischievous child. "Didn't you notice any new addition to the room?" She turned her head towards the balcony doorway.

He looked in the direction she indicated. "Two pieces of luggage! They're yours?"

She nodded and giggled with a large smile.

"When did you get them up here? How did you pull this off without me knowing?" His eyes moved across her face with confusion.

"I have my secrets." She grinned. "Being a duchess isn't always a bad thing. It has its perks."

Concern marred his brow. "What about your husband? How is he dealing with his wife flying across to the other side of the globe?"

"He doesn't know yet." She fingered the hair at his ear. "I'll let him know when I'm on your plane, flying to a new and wonderful world."

"I'm so very lucky to have met you—having you in my life." He looked in her eyes. "You mean more to me than—you're not ready to hear those words—not yet."

He kissed her again with love and not passion. She once more succumbed to desire—desire that went deeper than mere physical pleasure.

I pray to God I've made the right decision.
Will he hurt me? Is a goodbye inevitable?

Seventeen

SOMEWHERE OVER THE Atlantic in his jet, Trenton stared at Amelia sitting opposite him and pondered her seductive magnetism. Her luscious full lips, alluring eyes framed by long dark lashes, and vibrant red hair had captivated him at their first meeting and continued to have the same effect. He couldn't picture himself ever tiring of looking at her nor could he imagine his life without her. He had come to believe that somewhere, somehow, deep down he was put on earth solely to be with her. Nothing else pulled at him. It was Amelia and had always been Amelia. She was his destiny even before they met.

She sipped a glass of Lillet blanc. A tray of imported cheese and crackers rested on the small table between them.

Though his official divorce from Naomi was only months old, to him it seemed nearly a lifetime. He knew the marriage was over within six months of their wedding day, but believed marriage was a serious commitment, and remained true to his vows. Even those words had soured in his mouth whenever he remembered them.

"Why do you have that smug smile? Proud that you are traveling in the company of a duchess?" Her tongue lingered on her upper lip as she stroked the stem of her wine glass.

"Title or not, I'm proud to be in your company under any circumstances." He spread his arms along the back of the short sofa. "You are like no other woman I've met—there's a shitload of imposters out there trying to get their foot in the door, but none as genuine as you."

"That's high praise coming from a powerful man with extremely discriminating tastes." She patted the seat next to her. "Come, Mister Movie Producer, give me a lesson from the legendary casting couch."

"You don't need any lessons. You wrote the book. Such a tease, and I love it." He took a bite of cracker and chewed with deliberate seductiveness to match hers.

"My, my, I don't know if I can live up to such praise." She leaned forward and her décolleté caught his attention.

"You surpass all words to express your dangerous allure." *She knows exactly what she's doing—making me want her—making me want to grab her, tear her clothes off, and take her on the floor right now.*

"I see you crossed your legs." She took a piece of cheese with her fingers, and tasted the surface with her tongue. "Is your erection nearly complete for me? Do I need to lick this cheese longer for you to achieve the full desired effect?"

Trenton's face flamed. "You are so brazen. How do you do that—remain a lady while making such outrageous comments? Aren't you afraid of the flight attendant overhearing you?"

"Not in the least bit." She chuckled. "He looks a bit young. He might learn something."

"Do you miss those young male companions?" *Is she seeing this trip as a joke—a new experience she can cross off her bucket list?*

"You needn't be so polite, Trent." She looked squarely at him. "I make no pretense. I call a spade a spade. My 'male companions' are toy boys. Nothing more than to fill my time and my empty existence." She took a large swallow of wine. "I gave up that hobby, days after we met for dinner the first time. You became my new desire and remain as such."

"Hobbies can be dropped at will when the attraction wanes. I don't want to become just another statistic in your life." His senses sharpened, keen to read her true intent.

"You are not a hobby to me." She dipped her finger in the wine and slowly sucked off the drop. His pants grew tighter. "The attraction I have for you waxes, growing stronger and straighter, like a fine crafted stiff candle with a wick reaching for that elusive flame—that burst of fire that comes when sulfur ignites with oxygen."

He checked around for the attendant. The last thing he wanted was a witness to their wanton conversation—especially since Naomi's last call and threat. She eyed him with playful seductiveness, as a cat before a bird.

He had enough of her damnable teasing ways. "I think it's time for a tour of the jet."

Trenton stood and reached for her hand, fully aware that Amelia noticed the outline of his erection in his slacks as she sported an approving smile.

"You've already shown me the galley, cockpit, and where the steward sits during the flight." She grabbed her purse, then reached up and whispered in his ear, "What else could be so intriguing?"

The delicious heat of her breath fanned the flames of his passion. He wanted to be in her now, pumping with all his force, making her beg for more until she exploded around him, her juices bathing his cock.

Trenton led the way, while unbuttoning his shirt, and then unfastening his belt. "It's at the back of the plane—soundproof and very secluded." He opened the door, revealing an inviting turned-down double bed.

"You've thought of every eventuality." She opened her small pocketbook and pulled out a handful of brightly colored scarves.

He looked at the fabric in her hands. "What do you have planned? Blindfolds?"

I like the way she thinks.

"That's for you to wait and find out." Amelia slowly opened her blouse, button by button, revealing her white flesh by inches.

My God, she gets me so hot. I want to fuck her now! "Please speed things along. We'll be landing at JFK to gas up in just a couple of hours."

"It won't take as long as all that." She shimmied out of her skirt and stood there in a red bra and panties. "You'll be pleased ... very pleased." Her words hummed in his ears as he reached out to her. She pulled just out of reach. "Finish undressing. Get on the bed—in the middle."

He did as she instructed. "What are you going to do?"

Amelia's such an aphrodisiac. She should be patented.

She took a silk scarf and tied his wrists together above his head.

What is she doing? She better not have a whip in her arsenal.

His laugh had a nervous quality. "Pain is a turnoff for me. If that's on your agenda, we can stop right now."

"No pain. Pure pleasure." Amelia unfastened her bra, letting her full breasts show proudly with rosy erect nipples. "Like what you see?" Next, she pulled down her red panties, letting them fall to her ankles, and kicked them off. Her hands caressed her body, making him wish he was the one touching her, feeling her nipples in his mouth.

"Definitely. No man would not like your voluptuous lips and ... mouth." Amelia took another scarf and tied it around his head, over his eyes. "Darkness will sharpen your senses .... That's not too tight, is it?"

"The scarf? Not at all." He wondered what would be next.

He felt a silky piece of fabric lazily travel from his neck to his lips. Her hot breath was close to him following the teasing of what he surmised was another scarf. Goosebumps rose up on his arms. This electrifying feeling went lower down his chest. Her hot lips and moist tongue circled each nipple, and then Trenton felt her soft breasts graze over him, tickling the hair on his stomach, going ever lower and lower to his manhood. Her tongue made delicious flicks at the base of his desire. He didn't think it was possible, but his erection grew harder to the point where he thought he would explode. *Does she want me to hold back or come in her mouth?* Her lips closed around him, tantalizing with slow movements at first and then faster with teasing pauses. She caressed him with her tongue at his most sensitive area, as he had done for her during their previous lovemaking. *I can't hold back much longer.* Then all of a sudden, the luscious and exquisite sensations stopped.

What is she doing—a new form for torture—withholding what I want most?

He felt her lower herself down on top of him. Her warm folds surrounded his hard erection.

Her movement was slow and enticing, moving faster and then slowing to prolong the delicious pleasure. *I want to grab her and I can't! These damn restraints.*

His hands wiggled free and grabbed the firm flesh of her buttocks. He guided her movement, up and down, evermore rapidly. She gasped with each stroke. He removed one hand and flung the blindfold to the side, then firmly took hold of her breasts, her rhythm in sync with his. Faster and faster with trickling sweat glistening on their chests, their frantic movements brought them to the ultimate moment of ecstasy, spasms exploding through them as they moaned in unison. She collapsed on his chest.

The scent of her fragrance filled him and enhanced the closeness he felt for her. This unconventional woman with the "damn the rules" approach to life had captivated him. He wondered if she felt the same. He knew that Amelia was a woman who would not be rushed. He feared opening his heart would send her out of his life forever.

He stroked the damp hair at her neck as she snuggled into his chest. "You certainly are a woman of surprises. What made you think of the scarves?"

"If I don't show you what I like and my playful side, how will you know?" She lifted her head to look at him. He wanted to believe her eyes held love for him.

"So you would like to be on the receiving end of what you did for me?" He looked intently at her, trying to find a sign that this was so much more than sex.

"Of course." She gently kissed his lips.

"You'll have to give me about an hour to recharge the old batteries."

He looked at his watch. "Not even then. We'll be landing in New York in about forty minutes."

"You owe me one." Amelia gathered her clothes and went to the adjoining bathroom.

"Not to fear. I'll pay you back in kind ... with pleasure." Trenton started to dress and called out to her. "Don't you think you should call your husband?"

"I'll ring him when we land." Her voice faded slightly with the sound of running water. "All he assumes is that I went on holiday. I provided no particulars."

"Won't he worry? I know I'd worry. But ... I'm not Alistair." He feared her blasé attitude about her marriage could lead to trouble.

She came from the bathroom, fully clothed. "Not as long as he has his young men to entertain him. I certainly couldn't please him, though I tried when I was still a bride." She started brushing her hair in long strokes. "It was a long while before I knew the truth. All that time I felt rejected and ugly, a bride who repulsed her new husband." She paused brushing her locks, a vacant look to her eyes. "Maybe that's why I started taking up with all those boys—to soothe my devastated ego. I was only seventeen, you understand. Very naïve in that department."

He watched Amelia pile her locks up into a fashionable bun, fastened with an unused scarf from the pile on the side chair. "His inclinations are far afield from my tastes, though I don't condemn him for it, except the pain it has caused you. You've been through so much in such a short lifetime. I have many gay friends and associates. I never gave thought if they had to maintain a straight lifestyle for career or society constraints. It's different in the States than the UK."

"The UK is very open-minded, too. Only Alistair feels he needs the veil of a wife." She sat on the bed beside him. "Must be his Oxford upbringing .... Let's not talk about him. We have new adventures ahead of us."

That sounds encouraging. Will she still be in my life two weeks from now— or need to return to her former existence?

"WHY CAN'T I leave the plane to stretch my legs?" Amelia asked with raised brows. "It's not like we're on the terrorist list." She fidgeted on the jet's sofa.

"We're at JFK, but this isn't our final destination. L.A. is where we go through the customs drill." Trenton's face sported a boyish expression. "The US is very strict about entry these days—have been since 9-11. The airport fuel truck will be out to gas up the jet, then it's about five hours until we land, barring any bad weather."

With her international phone in hand, she walked up and down the narrow aisle, then sat down in a seat nearest to the cockpit door. She looked at the display and quickly dialed. On the fourth ring, Alistair answered.

His speech ran at a locomotive's pace, firing questions at her. "Amelia, where in bloody hell are you? When are you coming home? You took off without saying a word or leaving a note. I was nearly ready to call the police. Even Elizabeth wouldn't give me any information." His strident voice pierced her ears while a knot formed in her stomach.

She spoke with icy control, not caring who overheard her. "Where I am is none of your business, and when I come home is my decision, though I had only planned for a short trip—that could change. I'm always up for new possibilities—new horizons to explore."

"Damn and blast! Have you forgotten about the RHS Chelsea Flower Show?" The urgency in his voice screamed his desperation. "All the wives of my colleagues will be there, not to mention the royals. It reflects very badly on me if you ignore this social commitment."

She turned in her seat, looking at Trenton, and drawing strength from his concerned expression. "My missing a ruddy flower show reflects badly on you?" She strained to keep her voice void of emotion while rolling her eyes. "Your activities with your boys don't reflect badly on you? Why should my appearance be a yardstick to measure your moral character?"

"I don't mention your indiscretions, and you shouldn't mention mine—you're breaking the rules we have." He sighed. "Won't you please return *home?*"

"Return home, and return to the way I was, you mean." Her voice cracked. "I've sacrificed enough of my life for you!"

"Please, Amelia. Do this for me." She hated reducing him to begging. But, damn it all to hell and back—he brought this onto himself and it was long overdue.

"Look, Alistair, I only called to give you my contact information in case of an emergency of some sort—including any news about Stuart and Cindy." She related the Malibu address and phone number scribbled on the back of Trenton's business card.

"Amelia, will you please return in two weeks?" His persistence sounded pathetic and demeaned him.

"I'm signing off now. Amuse yourself with one of your boys at the club." Fearing he would try to contact her, she turned off her phone and slipped it in her pocket.

She sat there a moment, brushing away any remote feelings of guilt regarding her husband. *After the years of playing his sick charade, it's time I live for myself—make my life into what I want and not what others want for me.*

She looked at Trenton reading from a small stack of papers from the attaché case next to his expensive leather loafers. *He's so honest and loving, and in control at a moment's notice. Trent's not letting on he heard my responses to Alistair—that's for my benefit. He's doing what he thinks is best for me. Do I dare get closer to him? Can my emotions suffer such a strain?*

Amelia sat beside him, studying his intent expression. She found the fine lines at the corner of his eyes appealing and the look of his strong hands even more so. She wanted his hands on her body every moment and recalled with delight every embrace, kiss, and heated grabbing and tearing off of clothes. *He's a good four years older than me and yet turns me on more than any other man I've been with. Why?*

Trenton looked up at her while putting his papers aside. "What's up? Hubby not happy with you? You don't have to answer if you don't want to."

"Happy or not doesn't matter." She inched closer to him. "How about we take a nap in that comfy bed?"

"A nap sounds like just the ticket." His hand hid a yawn. "But I really need to sleep and get a jump on the jet lag."

"When do the pilots sleep?" She looked in the direction of the cockpit. "I don't want us making an unscheduled stop in the side of the Rockies."

"The pilot and copilot take turns." He patted her arm. "No worries.

You're in good hands."

She looked at his powerful fingers. "I'm looking at good hands right now, and I know where I want them—on my body."

A slow expansive smile framed his white teeth. "Just because I said I needed a nap doesn't mean I wouldn't mind a little activity to make me sleepy."

Grabbing his belt, she led him to the bedroom.

~~***~~

Clive sat at the club's stately leather-trimmed bar, waiting for Alistair to arrive. His friend and cousin-in-law sounded distressed over the phone and mentioned his main nemesis—Amelia. He wondered what new form of hell his cousin had devised for him to endure.

That bitch is always mixing things up, making me look over my shoulder, always wondering if she'll go public about the Penelope mess.

He looked at the antique clock hanging above the shelves displaying the best wine and spirits. Alistair was late by fifteen minutes. *Why can't he ever be on time?* He rubbed the pigskin edge of the bar as he scanned the room, noting what other friends were there. Sir Marmaduke was with a man he hadn't seen before—a blond solicitor type with an awkward demeanor. His manners were studied—not born to him. *Obviously, the club's standards are slipping. What's next? Accepting entertainers!* He brought the whiskey up to his nose, the ice tinkling in a pleasing way against the sides of the glass. He breathed in the rich aroma before emptying the glass.

A few minutes later, Clive spotted Alistair standing in the doorway perusing the room. He motioned with his hand to get his attention. Alistair rushed over, pulled up a stool, and ordered a scotch rocks.

Clive gestured to the bartender for a refill of his whiskey as he spoke. "It's not like you to be drinking before six. What is so important that you need a drink at three this afternoon—and with ice, of all things? What are you becoming? An American?"

"It's ruddy Amelia." He took a large gulp of his drink. "She's gone off with that blasted Yank movie producer to the States. Never left me a note and only called after she was halfway there. Gave me her contact information for any emergency here."

"She never fails to surprise." He leaned forward on his arms. "What's the issue? She'll be back after a week or so. She'll miss her boys. No man pushing forty would be able to keep up with their standards."

"Clive, this is different." He finished his drink in one gulp and motioned to the barman for a refill. "She was dead serious before she left—talking about her feelings, how she wanted a proper marriage with a proper husband—both of which I couldn't provide. Amelia was nearly in tears. I've never seen her like that before. I think Trenton Lowe is at the root of this. She even mentioned us not having children. She's totally gone bonkers."

"You are becoming a first-class bore. You've said all this before." He sighed heavily and unclenched his fists. "If what you say is true, sounds like Amelia is growing up and taking stock of her life." He fingered the bar napkin. "Would she really leave you for Lowe? After all these years?"

"I have a deep visceral feeling that she would and more—divorcing me in the process." His hand shook as he lifted his glass, ice cubes tinkling, the drink nearly spilling before reaching his lips.

"Steady on, Alistair. Don't make more of this than what it is." *He might have been right all along. If she truly divorces him, then I lose control of her money—especially the interest income. I can't allow that.* "Do you have her contact address and phone number of where she's staying on you? I think I should have that information since I might need to get in touch with Stuart .... Does she know your truth about your past?"

"No. She's never mentioned it. I don't know why others haven't mentioned those tasty details to her after all these years." Alistair took a creased piece of paper from his inside jacket pocket and slid it on the bar to Clive. "That's the only one I have. You'll have to copy it."

He took a fresh napkin from the stack on the counter, pulled a pen from his jacket, and proceeded to write down the important details. He passed the note back to his friend. "One never knows if or when this information will be needed. Keeping ahead of the course is always best. As to others keeping your secret, you might have friends looking out for you."

"What are you plotting, ol' man?" Alistair's eyes narrowed as he interlaced his fingers. "I want no harm to come to her. True, she has meddled in your life and put you in the situation of living here at the club, but still ...."

"I'm quite content." He chuckled snidely. "No hard feelings on that score. The food is good, the liquor is prime, and I'm not inconvenienced with mindless conversation."

"Glad to hear it." He stroked his chin. "One thing that does bother me—Amelia took all of her epinephrine injector medications for allergies—every single one of them. Why would she do that if she didn't plan on an extended stay?"

"She might have wanted to feel safe—packing more than what

would be practical." Clive took another sip of his drink. "I forgot. What did you say her severe allergy was? "

"Spiders. Not fancy or rare spiders, any spider bite will cause her death, provided she doesn't get an anti-allergy injection within minutes." He furrowed his brow. "Why do you ask? Planes are regularly fumigated, aren't they?"

"Of course, they are." Clive finished his scotch. "Don't mind me, I was just making conversation."

Hmm, there seems to be new possibilities.

Nineteen

"I WOULD LIKE to secure the services of an excellent lady's maid with cooking and housekeeping experience for a location in Malibu, California. I plan to cover all transportation costs in addition to regular fees. Would the assignment in the United States pose any inconvenience for your agency?" Clive asked over the phone in the drawing room of his private domicile in the club.

He eased back into a comfortable chair. The irritating street noise caused him to make a face. *For the sake of God, I'm on the bloody phone!*

The female voice answered in a professional tone. "Not an inconvenience at all, Mr. ... I'm sorry, I didn't note your name. Mr. ....?"

"Bradford, Clive Bradford. I have the pertinent information you will require. It's imperative that this gift remains anonymous." He was not as happy as he should have been—this woman's apparent inability to recognize his name grated on his ego.

"Discretion is one of the qualities that the Kensington Agency is noted for, as well as meeting the highest standards of our customers." She paused a moment. "I would need the exact location, date of employment, and advance for the services and transportation costs with a return ticket included with the first payment. We accept cash, credit cards, and bank drafts."

He gave the woman the necessary particulars, and added, "Payments will be made by bank issued draft. If it gets back to me that the recipient or any other person knows I secured this service, your business will be closed within a week. Are we clear on this? Remember, I *am* Clive Bradford, The *Duke* of Bryningmead."

"Of course, your grace. All will be as you require. No one will hear or read your name in connection with this transaction and contract." Her voice held a slight tremor. "The lady's maid won't even be aware of your identity. Do you prefer additional female services— hair dressing, mending, preparing tea sandwiches, and such?"

"I suspect all additional skills you mentioned would fit the situation the best." He made notes on a small pad of paper on the side table.

"Fine. Our employee should arrive at the stated location within five days, providing the agency receives payment by tomorrow." A polite cough sounded in his ear.

"You'll have the money by today's end by special messenger, with a signed receipt required upon receiving the draft. Email me the contract for my signature with the maid's mobile number." *There is no reason why the agency personnel should see my face. She has no proof as to who I am at the other end of the phone. Anyone can use my name.* "I believe this concludes our business. If I don't hear from the persons in Malibu that the maid has arrived, I will notify you and be most dissatisfied."

"Understood, your grace." She paused a moment as if thinking. "We are not ... in the practice of providing employees' mobile numbers."

"Make an exception. I will not abuse the privilege. Your agency will be well compensated for this consideration." She wasn't making this easy.

"Yes, your grace. As you wish, your grace." He swore he could hear a quiver in her voice—that pleased him.

Clive ended the call and sat there with a very satisfied smile as he tapped his fingertips on each other.

An English maid might make Amelia feel more at home, and I can keep a distant eye on her. The agency will be too fearful not to feed me information.

He scrolled his contact list on his phone, and swiped the number. A bank representative answered on the second ring.

"Please notify the bank president that His Grace, Clive Bradford will be visiting within the hour for a very private consultation and all the necessary documentation should be in order for my accounts."

There must be a way of tying up Amelia's money. If she wasn't around, she won't be able to expose my past and ruin me. That will take some thought and a great deal of planning. She's in my beacon. Now it's my delightful task to guide her to the rocks.

~~**~~

Naomi Lowe sat with her closest friend, Jessica Black, at a fashionable table in a high-end restaurant close to Rodeo Drive in Los Angeles. The two enjoyed fancy and colorful cocktails while waiting for their orders. The beautiful surroundings did little to lift Naomi's spirits.

"So what is this great chunk of news you want to share? Some new man on your heart's horizon?" Jessica asked.

"I'm far from ready for a new man to be warming my sheets." She fingered the paper cocktail napkin. "It seems that my ex has no notion of getting back with me—been keeping company with a royal during the filming in London .... At least that's what's been in the rags these days."

"My guess is ... it's more than keeping casual company." Jessica placed a napkin in her lap when the server brought their meal. "I've seen photos of the duchess boarding his jet in Gatwick airport." Her over-the-top Cheshire smile irritated Trenton's ex.

Naomi's eyes narrowed when a beautiful young model-type with a handsome stud walked past their table—another thorn stabbed her ego—a reminder of her fading youth.

"You're my best friend, remember?" She glared with flaming cheeks. "Why are you pouring salt into the wound? Not very friendly, if you ask me."

"I'm trying to get you to face the facts—get back to reality." Jessica stabbed an orange piece from the fresh fruit salad and brought it to her mouth. "It's time that you move on and quit lamenting your former marriage."

"I'm not ready to let go—not after what he did. Pushing me down the stairs and causing me to lose the baby." *She defends him enough! No sense in Jess knowing the reality—a stupid fall.*

"Let go of all of that. As I said before, you need to find a man to occupy your thoughts ... besides other things." She gave an impish grin before taking a drink.

"If I can't have Trenton, I don't want any other woman to have him." She cut into her fish filet as if cutting into his heart. "He needs to be as miserable as I am—he was the one who divorced *me*."

"Revenge and hate will only create lines." She motioned to the waiter for a refill of her drink. "And in this town, aging is the last thing you want."

"I don't care about lines." Naomi stiffened her posture in defiance.

"That's right, with your fat alimony checks, you don't have to worry about going back to modeling." She let out a deep breath and gazed out the window. "I wish I had a mega wealthy rich ex. If I did, I wouldn't worry about meeting the rent every month."

"You forget I have Jason—a son who makes certain that my nest egg doesn't grow too fat." She chewed with determination.

"You're a mother who spoils her son—like so many others." Jessica leaned forward. "You're not doing him any favors nor the girls he meets—no woman will be able to live up to your standards—creating a right little gigolo to torture some unsuspecting lady's soul and life."

"Jason likes the good things in life—takes after his mother." She pushed her half-eaten fish to the side when the waiter brought her another drink. "He has many good qualities."

Jessica glanced around for anyone who might overhear, and then lowered her tone. "Good qualities? Sucking the bank accounts of women nearly twice his age." Her grave face didn't upset Naomi. "That's the reputation he's cultivating—not one that will advance any type of career in this town."

"Why are you telling me all this?" She rolled her eyes. "First you eagerly dish out juicy details as to Trenton's activities and now degrading my son. You are on a fast track to losing my friendship."

"It's because I'm your friend ... you need to hear these things." She squeezed Naomi's hand. "You need to get a hold of your life and steer your son onto a more productive path."

"I guess you have my best interests at heart." She sighed. "It just difficult to hear." *I wish she wasn't so brutal with the facts.*

Jessica slid her plate to the side and leaned forward. "Has Jason mentioned that he's into making movies?"

Naomi's eyebrow arched. "No, he hasn't. Does that mean he's following in his stepfather's footsteps? Nothing wrong with that."

Her friend's tone lowered to a near whisper, "Trenton doesn't produce porn, nor stars in them."

She can't be speaking the truth! "How do you know this? From a boatload of unfounded gossip?"

"I wish I could be more reassuring and say it was." Her sincerity colored her words. "The guy I'm dating saw Jason in the film shown at a bachelor party at a private club. He said his name was even in the credits." Tears burned the rim of Naomi's eyes. "Too bad he didn't have the forethought to use an alias as most do."

"Couldn't there be some mistake? It can't be my Jason—not him! Maybe it's someone who's using his name—that's not unheard of." She took a napkin to her eyes, catching tears before they fell.

Jessica reached into her purse and pulled out her phone. She swiped the surface, typed something, and waited for it to load before she handed it to Naomi. "Pictures don't lie."

Naomi couldn't believe the photo—her son, completely naked with him on top of a equally naked woman in the middle of lovemaking. She could even identify the birthmark on his left buttock. Her world crumbled to infinitesimal pieces. A lump formed in her throat. Her only child had reduced himself to the level of scum, even lower than that—to that of a bottom dweller.

She shoved the phone back to Jessica. "I have no words." A tear trickled down her cheek. She hastily wiped it with her fingers and hung her head. Her voice cracked with pain and humiliation. "I need to leave. I need to be alone. Please don't call me for a few days." She slipped on her sunglasses and rose.

Jessica grabbed her friend's hand. Her eyes held hurt for Naomi.

"I'm so sorry. I'm always here if you want to talk."

Naomi nodded, gathered her things, and rushed out the door. She couldn't get to her car soon enough and believed all of L.A. knew the scandalous details Jessica had related to her. Anger bubbled up as a roaring cauldron—anger at Jason, anger at Trenton, and anger at that whoring duchess. It would take more than her deliberate stomping footsteps to put her world right again.

She entered the car, the heat slapping her face. She collapsed over the steering wheel; huge sobs escaped and she heaved her shoulders as tears blurred her vision.

Why did Jess have to show me that photo from the movie when she must've known it would hurt me? Yet, it's better I know now, while there might be a chance for me to do something to change his life. Why would he need to make money this way? Is this the tip of the iceberg? Is he involved in drugs?

Twenty

THE FRONT DOOR opened before Trenton had a chance to place the key in the lock of his three-story home on Malibu Road, and it startled him a bit. Alex, in his mid-thirties, stood very straight in casual beige slacks and a yellow polo shirt. His professional smile and the twinkle in his eye let the producer know the houseman had missed him. Amelia stood a step behind Trenton. The calls of seagulls and waves denoted tranquility. He hoped this locale would be irresistible to her, cementing the duchess to his home.

"Alex," he crossed the threshold into the sleek foyer and turned to introduce Amelia. "This charming lady is Amelia Hollingsworth, the Duchess of Steffenfordshire, and majesty of quick wit and outrageous comebacks."

The houseman extended his hand to her. "Alex Holt, your grace. Very pleased to meet you."

She waved her hand dismissively. "No 'your grace' for me, Alex. Call me Amelia." She looked at him a moment. "Australian, right?"

"Why, yeah." He smiled, then moved aside as Trenton's driver, Tom O'Neil, placed the luggage against the wall. "It was nice of you to notice."

Amelia beamed. "I'm fascinated by accents and the history behind them."

Alex attended to the suitcases. She followed her lover into the ultra modern living room of white and shades of blue from turquoise to aqua. Tall panoramic windows provided the most captivating and serene view of the Pacific.

"Call this place home for as long as you like." Trenton opened his arms as she walked to him. He embraced her and placed a kiss at her hairline. "I want you to feel comfortable here."

"The location doesn't matter." She looked up at him. "With your arms around me, I'm comfortable. Just keep the spiders away is all I ask."

"Spiders?" He laughed. "Are you afraid of them?"

"Worse than that." Her lips thinned. "One bite and I'm dead. That's why I keep an epinephrine medication pen with me constantly."

His eyes widened. "I'll let Alex know and make certain this place is insect-free. We do have it regularly treated by a pest control company so there shouldn't be a problem." He clasped her hand and led her through the doublewide sliding glass doors to the balcony perched over towering rocks. "Come. You have to get a better look at this. This is my oasis from all the cutthroat dealings of the day—production meetings of schedules, budgets, what the other studios are doing, and such."

Amelia squinted from the bright sun. The wind whipped her hair about her shoulders. She pushed the strands back in one smooth movement. "It's beautiful. Simply splendid." He came up behind her and encircled his arms across her upper chest. She put her hands on top of his and left a gentle kiss on his wrist. "There's parts of me out there ... little bits and pieces that haven't yet found each other to form a whole."

"Let me help you gather those pieces and bring them together." His lips brushed her ear before lightly leaving a kiss. The fragrance of her perfume brought a rush of glorious memories.

"That is a task I have to do for myself ... alone." She turned to face him. "Enough of this serious talk. I'm supposed to be on holiday with no thoughts of introspection." She looked to her right, past the circular table and chairs. "Um, a pool. That offers enticing possibilities." She gave him a sly wink that matched her enticing smile.

"If you're thinking of swimming au natural, the neighbors might object." He jutted his chin upward and to the side. "These houses are only twenty feet apart, give or take a foot. No diving. The depth is only six feet—basically a splash pool—a means for cooling off, not much more—can't even do a decent lap unless you swim along the edge, going around in circles."

Amelia glanced in the direction of a neighbor. "For your sake, I'll keep the swimsuit on. As you know, I've never minded being naked. Still ... it could be an interesting play pool, if you get my meaning?" She turned and gazed at the rocks far below transitioning into a pebble beach with a narrow strip of sand meeting the lapping waves. "Are all the beaches rocky like this? Isn't there any sand along the California coast?"

"There are sandy beaches, too. It might be fun to explore some of those." He kissed her neck, enjoying the smoothness of her skin. "There are so many sights I want to show you."

"You're a very sweet man and deserve the best of everything—including a good woman who doesn't possess a jaded heart." She turned back to the ocean. "I'm not that woman."

"You *are* that woman." He nuzzled into the back of her neck leaving gentle kisses. "I wish you could see yourself with my eyes, and then you'd know how beautiful and incredible you are." *Why is she pulling away from me? Regrets?*

"You're seeing qualities in me that are not there." She turned and cupped his cheek with her palm. "See me with clear eyes. Don't lose that wonderful objectivity that is your force in business." She reached up and left an innocent kiss on his lips.

"You deserve happiness, Amelia." He embraced her as she snuggled onto his chest and cherished the feel of her warmth radiating through his shirt. "Life is too short to deny yourself love."

Alex broke their private moment. "Sir, will you be dining in, or should I make reservations for you and Lady Steffenfordshire ... I mean, Amelia?"

Trenton looked at her for an answer. "Well?"

"I think a quiet night is in order. I haven't even unpacked yet." She patted Trenton's chest. "I'm downright knackered—truly very tired—my age must be catching up with me. Five years ago, I'd be ready to party most of the evening."

"Your fatigue has more to do with flying for over fourteen hours and less to do with age." *I won't suggest a night of love. She really looks beat.*

The houseman looked at him. "Are there any preferences for the menu, sir?"

Amelia piped in, not giving Trenton a chance to answer. "Pork of any sort will be perfect for me." She turned to him. "So sorry. I didn't mean to speak out of turn."

"Not a problem." He chuckled. "After all, you *are* my guest." He directed his attention to Alex. "You heard the lady."

The houseman went back inside to prepare dinner.

She went over to the table and chairs, and sat down, facing the blue ocean. Trenton pulled a chair close to hers and sat, barely believing she was truly with him at this moment.

Alex re-appeared with a tray of two glasses and a bottle of chilled Prosecco frizzante wine, along with a bowl of shelled pistachios, which he set on the table. She took a sip and smiled with approval. "Delicious. It dances on your tongue, but not stomp on it—a slight effervescence."

"Glad you like it." *I hope she likes everything here, and never wants to leave.* "I picked up a couple of cases the last time I was touring Italy while filming a movie."

She turned in her seat, and caressed the hair on his arm in loving strokes. "Trent, is Alex your cook, too?"

"Yes, he is. I don't have a big staff—driver, and houseman. The pool man and gardener visit once a week, a cleaning woman twice a month." He stroked her hand. "All in all, my life is as uncluttered as I can manage."

"From what I can tell, your world is far from simple." She took some nuts from the bowl. Her eyes never wavered from his as she spoke. "Meeting famous actors, big movie moguls, as yourself, and those red carpet events—all very impressive if you ask me."

"It's the town of make-believe with a veneer of genuineness and a phony core." He sighed as he watched the sun starting to set on the horizon, casting warm colors of red, orange, and gold on the azure waves.

"It's the same with royal society ... at least from my perspective." She sipped from the glass and focused on the scenic view. "It's refreshing to be away from all that. Here, I don't have to think of a new antic to shock the ruddy establishment."

He straightened in his chair and looked directly at her. "Is that why you agreed to fly out here with me?" *Have I been all wrong about her?* "I'm a vehicle to feed your rebellion?"

"No, Trent." She turned to him and cupped his cheeks with her palms. "You are so much more to me than another outrageous adventure to upset Alistair and the royals." Her eyes moistened. "I invested a great deal of thought about this trip. I'm here because I want to be with *you*—no other motive than that. For some reason, you instill a feeling of hope in me."

"Amelia, I want nothing but the best of everything for you—happy times, peace, contentment—all of it." He took her hands from his face and kissed her fingertips. "You are too special to suffer any hurt or disappointments."

She cast her eyes out to the sunset and bit her bottom lip. "Since my marriage, disappointment is expected on a daily basis." A painful sigh escaped. "I'm so very tired of it—all of it." She looked at him and smiled slowly. "I'm fortunate to have you as a friend." She laughed. It seemed forced, as if sadness tainted her joy. "Well, as you Americans say, 'friends with benefits'."

"Yes, friends." *I was hopeful she saw me as more.* "Our 'benefits' can lead to happiness—to a lifetime of love and sharing." *Why did I say that? I can't push her. She's like a spirited filly—can't be pushing her up to the next jump.*

"Not yet, not now." She gazed at her wedding band. "Things are far more complicated. Maybe someday you'll know all of it and understand."

He rubbed his knuckles against her cheek in loving strokes. "Try me. I have an understanding heart."

Her wistful smile tugged at him. He knew Amelia was the one to fill his life and home.

Will there ever be the right time to tell her how I feel? She spoke of hiding complications. What could those issues be to cause her such worry or fear? Behind her smiling eyes, I see a deep despair. I know I could make her happy if given the chance.

Amelia, will you ever open your heart to me?

Twenty~One

"BESIDES GOING TO clubs and squandering my money, what occupies your time when you're out of my sight?" Naomi scrutinized her son's expression as she sat in her Manhattan Beach living room.

"Hangin' with friends." He sat in a chair near the balcony entry and focused on his phone as he talked, clearly more interested in social media contacts than what his mother had to say. "What's it to you? I'm trying to find myself."

"Don't be insolent with me!" She folded her arms across her chest with a huff. "'*Find yourself*'? All you have to do is look under the nearest female. I know more about your activities than you think, and I far from approve of them."

He never looked up. "You don't know jack shit. What I do is my business." He angled his body away, showing most of his back.

"Turn around and look at me. I'm talking to you." Her muscles tensed as anger mixed with hurt burned through her. "You spend my money freely enough."

He slowly turned and faced Naomi. "You owe me." His jaw set in defiance. "I didn't crawl up your uterus to be born."

"Getting back to what you are doing ..." She wouldn't let him change the subject. "I saw a still photo of you—in a porn film!"

His expression froze a moment and then he looked down at the ceramic tiled floor. "Photoshop."

"Don't bullshit me!" *How can he continue to lie to me?* "I saw your birthmark on your ass!"

"It was someone else with the same mark." He crossed and uncrossed his legs as he continued, trying not to look at her. His razor smile cut her heart. "Christ sake! I'm almost twenty-one—legal next week. You can't control me—my actions or anything else in my life."

"You ungrateful bastard!" Tears rimmed her eyes as she sucked in air between clenched teeth. "I should have known something was wrong with you as a boy when you'd pull the wings off insects before killing them .... Have you given any thought as to how this reflects on me and what my friends will say?"

He brushed his hand through his hair. "That's the main issue, isn't it—your fucking reputation and social standing?" His sardonic grin fueled her anger. "I'm a product of you—your neglect, you not being there for my games in school, any of the events that were important to *me*." He pointed to his chest with a thumb. "I was merely an inconvenience to be tolerated. Hanging on the arm of my stepfather at the next red-carpet event was what mattered to you."

"How dare you say these things to me! Any events in your life that I missed were unavoidable. You're no better than your father, living dolce vita with his Italian whores at Lake Maggiore in Italy. When I married Trenton, I lost the pittance of alimony he paid me, and child support went out the window when you turned eighteen nearly three years ago and—"

Jason cut her off, "And if I had gone to college three years ago, you'd have collected a wad of bucks that I wouldn't see any of. I've been a money pot for you as a kid—that was my worth—child support to pay for designer clothes and beauty treatments."

He started pacing in front of her with only the coffee table separating them. His fists tightened and relaxed while his nostrils flared, his teeth clenched.

"You're exaggerating, and you know it." Naomi stood up and met him head on, seizing his shoulders, digging her fingers into his flesh. She wouldn't let him instill fear in her. "You've forgotten all about the fancy clothes, private schools, and yearly trips to Europe to round out your education."

"My father paid for those trips and schools *in addition* to the child support." He seemed to wait for her to speak. "I saw the bank records the last time I visited him before his death. The only good thing for you was he died a week after I turned eighteen—you got the maximum payout from him on that score. Records don't lie, *dear mother.*"

"Records can be altered." She let out a deep breath as a tear of frustration and anger fell down her cheek. "I don't want you in or involved with any porn films, porn actors, or anyone connected with that filthy industry."

Jason stood less than a foot from her face. His lips dripped pure hate as he exaggerated his words, "I will *see* and *do* whatever I want, including fucking in a porn film. Who knows, I might win a porn award as the best stud." *How can he talk to me like this?* "Besides, if you want my help, you will shut up, and keep out of my life— remember, you want to get back at my stepfather—can't do that without me."

His arrogance infuriated her. She ground her teeth as her eyes narrowed.

His quick steps took him towards the front entry. Naomi called out to him, "Are you using drugs?"

Naomi heaved a throw pillow at him as he headed away. The resounding sharpness of the door slamming was his answer. She hurled a glass candy dish from the table and watched it crash against the wall, shattering into fragments. She viewed her life in the same way as those disjoined pieces of glass on the ceramic-tiled floor. Her son drove her anger to the verge of filicide.

~~***~~

The outside gate alarm sounded. Trenton ignored it and assumed that Alex would see who came to visit. He heard the release buzzer, and lifted his head from a script he was reviewing when he heard Alex enter the living room.

"There's a lady's maid who can also cook, by the name of Jane Denton. This young lady, mid-twenties, said she was sent as an anonymous gift." Confusion plastered his face. "Are you dissatisfied with my cooking, sir?"

"Not at all." Trenton furrowed his brow. "This is very odd. I wonder if she's a journalist in disguise, or maybe a spy from a rival studio? Any references?"

"Yes, she has references and flew here from London." He paused a moment before lowering his voice. "She has a very upper-class accent. Do you think the duchess sent for her?"

"Have Jane wait in the foyer. I'll go ask the duchess." Trenton headed out to the balcony where Amelia sat in a chair, wearing an oversized hat, and large sunglasses. The ocean breeze played with her hair and hat brim.

She must have heard his steps as she looked up and slid the glasses halfway down her nose.

"Amelia, did you have an English maid come here to prepare meals for you?" He scratched his head.

"What? I might be forward in the bedroom, but I wouldn't dare insult Alex in such a manner. Why?" She looked as confused as he felt.

"Jane Denton is waiting in the foyer—said her services are an anonymous gift—came here from London." He sank a hand in his pocket. "She came with references—which I'll check, of course."

Amelia bit her lip and drew her brows together. "Alistair. It could only be him. He might have sent her—a peace offering to get me to return home. He could have sent Elizabeth instead. But, then he would lose his own cook."

"Would you mind talking with her and tell me in private what you think?" He started back to the sliding glass doors. "I don't know what to make of it. I don't let uninvited strangers into my home on a whim."

She nodded and followed him into the house. Alex stood by the sofa, looking hopeful that a solution might be forthcoming.

Trenton turned to the houseman. "Have Ms. Denton come to the living room." Alex started to leave to get the young lady. "No need for you to leave while we get to the bottom of this."

Moments later, Jane stood in front of them, looking eager and yet tired. Her prim clothing and demeanor spoke of someone trained in service. Trenton offered her a seat. Amelia's eyes narrowed, clearly sizing up both the woman and the situation.

This stranger immediately reached into an outside zippered pocket on her carry-on bag, and pulled out a sealed legal-sized envelope. On the front, in crisp black letters were the words "Trenton Lowe". She handed it to him.

He tore the envelope open, and read the contents—a letter of explanation and references accompanied with the required contact information. He handed the papers to the duchess. She scanned the page quickly, clearly looking for anything that might seem amiss. She shook her head and handed them back to Trenton. He looked at his watch and calculated the time difference. The would-be servant shifted her weight and bit her lip during the silent scrutiny.

"Please wait here," he spoke to Jane, "while I call about your references."

She smiled politely as he left.

In his study with the door shut, Trenton spoke on his phone to the agency's manager. "I don't understand any of this. Who sent her and why? I have never met this Jane Denton person in my life."

"As she and the letter explained, her services are an anonymous gift. We regard the secrecy and identity of our patrons very highly, Mr. Lowe. I can assure you that there is nothing to be worried about. Jane Denton is one of our top employees with high praise from our past clients. There is nothing dark and mysterious about this.... Of course, if you prefer to decline her services, the benefactor has included her roundtrip fare. She carries an open return ticket."

"No. I don't think that will be necessary at this point." He rubbed a kink at the back of his neck. "Thank you for your time and information."

Maybe all is on the up and up. I don't think a studio or a journalist had anything to do with this, especially since she flew here from the UK.

He returned to them in the living room.

"Amelia, it all checks out." He turned his attention to the young woman. "Alex, our houseman will show you to your room. He will be cooking the meals, too. You can prepare anything that the duchess requests, *if* Alex is not familiar with a particular dish or beverage—otherwise, you will be the duchess' maid. One important thing—keep all spiders away from Amelia. She has a deadly allergy to them."

Jane gave a small curtsey. "Of course. No harm will come to Milady. Thank you, sir. I'm certain I'll be very comfortable here and will enjoy functioning as Milady's maid." She turned to Amelia. "I was not informed that I would be caring for a duchess. I am extremely honored, your grace." She curtsied and cast her eyes downward.

"It's nice to meet you, Jane." The duchess waved her hand. "Please call me Amelia as does Alex. No titles for me—I abhor them just as much as I detest calling everyone 'darling'."

Jane took two steps back, then turned and left, following Alex to her room.

When out of earshot, Amelia spoke softly, "All appears to be proper. What do you make of this?"

"I was about to ask you the same." He scratched his head. "She seems okay. Her references all checked out. Would Alistair really be this kind to you—after leaving him so abruptly?"

"The money he's spending is originally mine, so it isn't a financial sacrifice for him." She looked out into space as if in thought. "I guess it's not such a stretch to think he'd do me a kindness, with an ulterior motive attached—even if it does scream of desperation."

"You're probably right." He rubbed his chin. "Yet ..."

Twenty~Two

"WHY THIS TRIP? And where are we going?" Amelia asked Trenton as they sat in his jet, waiting on the Tarmac. Sunlight streamed through the windows.

"After the endless meetings and all the daily screenings of the film, I thought we both could benefit with a mini-vacation." He secured his seatbelt. "The destination is a surprise." He shot her a wink.

"I was happy at your home. There's no need for you to entertain me." *I hope he's not jeopardizing his position.* She angled her head to see his face more clearly.

"No fun in that. What good is it to go to a new location and not explore the surrounding areas?" He raised his voice over the roaring engines preparing for takeoff. "There is so much more to California than Hollywood. You need to see some of its diverse sites."

"I won't discourage all the pampering you've treated me to since my arrival." *He is unlike any man I've known. Father would have liked him.* Her fingers interlaced with his and gave them a squeeze.

"You're entitled to all that and more." He glanced at his watch. "It's a short flight. When we land in Sacramento, I'll pick up a rental and drive to our paradise—only a little over an hour if traffic isn't heavy."

"Sounds utterly scrumptious." She felt the vibrations of the jet taxiing before takeoff. "Won't you give me a hint?" She hoped her seductive pout would melt his resolve and he would tell her.

"Everyone speaks English at our destination." He winked.

"Stop toying with me." She placed her hand on his knee and traced a design with her fingertip. "You're such a man of mystery."

"You've got me beat in that department." The feeling of his gentle kiss lingered on her lips. "Enigmatic runs in your veins."

~~***~~

The highway scenery of I-80 flew by from the view of the front seat of the Mercedes convertible creating a green blur peppered with bright wild flowers. Amelia was glad she had the habit of always stashing a scarf in her purse. She hated the feel of hair whipping across her face or nearly taking flight with a strong gust. To her, the weather was warm and delightful—far more pleasant than the all too frequent dank and dreary days of London.

She read the road signs indicating routes for San Francisco, but dismissed this as a possibility. She knew that city had its own airport. It made no sense for him to fly into Sacramento and then drive, if San Francisco was his goal.

Trenton checked the GPS navigator frequently. Amelia paid no attention. Hailing a taxi was her preferred mode of transportation most of her life. Rarely would she actually drive herself, unless it was an important mission that could not wait.

He turned on and off several roads after exiting the highway. State Road 221 gave way to new turns, and different streets towards the center of a small town.

The quaint weathered buildings both enchanted and opened her eyes to a new view of Americana. She hadn't noticed any signs indicating the name of the place. An old mill facing a river would make a lovely photograph if not a painting.

Maybe I'll take up drawing again. Father always laughed at my attempts. He's not here anymore to spoil my joy ... neither is Alistair. Trent wouldn't laugh—he's too kind for that.

Before she knew it, Trenton pulled up to the entrance underneath a grand portico.

He pushed a button for the canvas roof to appear from its hiding place in the trunk. "I hope you like Napa River Inn. It's the best in Napa and was once an old mill. I requested a room with a view."

"So, this is the famed Napa Valley that all the wine-tasting aficionados rave about?" She opened her door, not waiting for the hotel attendant. "It feels good to walk around a bit."

"Yup! Some of the best American vineyards are here. Though, Sonoma might argue that point." He tipped the attendant.

They walked through the entry and to the reception desk. She took a free pamphlet from the display and began reading, scanning the words. She pivoted at a snail's pace, taking in the country atmosphere and saw how this old mill was transformed into a luxurious and yet, a rustic inn. Trenton's adventurous nature meshed with hers as a piece in a puzzle. She looked up at him and knew he had come into her life at the right time. He could have pitched a tent, and she would've been happy.

After arriving to their room, Trenton strode to the glass doors opening to a small balcony and stared.

"Just look at that magnificent view of the Napa River." He placed his hands on his hips. "This is Captain Hatt's Suite. The brochure doesn't do it justice."

She came up from behind. "I'm enjoying the view in the room—in my mind's eye." He cocked his head at her with a question on his face. She jutted her chin. "That old comfy canopy bed looks inviting. Between the flight and the drive, a proper nap is in order."

"Why not?" A devilish grin matched his glint. "We need to check out all the room's amenities. Let's start with a shower."

The country chic décor of soft coral and warm beige, the romantic fireplace in front of the loveseat—all were enhanced by an enormous bowl of flowers on the table, which perfumed the entire space. The room lent a feeling of family comfort, and reminded her of childhood visits to her now late grandmother. *Days were good there. She was always so loving.*

Trenton headed to the bathroom, passing the wet bar. She leisurely removed her earrings before unbuttoning her blouse.

He called out over the running water. "There's even two robes here on the back of the door. Very plush." He stood in the short hallway, a white towel wrapped around his waist. She never tired of looking at his muscular chest. "Hurry up. A refreshing shower is waiting."

"A good soaping will refresh the libido," Amelia corrected, licking her lips.

She followed Trenton, eager to feel close to him, to feel his hands on her body, making her surrender and give up total control. His embrace transported her to a place of love and safety. Strangers' peering eyes and mean-spirited remarks couldn't touch her there— his arms held all that at bay ... even if only for a little while.

Steam clouded the mirrors over the sink with his message still visible. She smiled when she saw the double hearts he had traced with his finger. His thoughtfulness seemed boundless. Keeping her heart free from entanglement became harder each day.

He got in first to check the water's temperature. She took his extended hand, steadying herself. Under the stream, the warm water drenched her hair as she stood with her eyes closed. The dual showerheads were a treat she hadn't considered for her townhouse. Why should she? There was no one to share a shower with at her home.

Amelia sensed him near her and wondered when he'd make his move. Maybe he didn't want to make love. Or, was it the fact that her forward and outspoken ways had worn thin on him? This had been the longest relationship where she didn't have all the power. Silly! He'd just left her a love note on the mirror. Her momentary insecurities faded by his touch.

Trenton's soapy hands caressed her breasts as his mouth sought hers with hungry lips. He explored her recesses as their tongues mingled, sending sparks of desire surging through her. She rubbed her hands with his, coating her fingers with sudsy bubbles. Her touch traveled down his abdomen to the ticket of hair at his semi-erect manhood. His eyes tightly shut. His moans as she caressed his orbs and firm desire encouraged her, making her want him at that moment.

He slid his hand from her hard nipple down to her seat of pleasure. His fingers teased her with slow movements, then firmer, then backing off, driving her desire higher. Gasping breaths escaped as she swallowed hard, feeling his erection just touching between her thighs. Her hands gripped his buttocks as she tried to force him inside her. He grasped under her thighs, lifting her and simultaneously pushing her back against the marble wall. At last! He entered her in one delicious stroke. Her legs encircled him, holding tight, encouraging his every movement. Each stroke brought delicious sensations that made her crave more, and pleasure consumed her as he kept pace with her frantic breaths. Her hand gripped his shoulder, her fingers digging deep into his flesh.

She was so close. The pinnacle was there just within reach. Faster. Just a bit faster. His rhythm quickened. Her closed eyelids tightened as if making a fist and she bit her lip. Yes ... yes! The most exquisite feeling took over her body as she felt herself spasm around him and felt him find his own release in quick jerks. He held her there a few moments as her arms went limp and her wobbly legs released him. He rested his head on her shoulder, gulping big mouthfuls of air.

She felt his gentle kisses on her neck. "Are you completely satisfied? If not we can continue on the bed—no chair—I'm too spent for that."

"I don't have one ounce of dissatisfaction in me." She fingered his wet hair, drops falling on his shoulders.

"Are you sure?" His hand lightly touched her most sensitive area.

She abruptly pulled back and shoved his hand away. "Don't touch!"

"Just checking." His satisfied smile teased her emotions. "When I care for a woman the way I care for you—my pleasure is second place."

I've never had a man want to please me before without me paying him first. Every day, Trent's kindness and unselfish love only deepens my confusion.

London is safe and predictable—Trent is dangerous. Dangerous to my soul and others in my world.

Do I have the courage?

Twenty~Three

JANE'S CELL PHONE rang while she secured a button on Amelia's blouse. She knotted and cut off the thread, then looked at the display of "Caller Unknown". The ringing annoyed her. She wanted to make a good impression in hopes that this temporary assignment would morph into a permanent position and that meant making certain her grace's clothes were always in good repair.

"Hello." Her tentative voice mimicked her fingers fidgeting with her soft bangs.

"This is Mr. Clayton Smythe. I'm the new manager of accounts for the Kensington Agency. I'm calling to inquire if Her Grace, Amelia Hollingsworth is satisfied and how she is getting on."

"I'm sorry, Mr. Smythe." *The agency never mentioned him. I hope I haven't been sacked.* "The duchess is away on a brief holiday. I am not with her as she requested I remain in Malibu .... The agency never mentioned your name, nor your position."

"They wouldn't have done since I am relatively a new hire, would they?" *He sounds rather mature.* He cleared his throat. "Has she indicated when she plans to return to London?"

"No. She hasn't said anything about returning home. I'm hoping in any event that she would want to keep me on." *I shouldn't have said that.* "I am very happy working for the agency and wouldn't want you to feel I considered severing my association."

Restlessness filled her. Something wasn't proper. She stood and looked out the window at hunky men strolling on the beach with what must be their girlfriends and then turned back to her bed, sitting on the turquoise comforter.

"Quite." He chuckled. "One wouldn't blame you for wanting to better your life .... Considering that the duchess is such a prominent and esteemed client, I will be calling in from time to time as to her wellbeing. You needn't call the agency. I will keep them posted on the situation. Remember, part of your evaluation is based on your ability to follow instructions without question."

"Yes, sir. I understand." *I've never had a manager speak to me like this.* She twirled her chin-length hair with her finger.

"Right. I'll ring off now. Goodbye." His cool professional tone had a mysterious quality.

Jane swiped her finger to the recent calls section on her phone. She looked at the number. The country code was 1. That was the States' code. Why would an employee of the agency be using a phone that must have been issued from the United States? None of this added up. The area code displayed 617. She pressed the redial feature. A message flashed, "Incoming calls blocked."

Was that man a weird form of stalker? Was this a test of some kind to question my loyalty? If I call the agency, and this is indeed a test to see if I could follow instructions, would I then be sacked for not doing as told?

~~***~~

"Where would you like to dine tonight?" Trenton asked as Amelia gazed at the river from their hotel window. He read from a pamphlet the hotel offered. "Angèle offers country French and Celdon serves Mediterranean, Asian, and American fare."

"French, I think." She turned toward him. "Pasta and olive oil weigh me down—can't be gaining a stone or so."

"Stone?" His eyebrows rose. She loved his little boy expression.

"It's a measurement of weight." Her finger lightly touched the tip of his nose. "That's fourteen pounds. I forget that Americans aren't familiar with that term. Sometimes I think we share more differences than things in common."

"We share the same language." He embraced her and kissed the top of her hair, inhaling her fragrance.

"As I mentioned before, it only seems we do." She wished the moment could last forever.

"I'll call the front desk and see if we need reservations." Trenton went to the side table to make the call.

She loved him taking control, making dinner reservations and planning this trip. He was masterful without being overbearing— always considering decisions that might concern her.

This has to end, eventually. Why? Why should I not take this opportunity for true happiness? I'm scared. I've been in control for so many years, now there are times I feel blissfully helpless.

~~***~~

Seated at an outside table overlooking Napa River, Amelia felt a cool breeze play with her hair. She and Trenton sipped their after dinner cocktails. He enjoyed a scotch rocks, while she favored a strawberry daiquiri. The yellow and white striped umbrellas separating the tables along with strings of hanging white lights added to the romantic ambience. Murmurs from other diners rippled in the background.

"You were so quiet over dinner. Anything wrong?" he asked, sipping his drink, eyes on her.

"I'm sorry. Nothing is amiss." *I can't share my fears—not yet—not until I'm certain.* "I enjoyed our wine tasting excursion this afternoon. I never realized there were so many varieties of grapes."

"Don't change the subject .... What's troubling you?" He reached for her hand and gave a loving squeeze. "I could feel your thoughts all through the meal." His eyes scanned her face as if trying to read her feelings.

"I'm so afraid that all this will be over and just fade into a pleasant memory one day." She took a deep breath. "That's the way of my life. Momentary ... and then memories." She looked down at the table, then sipped her drink.

His voice lowered. "You can exist in someone else's drama ... or you can write and live your own script."

"Is that the movie producer speaking from a dialogue you've read?" *It's as if he's reading my mind.*

"No, that advice comes from years of making mistakes—some more painful than others." He lifted her downcast chin with his fingertip. "Look at me. Stop living for others and live for yourself. I'm not saying this with any ulterior motive. Even if I'm not in your future, live the way that is best for you."

She took a paper napkin to catch her tear before it fell. "I never had but one pet in my life—not because I don't love animals, but because I can't stand the final goodbye that must be. I've never allowed the thought of motherhood to clutter my brain either." She looked down at her wedding band. Knowing Trenton saw her truth caused a stabbing pain in her heart.. "The circumstances never afforded that opportunity—certainly not with Alistair. When a long-term relationship ends, it is so very painful. I learned that when Father died. Even though his plan for me was a hell he fashioned that continues from the grave, I miss him dearly. My previous existence was comprised of flirtations at my whim, which I never took seriously."

"I would welcome being a father." His eyes bored into her. "Am I *your* 'whim'? ... Are you looking for an easy way out?"

Her eyes met his. "I don't know what I'm looking for." *I see the pain on his face.* "Every day I spend with you makes the life I led in London ... so remote and foreign to me."

"You are one complex woman." He took a swallow of scotch. "In business, when I look into a man's eyes, I see his soul, and at that point I know if I can own him ... win the deal. I want your eyes to tell me that I can win your love."

Don't put this on me. I can't give you the answer you want to hear.

"Be happy with our 'friends with benefits' status." She sighed. "I'm so very tired of running."

"You've been listening, and that's a start." His eyes held hope.

"Listening isn't always agreeing." *I wish he wasn't so damn charismatic.* Amelia avoided his gaze. She felt he had started peeling her defenses away, layer by layer, like an artichoke. This new sensation unsettled her and she didn't quite know what to do about it.

A server came to the table. Trenton requested the check.

He glanced at the other diners, then back to Amelia. "Shall we go to the local nightspot, Silos? I hear the music is quite good."

The waiter presented the bill. Trenton pulled off some twenties from his wallet and laid them on the table. He mumbled, "Keep the change," then stood. She took his extended hand as he adjusted her chair.

"Music might be just what is needed after our deep analysis of my feelings." She laughed. "Seriousness in any form has never been my forte. As I said before, living in the moment is my shield."

"I concede." His broad smile lessened her concerns. "Come. Silo's is calling us."

~~***~~

Covered in sweat, Amelia woke up with a jolt, sitting up. Her damp skin glistened in the moonlight, her shivering uncontrollable, no matter how hard she tried.

"What's wrong?" Trenton rubbed his eyes, sat up, and brushed the moist hair from her face. "Bad dream?"

She hugged her drawn-up knees to her chest with eyes fixed to the darkness.

Her words came just shy from a whisper. "It's like you're in the ocean, and people are on the shore. You keep paddling and paddling towards them, but they keep getting further and further away. You're a bit of insignificant flotsam with no control—moving at the whim of the sea."

"You're not in that sea alone." He embraced her slender shoulders, his breath hot in her ears. "There's a raft within your reach. Grab it and hang on to me. Let me be your safe place."

A biting tear rolled down her cheek.

If it was only that simple.

Twenty~Four

JANE PULLED THE phone from her apron pocket. She looked at its face a moment, then scrolled to her contacts. Taking a labored breath, she stared at the number, and dialed. She bit her lip as the ring tone sounded, trying to gather her courage.

"Kensington Agency, providing the best for you. How may I direct your call?" the female voice asked.

"This is Jane Denton calling from California. I'm in the agency's employ. Please connect me with the Personnel Relations Department." She checked the time display on her phone and hoped she wasn't calling too late as she knew the personnel staff left early on Fridays. She leaned against her bed pillow and shot a glance at her shut bedroom door hoping that Alex was not prone to the rude habit of eavesdropping.

The call forwarding tone sang in her ears. Finally, a voice came on the line. "Personnel. Ms. Talbot speaking. How may I help you?"

"This is Jane, Jane Denton. I'm on assignment for the agency." Another deep breath escaped her lips. "I received an odd call from a person identifying himself as Clayton Smythe—the new manager of accounts."

"Yes. Mr. Smythe has recently been promoted from our Hyde Branch Office." Ms. Talbot's voice was cold, yet professional. "He is out for the day. Would you like to leave a message?"

"Was he in the States for the past few days?" She picked a piece of lint from the bedspread.

"No. He's been in the office—daily for the past month." Jane heard the clicking of a computer's keyboard over the phone.

"I received a phone call from a gentleman identifying himself as Clayton Smythe, checking on my assignment here in the States and the satisfaction of the duchess. He instructed me not to contact the agency about his conversation with me. Further, the number he called from had the States' country code with an area code of 617."

"That is quite peculiar." A moment of silence. "Could it be that someone is posing as Mr. Smythe? Maybe a bogus call?"

"Could anyone find out details about Mr. Smythe?" *Is this a harmless prank?* "Who has my phone number information—the international mobile the agency issued to me?" Anxiety laced with remote fear crept through her. Her palms gathered sweat.

"The agency of course, and a client engaging your service would be entitled to that detail." Jane heard more clicking from a computer keyboard. "I did a quick scan of your assignment, and there have been no irregular queries. No one has requested your mobile number. It's the end of the workday. Do you have any further questions, Ms. Denton?"

"No. Thank you for your time, Ms. Talbot." The foreign country code still bothered her.

Why would someone from the UK call from a phone that was issued in the States? Is Richard following me? She had told her ex-boyfriend to bug off months ago.

~~***~~

Amelia watched the vista of floating clouds and the terrain below through the window of Trenton's jet. She assumed they would be landing at LAX in a matter of minutes. She looked at her watch and mentally calculated arrival time. The steward didn't remind them to fasten their seatbelts for landing—that was odd in itself.

The mountains gave way to water—it had to be the beautiful Pacific Ocean. She looked at Trenton with mild alarm and then back out the window. "Is there trouble of some sort?" She tried to read his face for any hints of mechanical or weather concerns. "We're flying over water and not flying into a city."

He looked smug with the wisp of a smile. "You'll find out when we land."

"Aren't you the man of mystery." She left a gentle kiss on his lips. "Don't ever change—not a single hair."

"The unexpected is always exciting." He clasped her hand. "Isn't that what you live by—unconventional statements and actions?"

"That's a cloak to hide all the blackness." *I shouldn't have said that.* "When will we land?"

"In about twenty minutes or so." He leaned in toward her and glanced out the same window. "It won't be long now. I can already make out the coastline."

She peered out. The rocky coast beneath high mountains gave the impression of a tropical wilderness similar to the Hawaiian Islands bathed in turquoise waters.

Her stomach tightened and her knuckles turned white in a tight grip on the armrest. The airstrip came closer into view and didn't look very long—not compared to the commercial airports she took for granted.

Where on earth is he taking me? A third world country? Maybe it's a location for one of his movie projects. I hope there is running water. What if there are snakes? Or worse—spiders!

Air turbulence caused minor bumps. She held her breath and closed her eyes, waiting for either a smooth landing or a crash. Her stomach further knotted as she found it difficult to breathe.

He stroked her hand. "You can relax now. We've landed."

"When?" She glanced out the window, seeing the pavement and a forest beyond. "I only felt a minor bump. I thought that was the air current."

"I have an excellent pilot. He's flown many hours in the Middle East." Trenton released his seatbelt as she did the same. "I trust him with my life and the life of a very special duchess." He winked and touched the tip of her nose with a kiss.

"I'm such a ninny." She stood and gave a stretch. "Where are we, anyway?"

"Catalina Airport in California." He took her hand while the steward opened the door and released the steps to the ground below. "Catalina is the name of this island. We're headed for a private locale outside of Avalon." He gave her hand a squeeze. "I hope you like it as much as I do."

This unscheduled excursion brightened her spirits. She knew that eventually in the not too distant future, she'd be back in London, frequenting the same old haunts and seeing the same old faces. Amelia wondered if she'd be able to fall back into her old way of life. She inhaled deeply, filling her lungs with the clear and clean air.

Two taxis waited on the Tarmac. One of the cabbies stood by the open rear door. Trenton led the way and handed a slip of paper to the driver while she slid onto the backseat. Trenton sat close beside her. Stray hairs fell to his forehead.

"What route are we on?" she asked as they rode down the narrow winding road.

The driver answered while looking through the rearview mirror. "This is Airport Road."

Trenton smiled. "If you ask too many questions, you'll spoil the surprise."

"Since I've never traveled any further west than Manhattan, I doubt telling me the location would spoil the surprise." She gazed at the passing lush vegetation as the drive descended and took them closer to sea level. "Will the pilot fly back to L.A.?"

"No. I've treated both the pilot and steward to a short vacation. They're staying elsewhere on the island. The jet will park at the airport until our return." He looked at her from behind his sunglasses.

"Good people deserve nice things in their lives—including you." He kissed her cheek and squeezed her hand.

"I have nice things. You're a very nice and good friend with fantastic benefits." He was getting serious again—that would lead to topics she wasn't ready to explore at this moment—if ever.

"And what might those benefits be?" He started nibbling on her ear. A shiver ran through her and tickled a desire that never slept for long.

"Well, at the risk of being obvious, you're larger than an IHOP breakfast sausage." She giggled.

"Where did such a proper duchess learn of IHOP and breakfast sausages?" His eyes roamed her face. The way he looked at her did more than charm her body. Even in jest, she guarded her heart.

"My maid, Elizabeth, said that to one of her friends about a boy she had dated." She chuckled. "Later she explained what IHOP meant and what type of sausages they served. I think she said her last employer, Taylor, had mentioned that establishment. I like to think it was in reference to my menacing cousin, Clive—his sex drive consists of whatever specimen he's peering at through his microscope."

"He really bugs you, doesn't he?" Trenton stretched his arm across the backseat as his fingers caressed her shoulder.

"There hasn't been a word invented to describe him fully." *I wish I had never brought up the subject of my cousin.* She looked out the window at the passing scenery. "How much longer to our final destination?"

He cocked his head. "Not long. The winding road takes longer than a crow flies." He slipped his sunglasses lower on his nose and peered at her in a way that made her wish they were alone. "Do you have an urgent need to settle in?"

She smiled and licked her lips. "Yes. I have an urgent need ... and you are the one who needs to 'settle in'—settle in very deeply."

Twenty~Five

"THANK YOU MR. Lowe, for a wonderful introduction to the fun activities on Catalina." Amelia yawned from the white canopy covered bed, glanced at the discarded and torn condom wrappers on the nightstand, then ran her fingers through the thick dark hair on his chest to his abdomen, enjoying the feel of his rippling muscles.

"We didn't go on any excursions." He looked puzzled a moment, then smiled. "Ah, you're referring to last night—the way I warmed the bed and the woman in it?"

"Em, indeed. Delightfully warming." He stretched his long legs over the side of the bed with his back to her. Her nails raked down his spine in a teasing pattern.

He glanced over his shoulder at her. "Put your hair up in a bun or something."

She shimmied around to see the side of his face. "Why? We're going for a swim?"

"No swimsuits needed." He reached into his luggage and pulled out a red jogging outfit with a white stripe running down the side. "Here." He handed the garment to her. "You'll need to wear this. You packed athletic shoes?"

"Yes. I didn't know if I'd be walking where there would be rocks and such." He couldn't miss her dazed expression. "Why the special uniform? What have you planned?"

"It's another surprise." His fingertip lightly touched her nose. "I like to keep you off balance."

"As long as it doesn't involve spiders." *I love this side of him. No one else has tried to surprise me in so many years.*

He checked the bedside clock. "The taxi will arrive in less than ninety minutes. We'll grab a quick bite here, then off to our big adventure." He observed her stretching on the bed. "Get a move on and get dressed. We have to be there," he tapped his watch, "in a little more than an hour." She started to open her mouth. He cut her off. "Don't ask where. I'm not telling you."

Amelia took a moment to enjoy the ocean view and the circling porch fitted with a table, chairs, and chaise lounges.

It would be nice to share a bottle of wine there. Trent and I enjoying the view and revealing our secret thoughts—well, his thoughts. She shuffled to the all white spa-like bathroom.

After brushing her teeth, she entered the sitting area. He was already dressed and waiting in a chair. His neatly combed hair contrasted with the outdoor jacket, rumbled jeans, and scuffed running shoes. She quickly removed the white terrycloth robe and dressed while Trenton impatiently tapped his fingers on his knee. *He didn't approach me while I dressed. Did I wear him out last night?*

She slung her hobo bag over her shoulder. "All ready for a new experience."

"Off we go. Remember ... only a quick bite for breakfast." He took his wallet from the table near the fireplace and then walked to the door. "By the way, we spent the night in the bedroom of William Wrigley, Jr. and his wife. This was their cherished home. Inn at Mt. Ada is pretty significant with romantic history oozing from every brick and nail. Wrigley Road bears his name."

"Interesting trivia, Mister Producer." She entered the hallway. "You're so fascinating."

"You're the one who's fascinating—and I love ... it." He started down the stairs. "Don't change. Always be yourself with me."

"Change is a constancy that we must endure." *He almost said he loves me.* "However, my obligations are another constant trial—ones that I must eventually return to." *I don't want to get his hopes up.*

"No serious talk." He opened the door to the reception area. "The day is for fun."

She ran her tongue along her upper lip. "And so are the nights."

~~***~~

Seeing how the narrow road wound in snakelike patterns, Amelia understood why Trenton was in a hurry to leave their cozy suite. A sign indicated they were on Stagecoach Road. She took the epinephrine self-injector pen from her purse and shoved it in the inside zippered pocket of her jacket. *The last thing I need is to get bitten and face death in a matter of minutes.* She froze a moment. *Is there even a doctor or a hospital here?*

The car came to a halt in a clearing with an area for parking. Trenton guided Amelia to the waiting shuttle, which was filling up with other passengers. A driver in a blue shirt did a quick headcount against a paper and tickets he held. After a short journey, the small bus arrived at a building touting "Catalina Island Zip Line Eco Tours."

Trenton helped her out of the shuttle, clasped her hand, and hurried to the entrance. She overheard a passenger's comment.

"What's his hurry? Going to propose at the bottom?" Other

passengers' laughter riffled through the van.

She glanced at Trenton's flushed face and smiled, knowing that such a question was far from likely—especially since she had discouraged him on that point multiple times.

Wooden racks of helmets, harnesses, and rental jogging shoes were arranged neatly behind a long reception desk. She secured her purse in a locker provided and put the key in a zipped pocket on her jacket.

A young man smiled as he took the tickets of customers and explained the safety rules. She listened intently to the instructions and glanced at the pamphlet Trenton had handed her.

Now I understand why he wanted me to put my hair up. Excitement bubbled inside her.

The man continued to talk, "The excursion starts at over six hundred feet above sea level. The five runs total thirty-eight hundred feet. Average speed is forty to forty-five miles per hour. There are five lines and at the end of each is a guide who will check on any needs and give an overview of the importance of the surroundings. The experience will last about two hours. When on the line, please hold on to the hand bar and keep your arms close to your body and legs together. Wear the helmet we provide at all times. These instructions are for your safety." An employee handed out forms. "Please read over and sign the zip line waiver form and then you'll be on your way to a once-in-a-lifetime experience."

In harness and with hardhats in place, Amelia and Trenton waited on the platform with the others. She dared not look down over the railing.

Do I really have the nerve to do this? Picking up a man at the Savoy would be so much easier.

Then, it was her turn. She tried to concentrate on the guide's words. The height was dizzying. Her grip froze on the hand bar. The next thing she felt was his hand on her back giving a forceful push. Her eyes shut for a moment as cool air rushed into her helmet and tightened the chinstrap, and at the same time filled her with exhilaration, small fireworks bursting in her stomach. Not long on the line, she found herself enjoying the experience. *This is almost as good as sex.* She ventured to look down and saw bison grazing on a hillside, a fox chasing his next meal, beautiful flowers dotting the canyon, and an azure ocean lying beyond. Soon she was at the next platform. Trenton arrived minutes after her.

He spoke between labored breaths. "How ... did you ... like ... the first run?"

"It's wonderful. You're wonderful for planning this brilliant excursion." She kissed him gently.

"I always strive to please the number one lady in my life." His dancing eyes and easy smile softened her resolve.

Before she could reply, the next guide started talking to the group about the wildlife and indigenous plants in the area. His words floated above and couldn't intrude on her thoughts—thoughts of what a different life would be like in a different part of the world.

Trent could be my new beginning—maybe a new forever.

Having conquered her fears of the first zip line, Amelia thoroughly enjoyed the remaining four segments, gleefully observing the passing trees, and terrain.

She waited on the last platform for Trenton. He greeted her with a loving kiss and a warm hug that enshrouded her in a feeling of safety and calm.

"Did you enjoy that?" He guided her down the steps.

She couldn't resist his broad smile framing his white teeth, and pecked him on the cheek. "I absolutely loved the zip line. What made you think of that?"

"I had never been on an adventure like that, and I figured you hadn't either." He chuckled. "I wanted this to be a new experience for both of us—something that would be unique—create a special memory we both could share."

They were the last two passengers to board the waiting shuttle bus. Warm feelings flowed through her. She hadn't felt joy like this since she was a child and Aunt Betsy took her to Brighton Beach on holiday. It had been so many years, too many, since she had experienced this kind of all-consuming happiness. She knew Trenton was the reason for it, so why did her logical nature put up roadblocks to any type of future with him?

It's all fun and games now. Will that be the case days, weeks, months, or years from now? I shouldn't let my heart make these decisions. What if I'm just a diversion for him—the way all those young men have been for me? Am I more than a fanciful lark—to be enjoyed for the moment and then cast off like last season's fashion? I should run back to London before the magic fades and my heart is crushed. Yet ...

Twenty~Six

"TRENT, WHAT MADE you think of this place?" Amelia gazed out at the Pacific, enjoying the shades of gold and orange from the setting sun dipping behind the island. "Eating outside is refreshing. It's been too long for me—always dining inside of one restaurant or another." She leaned forward, primed to watch his lips and hear his words. The boys had never interested her beyond the bedroom.

"I usually eat outside if given the choice." He sipped a Wrigley Martini while she enjoyed a tropical fruity cocktail with a pineapple and orange slice garnish. "Business lunches and dinners usually require I eat inside." He glanced at the other diners on the patio. "Avalon Grille seemed the perfect spot for us." He jutted his chin. "You're looking out towards the east. No one on this side of the island will see the sun set—only sunrises."

"I'm looking in the direction of the California coast?" *He's fascinating. I never tire of listening to him.*

He nodded. "Not only that, Catalina has movie history. Marilyn Monroe lived here for several months with her first husband. In the 1930s, quite a few Hollywood stars, including Clark Gable, would use this island as a getaway destination. It's been a prime filming location for a lot of movies."

"Well, well, Mr. Lowe ..." she chuckled, "... aren't you the movie buff."

"Given the fact that movies are my biz, it's not surprising." The server placed their entrées in front of them and refilled their water glasses.

"How stupid of me." She knew color came to her face. "Of course you would know those things." She pushed the fattening sauce off her salmon before taking a bite. "By any chance, are you related to all those movie theaters that share your last name?"

"Don't I wish!" He took a bite of steak. "No. The names sound the same but are spelled differently. The 'e' is at the end of my name and not after the 'o'. Loew's been around since 1906 and merged with AMC in 2006. I don't hail from the Lerner and Loewe team either." He put down his fork and ran the back of his fingers against her cheek. "No more talk about movies and film—this is a vacation—*our* vacation."

She looked up at the darkening sky. Her lips curled into a small smile. "It has been a lovely, lovely reprieve from my London routine—one I could embrace for the rest of my life ... if only ..."

"If only what?" He inched closer to her. His eyes searched hers as if trying to discover her deepest thoughts. "What is this big thing that is holding you back from living your life as you want?" He rubbed her lower arm. "Is it Alistair? Is he the one who's tying your hands?"

She made a face and leaned into him. "Yes .... But there are things you don't understand."

"I can't imagine what the fuss is all about if you leave him." His light laugh brushed against her. "He likes men and so do you. It's not like the rest of the UK doesn't know that."

"But if I formally divorce him, then all my money from my dowry reverts back to me, even my money that Clive controls. Though, I wouldn't mind cutting off my cousin's grubby little fingers from my bank account." *How can I make him understand?* "My father was very *firm* in the marriage contract and the entail of his will." She lightly stroked the ridge on his hand. "Alistair would have to sell the estate, or think of a way whereby the country property could support itself. The majority of his associates think he made me wealthy and not the other way around. It's a matter of pride with him." She took a large swig of her drink. "Despite what *The Daily Mail* and all those other rags say," her eyes flared, "I'm not a heartless bitch."

"You mentioned some of this at the Manor." He wrinkled his brow. "Divorce him, and give him back some money to keep things afloat."

"That won't work. My father tied up the finances for all possible contingencies—a way of ensuring that Alistair wouldn't ever cast me off after he got all my money. If I divorce and then give him one penny, all my inheritance is lost—going to a charity my father favored." She sighed as she fought the tears forming in her eyes. "I don't know if I can hurt him so deeply—even if it's only financial pain. It's not as if he has an heir who would inherit." She used the corner of a napkin to catch a tear before it fell. "I could have had a child with one of the men I've been with. I'm certain that Alistair would have sung bloody praise—the world would see he fathered a child—it would fit in with his social scheme of things."

Trenton picked up another napkin and wiped her eyes.

She rutted her brow and swallowed hard. A shiver of fear stabbed her—revealing so much of her feelings—feelings long buried since her wedding night. "That would be a lie. I'd be the mother of a bastard.

I'd grow to hate myself and resent the child .... I may be many things, but to jeopardize a child's future reputation is not woven into the fabric of who I am .... I won't even get a pet because of the final goodbye that every cat or dog brings when they enter your heart. Rodney is my maid's Cavalier pup. I discouraged her dog from sleeping in my room—on my bed—I couldn't stand him breaking my heart."

I never intended to tell him my life's story. Why can't I keep my mouth shut? He's the only one I've ever opened up to like this.

"What you've told me explains a lot." His soft kiss on her cheek did little to ease the anxiety that tore at her fiber. "Your outrageous veneer is a smokescreen, covering all that deep pain."

"Don't .... Don't apply psychoanalysis on me." She pulled away. "See me for who I am, and what I've done. Don't make excuses for my actions—I don't." She set her jaw. "I married a much older man, as I said, an arranged marriage to a gay man who never touched me, and I sought casual lovers that I paid for. London society snickers and accepts the facts. Some comments I laugh off, others, well ... they hurt a bit."

He wrapped his arm around her shoulder. "Let's finish our meal and think of good things ... positive things." He lifted her chin with his finger. "No sadness allowed for the rest of the trip."

She looked in his kind eyes. "I make no promises."

His palm cupped a cheek as he spoke quietly. "As someone said somewhere, 'Be fearless in the pursuit of what sets your soul on fire.' Maybe I read that in a script. Still, it's good advice."

"Trent, we might be merely crossing and not on a single path together. Keep your dreams on the ground. I don't want to disappoint you."

"I'm not in the clouds. Never have been. I see with very clear eyes." He ran his thumb along her jaw then kissed her soft lips. That loving kiss moved her heart closer to his and made her decision that much harder.

~~***~~

Amelia was glad that Trenton had suggested a stroll after dinner. The cool damp sand felt refreshing under her bare feet and the salty taste of sea air enhanced this new memory in the making. They walked at the water's edge as the cool lapping waves washed over her feet and tickled her ankles. She liked the feel of the sand oozing between her toes. His arm at the small of her back was warm and comforting—creating a sensation of safety and contentment. He was good for her—good for her spirits and good for her soul.

He cocked his head to see her face. "Since you liked the zip line today, how about a new adventure tomorrow? Whale watching? Snorkeling? Or, we could do something else? There are plenty of nature trails—we could hire a guide."

"I wouldn't mind checking out the gaming back there." She looked over her shoulder in the direction of the Catalina Casino. "It's been ages since I played at the roulette table."

"I'm not much of a gambler. If we were in Vegas, I might give it a try." He drew her close and kissed her temple. "Who knows? You just might be my Lady Luck." He looked in the direction of the casino. "No gaming there. Only dances—always have been."

His phone rang. He twisted his face. "Lowe speaking." There was a long silence from him as he listened to the caller.

She eavesdropped to his replies as she stooped to pick up a pink shell. This would be a souvenir to remember him and their moments together. She brushed off the sand and slipped it in her pocket.

"I'm in Catalina getting much needed R and R after the wrap. What is the absolute latest I have to be there for the meeting? ... That soon, huh ... I'll be there ... No, don't tell anyone where I am .... This had better be worth it—cutting my trip short .... Later." He dialed a number. "Trenton here. Get the jet gassed. I have to leave tomorrow at one. Yeah, L.A." He shoved his phone into his pants' pocket.

Worry filled her as she looked at his face. "Trouble in movieland?"

"Not really, but it's something I can't ignore." He gazed out to the horizon as if in thought. "Reality of the biz is always at my heels ... ready to take a nip like a rabid dog. I play the game and survive. Unfortunately, I have a studio meeting the day after tomorrow. It can't be helped."

"I understand. I'm content to be in your company no matter the location." She glanced into his eyes for a moment, then softly kissed his lips. "It's you, Trenton Lowe, not your fame or fortune."

I hope his association with me hasn't caused himTrouble with his higher-ups.

Am I bad for him?

Twenty~Seven

AMELIA PLACED THE pink shell onto the night table next to her purse. She opened the French doors and walked onto the porch. Trenton had gone into the bathroom. She took the time on her own to enjoy the night and the moment. The sky was such a black endless velvet—a deepness she hadn't seen since traveling up to the Manor. Those were times when her surroundings mattered little to her. Now she relished the silence and twinkling stars that seemed to be alive. She wondered why this one man had caused her to see the ordinary with new and clear vision. What was the magic he spun around her? She turned at the soft sound of his footsteps coming up behind her and then turned her gaze back to the ocean.

His warm arms encircled her shoulders while she leaned against his chest. His hot breath caressed her as he kissed the back of her neck and nuzzled her hair.

She rubbed her cheek on the back of his hand and left a kiss. "It's hard to believe that I would want to be any place else other than here with you at this instant."

"Wherever we go, we bring our whole life with us. For some, they are happy with their lot. Most aren't because they're imperfect. When they obtain what they want, they want what they had." He turned her around to face him. "That's not me. I know what I have ... and that's enough for me ... you're enough for me."

"Those are very pretty words." Her eyes dwelt on his to capture this moment for her eternity. "You're making it harder for me to leave."

"You never have to leave." He held her tightly, crushing her breasts so tight against his chest that she could feel his heart beating. "Let me be all your tomorrows."

"My bitter truths never gave credence to 'tomorrows'—only the present." *I wish he would try to understand.*

He looked at her for a long minute as his lips parted. She rose on her toes, feeling his breath against her face. His warm lips caressed hers as he unfastened the buttons on her blouse. Her nimble fingers opened his belt and then slowly unzipped his pants. His ragged gasp escaped as her hand reached in and fondled him, feeling him grow hard and firm.

They quickly undressed. He took her hand to lead her back to the bedroom. She held back and cocked her head in the direction of the chaise lounge. The seductive cool air caressed her, sharpening her senses.

She beckoned him with a teasing finger. "We haven't christened the porch. Let's give Mr. Wrigley a memory. No one can see us." She licked her lips and coyly smiled as she eased back onto the cushion. "I bet they never did out here what we're about to do."

He stood before her naked—his erection hard and proud. "If they did—we do it better."

Trenton's knee spread her thighs apart as he leaned down on top of her, supporting himself on his elbows. She pulled him closer, clutching his shoulders, and kissed him, her tongue mingling with his, sending sparks of desire that tingled through her body. He broke away from her mouth and sought her rosy erect nipples. Her hand at the back of his head pulled him closer, begging him to put more of her breast in his mouth. Her moan crept out.

"Shush," he murmured. "Someone might hear."

His hand traveled slowly down her stomach followed by him mouthing her hungry flesh, and then his lingering tongue. His fingers parted her velvet creases, teasing her with each movement and stroke. She knew he could feel her moistness and stifled a near scream begging him to enter her. His kisses moved further to her sweet spot, ever teasing, kissing and then pulling away, and kissing again. She grabbed the back of his head, her eyes tightly shut. Through panting breaths, she whispered, "Don't please me like this. I want you inside me."

He replaced his mouth with his teasing fingers, then lowered himself down onto her, easing his erection into her, a fraction of an inch at a time. Not wanting him to tease her any longer, she pulled his buttocks hard, forcing him deep inside her, and wrapped her legs around him to keep him where she enjoyed it the most—that sweet spot that drove her wild. Her whole focus centered on the pleasure he gave her. Ecstasy surged through her body, sending electric twinges all the way down to her toes. She was so close. Her rhythm quickened, demanding he keep pace in frantic movement. She raised her hips with one immense gasp as her inner spasms caressed his pulsating manhood.

At that moment, she didn't care if Trenton had climaxed or not. He had transported her to a realm of complete satisfaction.

Their breaths slowed in unison. He raised his head and looked in her eyes, smoothing away the damp hair from her forehead. He kissed her earlobe and a drop of perspiration fell from his hair.

"From the vice grip you had on my ass and your response, I assumed I pleased you?" He rubbed the back of his fingers along her cheek.

"You definitely pleased me. I have never had such intense pleasure .... Were you pleased? You didn't give me much of a chance to mouth your glorious cock." She chuckled. "As you know, I'm not adverse to that."

"Yes. I well remember." He lifted himself off her and sat at the end of chaise. She moved her legs to give him more room.

"This was almost as good as making love on a beach, though I've never had the occurrence. I've heard that feeling nature so close at hand heightens the senses—all the senses." Her toes played with his back, drawing invisible small designs.

"It was better. There was no sand going up my crack." He hinted that he might have had such an experience.

"In the movies, it looks so romantic with the waves coming halfway up their legs—keeping pace with their passion." She looked up at the sky envisioning fantasy lovers caught up in rapture.

"You're remembering a movie of some sort, probably an old black and white tear jerker, like *From Here to Eternity* with Burt Lancaster—God rest his soul." His hand ran soothing strokes along her leg.

"Yes. That's the movie." She sat up and drew her legs away from his touch. "That is such an intense movie with palpable passion. Sex dripped off the screen in that love scene."

"Ah, but they were fully clothed in swimsuits." He stood and picked up their tossed clothing. "That's where the actors' talent comes into play. They didn't have to be naked for the audience to feel the intensity—the desire that must be satisfied."

"That describes us ... doesn't it?" *He says he feels something special for me, but isn't it just lust? And how do I really feel about him? He's different from my usual toy boys. They always satisfy me, but what I feel when he makes love to me is another sensation altogether.*

"I think we can't be together for twenty-four hours without jumping each other's bones, if that's what you mean." He chuckled and placed his hands on his hips. "That's not at all bad for a start to deeper things."

"Deeper things?" She stood up and walked close to him. Her fingers lightly caressed his flaccid penis. "You just explored my deeper things."

"Now you're being cute. I'm referring to love, a commitment between two people." He pulled his hips away from her teasing fingers. "You'll have to wait a while. The batteries need recharging. I'm not twenty anymore."

"The other night you were riding high most of the night." She reached for him again. He pulled away.

"That was an exception—not at all my norm." His eyes narrowed with a curious glint. "Aren't you completely satisfied? Is that why you're enticing me? You're left hanging?"

"Not in the least." He lightly touched her most sensitive area. She pulled his hand away. "Don't touch me there—not yet."

"Just checking. I care too much for you not to want your pleasure more than mine." He embraced her and kissed her neck. "I only want good things for you ... forever."

Forever? That's a big statement. Am I even capable of loving?

Twenty~Eight

TRENTON SAT AT the studio's oval conference table. This was where momentous discussions took place conferring on the major issues of a movie project, whether to sign a new actor, or toss another one out the window. This time was different as he looked at the other executives sitting across from him. He could feel it and see it in their eyes. Small talk among them filled the void until Aaron Krantz would make his appearance. The group avoiding Trenton in conversation was an omen. An inner squirm formed in his gut but he was careful not to let the others know his fears. At the opening of the door, the voices hushed. The tall and distinguished head of the studio entered the room, looming full of control and unrelenting power.

Aaron pulled out a chair from the head of the table and sat down, interlacing his fingers on the mirror-like oak tabletop. The air was already thick and heavy.

He eyed each one before starting. "I've called this meeting because I want everyone to be on the same page while *Duchess in Love* is in post-production. If you look over the pages in the folders in front of you, the production costs at this point are under budget, but not as much as we would have liked. Though the leading actors are all A-listers, we will need massive sales the first week if we want to have happy stockholders—more importantly, if we want this studio to survive." He paused and again made eye contact with every face at the table, one by one, making his point by his steely expression enhanced by his cold businesslike glare. "Everyone of you here is responsible for the success or failure of this film. You are all heads of your respective departments and must be accountable—no waste of time and money as production wraps up. Keep overtime to a minimum, if at all. I don't want to see that editing, sound, and the rest of it is going over the figures we budgeted for, for each department. The PR teams are under the same restriction. The financial margin is lean and every penny counts." He cleared his throat. Some members at the table rolled their eyes, but remained silent. "You all have your agendas listed."

They opened their folders, reading. After a moment of silence, the braver attendees discussed a few minor matters until the CEO said,

"This meeting is over and remember, watch the expenses." He lowered his voice and faced Trenton. "I need to speak with you after the others leave."

Trenton gave a weak smile while running his finger between his neck and shirt collar. *What have I done wrong now?* He watched the others depart, clutching their folders filled with goals and deadlines. Aaron walked to the credenza. He turned to Trenton, raising an empty crystal glass. "Scotch?"

Trenton nodded, and watched Aaron pour two stiff drinks from a Lalique decanter. "Do I need that to hear what you're about to say?" *The hammer is coming down and it's going to be brutal.*

"Probably not." He handed the drink to Trenton and pulled up a seat next to him, his thick fingers interlaced on the table. "Your liaison with the duchess is no secret, here or in the UK." He leaned in closer. "If you weren't behind the scenes, it could be bad press for a married actor."

"I haven't read or seen anything in *Variety* or the tabloids. Besides, I'm no longer married." *Is this the beginning of inching me out the door?* "I didn't think there was such a thing as bad press." He took a swallow of scotch and wished he could down it all and pour himself another. "Look at the box office response after that actor was arrested for showing up drunk and nearly naked at that party in France. The sales were higher than expected. There have been no negative photos of us in any of the press."

"True. But she *is* a married duchess." He furrowed his brow, eyes darkening.

"Her husband is agreeable." *What is he getting at?* "Hardly anyone not in the biz knows my name. I don't understand your point ... this isn't the 1950s."

"Because of Lady Hollingsworth, they are fast learning your name. A low-level buzz is circulating." His scrutinizing gaze unnerved Trenton. "Still, this could turn out good for box office. A few misplaced remarks in the right ears that the duchess might have inspired the movie you worked on. People would be clamoring to get a glimpse of the secret life of a real duchess."

"Are you suggesting I use my association with Amelia to further the success of the movie?" His posture stiffened to pencil straight. "I respect her too much to jeopardize her reputation."

"Reputation?" He laughed loudly. "You've got to be kidding. Lady Amelia threw that away when she married the duke. She and her toy boys are a joke in Europe and fast becoming the same joke here." He paused, eyeing Trenton's reaction. Clearly, he felt his position allowed him the freedom for such frankness just shy of rude. "You're far from twenty. What is the fascination? She wanted to try out someone near her own age? The rags have been tracking you two through London, Napa Valley, Malibu, and even Catalina. High power lenses don't lie, not to mention the great invention of camera drones. Your personal life is yours—as long as you keep the interest of the studio at the top of the list."

Rage surged through Trenton. His jaw set and he took a couple of deep breaths. He spoke through gritted teeth, "Don't insult Amelia. You don't even know her. You know nothing about her."

"Simmer down. I'm merely stating what everyone knows. You need to be aware of these things." He finished his drink. "Look. Try to keep free of nasty publicity—no outbursts in public—not that you ever have. You and Amelia can be a great asset for this movie. After the premiere, ship her back to London if you want to."

"I have no control over her. I won't use her for the studio. She comes and goes as she sees fit." *Of all the nerve! Amelia is nothing more than a commodity to him—to be used and tossed away.*

"Untie that knot in your dick. I'm not suggesting you share the between the sheets details ... just some social situations where you both can be seen at a restaurant or bar. Let the members of the public come to their own conclusions." Trenton wished he could wipe Krantz's smug smile off his face with a swift uppercut to the jaw. Aaron stood up from the table. "That about sums it up. Think about what I've said. It would be a shame for a producer to end up where he started twenty years ago—writing scripts for TV commercials."

Aaron extended his hand. Trenton rose and looked at him, not accepting the gesture. "I can smell the desperation. You reek of it."

Trenton's quick steps took him from the office to the carpeted hallway. He had hoped that slamming the door would let his boss know how despicable he was. He knew that the biz was ruthless, but had always been able to stay clear of that side of things. Asking him to exploit Amelia was too much—just too damn much. Even though it might cost him his job, he halfway hoped she would leave before the premiere. That would fix Aaron's ass. The rumored inspiration for *Duchess in Love* would be safe in London away from prying eyes, cruel whispers, and tawdry tabloid headlines.

Trenton walked to his car in the garage, his fists and jaw clenched, oblivious of his surroundings. He knew he should've stayed to speak with the editing staff, and sound department, but that wasn't his priority. Keeping Amelia safe was first in his mind. He had thought his prime task was keeping spiders away from her—and that was the only harm he needed to deal with. Now he had a viper at the top of the list and Aaron Krantz was the name of that snake.

He started the car, backed out and was soon on the highway, making the twenty-eight mile trek to his home. The more he thought about the studio's demands on his personal life, the more his anger brewed. He didn't want to send her away. If she stayed, how could he protect her from all the nasty gossip? True, Amelia had said she loved the attention of rumors in London. But those rumors she had control of, and not rumors created by movie moguls for the price of a ticket.

He recalled Krantz' words. Dread consumed his belly.

Deeper worry clouded his thoughts.

My God! If Amelia gets wind of how the studio wants to use her, she could think that I was up to no good—using our time in London and here to cement a relationship for the benefit of the movie, the studio, and my job. She's always been skeptical of people's motives—a bit cynical. If she gets any wind of this, I could lose her forever. She'd hate me. How can I keep her from the conniving truth? I don't want to lose her. She is so close to saying she wants a life with me.

Damn Aaron Krantz! He could ruin it all!

I must find a way ...

Twenty~Nine

AMELIA SENSED EYES boring into her while sitting at The Blvd outdoor dining area of the Beverly Wilshire Hotel with Trenton. She turned her head and glanced around, then took a sip of her drink before diving into the salad.

Having been in the tabloid spotlight for years, snickers and snide remarks were expected and commonplace. She relished them. It was her one claim to fame—her only claim to fame of any kind for that matter. This was different. She cared for Trenton and didn't want his reputation scarred on her account. She didn't notice any overt gawkers in the mix of people strolling toward her, carrying designer-named shopping bags down South Rodeo Drive.

"Deep in thoughts?" His charming smile and warm touch eased her worry. "Thoughts about me, I hope."

"Yes. You're never far from my mind." She leaned to him and left a soft kiss on his cheek. "I only want the best for you, even ... even if that means my returning to London."

A sharp ting sounded as he dropped his fork onto the plate. "I thought you'd be staying longer." His eyes grew wide with alarm. "You have nothing pressing in London. There's no reason." His jaw set and the muscles in his cheek twitched. "What's going on? You want to throw away what we have?"

"What do we have?" She felt tears welling up. "A friendship with side perks? You're too fine a man to ever be satisfied with that for very long. At some point, you'll want more."

"Only if you do." He squeezed her hand and stared into her face, then took a handkerchief from his pocket and wiped a falling tear on her cheek. "I'm happy if things never change between us."

"I'm glad you maintain the old fashioned habit of carrying a handkerchief," another tear fell, "forever ready to mop up my silly tears. You're the only one that gives me the gift of tears—I don't have to bury my emotions when I'm around you. I rarely cried before you entered my gray existence."

A very good-looking and well-dressed man in his early twenties came up to their table. "A gentleman never causes a lady to cry." He reached out as if to touch Amelia's cheek. She pulled back. "Especially one so beautiful." His cocky grin yelled disrespect.

Who is he? A paparazzo?

Trenton stood up immediately, shoving the chair beneath him. "I don't see where this is any of your business." His eyes narrowed. "Who are you working for? Who sent you?"

"Just an observation." It wasn't surprising that his snide sneer irritated Trenton. "I wouldn't mind getting to know her better ... after you're done with her of course. I'm willing to wait."

Trenton grabbed him by the shirt collar, tightening the garment around his throat. The man's face turned red from the strong grip, and Trenton shoved him backwards, causing him to stumble and fall into a planter. Dirt spilled onto the floor. A tense silence fell over the restaurant followed by cascading whispers and murmurs.

"If you ever come back to me or the lady again, you'll have more than a wrinkled shirt." He took several deep breaths. "Your face won't look so good in front of the camera." Trenton returned to his seat.

The strange man mumbled, "What the fuck?", jerking his neck, and stumbled off.

Amelia tried to compose the jumble of feelings that churned inside ... fear, anger, worry .... This was exactly the kind of thing she didn't want to happen—putting him in a position to defend her. At the same time, his taking control of the situation was extremely appealing. The only other man in her life who had ever stood up for her was her dead father.

"I don't want you to put yourself in a situation where you'll be injured—certainly not for me. He was beyond churlish—downright cheeky." *Will this incident be in the tabloids? Will his boss be angry with him?*

"No measly little punk will insult you—not on my watch." He picked up his napkin from the floor.

"I'll take that, sir." The waiter gave him a new one.

Another server refilled their water glasses and spoke in a low tone, "Well done, sir."

Trenton nodded, then asked her, "Did you recognize him?"

"Certainly not!" *Does he think my boys would travel the Atlantic to find me?* "And you? Was his face familiar?" The mere idea that Trenton thought she knew that lout infuriated her. Anger slid up and down her spine.

"No, never saw him before .... Let's enjoy our lunch. There might be a trinket we can find for you—a souvenir." He shot her a wink.

"My souvenir is lovely memories and that shell I picked up on the beach." She closed her eyes for an instant, reliving her treasured moment. *He shrugged off that incident quick enough, or he's putting on a proper face.* Her negative feelings softened. He had that magic to make everything right again.

"There are so many more memories I want to give you—memories of us." He lovingly kissed her cheek.

~~***~~

Amelia gasped as she entered the living room with Trenton. "Did you buy that plant?" She scrutinized his face. The new addition stood on the coffee table in front of the expansive leather sofa.

He hung his jacket on the back of a chair. "What?"

"That spider plant—did you buy it?" Her lips thinned, eyes glaring, as she dropped her purse to the floor.

"No. I didn't." He stroked his chin. "I have no idea where it came from."

"Whoever it was, they have a brilliant sick sense of humor." She eyed his face for a reaction, which told her nothing. "Who else knows about my severe allergy to spiders?"

"Only Jane and Alex." He placed his hands on his hips, eyes narrowing with concern. "I hardly think they would want to upset you."

She heard voices coming from the kitchen.

"Alex, Jane, please come here," Trenton said.

Alex wiped his hands on a towel as he entered, while Jane curtsied, then stood patiently still.

Trenton didn't give them a chance to speak. "Do you know anything about this?" He pointed to the plant. "How did it get here?"

Jane took a small step forward and spoke softly, "It arrived about two hours ago, sir ... while you and Milady were out. There was no message."

Amelia took a few steps to Trenton as she spoke to the servants. "Was there any card at all?"

"Only a blank card from the florist." Jane looked slightly worried. "I can get it out of the dustbin, Milady."

"Please do." As the girl started to leave, she added, "Tea in about an hour wouldn't go amiss."

Moments later, Jane returned, handing the card to the duchess. Amelia turned it over and back again. She didn't unearth any new information. She studied the name of the florist and their address.

"What is it?" Trenton sat down beside her. He took the card that nearly fell from her hands. "It's a typical florist card."

"It's not the card—it's where the card came from." *His reach is longer than I thought possible.*

"Why would anyone pay the exorbitant cost to have a plant air-shipped from Massachusetts?" His brow furrowed as he flicked the card.

She took the blank florist paper from him. "My darling cousin, Clive." *Why does he want to torment me?* "It's his message—I can never be far from his reach."

"That's a bit cynical." He rubbed his chin as if thinking. "Why do you think he's behind this and why is he fixated on you?"

"It's a strong assumption—no one else would want to upset me. He and I have a long history." She sighed. "I know all his skeletons. He won't breathe easy until I'm dead."

"I doubt it's as grave as that—excusing the pun." He put his arm around her shoulder, drew her close, and kissed her temple.

"I'm not overreacting. I know I'm right. To know him is to loathe him." Amelia put her hand in his and heaved a deep breath. She dug in her heels as her eyes pierced the image of Clive in her mind. "My determination will beat his any day." A forced smile revealed clenched teeth, then a deep breath. "Well, I won't let him spoil my lovely holiday. A shower is in order."

Amelia headed to the bathroom off from their bedroom. She stripped down quickly as the shower ran, steam clouding the mirror.

The water refreshed her and relaxed her muscles a little. With eyes closed, she stood there a moment enjoying the flow washing her fears down the drain with the suds. Trenton was her safe place. No one could truly reach her, not with him by her side. She reached for the soap from the shower's shelf and let out a shrill scream. "No! Oh God, no!" Her body froze, lead in her limbs. *I have to move. Got to get out of here.* She stepped backward, and screamed again.

She bolted from the shower and scrambled on top of the toilet seat.

Trenton burst through the door. "What is it?" His eyes were wide. "Are you hurt?" He stared at her naked body, shivering with fear.

Her bottom lip trembled as her shaking finger pointed. "In there ... three of them ... spiders! One is on the soap."

He pulled the curtain partially back and turned off the water. She heard his stomping foot on the shower floor. "I killed them," he said when he stepped out, droplets of water on his head and shoulders of his shirt. All should be well now." He searched the corners and nooks where other spiders might seek refuge. "No sign of any more."

She took a towel from his hand. Tremors filled her voice as she tried to cover herself. "I thought y— you had your home sprayed!

Did the company forget about the bathrooms?"

"Apparently, they did." He embraced her. "God, Amelia. I'm so sorry, and glad you're okay. I can't believe this could happen."

His warm arms couldn't obliterate the deep fear churning in her. She clung to him, her breath jagged. "You had better check the rest of the rooms."

When she returned to the living room in a fluffy terry robe, tea and dainty sandwiches waited on the coffee table. Trenton stood with his hands on his hips questioning both Alex and Jane.

"So no one was admitted to my home while we were out?" he asked.

"Yes. Absolutely no one." Alex looked at Amelia and then Trenton. "After pest control came in, when you first arrived from Catalina, I even went behind them after they left, and sprayed everywhere, especially around windows and doors."

Jane looked sheepish. "I think …. When the plant arrived, I placed it in the bathroom and turned on the shower for a breath of steam—it was looking a bit poorly." She twisted her fingers and bit her bottom lip while shifting her weight from one foot to another. "I read somewhere that plants thrive in steam if they haven't been watered for a while. After an hour, I brought it back out here. They may have been on the plant. I'm so sorry. I meant no harm, Milady."

"None done, Jane." Amelia pulled the robe closer around her and shuddered. *She looks crushed.*

"No harm done *yet.*" Trenton looked sternly at the young servant. "You both must be very vigilant—no insects of any kind. Spray daily if need be. And while you're at it, dispose of that damn plant—off the property."

Alex grabbed the green offending harbinger. He and Jane left while Amelia poured the tea.

"Well, that explains about the spiders. Just an innocent occurrence?" She dropped a lump of sugar into the cup and stirred. "I guess I'm getting paranoid. In London, Elizabeth sprays the townhouse every two or three days."

She reached for Trenton's hand. She needed to feel him—his strength, his guidance as terror still dwelt in her.

"Remember, Amelia." He eased down beside her, his arm around her shoulders. "I won't let any harm come to you … ever. This was just a very odd happening."

Was this a mere one-off incident or were those spiders planted by the florist—or someone else? Ridiculous! Still … I put nothing past Clive—especially not after Penelope.

Thirty

ARMED WITH A fistful of cash, Amelia delighted in shopping the fashionable boutiques on Rodeo Drive. Though she could have easily afforded this luxury herself, Trenton had insisted that he wanted to treat her as a way to show appreciation for her coming into his life.

Walking out of the dressing room, she twirled in front of a tall mirror checking the fit and color. The beach ensemble fitted her as if it were couture made to her measurements. She hadn't packed many clothes for seaside excursions. A familiar face caught her attention in the reflection in one of the mirrors—a male profile towering over the racks of clothing in the background. She frowned, brushed away any notion of concern, and returned her attention to the clothing.

A man's voice spoke, "Buy it. It suits you."

She whipped around. She remembered now why his face was familiar, and who could forget his boorish manner at The Blvd. "How dare you! You have no invitation into my life. Please leave. If not, I'll call for security." She gritted her teeth, pushed her shoulders back, and jutted her chin, ready to take him on if needed.

"That outfit looks better when you're wearing it than on the rack." He shot her a sly, confident smile. He appeared immune to her threat. "Even a room is enhanced when you walk into it."

She cocked an eyebrow. "Are you following me? There are laws against that." *Is my notoriety plastered on my face?*

He raised a store shopping bag. "Not in the least ... buying a gift for my mother."

"Really?" She wasn't convinced. "Obviously you didn't get the message to leave me alone at The Blvd."

Amelia left to change in the dressing room. When she returned to pay for the garments, the young man had vanished. A flood of relief surged through her. She decided it would be best not to tell Trenton of this odd encounter as he might overreact, causing him unwanted publicity in some manner, and jeopardize his position.

~~***~~

All was right in Trenton's world, enjoying the breeze at dusk with Amelia holding his hand, as they looked out to the ocean's horizon. Hands intertwined, they strolled along the boardwalk, the famed amusement park's lights dancing on the rippling waves. Families and lovers walking on the Warf's planks appeared oblivious to others. It was a perfect night with a perfect woman who he hoped would break down and finally admit she wanted him as much as he wanted her.

He felt a jaunt to Santa Monica Pier and the beautiful beaches might, in some infinitesimal way, sway her inevitable decision to return to London. Though she hadn't mentioned ending her vacation, that didn't mean she hadn't entertained that thought. He had purposely instructed Alex to keep all news about him confronting that lout, which appeared in the next day's tabloids, hidden from her. He hadn't heard back from Krantz, but that didn't mean he wouldn't in a day or so.

If I'm lucky, he'll think it's good PR. If not—it's another nail in my career coffin.

"By your serious look, your thoughts are worth more than a penny. How about a dollar?" he asked.

She flashed him a sideways glance then looked straight ahead, slowing her pace. "It'll be three weeks I've been away come this Monday. I should be either leaving or staying."

"Well, you know what I vote for—stay." He squeezed her hand. "You won't have a view like this in London, plus the beaches, famous Hollywood encounters, and movie premieres, not to mention having a movie producer warm your bed every night." He touched the blazed tendril at her ear, letting his finger trace the outline of her lobe.

She smiled. "That's the best of it ... the movie producer."

He stopped her, turning her to face him. He leaned in, their lips a scant inch apart. Her warm breath filled his being.

An abrupt shove against his shoulder ruined their moment.

"What the hell?" He spun around to confront the intruder.

The young man didn't give Trenton a chance to speak. "What are you doing with that old man? I'm the one who can *really* show you a good time." He shot a lurid wink to Amelia.

She glared with flaring nostrils. "Slither back to that rock you live under!"

On impulse, she grabbed her phone and recorded his picture.

"She only likes the beginning of things." The man sneered. "I'll be her next beginning."

Trenton's neck veins bulged with a visible pulse. He grabbed a fistful of the man's hair and with one swift movement, landed a blow on his face. Blood dripped onto the man's expensive-looking shirt. He grabbed a wad of paper napkins from his trousers and gave Trenton a look of disbelief.

"What the fuck man! You're fuckin' crazy." He wiped his nose and tilted his head backwards to ease the bleeding. "I've got a shoot tomorrow."

Trenton rubbed his knuckles and noticed he had cut himself on the man's pearly whites. "You're lucky I didn't aim for your eye," he said through gritted teeth. He grabbed the man by the shirt collar while others stood with their phones in the air, capturing either video or pictures. "I know you. You're the same asshole who bothered us at the restaurant. Who sent you? Naomi? Jason? Tell me you little punk." He raised his bleeding fist for another strike.

"No one! No one!" He pulled away trying to avoid another blow. His voice was meek and pleading. "I thought if the tabs could get a photo of me with you and the duchess," he looked at Amelia, "I might get a bit of free press—get my face out there."

Trenton felt her hand tremble on his arm. She glared at the man with panic. "Let him go. Just ignore him. Please, I want to go home."

Trenton released the young man's collar with a shove that nearly caused the intruder to fall backwards. The man caught himself in a stumble and fled down the pier back to the beach.

He saw the hurt in her eyes. "There's always some jerk-job out there trying to get a break and will do anything for it. Sometimes I hate this city."

She lightly touched his injured hand. "You're bleeding." She pulled out a Kleenex from her purse.

"It's nothing." He took the tissue and wrapped his oozing knuckles. "Sorry that idiot bothered us ... bothered you. Do you really want to go home?"

"After all the negative British publicity I've endured over the years ..." she let out a light chuckle, "that was nothing. Don't let him ruin our evening."

"I know of one way to make you feel better, and it's not here on this pier," Trenton teased.

"Since you're so modest, home might be a more proper setting." She licked her lips suggesting more. "Though I've never cared who watched."

"Not my style. I won't feed a voyeur's fantasy." *Did she ever have sex in front of others? Is she trying to shock me? How deep does her past go?*

No. She's too honest to be hiding something like that ...

Or is she?

Thirty~One

AMELIA REACHED FOR a travel magazine from the coffee table when Alex entered carrying a long florist box. A loving gesture from Trenton, believing that after he had put that punk in his place on the Warf, all would be right in her world?

Trenton entered the room.

Tossing the magazine aside, she went to him, stood on tiptoe, and kissed his cheek. He stared at her, and then looked at the delivery the houseman held.

"Don't make assumptions, Duchess." His devil-may-care expression turned to a frown, his lips turned sharply downward.

"Why not?" She flashed him a grin as her eyes twinkled. "You want to spoil me. I know of no better way to pamper me than with flowers. If you're lucky, I'll let you caress my naked body with one of those flowers."

Alex cast his eyes to the floor as if embarrassed. He handed the long box to her and then started leaving the room with swift steps.

"I didn't send them," Trenton said in a solemn voice. "Are they from Alistair? Begging you to return?"

She quickly lifted the lid and pushed the green floral wrapping away, exposing long-stemmed red roses. There was a plain white card, but not from a florist.

The words written on it filled her with cold steel fear.

Love your tricks. Next time, you're on top. I'll be in touch.

She dropped it and stared down at the carpet.

"What's wrong?" Trenton rushed to her, picked up the card, reading the message in a nondescript hand. "Alex, please come here a moment."

He had barely entered when Trenton hammered out his questions. "Did you see who delivered these flowers? Who's the florist? Did you recognize anyone?"

"I didn't see a van. A uniformed man came to the gate stating he had a delivery for Duchess Hollingsworth. I didn't recognize his face." He flashed a glance at Amelia and then back to his employer. "Since he knew Lady Amelia's name, I thought it was a gift from you, sir."

"Where's Jane? Did she see anyone?" Trenton rubbed his forehead as his brows drew together.

"It's her day off. She was out—still is." Alex stood there, looking helpless.

"I want to see the security footage." Trenton headed toward the kitchen and presumably to the surveillance monitors located somewhere near there.

Amelia eased down on the sofa. She felt her pulse race as she scrambled to make sense of this.

This has to be Clive's sick joke. But, why? I would think he's perfectly happy to have me out of his hair. Alistair? No. It's not in him. He finds comfort at the club with his boys. That toy boy type has crossed my path three times. Is he behind this? Stalking me?

Trenton returned. He must've seen the unspoken question on her face. "Nothing of any good. No monogram on his shirt. Couldn't even get a good look at his face with his head hanging down and a billed cap pulled down nearly touching his nose—like he didn't want to be identified." He went to her and wrapped his arms around her.

Fear filled her every cell. She shook. Her heart pounded against her ribs. She prided herself in being the woman who never let anything frighten her, and now she was torn to her center.

Trenton stroked her shoulders. "You're safe here. I won't let any harm come to you—even if it takes my last breath."

Amelia fought to keep her tears from falling. "It better not come to that. What if I'm bringing danger to you?" She snuggled against his chest and plucked at the buttons on his shirt. "Wouldn't it be better if I leave?"

"I don't feel threatened." He stroked her hair, instilling a safe feeling, causing her tremors to fade. "The studio's security rivals that of Fort Knox. No one can get to me at work."

Why don't I believe his words? This bastard has the cunning of an MI6 operative.

He lifted her chin with his fingers, forcing her to look in his eyes. "Who do you know that would play such a horrible joke? Someone from your past?"

"I don't think Reggie or the others even think of me. I've cut off contact with them since I met you in London." She bit her lip in thought. "My cousin Clive Bradford, the Duke of Bryningmead, would love to see me rotting in a grave—I know all his skeletons— his filthy secrets, you see. He doesn't feel properly secure while I still breathe air."

"If that's true, he has a long reach from London." He ran his hand through his hair. "Why go to all the bother when you're here and less likely to cause him trouble?"

"I won't put anything past his sort." *Clive? Really? It could be him and yet have nothing at all to do with that young man bothering me.* "He might want to cause trouble—mix up my holiday. If it is him, I'm safer here than back home. At least he can't get to me here—merely be a pest."

"I'd like to get to the bottom of this." He rubbed his chin as muscles in his jaw twitched. "Loose ends like this need to be tied up."

"If you don't mind, Trent, I want to be alone on the balcony." She angled her head to the large panoramic windows. "I need to hear the ocean waves and think a bit ...." She shot a glance brimming with hatred at the floral box. "Throw those blasted flowers in the dustbin. Better yet—burn them lest there be any insects."

He nodded, watching her walk to the terrace. She sensed his eyes on her while sitting on the chair at the small circular table gazing at the angry waves. The sea air blustered, whipping her hair about her face and reflected her worried confusion.

~~***~~

If there was one word that had always described Amelia, it was gutsy. She took pride in that moniker, but now with the recent events, she felt that rock of nerve begin to crumble. Her world was one of predictability where her control determined most events. These recent encounters with a stranger struck a new chord with possible dangerous results.

While on the patio, she pulled the phone from the pocket of her shorts and swiped the face to the photo section. She stared at the image of the unknown man—the intruder who dared to disrupt her perfect life—a life that she had begun to think she could share with a man who only wanted the best for her, who would be by her side without question.

Who are you? Why are you doing this to me?

She took a deep breath, then swiped the phone again and scrolled to the contact she wanted. Ringing sounded in her ear. With every tone, her impatience grew. *Answer the bloody phone!*

A man's voice answered. "Joe, here."

"It's Amelia—Amelia Hollingsworth. Can you talk?" She took a few steps and leaned on the railing, looking at the rocks below.

"Yeah. What's up? You and Lowe have been in the papers. Livin' up the Hollywood glam?" Her mind saw Joe with his white hair and welcoming smile—a charming diamond in the rough.

"Not bad news in the papers?" She started to pace, and glanced over her shoulder, relieved to see Trenton was not observing her.

"Nah, nothin' I'd worry 'bout. Why you callin'?" His voice was soft.

"There has been an instance, three actually—a man in his twenties who pops up and is annoying me. I think he's stalking me." She took another deep breath. "I recall you had helped Taylor and Cindy with their troubles and I thought you might do the same for me."

"Got a name?" he asked.

"No, I don't. But I do have a photo on my phone." *He might not be able to help at all.* "I could send it to you."

"Yeah, that'll do. I'm gonna need more than a pic. What has this creep done? Callin' and hangin' up?" She heard him take a swallow of something.

"No. But he's shown up at a restaurant, in a store where I was shopping, and again on Santa Monica Pier, plus an arrival of flowers with a note that was suggestive, ending with 'I'll be in touch'." She paused her pacing. The wind kicked up again. She smoothed her hair and tucked a wayward lock of hair behind her ear. "I'm fearful this is more than a playful flirtation."

"Any threats? A dead animal on the doorstep?" His tone held more than mere concern.

"No. Nothing like that. Do you think this man will hurt me or even *kill* me?" The vision of her murder—a man stabbing her from the *Psycho* film ran a deadly fear through Amelia.

"I can't say until I've looked into it, but probably not. You got any idea who else would want to pester y' besides this jerk? Maybe put him up to these pranks?" His voice sounded more serious.

"Clive was my first thought." Her lips trembled, knowing that there wasn't much her sinister cousin wouldn't do. "He's in London. If he *is* behind this, how would he benefit from it?"

"Maybe he's doin' it for Alistair. They're thick as thieves." His chuckle annoyed her. "The tabs had pics of you, and Lowe on that pier—one with him punchin' the punk in the nose. He sure as hell laid a good one on that prick."

"Oh, no. Unfortunately, he's the one." She hesitated. "So ... you think you can help?"

"I make no promises. Got a pal outta New York who owes me more than one favor." His voice lowered. "Look. If you'll feel safer, you can always come here to Bel-Air. Lar and Taylor would welcome you with open arms. Since Cindy's marriage, you're family."

"I don't want to impose on them." *I know he means well.* "It's best I remain here with Trent. If I leave, that man could follow me. That would only cause trouble for them. Do you think a private investigator here in Hollywood would help? Trent has a vast security system installed."

"Guess you're right 'bout not comin' here. Send me that photo and the exact wording on that card. It might come in handy. I'll check any PIs in the area. First, I'll see what my friend thinks. Gotta go and get workin' on this. Later."

She put her phone on the small nearby table. Joe's words made her feel better, but not by much.

Why didn't I stay in London? What if a woman is behind this? An actress who didn't get a role or was fired? Would causing me trouble be a way of getting back at Trent?

Thirty~Two

THE LOCAL PIZZA parlor had a warm charm and was a welcoming haven for Joe when wanting to get away from the many errands that Larry had him run. He sat in a back corner booth facing the doorway.

Watching various customers come and go was a cheap amusement. Joe sometimes wondered if he had lived his life differently all those years ago, would he now be a grandfather treating the grandkids to an outing away from the parents, teaching them the correct way to eat spaghetti or tackle a slice of pizza without allowing the cheese to slide off.

His thoughts shifted to more important matters. Amelia needed his help and he shouldn't've wasted time daydreaming when he had to call his old friend from the streets. Taking his phone from the table near his frosted mug of beer, he swiped the contacts list and tapped a name. The answer came on the second ring.

"Hey, Buddy. How goes it?" Sal Mourtos sounded in good spirits.

"You're happy. Got good news?" Joe chuckled. "Finally found a hooker who takes traveler's checks?"

"Knock it off." Honking horns came over the phone. "Never that damn lucky. Nobody uses them checks no more."

"Need a favor." He took a swallow of beer. "Kinda important."

"A whack?" Sal seemed hopeful.

"Will you get off that whack idea." Joe wiped his lips. "I've never asked you to whack nobody. Now, listen—listen good." He glanced around for eavesdroppers. All was clear. Joe lowered his voice. "Lady Amelia needs a PI—someone to check on her and a jerk pesterin' her—happened four times. A local guy would be fine if y' can trust him. She's a duchess and don't need no bad press goin' 'round. She's put her ass on the line for Lar and Taylor, plus Cindy and Stu. Don't need some shit yankin' her chains and causin' trouble."

"What you want done when this scum is found? Rough him up, break a few bones?" Joe heard him puff on a cigarette, the noise of more honking horns, and New York City cabbies yelling cuss words. "Can fix it so he won't be no use to no dame."

"Don't go off half-cocked, Sally." Joe let out an exasperated sigh.

"No harm—just find out who it is and if anybody else is behind this stalkin' thing ... Y' sound like you finally made your bones."

"I did. Self-defense–but I'm countin' it." Sal's voice lowered as if disappointed. "The boss don't think it a hit. So I ain't made yet—ain't a soldier—still a damn fuckin' runner."

"Killin' is no good—except for war." Joe noticed a little curly-haired boy peering over the top of the booth watching him. "Look. Gotta go. Get the job done. I'll send tabloid pics and the one the duchess sent me to your phone—she and this low-life. Call me. Later."

I hope to God Sal comes through. He won't talk—that much I know.

~~***~~

Naomi fidgeted on her sofa. She didn't know why her plan had not worked. Not getting her way angered her and strengthened her determination for an all-out war. Even a walk on the beach that morning had done little to soothe her tortured mind.

From the sofa, she looked up at the sound of the front door opening. Jason sauntered toward her with a cocky expression as if he had just won the lottery.

"You have no reason to look so smug. They're still together." She crossed her leg over the other and started moving her foot up and down with fuming irritation.

"It takes time, Mother dear." He plucked off a few grapes from the bowl on the low-lying table and popped them in his mouth.

"Time is not a luxury I can afford." She shifted in her seat—the power of her hate filling her. "I *told* you, I want her out of Trenton's life. No one dumps me and lives happily ever after."

"Simmer down." He chewed on a grape while strolling to the bar and poured Johnny Walker Black into a crystal glass. "I got that male model to follow her. I'm getting flack for his bloody nose—nearly cost him a gig he had the next day."

"A lot of good that did." She seized the drink from his hand and took a large swallow and handed it back to him. "What else do you have planned? Or do I already know—nothing!"

"Details cost money. People need to be paid to get things done—especially illegal things." His snide smile gnawed at her patience. "I'm short of funds."

"Aren't you always?" *He's taking my money and producing nil.* "Motherly generosity only goes so far. I'm not the Federal Reserve Bank."

"Ah, true." His mouth twisted into a sneer. "But you have secrets and I know them—your plan to torture my dear stepdad, for one.

Your socialite friends would love to chew on any of those details while sipping their fancy-assed drinks at a fancy-assed gala. Your name would be mud and you know it."

She swallowed hard. She knew he was capable of doing almost anything. She tried one last time. "Blood is thicker than water."

"So's soup," he scoffed with a self-satisfying tone. He took a large swallow of the expensive scotch, then shot her a scornful look with cold hateful eyes.

Naomi knew he wouldn't cooperate until she loosened the purse strings.

She reached for her purse on the coffee table and started writing out a check. "It won't be much. You had better not be spending my money up your nose. If you can't produce results, I'll take matters into my own hands and cut you off completely."

"That'll never happen even if you can't break up Trenton with his duchess." His boasting smile and sneering eyes flamed her anger. "Like I said, I know too much. There's no love lost between us. We are both self-serving. I'm a reflection of you. You can't stand the image looking back at you."

She balled her hand in a fist on her lap. "Are you smiling because you know the taste of shit in my mouth after what you said?"

"Just telling the truth." His arrogant smile boiled her blood. "Truth and you have never been on good terms." He took the check from her and waved it in the air with triumph. "Check and mate!"

Whistling, Jason strolled away toward the door. He called back without turning around, "Just because you're miserable, doesn't mean everyone else has to be."

She fought the tears welling up behind her eyes.

How did he turn out so cynical and heartless? Where did I go wrong? Still, he must love me in his own twisted way—or does he?

~~***~~

The muffled sound of music came from Larry's studio. Joe hesitated a moment before knocking on the door. He had always looked up to his adopted younger brother. Larry was the one who had talent and the smarts. His towering height made Joe feel small at times.

Melodic strains ceased followed by, "Yeah, come on in."

Joe entered and took an expansive breath. "Gotta talk to y'."

"Shoot." Larry rubbed his hands on his black jeans as he sat on a stool in front of an electronic keyboard. "By your expression, it can't be good."

"Lady Amelia called me askin' for help. She's stayin' with Trenton

Lowe." His thick fingers combed his hair. "She's been pestered by some jerk in L.A., kinda stalkin' her and ..."

"Why doesn't she or Trenton go to the police, Joe?" His brows lifted.

"I think she doesn't want the press to come down on Trenton any more than what they have—tryin' to do damage-control with silence." He slid onto a chair opposite Larry.

"I see your point." He held out his hands, palms upwards. "What do you want me to do? Put her up here for a while? I can do that. Lord knows she has helped this family numerous times. She didn't have to do that—putting her neck out for Taylor and Cindy."

A lump formed in Joe's throat, a feeling like he was in front of a cop or priest. "When I talked with her—"

Larry cut him off. "How did she sound? Concerned? Terrified?"

"Pretty damn scared, since you're askin'." *I hope Lar thinks of somethin'.*

"Any chance of her leaving him and coming here?" He looked hopeful.

"Nah." Joe twiddled his thumbs. "She's stuck to him like glue. Won't consider it."

Larry's face twisted. "That's odd. He's older than her."

"Maybe the duchess is growin' up." *He's gonna freak when I tell him all of it.*

"I suppose she won't return to London, right?" He twisted in his seat toward the keyboard. "I really need to get back to this arrangement."

"Lar, I need to tell you somethin' else." He stared down at the floor like a truant child in front of a principal.

"By the way you're hanging your head, I can tell you haven't told me the worst." Larry's eyes burned into him. This was going downhill.

He has to know the truth.

"Yeah, y' see, I kinda called a friend to help out." He looked his brother straight in the eye.

"Help out? How help out? Who did you contact?" Larry's neck vein grew large with a visible pulse.

"Sal, Sal Mourtos." *The shit's gonna hit the fan now.*

"Sal!" He stood up and faced Joe with only inches separating them. "That mob blabbermouth from New York! Have you lost all your senses? Good God, what were you thinking?"

"I trust Sal. He's a good guy. He wouldn't do nothin' to harm no one who's his friend." *Gotta make Lar understand.*

"He's a dumb jerk with underworld connections." Larry started to pace in the small room. Joe watched his brother's nervous steps keep pace with his rapid words. "I'm not convinced he's not connected to the Mafia no matter how much you try to sway me otherwise." He shook his head. "You could've put Amelia, Trenton—all of us in very serious danger."

"Lar, I only asked Sal to find a local PI to do a little surveillance. Nothin' more than that. A *PI* is no big deal."

"His definition of a PI and mine are probably very different." He paused his steps, eyes growing large, arms folding across his chest. "For all anyone knows, he could put a hit man on the job and that idiot of a stalker will end up with a toe tag."

Larry started pacing again as his face twisted and fists formed then relaxed.

"Nothin' like that. I swear." *God, I hope I'm right about this.* "I was firm with Sal. Told him straight out that only information was needed about the jerk, and no harm to nobody. He assured me that all would be good."

"I pray to God you're right." Larry paused his pacing and stood ramrod straight with a pointing finger. "If anything goes wrong, it will be on your head. One thing that's certain—Amelia will have to put her home in order, either here or there. She can't live in between—not now."

Joe stood up and started to leave, clutching the doorknob. "All will be good, Chief. Nothin' bad. Just a fact-findin' job."

What shittin' can of worms have I opened? Sal had better do as he said— no harm to nobody. Does he know a cool guy who ain't trigger-happy?

Thirty~Three

SAL RESTED ON a park bench overlooking the Brooklyn Bridge spanning the East River. He never tired of this view. When discouraged or just needing some quiet, this was his bit of calm. Eyeing pretty women strolling by or on a jogging run was a side perk. He looked at his watch. Five minutes to one. His old sidekick should arrive any minute.

Quietly, Elliott Crane sat down beside him leaving a foot between them. He looked straight ahead as he talked. "So, what's the deal?"

Sal did the same, staring to the horizon. "PI stuff, nothin' more."

"You yanked me from a whore for PI stuff?" he scoffed. "I'm not some punk comin' up the ranks." Elliott lit a cigarette from his pants' pocket, his hand cupping the flame. He took a deep drag and exhaled fully. "Who and what?"

"Some shit is tailin'—been stalkin' Lady Amelia Hollingsworth. She's a friend of Larry and Taylor's. Need to know if someone is behind it and who has eyes on her." Sal leaned forward with his elbows on his knees, and stared at the tuffs of grass poking through the beaten dirt.

"Royalty?" He sneered. "Why doesn't she have her own fuckin' security?"

"Don't know. Joe needs this intel." He looked at Elliott, stressing his point, "He thinks she's in some type of danger."

"Surveillance is fuckin' borin'." He took another drag on the cigarette. "It'll cost. No more free jobs."

"Joe will get the money. I'm sure of it." *I hope Joe can pay. Otherwise I'm stuck for the tab.*

"Where's the job? UK?" A patrol officer walked by. Elliott pulled up his collar, just touching his short beard by his jaw, hung his head and looked the other way.

"L.A. She's holed up in Malibu at Trenton Lowe's place." Sal sighed relief, as the cop was no longer in sight.

"Nice digs." He crushed the cigarette under his foot, mashing it into the dirt. Then lit another one from the pack.

"Need to cut down on those. Chain smokin' ain't good." He felt hopeful California would be the bait Elliott couldn't resist. "You gonna take it? Deal?" Sal offered his hand. Elliot turned his head the other way.

"Seven big up front for travel." His eyes fixed on the Brooklyn skyline. "Rest when I get back. I don't get the balance—you'll get hurt."

"How much more? Another seven?" *Holy shit, he could put a dent in my stash.*

"Ten. I'll throw in any needed whackin' and roughin'." Elliott's face showed no expression. It was all business.

Sal spoke between clenched teeth. Ice framed his words. "No *whackin'* and no rough stuff—only info. Enjoy the sun and the dames. It's a vacation for y'."

"For fuckin' sake, Sal. I'm a freelance mechanic—it's in my blood." Exasperation poured from his grimace. "Whackin' *is* my vacation." He chuckled. "I have a vacation every month—some better than others."

"Promise me no harm to nobody." *How will I explain this to Joe if there's killin'?*

"Yeah. Doin' what's right is in my gut. Some need to be dead." He puffed on his cigarette.

"Keep your idea of justice to yourself. No hit, no roughin' up." Sal offered his hand again. Elliott looked at it and then looked down.

"I'll do right by you and this Lady dame." He lowered his voice. "Got details?"

"Yeah. I'll text that stuff to you, pics, addresses—all of it." He stroked his chin. "When you gonna get there?"

"Soon. Gotta do research." His eyes bored into Sal's. "Don't need to know my business." His words held a death threat.

"Contact me when you can." Sal adjusted his seat as his throat tightened.

"Where's the money?" Elliott's expression turned deadly.

"Got it covered." Sal reached into his pocket and handed him a plain envelope. "Ten big in there. Only need seven more, right?"

"I'll let you know." He stuffed the packet in his inside jacket pocket. "Hollywood's expensive."

"Don't be a fuckin' loose cannon—only *intel*. Anyone comes up missin' or in a hospital, the deal is off." Sal watched for his reaction. There was none.

Elliott left, kicking a crushed soda can as his steps grew fainter.

Joe better not stick me with this. Frontin' him for the down payment was tough. I'm not a fuckin' bank. Friendship only goes so far.

Elliott never whacked nobody without a contract. Can he resist a kill? Yeah. He never crossed me.

~~***~~

On their return to Malibu from taking a ride up the Pacific Coast Highway, Trenton pulled over to a picturesque overlook spot. Though the parking area was small, he felt this would be a perfect view for Amelia to enjoy the ocean waves crashing onto the rocky cliffs below. During the drive, he had frequently checked his jacket pocket assuring himself that the contents were safe and hadn't fallen onto the car's floor.

She opened the door and stepped out to lean against the stony barricade. He took a moment to watch her. Amelia was so beautiful with that flaming red hair and flawless English complexion. It was not only her obvious beauty, but the loveliness beneath her surface, too. Her spirit and kindness had captivated him and there was no going back.

He got out of the car, glad to stretch his long legs, and walked to her. He slid his hand down the small of her back, heady with her fragrance as he nuzzled the sweet spot on her neck. He couldn't resist planting light kisses on it.

Amelia leaned on the rock barrier for a moment as if etching this instant in her memory. "I'm glad you took me on this ride. The view is stunning. It reminds me of the Cornwall cliffs."

She breathed deeply, inhaling the salty sea air, and tossed her head to dislodge a lock of hair that blew across her face. He had to agree with her that the scenery was magnificent, and the weather perfect, with small fluffy white clouds drifting across an otherwise azure sky. The breeze had whipped up white foam crests on the waves and they could hear the constant roar of the restless water smashing into the rocks far below them.

He wrapped his arms around her waist, touching her stomach. "I wanted to test the car out after the tune-up." He hesitated and cleared his throat. "After our first night ... when I saw you sleeping there, I couldn't see myself not greeting you every morning." He turned her, forcing her to face him.

She stroked his cheek and swallowed. "Yes, but ..."

He interrupted her with a gentle kiss. "Let me finish. I might be jumping the gun ... probably am ... but I need to say this."

Her eyes held encouragement as he continued, "I might sound like I'm saying words from an old black and white movie, but ..." He took an immense breath while pulling out a small black box from his pocket. "I love you with all my heart. I have never loved anyone as much as you. Will you accept my love forever?"

"I—" Her eyes grew wide and her jaw slackened as he opened the box containing a platinum ring with the six-carat pear-shaped diamond. "Will you?" *She's about to cry.* "Please be my wife."

She wiped her eyes with her thumbs and sniffled. "Isn't it customary to ask a single lady for her hand and not a married one? You wouldn't want to make me a bigamist, would you?"

"That's a mere detail." He stared into her eyes. "If you follow your heart, there is no possibility of you remaining tied to Alistair." He looked deeply in her eyes and cradled her face in his palms. "Haven't you sacrificed enough of your life for your dead father's wishes? It's time for you to find happiness on your terms—not based on the terms of others."

"What you say is true." He was still holding the ring in its box. She pushed his hand away. "I'm not free to say yes, Trent. Save it for when I'm certain of what I want my forever to be." She spoke so quietly the wind almost blew her words away.

A golf ball-sized lump formed in his throat. He swallowed hard and looked down at the dirt, and then stared into her eyes again. "Can I hope that you'll say 'yes' in the near future?" He closed the box and dropped the ring back into his pocket. At that moment, he wished she could read his mind. *Say yes with your voice and not just your eyes.*

"We all have hope." She placed her hands on top of his. "I can't commit now, but every fiber of my being wants to say yes."

"I'll cling to that then." He kissed her, crushing her breasts against his chest.

Will the day ever come when she'll be my wife?

Thirty~Four

HEADING BACK TO Malibu, they were both quiet, immersed in their own thoughts. Thankfully, the traffic was light. Amelia focused on the views of the ocean most of the time as Trenton maneuvered around the sharp curves. The drive hadn't ended as he had hoped with her wearing his ring. Yet, she hadn't rejected the proposal completely out of hand, and he felt this was the closest she had come to giving him the answer he'd longed to hear since London.

In his mind, a divorce was a relatively simple matter. The Hollywood crowd went from one divorce to another without batting an eye and didn't seem scathed by the experience. He was one of them after divorcing Naomi—another statistic. He shook his head. He had vowed never to walk down the marriage aisle again.

But Amelia was different, so very different and he truly loved her.

He frowned. Driving down the incline, when he pressed the brakes, the car slowed but not nearly enough. The taillights from the vehicle in front of him grew way too near. He pressed on the pedal firmer, and again. Nothing! Visions of a deadly crash flashed before his eyes. Now the other car's trunk was dangerously close. "What the fuck!" he cursed as he frantically swerved to the right onto the dirt shoulder, just missing a collision with another passing vehicle.

Amelia shrieked, "What are you doing? We're going to crash!"

Trenton yanked on the emergency brake as the car kept traveling with increasing speed. The sound of blaring horns seemed to come from everywhere. He glanced at her. Amelia's mouth opened wide as she screamed, with terror in her eyes.

He forced the gear into low, wincing at the automatic transmission's grinding sound. The car jolted, and slowed as it crunched over the large barrier of rocks, which lined the edge of the road to prevent vehicles from plunging down the cliff.

It came to a stop with the front wheels dangerously balanced over a stone hurdle.

"Thank God!" Trenton turned to Amelia. "Oh hell, Amelia. Are you okay?" He stared at her anxiously. If anything had happened to her, he couldn't bear it. Blood oozed from a cut on her forehead, but other than that, she seemed to be all right.

"I'm okay," she said in a frightened voice. Her bottom lip trembled.

Trenton dialed 911 with shaking hands and reported the accident, his voice frantic and filled with terror. Fishing out his handkerchief, he handed it to her to stop the bleeding. "Thankfully it doesn't look too deep," he said, peering at the cut.

He eased the door open and slid carefully out of his seat, his heart beating so hard he could feel it in his head. "Slip over this way to the driver's side—over the gear shift," he said, trying to make his voice calmer than he felt. "Slowly and carefully. Don't make any sharp movements." *Fuck. The way the car is teetering, it could roll off the cliff with a strong wind!* He reached for her hand, his palm sweaty from fear.

She was shaking, and looked deathly pale. He held onto her tightly. Tears ran down her cheeks as she stepped onto firm ground. The car rocked gently as he closed the door. Trenton took her into his arms, held her close, and tried to calm the terror he could see she felt. "Help will be here soon. You'll be home safe and sound." *Another foot and we'd have crashed to our death on the rocks way below us.* He tried to think clearly and couldn't make sense as to why this had happened. *Aren't mechanics supposed to check the brakes when a car is brought in?*

Amelia took a few deep breaths as she removed the handkerchief from her wound and looked at the blood on it. "I hit the windshield with a jolt. Next time I'll make certain I tighten the safety belt."

That doesn't make any sense. "Stay here away from the traffic. I want to check on something." He went to the near-teetering car, carefully reached in, and fastened the seatbelt. He gave it a yank. There was no resistance. It came free.

The belts have been tampered with—they don't lock in place! Someone wants us dead? That's crazy. What about the brakes, then?

He returned to her.

"What's wrong? What did you discover?" She stood rubbing her upper arms. Her shaking had changed to shivering.

"The seatbelts don't lock. That's why you hit your head. That should never have happened." He put an arm around her and she leaned into him.

He checked for flashing emergency vehicle lights on the road below them, and listened for the sound of sirens in the distance.

"Who would do this?" Her eyes held horrific fear—fear he had never seen in her.

"In some people, one evil leads to another, and they become a monster." He kissed the top of her head as she clung to him. "I have a good idea who that monster is ... and will not win on this one—

over my dead body."

"Your ex?" Amelia clutched his waist as if he was the only safeguard between her and death.

"Good guess, but no," he lied. "What made you think that?"

"The only thing you've told me about her is that she's outrageously irrational and insanely jealous."

Naomi is the only person who hates me enough to do this. Amelia's right— she's crazy enough, too—beyond reason. It can only be her. She must be stopped. Did she bribe the mechanic or have someone else do this when the car was waiting to be picked up?

~~***~~

The angry pounding on the front door caught Naomi's attention. She spit the toothpaste from her mouth. "I'm coming," she called out.

Jason forgot his key again? When will he ever learn? He's twenty-one going on twelve.

Her feet took her swiftly down the stairs from her bathroom to the foyer, and to the entry. "I suppose you forgot your ..." The blurred figure through the frosted pane didn't look like Jason. Unlocking the door and turning the knob, she slowly peered out, letting in a sliver of daylight.

Trenton pushed the door completely open and stormed into the foyer, nearly knocking her off balance. "Where is that bastard son of yours? He needs to answer for what he's done."

"What? Don't be ridiculous. I have no idea what you're talking about. Jason is not the cause of whatever you're accusing him of." Rage filled her as her mouth went dry.

She had never seen Trenton so irate. The vein in his neck bulged and his hands were balled into fists.

"While driving down PCH, my brakes failed and the seatbelts were tampered with—they wouldn't latch." His flushed face accentuated the fierceness in his eyes. "Amelia and I nearly became a statistic, crashing over a cliff."

"What makes you think Jason had anything to do with this? What did the mechanic say?" *He's unhinged.*

"The brake line had a hole in it and the seatbelt latch was faulty— there was no locking to the mechanism. I just had the car tuned up." He moved closer until inches separated them.

She took a few steps backward, feeling the wall. "That is no proof that my son was anywhere near your precious car. It's not in his nature to do such a thing."

"That won't hold any water with me—not this time. The one thing that keeps a person from being a criminal is a conscience—Jason has none." He took a deep breath as if to gain control. "The men at the service station told me they saw him, or someone who looks like him sniffing around the car in the lot after the tune-up." His hot breath and wild eyes caused her pulse to race.

"How would anyone be able to get into a locked car?" She raised a triumphant eyebrow. "He doesn't even have the keys to *my* car."

"I don't know that the car was locked. It could've been left open." He started pacing. "I've been going to that dealership for years. I have no reason not to believe and trust them."

"You're whistling up a drainpipe on this one. You've always had it in for Jason." She jutted out her chin to emphasize her point.

"If I dislike Jason, it's all *your* doing—spoiling him—giving into his every whim." He paused and looked directly at her. "What he has become is all your fault and no one else's."

"Have you gone to the police?" *If Jason is involved, this can be very bad.*

"What do you think?" He sneered. "Of course I went to the police. It was an accident—a report had to be filed. Thank God no other car was involved and we weren't seriously hurt—a small cut on Amelia's forehead."

"Are the police investigating?" Naomi felt inner tremors but she would never allow him to see her fear. She waited for his answer, hardly daring to breathe.

"The police felt the brake line and seatbelt latches became faulty on impact." She wished he didn't have her backed up against the wall. "The mechanic swears the car was perfect when I picked it up." Fire darted from his eyes. "*Someone* tampered with that damn car. That person wanted me and Amelia dead—pure and simple."

"You're talking about attempted murder!" Her jaw slackened. "How can you think such a thing about Jason?"

"You or him!" Trenton pointed his finger at her face. His jaw tensed several times. "You have often said that you don't like me dating anyone. I know you too well. In your twisted mind, your reasoning runs like an old murder mystery—'If I can't have him, nobody else can.' I swear, if anything happens to Amelia, you'll have more than the police to worry about."

"Is that a threat, Trenton?" *How deep does his anger run?*

He turned and started for the door, then looked over his shoulder at her. "I don't deal in threats—only promises."

He slammed the door. The sound of his footsteps faded off in the distance. Naomi sat down on a chair in the foyer, an icy chill flowing through her. She shivered and her pulse quickened as a dreadful fear consumed her—fear deep inside her gut, catching her breath with an icy stab.

If Trenton goes back to the police with his suspicions, Jason could be called in to do a lineup. Would my son be so diabolical? No. It's impossible.

Yet, he used to torture flies when he was little.

I'm overreacting—all children do that, don't they? Even so ...

Thirty Five

AMELIA ARRIVED HOME from her new bank in Malibu. She'd transferred funds from her London bank account and felt smug that she had arranged for automatic payments from the Trust for the care of Penelope, Clive's ex-wife in Switzerland. Clive had no moral right to manage her finances as he had done upon her father's death despite the directives of the entail in his will. Setting up a new account had taken longer than she anticipated. When Tom had pulled into the drive, her stomach pangs told her she had missed lunch hours ago.

Alex looked up from the counter as she entered the kitchen.

She cleared her throat. "Are there any of those delightful sandwiches you served yesterday left?" She grabbed the teakettle from the stove and went to the sink, filling it up with water. "I didn't stop for lunch and what I ate for breakfast didn't last me."

He closed his *Men's Health* magazine and went to the refrigerator. "Chicken salad on wheat, okay?"

"Anything at this point." She watched him turn on the fire under the kettle sitting on the stove.

"Do you want me to call Jane to serve the tea in the living room?" Alex's comment floated above her.

She stared down at the floor, then looked up at him. "Sorry. I was deep in thought. What did you just say?"

He turned his palms upwards. "Jane. Do you want her to serve you tea elsewhere?"

"Don't bother her. I'm comfortable eating here." She sat down on the stool at the counter. "If it wasn't for Clive—sending Jane to keep an eye on me—I'd be doing most things for myself."

He placed the small plate of dainty sandwiches and a teacup before her. "You're certain it was this Clive person?"

"That's my assumption. Can't be anyone else." She took a sip. "Has Jane mentioned his name—Clive Bradford?"

"No. Never." He poured hot water into her cup. She dunked the teabag up and down.

"Alex, I really don't want to talk about him. Go back to whatever you were doing."

Amelia headed for the living room with her snack.

She took the phone from her purse on the coffee table, stared at the contact list, took an enormous deep breath and pressed the number. Waiting for an answer, she tapped her foot repeatedly.

"When are you returning home?" Alistair obviously had caller ID on his phone. "It's been nearly a month since your impulsive departure."

"You're not entitled to my whereabouts—not when I've been trapped in this sham of a marriage." *He sounds tense.*

"However you see it ... you are still legally my wife." His voice took on a cold edge. "The Courts haven't enacted a change on that point since your childlike sojourn."

"What would you say if I didn't return?" *Is he going to be difficult?* "It's not as if we have a real marriage and all of the UK knows it."

"It's not the reality. It's the *look* of the thing that matters." She heard his labored sigh. "Besides, if you officially divorce me, my heir would be left with nothing. A title and little else."

She inched forward in her seat. "What in God's creation are you talking about? We have no children between us. A child between us? Ha! That would be an immaculate conception. You had the best man at our wedding stand in for you and rape me on our wedding night, as you are well aware. That total darkness trick nearly worked on my naïve seventeen-year-old brain, too. If it wasn't for him leaving the light on in the bathroom and opening the door afterwards, I might have thought it was you, which is what you wanted me to believe."

A dead silence. "Alistair, are you still there?"

"Sorry, I was gathering my thoughts." Another deep sigh came into her ear. His voice softened. "There's something I've never told you, because it was never necessary. You're forcing my hand now. Are you listening?"

He had her full attention and she frowned, wondering what he was talking about. "Go on."

He cleared his throat. "Years before our nuptials, I was married to another woman—she died of cancer, you see ... but not before she bore me a son. He's my rightful heir to the title and estate. He's been estranged since he learned of my true lifestyle."

She gasped, her posture stiffening. "You bloody bastard! You've kept this from me all these years!" She stood up and turned to view the Pacific, her heart pounding. "My father married me to an impotent old man—impotent to women—all for me to have a title! Not one person in the family or socially ever mentioned your past to me. All of this is simply horrid—all of them shielding you and your wretched reputation!"

"Please try to understand. A title is empty, nearly worthless without an estate." His voice verged on sounding pitiful.

"I can barely take all this in. I haven't said I want a divorce *now*." Her hand shook while holding the phone.

"I implore you. Don't. Nothing good can come of it." His voice assaulted her ears, just shy of a yell.

"You are bleeding audacious!" She walked onto the balcony to avoid the possibility of Alex or Jane eavesdropping. "Nothing good for *you*, you mean. I want something better for my life."

His tone held a desperate plea. "Maybe something better doesn't have to mean something else."

She leaned on the balcony's railing. "I am what I am, and I've lived long enough to know what I've got now, not to throw it away."

He wouldn't give up. "You sound confident. Trenton Lowe has done this to you—swayed your thoughts to him."

A light laugh escaped her lips. "Confidence never goes out of style."

He begged, stripping away his self-respect, "What can I do to have you like me?"

"Leave—leave my life." *How dare he!*

Amelia ended her call at the sound of footsteps, and turned to see Trenton approaching her. His face showed worry and stifled fear.

He pecked her on her cheek and leaned on the railing with inches separating them. She hadn't digested Alistair's startling news and now Trenton didn't appear to have anything positive to tell her.

"What is it?" She touched his arm. "You look absolutely dreadful."

His words were slow and measured. "I discovered that the seatbelts and brake line were definitely tampered with—vandalism. The police still think the damage was due to the impact when the car hit the rocky retainer."

"Who would do such a reprehensible thing?" She scanned his face. "Everyone likes you. You have no enemies. Except maybe your ex."

He said it wasn't his ex. Is Clive behind this?

"My ex does come to mind ... after her bastardly son." She watched his jaw set and muscles twitch in his cheeks. "Yet, there are crazies all around. It's not like we haven't been in the press ... then there's the stalker issue—pestering you."

"This stalker might be behind all of this—not your ex at all." She twisted her fingers. "I should return to London. I'm putting you in danger."

He clasped her shoulders and looked into her eyes. "I don't agree. You need to be here with me."

Amelia felt tears well up and a lump formed in her throat. She was still reeling from the information Alistair had just given her. A son and heir. She wasn't ready to discuss it with Trent, though. "There's no turning back once we're in this."

He cupped her cheeks in his hands. "We're already in this. I wouldn't have it any other way." He embraced her, kissing her hair.

"You need some serious convincing and I know just the man to do it."

"Sex won't solve this for us." She fingered the buttons on his shirt. "Only serve as a postponement."

"It will help us feel better." Clasping her hand, he led her inside and then to their bedroom.

Trenton pulled the drapes while she lit a couple of votive candles on the night table. The faint aroma of lavender relaxed her while she undressed. She wanted all her worries to diffuse into a whiff of smoke like the burning candles. She tossed her clothes on a nearby chair.

He waited for her between the sheets, dressed only in his shorts. He patted her side of the bed. "Come. Let me show you where you belong."

"On top?" The worry she felt earlier was washed away by his alluring smile.

She shimmied next to him. The warmth of his body and the touch of his sculptured chest awoke her libido, sending small electric sensations between her thighs. She brushed her face against him. He captured her head in his hands, raking his fingers through her hair, then grasped the nape of her neck. His lips parted, hot breaths searing her cheek. His thumb brushed the corner of her lips as she barely opened her mouth. He held her and kissed her hair and then her eyelids while his hands caressed her neck. His lips brushed hers, and she opened her mouth again to receive his hungry thrusting tongue, probing and tantalizing. She kissed him with all the fire that churned within her and placed his hand on her breast, encouraging him to go further. He eased himself onto her, while he nibbled the sensuous hollow at her neck. His mouth traveled to her breasts with his swirling tongue teasing her nipples to erectness causing her eyes to roll back in her head. His lips grazed over her abdomen as his hand left a trail of delightful sensations, while his fingers caressed her moist, velvety folds, exploring her, and sending her passion higher. She groaned.

Amelia wanted him to enter her at that moment. She spread her legs farther apart, inviting him to be one with her. The sensation brought by his hot tongue on her most sensitive part was so intense and so delicious she felt she might scream. She moaned—a moan of raw pleasure and the pain of not receiving what she wanted most, making her toes curl. "Trent, I need you *now*. I can't hold back. Fuck me!" His tongue moved faster to her sounds of near ecstasy on the brink, her hands grasped the back of his head. There was no turning back for her now. Ultimate pleasure was within reach, just a little more, don't stop! Shaking, a raging climax engulfed her. Her limbs went limp with satisfaction as the warm glow consumed her.

With her eyes still shut, she felt him slide up next to her and moved the wet hair from her forehead. She barely had the strength to touch his chest with her lead-ridden arm. He propped his head with his hand and gazed in her eyes. His satisfied smile showed that he received joy from her pleasure.

She took another deep breath. "You must feel frustrated. Let me do the same for you. It's your turn." She reached for his penis. He stopped her with his hand.

"I love you, Amelia." He kissed her eyelids. "I want to please you any and every way possible ... for the rest of my life. This moment was for you ... and you alone. My pleasure isn't important."

He held her tighter and smashed her words between them—words she held deep within her heart and which fear kept her from saying them.

Will I ever be at a place when I can say, "I love you" to Trent?

Thirty~Six

"WHAT IS SO bloody important to discuss that you had me meet you at your townhouse and not at the lab? You know how important my work is on this project. I'm losing valuable time. A bit cheek, if you ask me." Clive entered Alistair's library as he spoke before sitting down in a comfortable wingback chair. He lowered himself with a huff and crossed his leg in an angry fashion, his fingers gripping the chair arms.

"I wouldn't have taken you from your work if this wasn't urgent." Alistair sat in a leather-upholstered chair opposite with a small tea table between them. "It's about, about—"

"Get on with it man." He scrunched up his face while tapping on his watch. "I don't have all afternoon. I might be onto a breakthrough to cure Parkinson's—alleviate suffering."

"It's Amelia." Alistair inched forward in his seat.

"Good, God!" He rolled his eyes. "What has she done now—better yet, what hasn't she done?"

"She called from California—" Alistair focused on Clive's face.

"Malibu, to be exact." A snide smile curled Clive's lips.

"How do you know that?" *Why would Clive be that interested in Amelia?* He cocked an eyebrow in suspicion.

"I told you. I have eyes on her." He walked over to the bar and poured scotch into a crystal glass.

He's speaking pure folly—trying to ease my mind. Alistair looked down at his clasped hands. "I think I pulled a blunder, ol' man ... after she strongly talked about getting or seriously *thinking* of a divorce ... I told her about my dead wife and son."

"Crikey! Are you daft? What on earth caused you to make such a grave blunder?" Still standing, he took a large swallow of his drink. "She can strip you clean with only your title to keep you warm at night."

"Steady on, ol' man. I was desperate. I felt I had no choice." Alistair rose, facing him. "She hasn't done anything yet."

Clive stared across the room into space as he talked. "I had better tie up her funds at the bank. Thank God her father had enough sense to put me on her account before he died."

Alistair's tone turned grave as he looked up to his cousin. "If you take any action now, that could tip everything against me. I don't want to force her hand. Don't do anything rash."

"Anything else?" Clive sat back down, swirling his drink.

"She brought up our quasi marriage and how I had my ..." His voice softened. "... best man stand in for me on our wedding night."

"You did what?" Clive's eyes grew large with raised brows. He threw his head back with a loud laugh. "How did you pull that one off? Blindfold her?"

"Not exactly." Alistair poured himself a drink before sitting down. "The room was pitch-black. I thought she'd believe it was me making love to her, you see." He gulped a mouthful of scotch. "All would have gone splendidly if he hadn't opened the door to a lit bathroom—stupid ass. Oh, she carried on and on—cried for a few days afterwards but soon came to accept our unconventional situation. In the end, the job was done and the bride was no longer a maid."

"I have to hand it to you." Clive chuckled, his eyes with a mischievous twinkle. "You've got more nerve than I. It's no wonder she's been seeking other diversions all these years."

"I'm not proud of what I did." Remorse churned in his gut. "I was distressed at the time. I had a son and his legacy to think of—even if he hasn't contacted me in years. I couldn't afford to lose everything then, and I can't afford that now."

"Indeed. Amelia hasn't had a serious thought in her head since the day I've known her." He cupped his drink between his hands. "Lie low for awhile. See what her next move is. I'll do what I can from my end of things."

"What things are those?" *How far is he willing to go?*

"They are details best kept to myself." A sardonic grin emphasized his words. "Her nerve only runs so far and I know her breaking point. Nothing works better than the fear of the unknown."

"How can you do anything from here?" He rubbed his thumb along his forehead in thought. "You recently returned from Boston. Did you do something already—while you were at Harvard?"

"All is good. You have no worry—merely empty words from your wife who is as fickle as a bee in a garden. She's beyond any efforts of amelioration." He checked his watch again. "Now, I'm going back to work and put my time to a more productive use other than worrying about Amelia whose brain is vapid ninety-nine percent of the time."

Alistair watched his cousin-in-law walk out of the room, hearing him open and then close the door. He didn't feel reassured.

Would Clive be a danger to Amelia? No. It's not like him.

He sounded serious—deadly serious.

~~***~~

Amelia spotted a plain florist box sitting on the coffee table as she and Trenton entered the living room. Alarm tinged with fear ran through her and a lump formed in her throat.

When will this hell stop! Does Clive want me dead or merely to go insane?

He called out to the houseman, presumably in the kitchen, "Hey, Alex, when did these arrive? Did you see the name of the florist?"

Alex entered wiping his hands with a dishtowel. "About an hour ago. I checked the security footage. A man in a uniform placed them at the gate then pushed the buzzer and left. There isn't a clear look at his face—appeared to be in his twenties. I didn't see a delivery truck."

Trenton lifted the lid. He jerked the card from the cluster of long-stemmed red roses. His brows pulled together, forming an angry crease between his eyes as he scanned the words.

His mocking tone drove more fear into her as he read the message aloud, "*'I love it when you're on top. Remember, I'm in control.'* That sick bastard!" He looked at Amelia and then back to the houseman. "Jane!" he yelled.

The maid walked into the room, her face pale.

"What do you know about this?" Trenton asked, tapping the box a little harder than necessary with a finger.

Jane looked at Amelia and then swallowed hard. "I only know what Alex knows, sir," she said to Trenton.

He turned to Alex. "I want to see that video for myself. Amelia, if you need me, I'm in the security room." His voice trailed off as he started to leave.

"I'm going for a walk on the beach," Amelia called to Trenton.

She grabbed her cell phone, walked through the sliding glass doors, and down the steps onto the beach. The salty breeze and sound of the rolling waves did little to assuage her mounting anxiety. She swallowed a large lump in her throat several times. Her mouth was so dry. She wouldn't allow the panic to emerge and control her thoughts and obliterate her common sense. Fear pressed on her spine, her posture stiffened.

She tapped her contact list and pressed Joe's number. It rang once, twice, three times.

Answer! Answer! Damn it, Joe, answer the bloody phone!

"Yeah, Duchess. How goes it?" His warm voice was nice, but couldn't ease her turmoil.

"Not good at all. Things are escalating." She removed her sandals and carried them with her free hand. "I don't want to leave ... but, but maybe I should take a break and hide out in Cannes."

"Hold on for a damn moment." His voice lowered. "That won't solve a thing if this is because of Clive and you believe he's behind this harassment. It's what he wants—separatin' you from Trenton. Besides, you won't be any safer—not with him on your tail. You're safer with Trenton where he has security and can keep you safe."

"I'm not entirely convinced." She paused, facing the waves and digging her toes into the moist, cool sand. "It's more than a flirtation in a public area or flowers arriving with salacious messages."

"Amelia, tell me." She heard someone shouting and a siren over the phone, as if in a public area. "It's important. I need all the facts for the PI."

"There is someone definitely looking into this?" Everything was so uncertain. She needed to feel wrapped in a secure cloak—only Trenton could provide that.

"Yes. I contacted my friend, Sal, in New York. His PI buddy is on the case." He took a drink of something.

"What's this PI's name? Can I contact him?" His words didn't make her feel any better.

"Nope. Sal doesn't share that intel." Joe's voice turned brotherly. "Now ... tell me all of it."

What if Sal didn't contact this detective friend at all and only told Joe he would?

"When Trent and I were driving back to Malibu on the Pacific Coast Highway, we nearly died or could have died in a crash, careening over a cliff into the ocean." Amelia tried to stop her hands from trembling as she relived the event in her mind.

His voice raised a decimal. "Someone, someone shoved you off the road?"

"No, no ... the brakes failed." She took a deep breath trying to regain control and steady her voice. "Trent said the seatbelt latches were tampered with, also."

"Any injuries? You and he okay?" He paused a moment. "You wanna come here and stay with Larry and Taylor? He said he's good with it."

She began strolling away from Trenton's home, brisk waves lapping on her toes. "No. I fear I would only be putting them in danger."

His tone grated as if his throat had dried. "How do you know all this—about the car? The cops tell y'?"

"The police don't think there is anything sinister about this at all—

merely a malfunction." She sighed. "It's all quite exasperating. There isn't much that frightens me, but this is different. I'm being watched and I don't know by whom. Trent told me that a young man was walking around the car in the mechanic's lot. It could be nothing, but now I'm beginning to think otherwise." Her voice started to tremble. "Joe, I fear Clive has hired someone to kill me. Alistair doesn't have the stomach for it—with Clive, I'm not so certain that murder would be beyond the pale for him. All these flowers are in a plain box with a card and no identification at all as to the florist."

"That sounds like an old cloak and dagger mission out of the Cold War." He took another swallow of something. "Doesn't Clive do work for MI6?"

"On and off. Not on a steady basis." *No MI6 agent would terrorize a private citizen.*

"Maybe he got an idea to play around with your head a bit—use some of their tactics. Kinda hopin' you'll return to London and the status quo."

"It feels more serious than a ploy to me." She turned and saw Trenton heading towards her. "Flowers arrived again today—that makes at least two anonymous deliveries so far."

"That's not a flood. Just wait and see what turns up." Joe offered nothing to sway her fears.

"If Trent wants to hire a local private investigator, I won't discourage him." He stood in front of her with a curious expression. "That way, both men could compare notes and get to the bottom of this."

"Won't work. Sal's friend works solo." He laughed quietly. "Just stay close to home and do what Trent tells you."

"Yes. I will. I need to ring off. Love to Larry and Taylor ... Joe ... thank you for all you've done." She slipped her phone in her pants' pocket.

"What did trusty ol' Joe have to say? Anything encouraging?" He reached for her hand as they walked back to his home.

"He has a friend, Sal, who has a friend who is a private investigator." She looked at his face for a reaction. "Apparently, that detective from New York is already searching out who the source is for all my stalking issues."

"You trust him?" He paused and looked straight at her. "You know nothing for certain—only what Joe said his friend related to him."

"Yes. I *do* trust Joe. But I know nothing about his friend." *Was Sal only appeasing Joe?*

"I think I had better get my own investigator—here—a local man who knows the area." He brought her hand to his lips and left a kiss.

"You're right, of course." A smile turned the corners of her mouth up. "You take such good care of me. I feel so safe in your arms."

She reached up on tiptoe and kissed his lips—a kiss of love and not lust. His arms encircled her waist.

Trent makes all that wrong seem to fade when I'm in his arms. Problem is … there are times when he can't be with me.

What then?

My death?

Thirty~Seven

JASON WALKED WITH a cocky stride toward Naomi. His self-assured smile irritated her. She wondered how the blond blue-eyed three-year-old boy who would giggle on her lap had turned into this monster who clearly loathed her.

Sitting on the sofa, she watched him flop down in the opposite chair.

He jutted his chin and raised an eyebrow. "So, Mommy dear, what was so damn important that you pulled me away from a most agreeable sweet young thing?"

"Has your head been up your ass all these years?" Her voice remained quiet and controlled. "Have you learned nothing from me?"

"How to be selfish and devious, if that's what you're referring to." His snide laugh erupted. "Plus, a love for the very decadent rich life."

"That stunt you pulled with Trenton's car was sheer stupidity." Her lips thinned into a grimace. "What were you trying to do—kill him?"

He gazed up at the ceiling. "The duchess was with him—or so I read in the papers."

"Don't get cute with me!" His feigning ignorance piqued her even more. "I know you had something to do with that accident."

"Mechanical breakdowns happen all the time." He grabbed an apple from the fruit bowl on the coffee table and polished it on his jeans-covered thigh. "Some are more convenient than others."

The sound of him crunching into the firm fruit drove her restrained anger to near explosion. "You are so smug, so certain you have all the answers without a thought to the consequences." She crossed her arms, her defiance meeting his head-on. "Listen to me, and listen good. If Trenton dies, there will be no more money—not from me. If my cash flow dries up, so does yours."

He wiped a drop of juice running from the corner of his mouth with the back of his hand. "I didn't say I caused his brakes to fail or his seatbelts to loosen."

"How did you know about the seatbelts?" *My son's a murderer?*

"It was in the papers." He took a swallow from her water bottle on the table.

"No. It wasn't." Her eyes narrowed as she unfolded her arms and leaned forward. "Only someone who tampered with the car would know that." She let out an exasperated breath. "Trying to get a straight answer out of you is like pinning Jell-O to a wall."

"Look. *I* did not touch his sainted car." He crossed his legs as if emphasizing his point. "All turned out well for them."

"She's still with him—that's not good for me." Naomi went to the bar and poured a fresh margarita from the frosted pitcher into her glass as she spoke. "I've been doing research on the Net. Seems Amelia is deathly allergic to spiders—so deathly that she carries an epinephrine pen with her at all times." She turned with a satisfied smile. "Why don't you do something with that?"

"I can't believe my sweet-hearted mother, who lives in Margaretville constantly, would propose that her innocent son should contemplate such a delightful and sinister deed." His tone mocked her with every inflection.

"Cut the bullshit, Jason." She resumed her place on the sofa, then took a large swallow of the citrus mixture. "What are you going to do with this information now that you have it?"

"You're telling me to commit murder." His eyes met hers with serious intent. "I would be the one charged—not you." He chuckled. "Unless, I tell the cops you put me up to it."

She took another gulp of her drink. "No—I'm not proposing murder. She'll use the epinephrine pen to save herself. Anyone with an ounce of sense suffering from an allergy carries them." She posed a stern warning. "Besides, it's only murder if she dies. I prefer to think of it as an unfortunate accident." Another swallow of margarita. "Don't try to double-cross me, you grubby little bastard— I've been a master at it a lot longer than you."

"If you don't like what I am, then look at yourself in the mirror." He cocked his head. "I learned from the best."

She cocked her head. "Jason, hello! Copernicus called and you're not the center of the universe!"

He swallowed a mouthful of apple. "No. You think you are, dear mother!" He lowered his voice to saccharine sweetness. "Don't forget to grease my palm."

Why is he always so cruel? She paused before reaching for her wallet in the purse on the carpet, shooting him a look that showed how she hated the direction of this conversation. "Is there no love between us?"

"Maybe from you. From me? That will cost you." He held out his hand. "I'm short of funds. Spiders cost money—the most poisonous cost a lot of money."

She gathered a wad of one hundred dollar bills. "You said you're in with me on this. Looking at the sneer on your face, I'm not convinced."

"You won't know until you pay up." He snapped to his feet, yanked the cash from her hand, and quickly headed to the door.

"I only wanted her to be scared away." Naomi watched him walk from her. "How will you get them into the house?" she called out to him, seeing his confident swagger. "If you can't get this done, I will and hell's coming with me!"

"The less you know, the better. Remember, the best way to rid yourself of a problem is—permanently." He chuckled, then slammed the door sending a chill though her.

I never told him to murder Amelia.

What is he? A psychopath?

I should try to stop him, but I don't think he'll listen. There's no going back now. If Jason goes down, will he drag me with him?

~~***~~

Trenton thought the secluded cove up the coast not far from his home offered a respite from the media's prying eyes. He and Amelia would be free from the worries of clicking cameras hungry for the next scandalous shot to grace the front page of the following day's news. The high cliffs, vegetative overgrowth, and setting sun gave that feeling of complete isolation.

With their fingers entwined, Trenton led her down the winding path to the shore while carrying a basket Alex had prepared along with a camp light and a blanket. He found what he thought would be the perfect spot. No one could want a more pristine location for washing away whatever life's cares threw at them.

He spread out the blanket and placed the basket and light nearby. Trenton watched Amelia kick off her sandals and sit down. She drew up her legs with her arms hugging her knees, and gazed out to the orange and blue horizon cast by the sun ever sinking lower, painting hues of dusky lavender in the sky. Her silhouette framed by red hair and enhanced by the dwindling glow made her more beautiful than ever to him. He had never felt this way about a woman—certainly not about Naomi. His love grew daily. She was constantly on his mind during every aspect of his day—driving, during meetings, looking in shop windows wondering if Amelia would like this or that, even the lock of red curl hugging the curve at the back of her neck when she wore her hair up.

"You seem deep in thought." He placed his arm around her shoulder. "Care to share?"

"What did Alex pack for us?" She turned her attention to the basket.

She's changing the subject. Why? "Whatever it is, his taste is perfect—like the woman I'm sharing this moment with."

"Don't put me on an unobtainable peak." She looked at him. "I have long since tumbled from such loftiness."

"I see you with clear eyes." Trenton spoke while opening the basket, and pulling out a bottle of red wine, two glasses, napkins, pre-cut pieces of cheese, fruit, and crackers. "There's been no illusion from my way of thinking."

"Have you not been reading the newspaper headlines involving me?" Her brows rose.

"I don't pay attention to that trash." He offered her a glass of wine. She took it as their eyes met. "I think when you're our age, you don't get bothered by petty gossip the way we did when in our twenties."

"Maybe you should." She sipped from the glass. "... at least some of it."

"Is this why you've been avoiding giving me a direct answer to my proposal? You think I'm not aware of your past?" *Is this her way of saying no? Leaving me?*

"If I do get a divorce from Alistair, how would that impact your career?" Her finger drew a random pattern in the silvery sand. "Wouldn't there be ramifications?"

"If there were, I could handle them." He squeezed her shoulder wishing she would let him fully into her world—into her heart.

"Do you trust me?" Her long lashes held back tears. "There have been many others before you. Aren't you afraid I'll grow tired of you?"

"I try not to think about your other flirtations." *Another roadblock from her.*

"Flirtation is such an innocent word. It cloaks the fact that I acted no better than a cheap whore." A tear fell to her cheek. "Then they *have* plagued you—my many illicit liaisons? Or at the very least ... they have crossed your mind." She drained the remaining wine from her glass and placed it back in the basket. "You had better think about what I've said before I accept your ring ... *if* I accept your ring."

"Why are you torturing yourself like this—dragging up your past?" He stroked her cheek with the back of his fingers, wanting to absorb all her hurt and set her spirit free to love and trust.

"If I didn't care about you so dearly, I wouldn't bring up any of this." Another tear fell, glistening in the dusky light. "I couldn't bear it if I was the cause of any pain to you—in your career or otherwise."

He wiped her tears away with his fingers. "Others might cause me pain. Not you. You have brought such joy into my life. I can't picture a tomorrow without you in it—just as you dwell in my heart, and always will." Reaching behind, he placed his glass in the sand.

"Beautiful words can wither and die in the harsh light of cold reality." She looked down at her hands.

"Let me show you my reality." He leaned forward and gently kissed her lips, easing her backwards onto the blanket. She tasted warm and soft as a fine wine.

Trenton lost himself in sensations, the smell, taste, and the feel of her. His lips continued along her neck to her collarbone before trailing up to taste her other ear. Warmth consumed his every fiber. He wanted her to need him, to want him as much as he ever wanted her.

Amelia's parted lips drew his gaze. He kissed her ... her tongue roaming the recesses of his mouth, furthering his desire. His hand cupped her breast through her sundress. Again he left trailing kisses along her neck to the delicate white shoulders he craved every time he looked upon them. He slipped the straps off her shoulders and pulled down the bodice of her dress, exposing her bra-less nipples, which rose erect from his hot lips. She moaned at the heat from his mouthing and teasing licks.

His hand traveled from her lower leg to her knee. Another moan escaped her. Lightly, his fingers traveled agonizingly slowly up her thigh and lingered at the edge of her panties. He knew what she liked and how to tease her to near screaming. She parted her legs—a clear invitation. He gently caressed her over the thin fabric, feeling her grow firmer under his touch. She pulled his hand away and wiggled out of her panties, then hiked the hem of her dress up to her waist.

Viewing her nakedness, Trenton swallowed hard. He tried to ignore his erection. Once again, the pleasure had to be for her—solely for her.

He lay beside her. Beginning at her knee, his fingers slowly traced the length of her other thigh to the crease of her groin and toyed with her thicket of hair, barely touching her sweet spot. Her hips rose up to his hand, as if begging for more pleasure. His palm pressed against her causing her to moan as her tongue wet her lips. She reached out to him. "Trent, I need you."

"Not yet." His massaging grew firmer, and then he slipped first one and then another finger inside her heated core, reaching her internal pleasure trigger. He moved them slowly at first, and then faster when he heard her panting. Her back arched to beg him for more. Bending down, his lips brushed over her most sensitive area, heightening her desire. His tongue caressed her lightly there. Amelia moaned again. Her hands clamped the back of his neck as her groans grew louder. He knelt between her legs. Encouraged, he gave her more of what she desired, faster until he felt she was on the brink. "Yes," she cried out. "That's it. Just like that. Don't stop."

He slowed his movements down, teasing her. "I can't take much more of this. Either fuck me or bring me off." Her eyes were tight shut and she let out whimpering gasps. She writhed under his teasing touch. He moved his tongue and fingers faster, giving her what she needed to climax.

Her hands froze on his neck as a wave of spasms flowed through her limbs. "Yes! Oh God, oh God, you're so amazing!" she cried as her chest jerked and heaved.

Her clasp relaxed from him, and her heavy panting slowed. He touched her lightly.

She pulled his hand away. "No. Don't."

"Just checking that you don't want more." He wiped his chin with a napkin and then lay next to her, propped up by his elbow.

"You've done that twice before—checking to see if I'm pleased." She toyed with a strand of hair that fell on his forehead. "No man ever cared that much about my pleasure—only you."

"I love you, and I want you to be completely happy in every way. My satisfaction is secondary." He kissed the hollow at the base of her throat.

She stared up into his face, an expression of complete fulfillment on hers. "Maybe I happen to feel the same." She carefully unzipped his pants and reached in. "Satisfaction is a two-way street." She licked her lips.

Will she ever believe there is more than sex between us?

AMELIA SCREAMED AND screamed, her eyes wide with terror, her naked body vulnerable. Black spiders crawled all over the shower curtain. Her heart pounded and her hands shook so much it took her three tries to grab the bug spray from the cabinet under the sink.

She shot the stream of poisonous mist all over the curtain, tears running down her face.

Jane came rushing to the doorway of the master bath. "Milady! Are you all right? I heard you scream. Was the water too hot?"

"Those bloody spiders again." She gasped. "Here, you do it." She handed the insecticide can to the young girl who appeared almost as startled as Amelia. "Spray everywhere—in the closets, too." She pulled a towel off the rack and wrapped it around herself as she backed out of the bathroom, bumping into Trenton.

She turned, heaving in sobs and pressing her breasts into his chest as he threw his arms around her, his face pale, his warmth welcoming. "You weren't bitten?"

"No. Thank goodness. Nothing as drastic as that." Amelia broke free, brushed by them both and went to her purse on the dresser. She pulled out two epinephrine pens and inspected the expiration date.

"Anything wrong?" He came up to her, placing his hand on her shoulder.

"No. I have almost a year before I need replacements." She glanced at Jane spraying the room at the baseboards and window frames. "You had better call another exterminator. The business you contracted didn't do their job properly." She stepped into slippers and eased into a satin robe, the fabric feeling cool against her skin.

Trenton and Amelia returned to the living room. Another florist box lay on the coffee table. He made fists repeatedly. She stared at the delivery, then tore the lid off. The white card rested on top of the green floral paper. She read it aloud, *"The blindfolds were fun. Next time—handcuffs?"* Her hands trembled as the message fell from her hands. "Trent, very little if anything has ever scared me, not even that devil, Clive. I'm beginning to feel otherwise. This is becoming more than a stalking nuisance—this is turning dangerous."

He embraced her tightly as she rested her head on his chest, her breath coming with great heaving sobs. "I won't let anyone or anything harm you." He kissed the top of her head as he stroked her hair. "Your safety and happiness is my sole mission."

As if on cue, the house telephone rang. Alex answered and handed the receiver to Amelia. "It's for you, Milady." The houseman left the room.

"For me? That's rather odd." She took the phone from him. "Hello. Amelia Hollingsworth speaking."

Trenton looked on with a curious expression and mouthed, "Who is it?" She waved her hand for quiet.

"This is Naomi—Naomi Lowe. You need to know a few things about my ex-husband—the man who's warming your bed every night."

"I have nothing to say to you." She sat on the sofa, put her hand over the mouthpiece and whispered, "It's Naomi."

"Hang up on her." Trenton's veins in his neck bulged and his nostrils flared. He let out a long sigh. A look of dread and apprehension lived in his eyes.

"You might have nothing to say, but I have plenty for you." She chuckled. "Tell Trenton to cool his jets. I can hear him over the phone."

Amelia pressed the speaker function and put her finger to her lips for him to be quiet.

"Go on." Amelia crossed her arms and stared at the speakers. "I'm listening."

"I can tell from the echo, you have me on speaker. Doesn't matter. I don't care who hears what I have to say." Her shrill laugh had a tinge of sarcasm. "Trenton, you might want to hold your words until I'm finished."

"Get on with it." Amelia rolled her eyes.

"Has Trenton told you about the others before you and after me?" Amelia's breath caught in her throat a moment. *She's desperate.*

"Whatever he has shared with me is none of your concern." She studied Trenton's reaction, his head shaking in denial. "I really don't care what your feelings are on the subject."

Another laugh. "That's just your defenses speaking." Naomi paused as if gathering her thoughts. "We have a bond—Trenton and I. He will not keep you for very long."

"You know nothing of our relationship." Amelia's lips thinned. His quiet appeared to disarm Naomi. He gave no reaction.

"There have been three, no wait ... four others before you since our divorce." Amelia visualized Naomi's crazed expression.

"As I said before. I'm not interested." She watched him turn his back and look out to the ocean through the expansive windows then turned her gaze back to the phone's speaker.

"Those affairs didn't end because the lady grew tired of him or his money." *She's dragging this out to torture me.* "He dumped them, like yesterday's news in the trash—the same way you toss out your boys back in merry ol' London. He even presented a ring to one of those placeholders."

Trenton spun on his heels, his eyes wide with anger. Amelia gestured for him to remain silent.

"You see, Duchess Amelia, you're nothing but a placeholder—like all the rest. Whether he's presented you with a ring or not, he'll come back to me. I know his secrets. I keep his secrets."

"I trust him completely. You have no power over him or me." Amelia started to pace. "You would be the last person on earth that he'd return to."

"He'll tire of your fancy Mayfair accent and English ways." Naomi's voice turned colder. "If you don't believe me, check the old newspapers."

"I wouldn't put forth the effort." Amelia walked to Trenton. She needed the safety of his embrace.

"Why don't you ask him about the unborn baby he murdered—pushing me down the stairs?"

Trenton spoke up, as he could no longer hold his words. "That was an accident and you damn well know it! That was years ago."

Naomi's tone grew as hard as iron with darts piercing the air. "There is no statute of limitations on murder, dear Trenton. All I need to do is make one call to the police. If I can't have you—Amelia and no one else will. I'll stake my life on that!"

Trenton wouldn't let it go. "Is this how you live with yourself—by rationalizing the obscene into the palatable?"

"Well, at least I have your attention now." Another diabolical laugh. "Be a good boy and ship out that English crumpet on the next plane."

"Hell will freeze over first! I never hated anyone before ... now I know what it feels like." He walked over to the phone and abruptly ended the call.

Amelia eased herself on the sofa as tears filled her eyes. He sat down beside her and clutched her shaking hands in his.

Her lips trembled. "Trent, is any of what she said true?"

"None of it. You can search tabloid papers for all eternity and won't find a bit of dirt." His fingers wiped a tear from her cheek.

"Don't give Naomi the power of control over you. She's very bitter since the divorce. Our marriage was a constant battle after the first three months. Her jealousy and imagining me with another woman is what ended our relationship. I never cheated on her and never raised a hand to her." He took an enormous deep breath and balled his fists. "God, I'd drive a stake through her heart, but I don't think even that will kill her." He kissed her temple and looked into her eyes. "You believe me don't you?"

Amelia nodded as she sniffled. "Don't ever break my heart, Trent. I couldn't endure that."

"You have my guarantee on that score." He kissed her hairline.

"Don't you think it was a bit odd that she called after me finding spiders in the bathroom? It's almost as if she could see through the walls." Her mind swirled with abject terror—images of Naomi wielding a knife over her lifeless body.

"Now you're sounding paranoid." His fingers lifted her chin. "I think it was pure coincidence. Naomi doesn't have those types of connections."

"What about her son?" A tear rested on her eyelash as she fought off the need to cry again.

"Not very likely. He's too interested in women and drugs—not his style." His eyes held a fear that belied his words.

"What if Naomi asked him to torment me?" *He's telling me what he thinks I need to hear.* Goosebumps scrambled over her body.

"He's never followed her rules. Always too obstinate." Trenton squeezed her shoulder as if to reassure her.

Maybe I was wrong about Clive. Naomi is trying to drive me away. Yet Clive is aware of my allergy. Who else would know the symbolism of that spider plant when it arrived?

Thirty~Nine

AMELIA AND TRENTON sat in the luxurious velvet seats waiting for the private fashion show to begin. Even though she was accustomed to shopping in the establishments donning the royal warrant in London, this was all the more special for her—he had made the arrangements, telling her he wanted her to feel special in so many ways.

When purchasing anything in London, it was on her terms and with her own money. This was different. His income would fill her closet with a glorious new gown. For what purpose? He didn't say. Maybe it was on a whim for a future social obligation. Deep down she hoped this wasn't a going-away gift on his part. Naomi's words haunted her, though she tried to push them back. *He dumped them all.*

Haute couture models strutted past as she eyed the various lines, fabrics, and colors. She had learned at a young age from her late mother what colors and styles flattered her completion, hair, and figure. A pale combination of aqua and turquoise chiffon image ending with a slight train floated by, the young lady pausing briefly. Amelia nodded and smiled, then made a note of her choice on a pad.

Trenton inclined his head. "You have excellent taste. That's the one I would have chosen for you. Classic Grecian lines for a very classy lady." His finger playfully touched the tip of her nose.

"I wish you'd tell me what this is all about." She faked a pout. "I know you must have something in mind—something you've penciled in your journal."

His brows rose. "Journal? I don't write down my memoirs."

"I forgot your American English terms. I mean your datebook." She chuckled. "As I've said many times, it only seems we share the same language. Back to this exorbitant gift—why purchase a gown that I can only wear at a formal function?"

"If I do have a special occasion in mind, then it's a secret." He leaned closer to her. "If I don't, then it's just a gift for the most special woman in my life."

André, the designer and owner of his fashion house approached them. She showed him the number of her choice from the paper she held. "If I may, Duchess, it is necessary for you to come back with me to the fitting room so that we can obtain your measurements.

Everything must be sewn perfectly."

Amelia flashed a glance at Trenton. "My, my, Mr. Lowe knows how to treat a lady."

He smiled and squeezed her hand as she rose. "Only the best for my duchess."

She followed André to the back, then entered a room with multiple floor-length mirrors and lush beige carpeting with an elevated two-foot high pedestal in the center. He motioned for her to stand on the platform and then clapped his hands sharply twice. Three seamstresses appeared with tape measures around their necks, and one held a pad of paper and a pen. André spoke to the assistants in his native language. She was glad for the French lessons she had endured from a young age.

Amelia spoke to André in his mother tongue, "I understand everything you are saying. I learned French since I was five."

He turned a multitude of colors. "Pardon, pardon, Duchess. I had no intention of offending you."

"No harm done," she spoke in English. "I thought it would be best for you to know I'm fluent in your language before you embarrassed yourself by saying something you would rather I not hear. For the record, I will be wearing three inch heels with the gown."

André spoke to the three women, *"Commencez!"*

Silently, they went to work measuring every aspect of her body from her neck down to her toes. All went with the utmost efficiency. Just when she thought this was the end of the fact-finding, the three repeated the process, presumably to be certain of their findings. Amelia was thankful she hadn't worn bulky clothing, as she would have refused to change into a plain dressing gown.

While walking back to Trenton in the showroom, she dialed Joe's number on her cell phone. The last arrival of flowers and recent encounter with spiders unnerved her, no matter how stoic her façade.

"Joe, any news from your friend's PI chum?" She entered the main room, walking around the small runway.

"Yeah, talked with Sal." She heard chirping birds and assumed he was outside somewhere. "Says his buddy is on the case—should be out there in L.A. by now. He'll report back to Sal, and then Sal will call me."

Trenton turned to her and clearly listened to her responses. "I would feel better if this private investigator would contact me or Trent. The way it is now, any future information you relate is third hand at best." Trenton motioned to her that he wanted to speak to

Joe. "Wait a minute, Trent has something to say."

She handed him the phone. "Joe, what is the name of your friend—the one who has this PI in New York?"

"Sal Mourtos—an old friend. I think I already told you that. I don't even know the name of this snoop buddy."

"I'm not entirely comfortable not knowing his name. I've already hired my own PI out here." He hesitated as if in thought. "Wouldn't it be smart if both PIs could compare notes? Force in numbers?"

"Sal is very firm 'bout keepin' this guy's identity private. Might be somethin' they have agreed to." Trenton held the phone slightly away from his ear so Amelia could hear. He gave Joe his cell phone number.

"I need. No, *we* need to know who is ordering these flowers with suggestive messages. There is no identification as to the florist or the person. Plus, the appearance of spiders is just too odd considering that I've had two exterminators come out to the house. I've hired extra security, too." His brow created deep furrows. "I'm not convinced that our car accident, faulty seatbelts, and failing brakes were a result of the crash. The police felt that was the case—I'm not so certain, and my mechanic agrees with me."

"Any ideas who has a beef to grind with you and Amelia?" She twirled a lock of her hair and bit her bottom lip while listening.

"Amelia feels that her cousin Clive is behind this. Me?" He eased to the empty public waiting room of the design house with Amelia close behind. "I have an ex who's not happy that I'm not single. She's a remote possibility—I'm not sure she has the guts to pull off such a deadly stunt."

"I'll call you or Amelia as soon as I get any info from Sal. I'll text your number if needed." He swallowed something. "Look, I got a call comin' in. Later."

As they approached the door, she saw the fear in his eyes as he spoke. "I don't feel reassured."

"Why?" She nudged him as they stepped onto the sidewalk.

"Just because Joe trusts what his friend Sal tells him, doesn't mean I do." He slipped on his sunglasses. "Sal could be telling him anything. We have no proof that Sal's PI friend is truly out here on the case. We don't even know if there *is* a PI friend in the first place."

"I've known Joe for a number of years." She glanced at a shop window displaying the latest fashion on a mannequin. "I've never found him to be dishonest." She grabbed his arm as her eyes narrowed. "Larry trusts Joe with his life. Joe has been very straightforward in his dealings—if he believes his friend Sal, then I believe what Sal has told him."

He stopped and kissed her cheek. "Keep those positive thoughts. I pray to God this all comes to a peaceful end. I want the only flowers you receive to come from me."

~~***~~

Amelia sipped her early morning tea on the balcony. Trenton had already left for the studio for some sort of important meeting. He had mentioned earlier that the editing was completed on the London movie project and distribution was next on the agenda along with scheduling the all-important movie premiere.

She took her mobile phone from the table and scrolled the contacts list. She stopped at the name of Mr. Hargrove, her solicitor.

Her hand trembled as she brought the cup to her lips.

Dare I do this? Take a step that will change my life forever? Change Alistair's life? What if this doesn't work out with Trent? What then? Live on the French Rivera with one new boy after another until I become a pitiful joke—wrinkled hands and Botox keeping the lines away with men young enough to be my grandsons?

She bit her lip as a lump filled her throat. She swallowed hard.

Life was so simple before Trent. My biggest decision was what to wear, eat, or who to sleep with for the week. I know for certain, at least at the moment, that Trent loves me. Will he feel the same a year from now?

She took a couple of labored breaths, calculated the time difference in London, then pressed Mr. Hargrove's number.

It rang five times before the receptionist answered. "Mr. James Hargrove of Hargrove and Wright solicitors. Whom may I say is calling?"

"This is Duchess Amelia Hollingsworth. Is Mr. Hargrove in? I need to speak directly to him." Her palms grew moist as her hand shook.

"Yes, he is. Please hold on the line while I put you through." Her voice was professional to the point of leaving a chill in her ear.

"Amelia, it's so good to hear your voice. I take it you've come to a decision about your marriage since we last talked."

"Yes. I have." She took another deep breath. "I feel a divorce and not an annulment would be best. Alistair confessed that he has an heir—a son from his dead wife years before he ever married me."

"Well, I dare say, that does paint a different hue onto the canvas." She heard his sigh. "Not consummating his marriage to you on your wedding night would be difficult if not impossible to prove in light of his prior legitimate issue. You are correct in your assumptions of an annulment not being viable. The courts would find that difficult to believe with an heir in the history. A divorce is straightforward, provided he doesn't object legally." His tone softened. "Are you certain this is what you want? Your life will be very different for you and Alistair. Your title will be downgraded from duchess to lady."

"Quite certain. I don't care about titles. There is no love—never has been love between us." She twisted her face while biting her bottom lip. "Please draw up the papers and mail them to me straight away."

"I'll post the petition for divorce to you by the end of the business day. You must sign it with a witness of your signature—someone with a notary—perhaps at a bank. Then the court will issue a Decree Nisi. If Alistair doesn't pose any objections, you don't need to appear in court. If he does, then you must return to London. Should that happen, I advise you to stay in a hotel and only return to your townhouse to collect your possessions." She heard him cough. "Are you planning to confiscate all your assets that you brought to the marriage as stated in your late father's entail? Do you want to leave any money for him to maintain his estate up country? What about your money that Clive controls?"

"I don't want to leave anything for Alistair. He can keep the townhouse. I've already transferred my money that Clive has been managing and using for Penelope's care to a bank here in Malibu. I've set up a Trust for her. If he visits the London bank, he won't find a penny." She felt courage build within as she made a fist. "Considering the lie my gay husband has been keeping all these years, I'm being quite generous in allowing him to have the townhouse. Yes, he's been kind to me, but no more loving than that of a brother. For God's sake, he had his best friend pose as him on our wedding night—using the pitch-blackness to cover his identity. That's a deplorable way to treat a virgin bride of seventeen years." She tapped her foot repeatedly as the memory burned in her mind. "That was totally egregious."

"Indeed. After what you told me, it's a wonder you've stayed with him this long." He let out a sigh. "His homosexual activities will be cited as reason for divorce, and I might have to mention your clandestine affairs as well. Is your address the same as you told me since our last conversation—on Malibu Road?"

"Right. Use whatever facts you deem necessary. Yes. I don't intend to move elsewhere." *I've taken the first step—the biggest step in my life.* "If Alistair objects, how will I know?"

"His lawyer will file an objection and I will be notified, whereupon

I will then call you, and as I said, you'll need to return to London. If we don' t hear anything within two or three weeks after the Decree Nisi is issued, then all will appear favorable for your marriage to be dissolved. Then I will petition the courts to issue a Decree Absolute. Six weeks after that, the final decree is granted, and you will be free to remarry." His voice lowered. "You are serious? Are you completely certain this is the correct course? No doubts whatsoever?"

"I am more certain of this than anything else in my life." She took a couple of deep breaths. "It's time I live my life for my happiness and not for someone else—living or dead .... So it's about eight weeks from today before I'm a free woman?"

"I would say that, barring any objections." He coughed again. "It's all rather cut and dry."

"Thank you, Mr. Hargrove. We'll be in touch." She ended the call.

Tears filled her eyes and a tortured heaviness filled her chest. The sorrow was not for Alistair, but for all the happiness she might have enjoyed with someone else, and children she might have had.

Trent is my future. I hope his love will not fade. New relationships are bright and shiny until time tarnishes the love with sameness and dreaded boredom. May I never become that tiresome person in his life.

Forty

AARON KRANTZ PATTED Trenton on the back as he came up behind him, before sitting down at the table of the studio's commissary. Trenton knew it was his "lord and master" without looking. No one else had that commanding gait nor the friendly pat that oozed total authority. Even the hum in the room diminished when Krantz was around. The last thing he wanted was another pitch fest as to how he needed to capitalize on his relationship with Duchess Hollingsworth. He had purposely chosen a table at the back of the room in the corner, facing the food line to avoid this somewhat irritating man. Trenton didn't have the means to start his own studio and Aaron knew it, seeming to relish in having Lowe by the short hairs.

"Glad I caught you." Aaron pulled up a chair. He practically drooled from the prospect of making a big first week in ticket sales from *Duchess in Love*, his eyes bright and eager. "Have you spoken to the duchess about the promotion—intimating that the movie reflects aspects of her life?"

Trenton looked up from his lunch. "I don't want her to feel used ... to surmise that my only interest in her is the damn film."

"Of course not." He drew his hand over his mouth to the bottom of his chin. "It would be even better if we could run a slug line that is based on her. That would really swell the box office."

"You want her to take the next jet out of here for London?" He laughed, not caring how his boss would react to his comment.

"No. That is not my intention." Aaron nudged his elbow against Trenton's forearm. "I'm thinking of ticket sales." Greed oozed from his eyes and dripped from the corners of his mouth. "I see no reason why she would mind. Her reputation is infamous on both sides of the Atlantic. What's the problem?"

"The problem is ... is this. Amelia controls the gossip that swirls around her. She acts out for her own amusement and not that of others—box office or otherwise." *I work for a stupid ass.* "The studio setting her up as a publicity stunt won't set well with her. If it was her idea, well that's one thing—but it's not."

"Well, present it to her as if it *is* her idea." Aaron rubbed his palms together while a gleeful smile emerged.

"And just how am I to accomplish that?" He chuckled. "Casually say, 'Oh by the way, your idea to allow the studio to promote the movie as your life is a fantastic idea.' She's too smart to buy that one, no matter how many glasses of champagne I serve her."

His boss leaned into him and spoke in a low tone with a determined crinkled brow. "You'll pull it off. I have faith in your power of persuasion." He winked as he rose and flashed a snide smile. "You will ... if you enjoy your position as chief producer of this studio."

Trenton clenched his teeth and resisted a well-deserved retort while he watched the pompous executive stroll to the door. Restrained anger brewed.

He's the rooftop here. He waves his sword in the air with grandiose strength enforcing his rules. I have no wish to replace him. I merely want to survive in his kingdom—that is no easy feat.

He thought of Amelia and took his cell from his inside jacket pocket. Before he could dial a number, his phone chimed. No one responded to his "Hello". The caller hung up. He scrolled to "received calls" and noticed "unknown name" with an area code of 617. Trenton jotted down the number, date and time on the napkin from the table, folded it neatly, and placed it in his breast pocket. He searched the Net and discovered that number belonged to the Cambridge area of Boston. Now he had a new worry.

Was that person from a call center—a robot call, or connected to Amelia's troubles?

~~***~~

Trenton's phone chimed again as he was driving home. His face twisted. *Of all the wrong times to get a call.* He picked it up off the passenger seat and looked at the caller ID. He recognized it immediately as Juan Sanchez, the local PI he had hired, and pressed the speaker button.

"What's the news?" He looked in his rearview mirror as a large semi appeared, barreling up from behind, sending diesel exhaust upward.

"I called in some chips and contacted nearly every florist in L.A. Finally, I hit paydirt. Seems the original order came from Boston— Cambridge to be exact. The prepaid credit card used was in the name of Steven Dunn. I dug some more and this Dunn guy is dead complete with a death certificate issued in 1985. A very crafty person went to great lengths to pull that one off. Still, it comes to a dead-end, excusing the pun. All the other flower deliveries were from different burner phones with a 310 area code—L.A. to be exact."

Trenton's grip tightened on the steering wheel as he looked into the rearview mirror. The truck was closer. "Who's this pain in the ass?"

"It's from a burner phone—no name, no ID." He heard him puff on what must be a cigarette. "You know anyone in Boston?"

The traffic slowed to a near stop causing him to slam on his brakes, jerking the car forward and back again. With the car accident fresh in his mind, he couldn't help wondering if his brakes would hold despite the fact that the repairs were guaranteed by the mechanic. He let out a huff when noticing the truck's brakes kept their vehicles from crashing, even if it was only by inches.

"Trenton, you still there?" Juan's voice rose.

"Yeah. Still here." He wiped perspiration from his forehead. "I'm in traffic. Seems to be a collision up ahead—typical for L.A. Anything else about this unknown jerk?"

"I have all the dates recorded for my final report." He swallowed something.

"Juan, I received a bogus call today from a 617 area code." He took the napkin with the scribbled number from his pocket and read the numbers off to the PI.

There was a moment of silence. "That's the same number I have—the burner cell out of Boston. You know of anyone there? An old rival of some sort?"

"My ex is from Boston. Her family still lives there." Anger twisted and churned in his gut. "I had no idea that vile bitch would go to such lengths to wreck my life."

"Hang on a minute. We need more to go on before we can assign a name and you can go to the police." A light chuckle escaped. "Are there any other possibilities? Someone a bit remote?"

"Amelia feels her cousin Clive is behind the harassment." He inched the car forward a few feet and then stopped. "My ex-stepson, Jason Banner. He's not likely as he rarely does anything that Naomi wants."

"Are they close?" Juan seemed interested as if he was thinking of a possibility.

"Only when she pays him—with my money of course." He let out a sarcastic laugh. "Far be it for her to actually hold a job. Never worked a day in her life from what I know."

"What about this Clive person? What's his last name?" Another pause. Trenton assumed he was taking down notes. "He nearby or in Massachusetts?"

"Clive Bradford, the Duke of Bryningmead, is tucked away in

London, working for MI6 or doing research of one type or another." *Maybe Clive shouldn't be written off.* "He and Amelia have been at each others' throats for years."

"Interesting. Not likely considering his location and where these calls to the florist have been from." He took a deep breath. "Any idea about your crash on PCH? Got a name for me?"

"None on that score—not more than what I already told you. Jason or a goon buddy of his." The traffic sped up as he passed a mangled car on the side of the road with emergency vehicles flashing their lights.

"I'll keep digging on my end." He coughed. "Call me with anything—no matter how insignificant."

He needs to lay off those cigarettes. "Will do. One last thing. A friend of Amelia's—Joe Winton has contacted his friend Sal Mourtos out of New York who has a PI friend. Supposedly, this PI is on the case, too."

"Got a name?" Another cough.

"Seems Sal won't share that info." Trenton changed lanes to exit off the highway and onto Malibu Road. "Guess the PI doesn't want to be known."

"Typical, especially if he has a shady past." His voice faded. "I won't be able to check him out with nothing to go on. He's probably on the up and up."

"Oh, I nearly forgot ... I've had a rash of spider invasions. Had the exterminators out a few times, plus spraying the place inside." Trenton decreased his speed, enjoying the tree-lined road with dappled sunlight.

"How is that important?" Juan coughed again. "Malibu is noted for all types of creepy crawlies."

"Amelia is deathly allergic to them." He slowed the car as he approached a traffic light. "She even carries an epinephrine pen with her wherever she goes."

"Who knows about her allergy?" Sanchez seemed interested as his voice lowered.

"I imagine her family—Alistair, her husband, and of course Clive." He adjusted himself in his seat. "Could Clive have some way of infecting our home with spiders?"

"Nah, it doesn't seem likely ... unless he has friends in L.A. Does he? Have friends out here?"

"None that I'm aware of." *Could Amelia be right?* "As far as I know, he rarely travels beyond the UK."

"The spider invasion might just be mere coincidence." He puffed again. "Still, I'll check it out."

He was only a few miles from his house. "I'm nearly home. Call me at any time. I fear Amelia is in real danger."

"Calm down. Most of these stalking cases are harmless." His voice lightened. "Don't alert Amelia too much. You don't want her imagination getting the best of the situation. We don't have a prime suspect yet."

"You're right. I'll play it down. Gotta go." Trenton turned on his left signal a few houses before his home.

He pulled into the drive and pressed the gate's security code.

Juan's right. Amelia might be blowing everything out of proportion. Or not.

Forty~One

THE COOL WATER relaxed Amelia as she reclined on the swim-out of the infinity pool. The breathtaking view of the endless horizon with low-lying clouds kissing the Pacific added to her enjoyment and fueled her introspection. She knew her decisions had life-changing consequences. At last, she had harnessed the courage to take charge of her life. For good or bad, this was her life and she would live it as she wanted—a life with true substance.

Trenton would be home at any moment and she hoped he would join her before Jane and Alex returned from their day off. She toyed with the idea of cooking dinner for him instead of heating up what Alex had prepared, but gave that up as a poor idea as she barely knew how to scramble an egg. Maybe if her mother hadn't died when she was a child she would have learned more domestic skills. But being the daughter of an earl didn't lend itself to such training. The proper way to curtsey before the royals during her first season, planning a lavish dinner, and excelling in polite conversation was the bulk of her upbringing. All useless skills for a real life—a life denied her.

She arched her neck backwards at the sound of footsteps on the patio. Trenton stood above her head with hands on his hips. His smile broadened as he eyed her shapely form in her leopard print bikini.

"All finished with those pressing meetings that kept you from my side?" she purred. "Why not slip into your trunks and join me? I can't mix many cocktails, but I make a wicked G and T—utterly sinful, like yours truly."

"Gin and tonic?" He knelt down and placed his fingers in the water. "Not to my taste. After I've changed, I'll fix a gin for you and bourbon for me."

Trenton strolled back into the house.

Her thoughts turned to her pending divorce.

Would Alistair prove difficult? He might, especially if Clive gets in the mix.

In his navy swim trunks, Trenton returned with a worrisome expression, a drink in each hand, and a large turquoise beach towel over his shoulder. She accepted the gin from him and sipped on the straw while he dropped the towel in a heap near the pool entry. He slipped into the pool and sat on the top step, still holding his drink. She placed the cocktail on the pool edge and eased from the swim-out to the steps.

Looking up at him, she linked her arms around his knees. "There's a mean old thundercloud on your face. What's upset you? Unpleasant news in Hollywood heaven? Some starlet failed the casting-couch audition?"

"It's a bit more serious than that." He took a swallow of bourbon.

Her finger doodled on his knee. "Well, just don't stare at your drink and sulk—talk. Talking always makes it better, or so you've been telling me all these weeks."

His lips thinned, as he looked outward above her head. "It has to do with you and what they—no, my boss wants me to ask you."

"Now you must tell me." She positioned herself beside him. "It can't be that bad, unless they are asking you to pack me off."

"Nothing like that." Trenton stroked her cheek as his eyes searched hers. "Quite the opposite." He downed half his drink in one gulp. "Krantz wants to promote the new movie based on your celebrity—telling the theatergoing public that it's loosely based on your life. He feels the ticket sales will go through the roof."

"Truly? Me? I'm known as a celebrity?" Her brows rose. "Wouldn't that just curdle old Clive's clotted cream!"

"You mean, you're okay with it?" His face held hope. "It would push you into the media—newspapers, maybe even an interview or two."

"How would Mr. Krantz react toward you if I decline?" *This must be important to him or else he wouldn't look so serious.*

"He wouldn't be happy." He stared at the rippling water.

"Not happy with me—or with you?" She touched his chin, forcing him to look at her.

"Me—he'd be upset that I didn't persuade you." He took a deep breath. "I don't want you to feel you must agree to his harebrained scheme. I never want you to feel used. I'd never do that to you."

"Bosh!" She laughed. "I trust you more than that. By the way, what is this movie about, besides a contemporary duchess?"

A glint rested in his eyes. "An updated version of *Lady Chatterley's Lover.* Its title is *Duchess in Love.* Now you understand my reluctance to even ask you."

"Definitely! Tell Mr. Krantz that I agree. With that title, I have to be in on this. That old novel could be the bible of my life—before you ... no longer, of course." Her throaty laugh escaped. "Based on my reputation with the royals, this is just too perfect. Oh how I'd love to see Clive's reaction on that one—might even cost him his discretionary title of duke." She licked her lips with a slow savory caress. "I couldn't care less what the royals feel at the palace. It's not like they haven't had their share of scandal in years gone by."

"I am so relieved that you're not upset." A smile tugged at his lips before he bent and kissed her gently. "The title could've been better but it's what Krantz wants and he *is* the boss. You have no idea how I agonized ever since I returned to work and he first brought it up."

"Trent, when we first met—at the wedding, did you know I was a duchess who could help your film—researching my life with due diligence?" She held his eyes with her own.

"Not in the least." He tilted his head, a boyish smile beamed. "I didn't even know who you were, let alone a duchess. The screenwriters and researchers dig out the background stuff for the characters they create—culture, language, customs." Knitted lines creased his forehead. "I hope you don't think our meeting was a put-up job to further my standing at the studio. That's *not* who I am."

"Never. I know you wouldn't do such a thing. It was stupid of me to even ask." She cupped his cheeks in her hands, "I only want the very best for you ... if I can help on that front, then I will."

His lips pressed hers gently, washing away her foolish doubt. "You're the best for me."

"I have some news of my own." She took a large gulp of her G and T, then swallowed hard, gathering courage. "I called Mr. Hargrove, my solicitor."

Trenton's brows drew together. "Really? And?"

"And ... the papers have been drawn up, signed by yours truly, and returned to him—legal papers petitioning the court for my divorce. Might have already been presented to the magistrates and ... Alistair, of course."

Maybe I should've waited telling Trent until things were further along.

Trenton's lips curled into an expansive smile, joy emitting from his eyes. "You have made me one lucky man." His arm encircled her waist. "I know of a great way to celebrate." Light kisses teased her earlobe, his hot breath stirring her libido.

"I like the way you think, Mister Producer." She placed her hand on his chest, her fingers toying with his hair just above his six-pack. "Don't plan on whisking me away to a vicar anytime soon. If Alistair doesn't contest, I'll be a free woman in eight weeks. However, ol' Clive might stir him up to make a fuss, which means I'll have to return to London and appear in court."

"Why would Clive want to do anything to bring you back to London?" Worry lines formed at the corner of his eyes. "I thought you said he was happy that you were far, far away."

"Darling," she tapped his chin, "he will do whatever it takes to make me the most miserable that any human being could suffer. He has never liked me—downright hates me, if the truth be known." She sighed and turned her eyes to his. "Hubris gives him delusions of grandeur and is his gravitas. Remember, I told you, I know all his dirty little secrets. Whispers become murmurs before blossoming into delicious gossip—that's my power over him."

"I didn't think much of Clive after briefly meeting him at Stuart's wedding—pompous and self-absorbed." He gulped a mouthful of bourbon.

"Enough about my troubles." Her fingers ran up and down his thigh in the water, creating tiny ripples, glistening from the low sun. "Any news from that private investigator you hired?"

"Nothing earth-shattering." He signed and looked up at the puffy clouds. "No prime suspect yet. He did find out that those flowers were ordered from a burner phone bought in Boston—the Cambridge area."

"Truly?" Her mind went racing, trying to recall her conversation with Clive at the wedding reception. Her forehead creased with fine lines at the corners of her eyes. "Where is Harvard located?"

"In Cambridge. Why?" He turned and looked directly at her. "What's wrong?"

"My cousin said he was invited to lecture at that university at the reception. I think I overheard him tell that to Alistair." She rubbed her forehead. "He's the one—it has to be him."

"Not so fast." He stroked her hair. "Naomi has relatives in Boston. I think she is far more lethal than Clive. He wouldn't want to risk his cherished title. If the cops nabbed him in a crime, he'd lose his title, right?"

"He'd lose not only his title, but his career, too." Amelia let out a ragged breath. "Enough of this troublesome talk. I want to feel nothing but joy around you—Clive and Naomi are not contributors on that score."

"What do you have in mind?" He undressed her with his eyes.

"You said we need to celebrate my agreement to Mr. Krantz's plan ..." Her hand crept down his tight abdomen to the waist of his trunks and lingered there before slipping a finger inside the elastic band. "Making love in a pool can be sensational."

"Not with the neighbors and their telescopes." He jerked his chin upward and to the side. "Besides, the sun is just setting."

"If it was dark, would you?" She delighted in teasing him.

His lips brushed hers before answering, teasing her with a near kiss. "Not on your life. The last thing I need is to see my bare ass in tomorrow's tabloids."

She reached into his trunks. She relished in feeling the beginnings of an erection to her teasing caresses.

"Not here, Amelia." He removed her hand, then kissed her cheek. "We'll continue this privately ... in our bedroom."

I love that he can't be controlled. Every day he seems more a part of me.

Forty~Two

EXCITEMENT PEPPERED WITH anticipation danced in Amelia as she sat in the backseat of the stretch limo. This feeling was long forgotten since childhood on a Christmas morn. She had not a fathom of an idea as to what to expect. Trenton requested she wear the haute couture gown he had gifted her, and she could only describe him as 'dashing' in his impeccably-tailored black tuxedo. The traffic flowed smoothly until they approached L.A., but it didn't worry her. She delighted in the pampering, and enjoyed splits of chilled champagne.

Trent thinks of everything, right down to the last detail.

She wiggled her toes in the strappy silver sandals. "Now I understand why you wanted to leave so early. The traffic is horrid."

"You haven't asked me where we're going." His arm extended across the back of her shoulders.

"That would spoil the surprise for me." She glanced at him from beneath her long black lashes.

His sly smile emerged. "I thought you were a woman who wanted to know all—to be in control of things."

"I was, until ... until you." Her fingers stroked his knee. "I don't mind relinquishing some of my power to you."

"Good to know." He leaned in and kissed the gentle curve of her neck just below her ear. "Hmm, I love that fragrance. You were wearing that when we first met at the wedding reception. What's it called? I'll buy you a tub full so you can bathe in it."

"Can't you guess?" She extended her neck to receive more of his kisses. "*Scandalous* by some French perfumer, Monsieur What's-his-name." She reached for her small aqua evening purse that had slid off her lap and onto the floor.

He checked his gold Rolex and fidgeted in his seat as the limousine turned onto Hollywood Boulevard. Seeing the row of shiny black vehicles creeping behind each other reminded her of the black taxis in London pulling up when the theaters let out late in the evening. *This is an important night for Trent.* As hard as she tried to see, their car was too far back for her to distinguish any famous personage exiting at what must be a theater's entrance.

"Did you expect this?" His palm met hers as his eyes brightened like a schoolboy at Christmas. His thumb caressed the top of her hand.

"I'm still not certain what all this fuss is about." She looked at the tourists behind the barricades holding their phones in the air, and others with cameras. Muffled shouts and yells from the crowds thrilled her, as if she was in a different world—Trenton's world. "Is it a charity function where you'll introduce me to a few Hollywood stars?"

"You could say that." He let out a devilish chuckle.

Her fist pounded his chest playfully. "Will you tell me or not? Now's the time to tell all."

"Well ... since you agreed for the studio to associate your personage with the movie," he paused, keeping her in suspense.

"Get on with it. Tell me!" She pinched his arm.

"Ouch!" He looked smug. "They, Mr. Aaron Krantz in particular, wanted you to attend the movie premiere. He pulled out all the stops on this one—crossing searchlights will be illuminating the sky when we exit, media contacted, and a special post premiere party. I assume Wolfgang will be doing the catering. When we arrive, if there is a question you don't feel like answering, look at me and I'll take over talking to the reporters—this is all new to you."

"I hope it will be a jolly good crack." She peered through the window, searching for a famous face.

"Good crack?" His eyes widened. "What exactly are you referring to?"

"It's Irish for a good time—a happy atmosphere." *I must've said something wrong.*

"Well, please don't use that expression with anyone you meet tonight." His small laugh escaped. "They will assume you're looking for crack cocaine. And, *that*, I don't need to be associated with in any shape or form."

"Right." *I better brush up on American slang.*

Behind two black stretch limousines, she clearly saw the famous actors and actresses as they exited.

She leaned forward and tapped his knee. "Is that Jude?"

"Yes it is. He has the lead." He smiled as if pleased that he had impressed her. "The leading lady is the same from one of the remakes—the blockbuster, *Titanic*."

"Was Kate chosen because of her red hair—like mine?" She kept her eyes focused on the famous stars walking on the red carpet up ahead.

"Talent rules in this town and if they are box office—will sell tickets on name recognition." He rubbed her shoulder. "Hair color can be changed for whatever the role dictates. They both have English accents and are extremely talented."

"Yes. But Kate is from Australia." Amelia demonstrated that she did have some knowledge of his world. "She mimics an excellent English accent."

Only one car length behind a limousine, her eyes widened as she saw the front of Grauman's Chinese Theatre. The photos she had seen in a magazine didn't do this famous landmark justice. The ornate exterior resembled a giant, red Chinese pagoda with a huge dragon in a snakelike position over the front. Two lion-dogs of stone guarded the main entrance with silhouettes of tiny dragons running up and down the sides of the detailed copper roof.

With such flamboyance, what does the interior look like?

Finally, the driver pulled up to the front of the theater. Velvet ropes flanked the expansive red runner going up the steps and to the entry. A male attendant opened the back passenger door. Trenton exited first and then extended his hand, assisting Amelia onto the carpeted walkway. Microphones held by hungry reporters and flashing cameras assaulted them from all angles. Clearly, he squinted due to the cameras' bright lights while she smiled as if this was all commonplace.

A fashionably dressed woman sardined her way through to be the first to question the duchess. "You have a lovely accent."

I haven't spoken yet. What an idiotic statement. "So do you," she quipped. *This is going to be great fun.*

A man from a television entertainment program edged his microphone close to her face. "Duchess, are you looking forward to seeing your life portrayed on the big screen?"

"That depends on the script and the actors. I imagine they are all very talented." She slipped her gloved hand into Trenton's crooked elbow.

Another man pushed forward and raised his voice over the others. "What did you think when Mr. Lowe pitched the script to you for your personal endorsement?"

She set her jaw for a moment. "I was tremendously flattered—wouldn't you be?"

The same man directed his attention to Trenton. "Mr. Lowe, how did you find the duchess?"

Amelia couldn't resist answering for her lover. "He found me very talented, indeed."

The reporter nearly drooled from her remark. "Talent in what area,

Duchess?"

She sported her trademark impish smile. "You shouldn't have to ask, you should already know. If not, see the movie."

Another female reporter approached. "How much of the movie is actually about your colorful life?"

Amelia spoke in a flat tone, "I have to see the movie first."

The same female continued, "Who are you wearing?"

"I wear Trenton Lowe. Sometimes he wears me. If you're referring to my gown, André designed this lovely creation of Chez André."

A man called out from behind the throng of reporters, "Who are the young actors playing your lovers?"

Amelia looked at Trenton. He took his cue. "The studio is expecting this to be a smash hit."

The same voice asked the producer, "Do you feel an Oscar is in the future?"

He started walking to the steps. "That would be nice. Thank you for your questions. We need to get to our seats."

He whisked Amelia up to the steps while mumbling, "Say no more. They have high-powered mics everywhere."

Once inside the sanctity of the lobby, she gazed at the décor of a dazzling blur of exotic Asian motifs with elaborate murals depicting life in the Orient. Bold red and gold columns and the colossal, intricate Chinese chandelier seemed a bit ostentatious to her.

"Amelia, you handled that verbal third degree from the reporters with aplomb." He boasted an approving smile.

"As you Americans say, 'this ain't my first rodeo'." She flashed him a wink, then whispered in his ear, "I'm not wearing any panties ... chew on that thought for the evening."

His tongue slowly grazed his bottom lip and a seductive smile appeared.

I've got his imagination fired up now.

Trenton handed the tickets to the usher. He escorted them to their reserved, bright crimson VIP seats. Her heels sank into the vibrant scarlet carpeting.

He offered historical tidbits, as he seemed to want her to know the importance of this location. "Sid Grauman built this place. It opened in 1927 with the original silent version of *King of Kings* produced by Cecil B. DeMille. Millions of tourists flock here yearly—mostly to see the forecourt with its foot and handprints of the stars. It's been modernized now, with a state-of-the-art IMAX screen."

As he talked, she looked up at the spectacular chandelier illuminating the center of an ornate starburst with a ring of dragons, and another circling a ring of icons from scenes in a Chinese drama.

Trenton continued to relate trivia of this famous landmark. "A Chinese electronics company bought the rights to change the name to TCL Chinese Theater on the marquee." He chuckled. "Of course, it will always be called Grauman's Chinese by the public. Trying to rename something as iconic and historic as this place is like trying to rename the Eiffel Tower."

"It must have cost a quid or two to purchase the rights to rename this theater." She looked at the walls displaying glowing Oriental lamps, hanging between intricately carved stone columns. Black and white murals of trees and pagodas filled the spaces in between.

"About five mil, give or take a two." He pointed discreetly behind them. "See those four private opera boxes?"

"Yes. Who are seated there? I can't quite make out their faces." She wished she had packed her opera glasses.

"That's reserved for celebrities—those stars who arrived before us and are starring in this film." He smiled with delight as if he wanted to please her in every way. "There's a VIP lounge on that same level."

"I wish it wasn't so dim in here, then I might be able to see Kate and Jude's faces more clearly." She glanced around at the others in the theater and wasn't certain if there were any recognizable faces.

He patted her hand. "You'll meet them up close and personal at the post party located at the Wilshire. Like I said, Krantz spared no expense. I only hope the film doesn't offend you. Hollywood can be brutal at times."

"Are you warning me off?" *Just how much of my life will be on display?*

"No. I want to remind you that the plot is based on fiction and not real facets of your life." He tilted his head so their foreheads touched. "Your name is just as big box office as that of Jude and Kate's."

She flipped the pages of the program, squinting to read the words. Under the movie's name was printed "based on the life of Amelia Hollingsworth, the Duchess of Steffenfordshire". Farther down was Trenton's credits as producer with the studio's name. This accolade gave her a thrill. Exhilaration bubbled up inside her—a feeling quite new in her life. Her old life had been so predictable in the past. She looked over at Trenton.

I am lucky to have Trent in my world. Almost twenty years wasted. And for what—the delight of a new boy at my whim?

Forty Three

"SO WHAT DID you think?" Trenton looked earnestly at her face. He hoped the film didn't offend her.

Amelia and he waited in the back of the lobby, letting the film stars exit first hoping that the throng of paparazzi would be on their quest to the Beverly Wilshire Hotel.

"I think it was closer to my life than what I would have cared to reveal." Her eyes latched onto Jude's as she watched him walk past her with Kate. "You should have given me the script."

"What upset you?" *I wanted to honor her. Now she's thinking I tricked her in some way.* "Associating you with the film came up rather sudden and Krantz had already put the PR cogs into motion."

"All those escapades of that duchess with meaningless liaisons until she finds that one special man in her life. I'm far more outrageous than the character—she was too tame and polite." Her brows drew together. "It makes me feel that someone was watching me from a peephole somewhere. Yet, the ending was touching, even if her lover died." She clasped his hand and gave it a strong squeeze. "You must promise me that you won't die."

"Dying is not on my agenda—keeping you happy is my concern." He chuckled. "If I can placate my boss in the process ... well, all the better. As to the tameness—the studio didn't want to go beyond an R rating."

"I see your point." She looked in her purse as if checking on something, then snapped it shut. "Still, I don't form my sentences like the words Kate spoke."

"That's the whole idea." His eyes widened. "It's not about *you*. It's a fanciful story with your name tied to it."

The last of the cast and crewmembers walked past them to the entry. Soon, the technical talent would follow along with those in the art department, costumes, and musicians.

"When should we leave?" She appeared anxious to arrive at the hotel party.

Trenton peered through the glass door from a distance. "All the tabloid types seem to have left." He nudged her elbow. "Let's go. Our limo should be parked somewhere across the street."

~~***~~

Delighted to see Larry, Taylor, and Joe at their assigned table, Amelia beamed as she sat down. Excitement overflowed her every cell to the point where she forgot to allow Trenton to introduce the others seated with them.

"It is splendid to see you all." She leaned into Taylor. "How did you manage it—getting tickets to the premiere?"

"Larry wrote the score, so it was a given that we would be invited." Taylor jutted her chin to Trenton. "Mr. Lowe, I mean, Trenton saw to it that Joe would be included."

Larry interrupted, "This is a real thrill for me. It's my first premiere." He glanced about the room. "The studio knows how to throw a party."

Joe added his two cents, looking at Trenton. "Mighty nice of y' to invite me." He raised his water glass in tribute to the producer.

Amelia touched Taylor's hand. "It's so good to see you again— well, to see you all again. The last time we met was at the reception." Her voice lowered. "I have so much to tell you."

Joe spoke over the rest, "They got any beer here?"

A server must have heard his comment and came to the table saying, "Right away, sir."

Trenton coughed. "I hate to interrupt this reunion. I'd like to introduce the other valuable members at our table." He gestured to the first couple. "To Joe's right is Anne Jackson and my priceless AP, Duane Jackson. He's an indispensable assistant producer to me—seeing to details when I'm pulled elsewhere. To my left are Jeff Towers and his lovely wife, Suzanne. Jeff is my associate producer who is always keeping me on my toes." He took a breath. "I'm pleased to introduce my lovely companion, Amelia Hollingsworth, the duchess of Steffenfordshire, who graciously agreed to allow her personage to be associated with this film, then Larry and his wife, Taylor Davis. Larry is our composer extraordinaire for the film. Joe Winton is one helluva guy who keeps Larry in line."

All exchanged pleasantries. Each returned to their own private conversations.

"Amelia, how are Cindy and Stuart?" Taylor asked.

"They are getting on brilliantly. I haven't heard of anything to the contrary." Amelia lowered her voice. "I have big changes in progress."

"I'm all ears." Taylor leaned in closer.

"My solicitor filled a petition for divorce from Alistair." Her eyes brightened. "If he doesn't contest the proceedings, I'll be a free woman in six to eight weeks."

"Do you think he will—contest I mean?" Taylor bit her lip as if in thought.

Amelia eagerly shared the details. "If he doesn't object, he'll forfeit all my money. He shocked me beyond compare," she lowered her voice to a near whisper, "right out of the blue, Alistair tells me he has a living male heir from a dead wife eons ago—the cad."

"That must've been a bombshell for you." Concern showed on Taylor's face as her eyes grew large. "That is the last thing I expected you to say about him." She fingered her napkin. "I guess you and Trenton are an item? Will that continue if Alistair poses problems?"

Lines knitted Amelia's brow and she bit her lower lip as if a gray cloud came to her. "Alistair's possible roadblocks? I'll deal with that if I must." She took a sip of water. "Trent and I being 'an item'? That has a lovely sound to it." Her eyes twinkled. "If he has anything to say about it, we are. I haven't accepted his ring yet—appeared to be five or six carets, pear shaped, looked like a platinum setting—I want to be certain that I can love him for more than a couple of months—that I can love him for the rest of my life."

"That doesn't sound like the carefree Amelia I know." She chuckled. "Seems Trenton has brought out your serious side .... What about your tiaras and jewels? Are you leaving them behind?"

Amelia glanced at him, smiled, and then back to Taylor. "Trenton has brought out many good qualities that I didn't know I possessed." She leaned in closer and lowered her voice. "The matter of my jewels? Elizabeth has the key and knows where I hid them. I'd never trust them to a bank vault—not with crafty Clive. He's in league with Alistair."

Two waiters appeared at their table and poured champagne into everyone's flute.

Trenton raised his glass, prompting others to do the same. "I'd like to toast all for a fantastic job done in the creation of *Duchess in Love*. Your individual talents have made this film a future success." He looked at Amelia. "And to the lovely and vivacious duchess who was willing to associate her name to this movie."

All raised their glasses, and said in unison "To Lady Amelia" before tasting the champagne. Color came to Amelia's face. This form of accolade was new, causing her to feel a trifle embarrassed. She nodded back with a smile. "Thank you, all."

Taking her purse, Amelia stood and placed her napkin on her seat. "Taylor, I'm off to the loo. Wantt to join me?"

Her friend shook her head. "I've been before we were seated."

"Right." She flashed a smile.

Amelia left the group and found an attendant, who directed her to the restrooms.

When she came out of the stall, a blond, blue-eyed, petit woman stood at the vanity, touching up her lipstick in the mirror over the sinks. Amelia dug into her purse and extracted a small comb, and set the purse on the vanity next to the woman's pocketbook.

"A lovely evening, isn't it?" She spoke to Amelia's reflection.

"Smashing, in my estimation." Amelia looked at her. "I'm terribly sorry. Have we met?"

"No. But I've seen your picture in the media." She held a knowing smirk on her lips. "You're the famous Amelia Hollingsworth, a duchess—*the* duchess—the one the movie is all about."

"And you are?" The duchess extended her hand.

She doesn't resemble any of the actresses in the film—or any film for that matter.

The strange woman carelessly swiped her hand, knocking Amelia's purse onto the floor. The contents spilled out all over the tiles.

Amelia bent to retrieve all her things, but the woman crouched down over them, effectively blocking her. "I'm so sorry," she said, returning the items into the evening bag. She handed the purse back to Amelia. "Sometimes I'm clumsy—must be due to meeting a famous duchess."

"No bother, really. All is right." Amelia took one last glance in the mirror and left.

She certainly seemed flustered. Am I becoming a celebrity?

~~***~~

Through the large archway, Trenton spotted Juan leaning against the bar, away from the premiere party. He walked quickly toward the PI. "Sorry I couldn't find a way to get you into the ballroom. Tickets were tight." He watched him take a swallow of his drink. "So, what do you have for me? Anything suspicious here?"

"None that I can find." He motioned to the bartender for a refill. "Any more encounters with that jerk since you bloodied his nose?"

"No, thank God." He rubbed his chin. "We've had an invasion of spiders. I don't know if it's deliberate from an outside source or just a normal happening. I guess I'm more aware of those nasty critters because of Amelia's allergy."

"For someone to plant spiders in your house would take a fair amount of planning—have an intimate knowledge of your surroundings and routine." Juan's eyes narrowed. "Any idea on that score?"

"My ex comes to mind." He shifted his weight to the other foot. "But she's tucked safely away on Manhattan Beach."

"Are you certain she hasn't been sniffing around somewhere?" He turned his palm upward. "She would have means and motive. Spiders aren't exactly foreign beings and difficult to obtain."

Trenton scanned the patrons in the lounge. "Well, I don't see her here."

"I doubt she'd risk discovery by trying to crash a Hollywood party." Juan ran his hand through his hair as a pretty girl passed by, and watched her curvy hips sway. "Don't forget to send me a photo of her. Blue-eyed blonds aren't much of a description to go on—not in this town."

"Sorry about that. It slipped my mind." Trenton took his phone from his tuxedo jacket, scrolled the photo section, selected the image, and then tapped send. "You should be getting her photo in a minute or so."

Juan looked at his phone. "Got it."

Trenton took a few steps backwards from the bar. "I need to be getting back to the rest. Keep me posted."

~~***~~

Amelia noticed a man weaving through the tables, clearly headed for where they sat. He reeked of self-importance. Trenton scrunched his neck down and hunched his shoulders like a tortoise trying to avoid recognition by a predator.

He mumbled to Amelia, "*God* is approaching. Don't let him fluster you."

"Your boss?" She eyed the older gray-haired man and then looked straight ahead at Suzanne. "I can handle him."

"How?" He seemed mildly puzzled.

"I'm the duchess. I hold the trump card. No *me* in the credits equals no box office." Her sly smirk exuded confidence.

He touched her hand. "That's my girl."

Aaron gripped the backs of their chairs and leaned toward Amelia. "I just had to meet the beautiful and captivating Duchess Amelia," he said with a smile. He held out his hand.

"How do you do?" *I didn't think anyone could be more pompous than Clive.*

He took her offered hand and forwardly kissed it. She caught Suzanne and Anne rolling their eyes, and stifled a giggle.

"I and the studio are most grateful that you have agreed to endorse the film. I trust you enjoyed the movie?" He was still holding onto her hand, and his schmoozing was enough to sicken anyone.

"Yes. Very much." She smiled at Trenton and pulled her hand back. "If it wasn't for the aptness of Mr. Lowe, I would have never known of this wonderful opportunity to promote such a treasure. Of course, the musical score by Mr. Davis contributes immensely to the emotional feel of the scenes."

Larry nodded and Taylor smiled discreetly.

Amelia enjoyed this banter she'd devised. "I trust you have been treating Mr. Lowe and Mr. Davis with the appropriate appreciation for their vast talents."

Aaron appeared taken aback. "Of— of— of course, Duchess." He flashed a glance at the two men. "They will be well-compensated for their contribution." He appeared mildly unnerved. "You know, this party is the place to be and be seen."

Amelia pursed her lips. "Of course. Wherever *I* am, is the place to be ... and *I* am the one to be seen."

Krantz shifted his weight as he straightened, clearly feeling intimidated. "Very nice meeting you, Duchess."

"Yes, it was, wasn't it?" She flashed a confident and controlling smile to the man who liked to think he had the upper hand in all situations.

Aaron looked sheepish and caught his breath before continuing, "... and nice meeting you, too, Mr. Davis. Glad you could attend our gala." He cleared his throat and took a step back. "I need to move on to greet others."

Larry smiled and nodded in response.

They all watched Krantz leave and waited until he was out of earshot.

Trenton looked at Amelia with a broad smile, and kissed her on the cheek. "Very well done ... masterfully done."

The rest raised their glasses in tribute to Amelia's display of handling the grandiose man.

Amelia looked at each one at the table as she spoke. "Is his only gravitas pomposity? What a pity if it is and my condolences to all of you under him."

Taylor spoke in her ear. "You certainly put him in his place."

"Putting one in their proper place is sometimes necessary to level the stage." She took a sip of champagne. "Why does the world have to be peppered with so many *Clives* out there? Now that he has been taken care of, let's enjoy the rest of the party. I doubt he'll grace our table again for the duration of the evening."

Trenton turned and gestured to the headwaiter, who promptly approached, and whispered something in his ear. He sported a Cheshire smile.

"What are you up to now?" Amelia couldn't contain her curiosity.

"Something that I hope will please you." He kissed her cheek.

Moments later, Kate and Jude approached their table. Her eyes widened as the others watched.

Trenton rose, introduced the guests at the table and then gestured to Amelia. "Kate and Jude, please allow me to introduce Amelia Hollingsworth, the Duchess of Steffenfordshire—the person who was so gracious as to associate herself with our film." He sat down again.

Jude bowed and kissed Amelia's extended hand. "It is a supreme honor, Your Grace."

"I'm not the bloody queen." She let out a small laugh. "Dispense with 'your grace' for me. 'Amelia' is perfectly acceptable."

Kate shook the duchess' hand briefly. "It's my pleasure to meet you. I hope I did your character justice."

"Quite. Very well portrayed." She cocked her head. "Did you find the role challenging?"

The actress' strawberry blond locks emphasized her reddened face. "Yes ... a bit. I wanted to emote the torture of the unspoken words—the turmoil of the character searching for that one true love in her life."

Amelia looked at Trenton for a moment. "Yes. Your performance was dynamic and sensitive. The underlying emotion was clearly present." She looked at Jude. "If I didn't know better, I would have sworn you were portraying Trenton Lowe." She glanced at Trenton and then back up to Jude. "Was that your notion or that of the director?"

"Not in the least, Your Gra—I mean, Amelia." An uneasy expression crossed his face. "I felt the role demanded a certain strength to meet the lead female's character." He flashed a glance to the actress. "Kate made it quite easy for me."

"You weren't so bad yourself, Jude." She smiled with admiration at the leading man. "Talent always feeds off other talent and makes the process flow—basically you feed off one another's great performance."

Amelia looked at Kate and then at Jude. "Fascinating. I'm a bit lost in the wilderness when it comes to making movies." She patted Trenton's hand. "With Trent's help, I'm learning the ropes."

"It's been an extreme pleasure meeting you, Duch—, Amelia." Jude beamed, showing perfect white teeth.

Kate chimed in, "A pleasure for me, too."

The actor nodded. "We must return to our seats. Thank you for receiving us." He took a few steps backwards before turning and headed away from them.

"My, my, that was a thrill. Jude is well-schooled in proper forms of address, even though I find the whole protocol damn stuffy and ridiculous." She looked at Trenton. "Did you orchestrate that lovely encounter?"

He shrugged his shoulders. "They mentioned wanting to meet you—I merely took advantage of the opportunity on the mat."

She kissed his cheek. "You're always thinking of ways to please me."

Taylor leaned to her. "He's a keeper."

~~***~~

On their way home from the premiere party, Trenton and Amelia sat quietly in the backseat. She had hoped she hadn't been too intimidating with Aaron. The last thing she wanted was to cause him trouble with his boss. Yet, it was delicious fun to put that pompous ass in his place.

"Did I speak out of line with your superior?" Her fingers ran up and down his thigh.

"Not at all." He angled his position towards her. "If he didn't know it before, he knows it now—you have a mind of your own."

"And don't you forget it." She glanced at the tinted privacy window between the driver and the backseat. "Can the driver see through the window?"

"Yes, a bit. There's a solid privacy panel." He pushed a button on the controls and the pane quickly rose. His forehead furrowed. "What do you have in mind?"

"You'll find out soon enough," she purred as she licked her lips. "Ever had a woman in a limousine?"

Before he could answer, her lips met his—her tongue searching the recesses of his mouth. The spicy smell of his cologne fueled her desire and she moaned at the feel of his manhood, his erection already huge and hard. She unzipped his trousers and it sprang free. "Naughty boy," she whispered as she ran her hand up and down it. He gasped, and buried his head in her neck leaving tantalizing kisses and traveling to the top of her cleavage. He slid his hand up her leg, under her skirt and caressed her moist center. She moaned with him as her breathing quickened from his teasing touch.

She *had* to have him, to feel him deep inside her—she couldn't wait any longer. With heated desire pulsing through her, Amelia lifted her skirt and eased herself onto him, inch by inch relishing the wild sensations that gripped her as his hot and hard erection slid into her. Her head rested on his shoulder and she fingered his hair, panting with desire.

"Now I know why you didn't wear any panties." He breathed in heavy pants. He grabbed her buttocks and guided her movements, faster and faster.

She couldn't tease him by changing her tempo, and she didn't want to—the urgency of her need equaled his. Frantically, she moved in unison with him, sweat trickling from her hairline and down between her breasts.

Her climax was within reach. "Yes, yes, yes!"

She clenched her teeth as her spasms melded with his—both heaving and shaking as their ecstasy controlled them.

Amelia lifted her head, still breathing hard, and played with a lock of damp, fallen hair on his forehead. "That was a first for me, darling."

"I'm glad I was the one you chose to share this moment with," he said, his voice hoarse. He kissed her lips gently. "I want to be part of all the firsts in your future."

She grinned. "That was so hot. I should go without panties more often."

He caressed her ear, his eyes delving into her. "I was hot ever since you told me you weren't wearing any. I spent most of the evening glad I was sitting."

"That was the whole idea, darling—" A mischievous glint colored her eyes. "I wanted you to think of me the entire evening."

Forty~Four

"WHAT PROMPTED YOU to take me on a nature trail?" Amelia gave Trenton a sideways glance.

"I thought I'd expose you to more of Malibu besides the beaches and ocean views." His eyes held steady on the smooth paved walkway. "I come here to clear my head sometimes—when all the stressors of the studio tend to overwhelm me. It's a small pocket park with only a third of a mile of trails. Still, if you ignore the houses on the hills, you could almost feel you're in a forest or field."

"Well, after today's reviews I read in the papers, your stress level should be in the negative range." She gave his hand a gentle squeeze. "And I quote, '*Duchess in Love* is anticipated to be a strong contender for an Oscar.' I might have the photo of us on the red carpet framed. You looked so dashing."

"You by my side made the photo important for me. I'll contact the paper and see if they'll give me a print so I can have it on the mantle and see those beautiful beguiling eyes every time I enter the room."

She smiled. He always had the knack of saying the right thing.

His tone turned serious. "As to an Oscar, I won't hold my breath nor order a new tux anytime soon. Politics is as heavy as thick slime—including the Academy of Motion Picture Arts. For the most part, it's a fair system ... but there can always be the influence of others. Still, I expect the box office to swell all because of your endorsement."

"It's a dreadful shame that talent should be judged in such a slanted way—boiled down to who knows who, and what social connections they have. I agreed to endorse the film because of you—you have opened my eyes to a new world—new possibilities." A cluster of gold and yellow flowers caught her attention as their leaves fluttered in the breeze.

"Such is the way in most of the world—connections rule all." He led her to a wooden bench where they sat down. "I'm glad I had—no, have—a positive influence on you .... I recall you received a glowing review yourself—'Amelia Hollingsworth, Duchess of Steffenfordshire, was a delight with quick and witty quips that enchanted with adept aplomb—a true asset not only to *Duchess in Love* but to Hollywood.' See, I remember things, too—things about you."

"I'm very impressed." She looked upward towards the blue sky with cotton candy clouds. "I've never been the center of anyone's life—except my late father's .... It's a feeling that I don't know how to manage—not yet anyway."

"You're managing very well." He dropped a gentle kiss on her cheek. "May you never return to jolly ol' London."

"London isn't right jolly for me—rarely has been." Her eyes narrowed as she visualized faces from her past. "I detest those pompous arses. The women blossom on a diet of fine conversation, porcelain, and pearls. The men thrive on their clubs, fine brandy, and lucrative business dealings—some honest, others not."

"You sound so bitter." He angled his head to her while rubbing her shoulders.

"I am in some things, but not in the important matters ..." Her fingers traced his hairline where a lock fell onto his forehead. "... like you. You're very important to me."

"Important enough to marry one day?" He paused his breath, cocked his head, and raised hopeful brows.

I want to say yes to him so very badly. I can't ... not yet. "One day ... not now."

"Well, that is something, I suppose. I think you said what you wanted me to hear." Disappointment crept from his strained smile. "Do you want to go home—take a shower or something?"

"I want to be alone in the truth with you." She sighed with a heaviness, holding onto words she wanted him to hear and couldn't reveal yet. "Our truth is us, here, now, without the chatter of others that adds to the noise and cuts into our substance."

"Those are mighty deep thoughts from the carefree lady I met at a wedding reception." He stroked the top of her hand. Tenderness filled her heart. His touch felt so right, so very perfect.

"I think I've grown up some since then." She laughed as if mocking her existence. "A bit late to be growing up at thirty something."

"Grown up or not," he kissed her gently and then looked into her eyes, "you are perfection."

~~***~~

Amelia approached Trenton, who was sitting on the living room sofa, engrossed in a script. He looked up.

"You have a ton of worry on your face. What's up? You look pale." He placed the script down on the sofa.

"I had to vanquish another spider again with the ubiquitous bug spray in the bedroom." She made a face as she flopped down beside him, grabbed a pillow, and hugged it to her chest. "Those exterminators you hired are total idiots if you ask me. I hope they offer a guarantee of some sort considering the multiple times you've had them out here."

He frowned. "The last time they were here, we were shopping for your gown. Alex told me they spent nearly two hours spraying every nook and possible hiding place for those insects."

Her brows lifted. "Then, how are the spiders getting in? It makes no sense."

He patted her hand. "We live in a climate where insects flourish. Sometimes it seems to be an uphill battle."

"Uphill battle or not, I don't relish ending upon a slab in the morgue due to one of those monsters." *Is that all it is? A matter of climate?* "I hate to think that a mere spider could send me packing back to London."

"Perish the thought!" He embraced her with his arm on the back of the sofa, drew her closer, and kissed the top of her head. "I never want you to leave. I'll remind Alex and Jane to be more vigilant and to do a routine spider search."

She angled her head to him to see his face. "If we didn't have an ocean and a continent separating us, I'd swear that my loathsome cousin was the root cause of this invasion."

Does Clive have friends here in California? I don't recall him mentioning anyone in the States.

"You're sounding paranoid." He straightened and looked at her with narrowing eyes, as if searching for more.

"You haven't a fathom of an idea of how much hell he's caused me, not to mention others in my life." She looked up at the ceiling for a moment. "The only kindness I can find in him is his charity work at the free clinic. I hate to admit it, but he's restored and saved many lives."

"So, he does have redeeming qualities." He tilted his head in a questioning fashion. "Want to share his dark side?"

"I can't. Those secrets belong to others." She huffed. "His good deeds are the only thing that keeps him from being a complete psychopath." Her gaze went off in space. "He only does good for the accolades that he'll garner—surely not for any true sense of altruism."

"I'm glad I didn't exchange more than a few words with him at the wedding." He picked up the script. "I want to be under his radar. From what you said, he makes Krantz seem like a benevolent saint."

"Would you mind terribly if I invited a friend here for a visit?" She hoped her pleading tone would result in a positive response.

"You shouldn't have to ask." His smile broadened. "The only thing I'd deny you is returning to London."

Her face twisted. "If Alistair contests the divorce, then I'll have to return."

"May that never happen and you remain here ... forever." He gently kissed her lips to seal his wish.

She noticed the script in his hand. "I'll leave you to your reading." She rose and headed to the bedroom while saying, "I forgot to change out the contents of my purse from the premiere night." Near the hallway, she turned to him and licked her lips. "If you get tired of reading the next blockbuster, you can assist me ... on the bed."

"What a luscious thought." He made no effort to follow her and flicked the script with the back of his hand. "I have to finish this read."

In the bedroom, Amelia pulled out the items from her evening bag onto the bed. Something was missing. She looked in the purse again. It wasn't there. She frantically upended the bag and shook it. Where was her epinephrine injection? She could be dead without it.

She called out, "Trent, please come here. My medication is missing."

Seconds later, he stood at the foot of the bed with hands on hips. "What's wrong?"

She looked up at him with exasperation. "I told you. My epinephrine injector is missing. I never go anywhere without it. I've checked both pocketbooks—it's not there!"

He went to the bathroom and came back a few seconds later. "I found this one in the cabinet." He handed it to her.

Amelia let out a grateful breath and took the medication from him, placing it in her all-purpose daytime bag. She searched her memory trying to recall how it came to be lost.

"I must have lost the other one in the ladies' room during the premiere party." She glanced up at him. "This blue-eyed blond lady clumsily bumped my purse. It fell onto the floor and everything tumbled out. She insisted on replacing my items herself—wouldn't let me help. She seemed to know me as being a duchess—acted more as a servant would. It was a bit embarrassing to be known by a stranger."

Trenton stroked his chin as his brow creased. "Was she tall or short?"

"Petite, actually, and she seemed nice." A twinge of fear slid up her spine.

He went to the bedroom closet and pulled out an album. He flipped through the pages, stopped, and walked to her. "Is this the woman you saw who helped you?" He held the book out for her to see.

Amelia stared at the picture. "Yes. That's she. Who is she? A relative?"

His teeth clenched. "That's Naomi—the bane of my existence. I wouldn't put it past her stealing your injector pen."

"What a horrid thing for her to do." *Could she be in league with Clive? Ridiculous! My imagination is getting the better of me.* "If it wasn't for my spare medication, I could've ended up dead—especially with the invasion of those little black monsters here."

"I wouldn't doubt if that was her intention." His jaw set. "I knew she was vengeful—just never knew how much ... until now."

Her fingers clasped his arm. "Come on, Trent. You're talking about premeditated murder."

"Exactly." Muscles in his jaw twitched as he looked through the expansive window.

I'm not safe in London—not with Clive nipping at my heels.

Now, here? If Trent speaks the truth, I'm in just as much danger!

Forty Five

"TOM, WHERE ARE we headed?" Amelia asked the driver as she sat in the backseat of Trenton's Mercedes sedan, his second car. "To Mr. Lowe's studio?"

"No, Lady Amelia." He looked at her through the rearview mirror. "I think he intended this as a special treat for you while he's working."

"This is Pacific Coast Highway." *This is the road we were on when the brakes failed.* She tried to calm herself and looked at the gorgeous ocean. *The Thames can't compete with this view.* "I believe the locals call this road PCH."

"Very good, ma'am. You're catching on." He turned on his right directional signal while decreasing the speed, turned into the parking lot, then stopped at the entrance.

Tom assisted her out of the backseat and then led her to the restaurant's door. The headwaiter sported a welcoming smile and extended his hand. She read his nametag.

He's very friendly, a bit old. Reminds me of Father.

"I am Mr. Carlo Bennetti. It is our extreme pleasure to welcome you, Duchess—your grace, as our guest at Moonshadows." His smile stuck as if frozen by a bad facelift, or else she was the first royal he had ever met.

"I'm delighted." *Did I say that correctly? Back home I would have merely smiled. American customs still leave me bewildered at times.*

She shook his hand, then followed him into the restaurant, glancing at the relaxed and elegant décor of dark beige, white, and rustic chairs at dark plank tables—all lending a beachy feel.

Perched over a cliff, it afforded views of the raging Pacific through the nearly floor-to-ceiling windows. In the distance, crashing waves caused the spindrift to spray up against the rocks, just as Clive had unmercifully battered. trying to ruin her life and those she cared about.

Closed umbrellas on the patio flapped in the blustering wind from the center of tables. A rope secured the chairs in place. Other diners chatted in subdued tones and took no notice of her. Amelia was glad for that. She recognized some of their faces from various movies, but didn't feel a thrill—not the same exhilaration she would have felt before entering Trenton's world.

"I have chosen an inside window table as the wind has kicked up and thought you would be more comfortable here." His expression showed him wanting approval. "Unless you would rather chance it and brave the weather?"

"This will be fine." She flashed a brief grin as he pulled out the chair and assisted her to sit.

He placed the menu before her. Another waiter served her water while a third placed a flute of bubbling champagne on the table. Amelia scanned the menu and gave her order.

Remembering her earlier conversation with Trenton, a thought came to her. There was no logical reason for it, but it compelled her to act at this moment. She took her phone from her purse and scrolled her contacts list until she found the name.

A moment passed before the ringing sounded in her ear. She shifted in her seat and tapped her fingers on the table.

"Elizabeth, this is Amelia." *I hope she fancies a bit of travel.* "Can you talk so no one hears you? Where's Alistair?"

"His grace is at the club or laboratory. Simon, the new houseman isn't even here. It's his day off, Milady." Amelia heard Rodney, the King Charles Cavalier spaniel barking in the background. "Are you coming home?"

Relief filled her. Alistair wasn't home. "Not bloody likely." The server placed the truffled chicken on the table before her. She nodded to him. "I want you to pack up every stick of my clothing and ship them to me—better yet, bring them to me. Include all my other personal items—books, objets d'art—all of it. None of my belongings are to be left there. Don't forget the tiaras and all the jewels, too. You know where I have them hidden and you still have the key, I trust?"

"Yes. Your jewels are safe." There was a pause as if Elizabeth was in shock. "Fly out there? To Hollywood? Are you quite certain, Milady?"

"Quite certain. I'll text you with the address and email the first-class airline ticket." *I hope Alistair doesn't realize she'll be gone.* "Elizabeth, listen, this is *important* ... you must not tell anyone that I called nor the instructions I just gave."

"No. I won't tell a soul about your call and what you said. What about Rodney? He'll need a ticket, too." Her voice lightened. "His veterinary medical papers are all up to date. There shouldn't be a problem with the airline officials." She sounded excited. "I've never been out of the country. This almost seems like a jolly good holiday for me."

"If all goes well, it will be more than a holiday—it will be a change of life—if you find that's what you want." *I know I can trust her. The only problem could be Alistair and Clive—especially Clive, if he learns of my plan.* "Has his lordship said anything about me?" Amelia glanced around the restaurant, scanning for eavesdroppers. "Received any mail or papers that disturbed him?"

"I don't know if this is significant, but, but he was right somber a few weeks back after opening a large envelope and reading what appeared to be legal papers."

If he was going to contest the Decree Nisi, I should think I would have been notified by now.

Amelia listened closely to Elizabeth. "I never mentioned that I saw him and what he was reading. He hurried out the door. His grace mentioned he was going to the club, he did. He didn't return for almost a week."

Alistair found solace in his brandy and a young man's trousers.

Amelia took in a deep breath and let it out. "Right." *She must get out of there.* "I know it's dreadful to leave Simon to get on by himself, but there is no other choice."

"Oh, he'll be all right, Milady." Elizabeth chuckled. "There's barely enough work to be done for one, let alone two. His lordship rarely eats home anymore. And I dare say, Simon is capable of doing the light clean-up. The housekeeper still comes in for the heavy cleaning once a week."

"I'll ring off now." She took a forkful of food to her mouth. "Remember, pack *everything* I own. Take the jewels in your carry-on bag."

"Yes, Milady. Right away, Milady."

A satisfied smile came to her face.

Elizabeth has always been loyal. Now I have to break the news to withering Jane. She's nice, but such a bore.

~~***~~

Trenton repeatedly pressed the doorbell. No answer. He pounded on the front door with his fists, his fury growing with each blow.

"Naomi! Answer the damn door! I know you're in there. Your car is in the drive." He noticed a nosey neighbor peering from a window. He took a few deep breaths in an effort to prevent himself from losing total control.

A voice came from the interior. "Why should I open the door? Not with your temper. I don't trust you."

"I have *never* laid a hand on you and you know it." *Now she's playing the battered wife routine?*

The door opened a crack. He saw a sliver of her face. "What do you want?"

He pushed the door open and entered the foyer. His voice blasted off the walls. "I want all of this to stop! And, stop it *now*! Leave Amelia alone!"

She glared at the neighbor and closed the door. Naomi almost seemed pleased by his outrage. "I could care less about that whoring duchess."

He looked for a glimmer of uneasiness in her face and found none, his volume climbing, "The flowers, the stalker, spiders, and now stealing her allergy medication. This has to stop!"

"You're talking like a crazy fool," she huffed, while taking a couple of steps backwards. "You need to be locked up instead of producing movies and kissing Krantz's ass."

"It takes one to know one, baby." He glowered at her, his eyes narrowing, his hands balling through into tight fists. "Your Boston relatives could've sent the flowers. I don't put anything past Jason—he's been doing your bidding all his life. But to steal Amelia's medication—*that* verges on premeditated murder!"

"Yah-dah, yah-dah, yah-dah," she mocked. "Put it on a CD and save your breath. I've heard it all before." Her eyebrow cocked. "What makes you think that *I* was the one responsible for the missing epinephrine? She's so empty-headed, she probably misplaced it."

"I never told you the name of her medication." *I've got her now.* "How did you know?"

"You told me the last time you crashed in." Naomi bit her lip and avoided his eyes.

"No, I didn't." His chest heaved, and he resisted the urge to strike her. "You wouldn't have known that unless you were the thief—creating an opportunity, following her into the bathroom at the premiere party, knocking her bag over and then insisting you put her items back into it." He let out a sarcastic laugh. "You had this all planned from the beginning." He ran his hand through his hair. "My God!" Trenton's eyes widened as he realized the depth of Naomi's evil. "You wanted her dead from the very beginning."

She went to the door and opened it widely as if to give any spectators a clear view.

"Please leave and stop harassing me," she growled in a raised voice, clearly for others to hear. "If you act like this again, I'll call the police."

"I'll leave—gladly." He stepped to the threshold, then turned to her with a pointed finger. "Your little display is pathetic! Anyone who knows you won't believe for a minute that you are a victim."

How can I stop her? I have to do something. What? Ship Amelia to another country? How could I be sure she would be safe anywhere?

"WHY DIDN'T YOU want to meet at a fashionable restaurant or café instead of here on your balcony?" Jessica flashed a glance to the beach. Yells and cheers came from a group of volleyball players. "I must admit—the view is inviting. I never tire of looking at gorgeous, shirtless men flexing their muscles." Sitting across from Naomi, she sipped her Mai Tai and looked vaguely curious with a slight smirk. "This is all a bit of cloak and dagger."

"Plotting doesn't need easy ears around—ready to pick up juicy details, then run with them for the next day's papers." Naomi winked at Jessica and licked her lips as a cat would before a saucer of cream.

"You're sounding absolutely Machiavellian—and I love it!" She leaned in closer over the small circular table.

Naomi refilled her friend's drink from the tall glass pitcher sitting in the middle. "Trenton stopped by the other day all riled up about his duchess being bothered."

"In what way?" Her eyes brightened, mouth on the verge of drooling. "What have you been up to? Found a way to ship her off to merry ol' England?"

"Maybe." A smirk pulled at her lips, and she fingered a napkin. "He's not one bit happy about the anonymous flower deliveries, and encounters with strange young men. He intimated that I had one of my relatives in Boston send the flowers."

"Did you?" Jessica purred.

"Once or twice." Satisfaction filled her every cell. "I must have a helper I don't know about. Or Amelia has more enemies lurking about." She enjoyed a large swallow of her drink. "Jason is very loyal and loves to see his mother happy."

"He's loyal to your money is more like." Her matter-of-fact tone pricked Naomi. "Unsolicited assistance is a blessing."

"He's no dummy—I'll give him that much." She looked out to the Pacific's rolling waves. "Trenton put two and two together and discovered I encountered Amelia in the ladies' room at the premiere party."

"That must've gone over like a ton of bricks." She took in an expansive breath, eyes wide with eager anticipation. "Did her royal highness recognize you?"

"If she did, she didn't let on." Pleasure filled Naomi. "I wasn't impressed. I'll bet you my next month's alimony that her flaming hair is out of a bottle from a high-end coiffeur."

"Collars and cuffs not matching is common in this town." Jessica ran her fingers through her hair. "Mine haven't matched in years." She chewed on the pineapple garnish. "Since the duchess is still in his life, have you given up? Seems Amelia is cemented to his hip—especially since the studio has her name connected to the movie."

"But, another accident might remove her not only from Krantz's plans but from Trenton as well." She couldn't withhold her scheme a minute longer. "The minor crash on PCH didn't yield any results—pity. Brakes can be so unpredictable."

"You're starting to scare me." Jessica's eyes narrowed, and, her lips parted slightly. "What are you getting at?"

"It would be a shame if Amelia has lost ..." Naomi reached into her purse sitting on the ground next to her ankles. "... this." Her hand held an epinephrine injector pen.

Jessica took it from her and read the label. Shock blanketed her expression. Her voice lowered with hardly enough breath to speak, as if she were revealing nuclear codes. "What you're suggesting is just shy of murder."

"Yes ... just shy." She took the medication from her friend and replaced it in its hiding place in her purse. "I didn't say this was *actually* hers." She let out a throaty laugh. "Allergies can be such a pain—a deadly pain for some, or so I've read."

"Did you somehow steal that medicine from Amelia?" She pulled her chair closer to Naomi. "Tell me!"

"Secrets are fun." Naomi nodded to Jessica. "Let me top off your drink." She grabbed the pitcher and poured. "Enjoy the view. That muscle builder is flexing those fantastic biceps again."

~~***~~

Alex had told Jane that he would be out and that he wanted to pick out the fresh produce himself, never trusting the judgment of the shop owner as to what was ripe or spoiled as part of a food delivery. She was alone in the house with Amelia and thought she'd ask permission to stroll on the beach if she wasn't needed for a task.

Jane enjoyed her assignment, yet still had moments of uneasiness attached to it. The call she had received from the head of the department of her agency didn't set quite right with her, and then there was the car accident Amelia and Trenton were involved in on Pacific Coast Highway. But those incidents weren't enough to send her packing and off to London. She brushed her negative feelings aside. "Oddities happen to everyone without a sinister force being the motivating cause," she told herself quietly in her room.

On her way to the beach, as she was about to open the side door, there was a gentle knock. She glanced at Amelia sitting on the balcony under a large umbrella.

Looking through the peephole, she saw no one. Slowly, she opened the door. A lush green potted plant sat on the stoop. She picked it up, and searched briefly between the leaves for a card. There was none.

I wonder who left this? A neighbor? Duchess Amelia is a bit of a celebrity. Maybe a fan made this delivery.

She looked at the tall security barrier.

How did this person get in? Climb over the fence?

Jane closed the door, and promptly carried it out to Amelia, still on the balcony reading a novel.

"Milady." She took a few steps forward. "This plant was outside the door. I think it's a gift for you."

"Charming." The duchess returned to her book. "This story is jolly good. I can't stop reading."

"What is the title?" Jane tired to get a good look at the cover.

"*Redneck PI.*" Amelia's eyes moved back and forth along the printed page. "Trish Jackson writes a marvelous plot—romance, intrigue, crime, mystery—it has all of that and more, and a setting totally divorced from what I'm familiar with. Trenton might be interested in making a film based on this tale. He needs to contact the author. Maybe this Trish Jackson person could write the script."

"What about your cousin, Lord Stuart Dumont-Bradford, Milady?" *Wouldn't the duchess want to help her relative over a stranger?*

She placed the book down and slid her sunglasses slightly down her nose, exposing her eyes to Jane. "His novel needs a bit more polish before I could bring up that subject to Trent. Stuart is busy with the revisions as we speak." She chuckled. "Whether family or not, talent should always be recognized ... and rewarded."

"You're very kind, Milady." Jane looked down at the plant and then back to her mistress. "Where would you like me to put this? In the living room?"

Her brow knitted as if in thought. "No. Place it in the master bedroom. It will brighten things up a bit. After I finish this chapter, I'll take a nap. No need to turn down the bed."

"Right away, Milady." She watched Amelia adjust her sunglasses and return to reading.

In the bedroom, Jane nearly tiptoed on the plush carpet as if she were treading on sacred ground. Tending to a duchess and one associated with Hollywood would look good on her résumé if she ever found the need to seek a new assignment.

She placed the plant on the left nightstand—Amelia's side of the bed. Pleased, Jane stepped back and surveyed the placement.

Milady will have a cheerful plant to look at every morning when she awakes.

Jane fluffed the pillows and left, humming a familiar tune. She yawned. She opted for a nap instead, feeling the bright California sun would play havoc with her milky white skin. She could always stroll on the beach later when the sun wasn't so fierce.

Forty~Seven

"IS THE DUCHESS here?" Not seeing Amelia, Trenton called out as he walked from the foyer into the living room, hoping someone would answer. He heard a door open and then shut.

Jane came from the guest bedrooms' hallway, hiding a yawn with her hand. "Terribly sorry, sir. Milady said she would be enjoying a lie-down in the bedroom."

"Has she been asleep long?" He started to the master bedroom then turned for her answer.

"I would venture to guess for an hour or so." She twisted her fingers.

Jane's footsteps on the hardwood floors faded away.

Trenton paused.

Should I wake her? Maybe not. Amelia's been under a lot of stress.

He opened the door a crack. It took him a brief moment for his mind to register. "Amelia!" He flung the door open. "Oh, my God!"

His eyes darted about the room, trying to take it all in, and at the same time, he didn't want to believe it. He felt for a pulse in her neck with shaking hands. She was still breathing—just barely, thank God. He whipped out his phone and dialed 911. It rang, once, twice, three times ...

"Answer the damn fucking phone!" A pulse pounded in his head and rang in his ears.

The grotesque swelling on Amelia's body obliterated her beauty. One red welt melded into another; even her ears were swollen.

Trenton dashed to the bathroom for the lifesaving injection when the operator answered, "What is your emergency?"

He took a deep breath and tried to gain control of his voice. "This is Trenton Lowe, on Malibu Road. Amelia Hollingsworth has suffered an allergic reaction. She's barely breathing." He opened the medicine cabinet and flung items out of it. Fuck! It wasn't there.

"Mr. Lowe, we have EMS on their way from your phone's GPS. They should be there in a few minutes. Is she conscious?"

He went back to the bed and looked down at her, his heart pounding. "I don't think so." He lifted her hand. It fell back on the bed like a rag doll.

He leaned close to her ear and yelled, "Amelia, Amelia!" Trenton answered the dispatcher, "No. She won't respond."

"What is the nature of her allergy?" the calming and professional voice questioned.

"Spiders. She always has an epinephrine pen with her. I couldn't find it in the bathroom cabinet—where she always keeps it." His eyes scanned the items around the bed. "No, wait. Here's the pen— on the floor." He picked it up. "It's been used—she must have injected herself."

Why didn't she call for help?

"Fine. That's a good thing." He heard other voices in the call center's background. "Loosen any clothing she's wearing." He cocked his head. Was that a siren outside?

The doorbell rang and loud knocks sounded with a burly voice, "EMS here for an emergency."

He ran to the front door and flung it open, the phone still held at his ear. Jane rushed from her room.

"Mr. Lowe. Since EMS has already arrived, I'll end this call and let you answer their questions," the call center voice stated.

He stuffed the phone into his pocket and pointed. "She's in there."

The team of three men carrying their portable stretcher charged to the bedroom. One man spoke into a mic attached to his shirt, giving a report to what must have been a doctor.

Trenton's words came rapidly and pressured. "I found her like this. She's severely allergic to spiders, carries an epinephrine pen at all times. She must have used it." He handed the spent medication to the man. "I have no idea what bit her."

The first man took charge. "Calm down. Please stand over there." He pointed to a chair by the window. "We will do everything we can and report to the emergency doctor at Malibu Memorial."

"Why not Cedars Sinai?" This made no sense to him. Trenton wanted what he thought would be the best hospital for her.

"We are forced to bring all patients to the closest emergency facility—it's protocol." He placed a warm hand on his shoulder. "She will receive expert care. What's her name?"

"Amelia Hollingsworth." He felt a sick reality fill the pit of his stomach as her color turned to pallor circling the red swollen patches.

The paramedic at her head called out her name, "Amelia! Can you hear me?"

There was no reaction, not even a flutter of her lashes.

He watched the three men go about their duties with the precision of a finely tuned watch. An IV started in at the crook of her elbow, an injection at the IV site of what he hoped would be lifesaving medicine, a small plastic clamp on her finger, electrical wires of some sort attached to her now bare chest, a pressure cuff around her arm, and the third attempting to pass a tube down her throat.

The men's conversation floated above his head and it felt as if he were hearing a voice-over from a movie. "Can you intubate? Need to do a trach?" ... "I think I can pass it—it will be tight—lots of edema. Got it. No need for a tracheotomy." ... "BP?" ... "60 over palp. Heart rate 152. O2 sat 84." ... "Epi bolus given. Epi drip infusing." ... "She can't keep that rate up for much longer or we'll lose her. What beast bit her?"

He stared at her erratic heart rate pattern on the monitor, not understanding what it meant. He did know that it didn't look good.

One of the men looked at Trenton as he slowly squeezed what looked like an air bag in a rhythmic pattern. "What bit her?"

"I—, I don't know." He felt helpless. His mouth went dry as all his future dreams with Amelia seemed to fade into a black fog.

The other man spoke firmly. "Jack, don't move. I see it. Red hourglass on its back. Black widow."

The man they called Jack froze, barely breathing. "Those things are deadly. You don't have to be allergic to them."

His partner took a small glass jar in one hand with the lid in the other and slowly moved to the pillow by Amelia's head. In one swift movement, he trapped the killer in the container.

The other two men placed her on the stretcher and hurried out the front door.

The lead paramedic turned to Trenton. "We'll meet you at the emergency entrance. Drive safely. We don't need to be responding to a car wreck with you at the wheel."

Before he could speak, they were out the door with the blaring sirens fading as they drove off.

He stood there and stared at the open entry with lead-laden limbs, not wanting to believe any of it. Jane's stiff body caught his periphery. He glared at her with a horrified, unspoken question on his face.

"How? How did this happen? Where were you? You're supposed to be looking after Amelia." He took two slow steps towards her. "Didn't you hear her call out? She must've called for help."

"S- s- sir," her voice trembled, "I was sleeping, too. Milady said she would have a lie-down, and I decided to do the same. I heard nothing."

His eyes narrowed. "Of course you wouldn't—not with your room at the opposite end of the house. Did you or Alex spray for bugs?"

His brow knitted; whipping his head side-to-side, looking for the servant. "Where is Alex?"

"He's out food shopping. He told me he sprayed this morning while Milady was on the balcony." She grimaced and twisted her hands together.

"What is it?" He gripped her shoulders and gave a mild shake. "Tell me!"

"I— I placed a plant in her bedroom that someone left at the door." Water rimmed her eyes. "I thought it was a nice gift from a neighbor friend."

Trenton spun on his heels, and rushed back to the bedroom. He spied the plant on the nightstand and approached it slowly as if it were a nuclear weapon ready to blow at any minute.

Bending over, he examined it closely. There! He stepped back. At least six black widow spiders were crawling in the dark recesses of the leaves. "Shit!"

He turned to Jane who was now staring wide-eyed from the doorway. Somewhat nervously, he picked up the plant, holding it at arm's length and walked to the kitchen, taking care not to bump it on anything. Jane followed. He set it on the counter and backed away. "Seal it up in a plastic food bag, but be very careful. It's loaded with spiders! Black widow spiders!"

Her face held a question.

"The police will need this as evidence. I have to hurry to the hospital." Her widened eyes and dropped jaw had no effect on him. He fished for the car keys in his pocket, grabbed Amelia's purse from the foyer table, and ran out to the car.

Trenton wondered if Jane was complicit or not in Amelia's deadly encounter. All he knew was that the love of his life lay on a stretcher gasping what might be her last breaths. He shuddered at the thought of never again hearing her laugh or seeing her devilish expression that he loved so much. Tears blurred his vision as he maneuvered down the narrow road.

She has to come through this! She must!

Naomi has gone too far. She knows no limits.

I will deal with her in my own way!

She will pay for this.

Forty~Eight

TRENTON CLUTCHED AMELIA'S purse as he rushed to the reception desk of the emergency room. Bright overhead lights, crying babies, and that sterile hospital smell assaulted his senses. He didn't care that others had loved ones in dire need or not. Amelia was here and he didn't know if she was alive, dying, or already— God forbid—dead. An older nurse behind the reception desk looked up at him with a professional and kind smile. He didn't give her a chance to speak.

"Amelia. Amelia Hollingsworth was brought in for an allergic reaction. I need to see her immediately. I'm Trenton Lowe—her close friend." He heard the tremor in his voice and tried to swallow, his mouth dry.

"Do you have any identification, Mr. Lowe?" She smiled briefly.

He fumbled with shaking hands, and pulled out his wallet from his pants' pocket. He dug for the driver's license and handed it to her. She scribbled down her needed information and handed it back to him. Then she phoned what he assumed was a nurse or doctor caring for his Amelia. He tried to decipher information about her condition through the brief conversation and the nurse's expression. He knew no more than before.

"Mr. Lowe, at the sound of the buzzer, open the door to your left and follow me." She had no smile. A serious, deadly serious expression sheathed her face.

Oh, God! This isn't good.

The buzzer sang and he passed swiftly through the door and followed the nurse through a maze of drawn-curtain cubicles. Moans and crying came from them—and he wondered briefly at their stories—a car accident, drug overdose, heart attack, or whatever horrible fate had brought them here to this haven of mercy, pleading for one more chance at life.

The nurse turned and stopped at a corner bed. She pulled the curtain, revealing a woman he hardly recognized. His Amelia looked worse than before, if that was feasible. Every possible and conceivable piece of medical equipment seemed to be plugged into her frail body.

Another nurse said with a gentle, low voice. "I'm Ann .... I can imagine that all this looks frightening. Ms. Hollingsworth could not breathe. The tube in her mouth with that air compression machine attached is breathing for her. It's called a ventilator. We are watching her blood pressure and heart rate though this monitor." She pointed to the screen above the head of the bed. "The IV has medication in it to decrease her swelling and reverse her allergic reaction. The pulse-ox probe on her finger records the amount of oxygen in her blood. A urinary catheter was inserted to drain her bladder." She paused her dissertation, clearly letting him absorb all the information. "Ms. Hollingsworth is in no pain."

His tear-filled eyes turned to the nurse. "Will she be okay? Will Amelia recover?"

"Only a doctor can answer those questions." She glanced to the nurses' station and then back to Trenton. "Dr. Carter is our chief ER doctor and he contacted Dr. Rosenman, our chief allergist, who is assigned to her care and will be her primary doctor. He's here now. Would you like to speak with him?"

"Yes." Trenton wiped his red eyes with the back of his hand, his bottom lip quivering.

He watched the nurse go and say something to the doctor studying the computer screen. His breath came in huge gulps. He looked up to the paneled ceiling to fight his tears from falling and then back to Amelia. Her helplessness tore at every fiber of hope he held onto. If the medicines they were pumping into her veins were working, why didn't she look any better? Instead, she looked worse than when he found her on the bed. Were the doctors giving her the right treatment?

Why didn't I insist they take Amelia to Cedars? If I had, would she be talking to me now—making me laugh at her witty quips?

A soft voice came from behind him. "I'm Mrs. Greyson from billing."

He turned, hardly comprehending her words. A plump woman with brown hair and kind eyes held a clipboard stacked with forms and a hand-held scanning device.

"Mr. Lowe, the nurse said that you are Amelia Hollingsworth's significant other, am I right?" Her kind smile didn't soften his fear.

"Yes." He looked back at his love. His hands gripped the side rail drawing the skin tight over his knuckles, turning them white. "Look, all her medical expenses are to be sent to me. Give me the damn papers and I'll sign them."

"Certainly, Mr. Lowe." She handed him a pen and the required forms with a large X marking the areas for his signature. "By signing

where I've marked, you agree to being the primary person responsible for her medical expenses."

She pressed his arm, her voice soft and sincere. "I'm very sorry and
hope your friend will recover soon."

Trenton scribbled his name, handed the papers on the clipboard
back to Mrs. Greyson, then returned his attention to Amelia, praying
that her death wasn't inevitable. The woman turned to leave. A
thought came to him.

He opened Amelia's purse and handed her wallet to Mrs. Greyson.
"You might find info in there for her records."

Mrs. Greyson smiled, took the item, opened it, pulled out a card of
some sort, jotted down data, swiped the barcode through her
portable scanner, then handed the wallet and card back to him.

She left with quiet steps.

Dr. Rosenman approached the bedside and introduced himself.

Trenton shook his extended hand, not feeling the contact. "Will
she be okay? When will she wake up?"

"We are hopeful, that is, Dr. Carter and myself—providing she
responds to treatment. We have her on the maximum amount of
medication. Ms. Hollingsworth is in a drug-induced coma in case
there is any swelling on her brain. We won't know more until we do
more tests—that can't happen until she's stabilized. The ventilator
supports her breathing so she can rest."

"What if she doesn't respond to everything you're doing? What
then?" *This is bad—damn bad!*

"I should only be discussing these details with her closest living
relative." He shoved his hands in his pockets. "Does she have a
living will?"

"I don't know." Frustration welled up inside him. "Look, she's
going through a divorce. When she's free, we'll be married." He
hoped the doctor wouldn't notice there was no notation of an
engagement ring in her chart. "Her estranged husband is in London.
It's difficult to contact him. I'm her only friend here. I'm the *only*
person who cares if she lives or dies." Pleading painted his face.

Dr. Rosenman let out a ragged breath and ran his hand through his
silver hair, looking down at the floor as if he was deciding if he
should discuss Amelia's situation with him, and then turned his
attention to Trenton. "It could be grim. If the medication fails to
relieve the edema—swelling that is, and fails to neutralize the poison
in her, she could go into multi-system failure—all her organs will
stop working as they should."

I'm not believing any of this. It can't be true—not to Amelia. "What is the likelihood of her not getting better? Be honest, doctor. I need to know."

"Fifty-fifty at best. We'll know more in twenty-four hours—thirty-six at the longest." He bit his lip as he looked at his severely ill patient. "She will receive the very best care. We're transferring her to ICU in a few moments. The nurses are finishing the necessary forms now. She's received anti-venom vaccine—multiple doses. Both Dr. Carter and I will continue to supervise her progress." He patted Trenton's shoulder. "We will be checking with the nurses frequently. Orders are written for two nurses to be in attendance at all times."

"Two nurses?" *This is sounding worse by degrees. What is he holding back?* "Isn't that unusual?"

"As I said, Mr. Lowe, we are giving your fiancée the best care." He started to leave. "You'll be able to go along during the transfer. I'll be up there shortly."

A male voice came from behind him. "Excuse me, sir, I'm a respiratory therapist. I need you to move away so I can prepare her for the transfer to her room." Trenton watched Amelia's chest rise and fall as the therapist disconnected the ventilator and attached an air bag, squeezing it slowly and releasing it as the paramedic had done at his home. "This is called an ambu bag. It will breathe for her until I reconnect her to a ventilator in her room."

An orderly and two nurses appeared and helped to prepare Amelia for her journey to her new room in ICU. They wasted no time in boarding the elevator to the second floor, a nurse on each side of the stretcher, keeping close eyes on the portable monitor resting on the blanket at Amelia's feet. They walked so fast he felt they were just shy of a fast jog—which increased his fear.

Trenton read the signage and realized the operating rooms were on the same floor. This gave him no additional comfort in knowing emergency surgery rooms were close to the ICU. He reasoned that any needed operation would only indicate her deteriorating condition.

He held her purse tightly, fingering the straps, as if in some miraculous way, this caressing of something of hers would create a magical power causing her to wake up and recover in minutes. He knew it was a silly thought and on the same level as children who avoided stepping on pavement cracks to keep their mothers free from injury.

He perched on a chair in the corner near the head of the bed, feeling small and helpless, and watched at least six people scurry around Amelia, attaching the same type of equipment he had seen earlier, emptying her urine bag, then writing something down on a scrap piece of paper pulled from a pocket, checking her IV site in her still grossly swollen arm, then applying ointment to her lips and her swollen-shut eyelids. He was relieved to see the ventilator was again causing her chest to rise and fall with unwavering accuracy.

After all was connected, the respiratory therapist stood by the head of the bed adjusting various dials for what Trenton believed to be the best settings to keep Amelia breathing. Two nurses remained. He answered one of the nurse's questions about Amelia as best he could and watched her record them on the bedside computer. Trenton knew they had introduced themselves, but he had forgotten their names as soon as the words left their lips. He read their nametags to jog his memory.

He looked up at the older nurse standing at the bedside, double-checking the ventilator settings. "Pat, may I stay here." He raised his brows in a pleading gesture. "I don't want to leave her. I *won't* leave her."

Her warm smile reassured him. "Yes. Both doctors wrote orders that you are permitted to stay as long as you like, whenever you like. I'll be personally taking care of her with Barbara. If her swelling worsens, we'll need to cut off her wedding ring. Here are the items we removed. Please sign the paper attached and give it back to me. That form merely states that you now have possession and responsibility of the listed items." She handed him a clear bag containing Amelia's jewelry. He scribbled his name where needed. The other nurse smiled, and returned to her charting.

Pat looked kindly at him. "I suggest you find some time to rest. You'll be doing Ms. Hollingsworth no justice if you become ill. Would you like a cup of coffee or a soda?"

He shook his head. "I can't rest at home—not yet anyway." He gazed at Amelia as he spoke. "Pat, you're the charge nurse. Is it typical for charge nurses to care for a patient? Don't you run the ICU?"

"Ms. Hollingsworth is a special case. The nurse manager will be arriving to take over my position." She smiled warmly again. Her kind eyes couldn't veil the truth he saw.

Does Pat expect Amelia not to survive the next few hours?
This will be the longest night of my life ... and the most tortuous.

Forty Nine

TRENTON STAYED AT Amelia's bedside the entire night. He couldn't really sleep with the bellow-like swooshing noise of the ventilator pushing in air and then sucking it out of her lungs. When he did doze off, the nurses checking the various monitors and her vital signs interrupted his sleep. Though he had no medical knowledge, he knew the decreasing hourly amount of urine that the nurses emptied and measured from the catheter bag couldn't have been a good sign. He wondered if this was one of the first signs of multi-system failure that the doctor had warned him about earlier.

The first night nurse came in and hung another small bag of IV medication, connecting it to a port in the main IV tubing. He rubbed his eyes to focus on exactly what it was—maybe a new wonder drug that would miraculously bring Amelia back from the brink?

The nurse must have anticipated his question. "Dr. Rosenman ordered new steroid medicine." She jotted on a piece of paper, noting data that the various monitors displayed. "I'll be going off duty in thirty minutes. Pat will be relieving me. The other nurse is giving report to her now." She smiled gently. "That way, Ms. Hollingsworth is never without a nurse at her bedside."

"Is she better?" He looked at Amelia's still edema-laden face. "Her hives have gone. That has to be a good sign. Right?"

"There has been no change in her vital signs." Her brow furrowed, filling him with alarm. "No change can be a good thing. There are more doctors who will be in later—a cardiologist, pulmonologist, and a nephrologist."

"Why?" *She's dying?* "I noticed that her urine in that bag," he pointed to the drainage, "is a smaller amount each time it is emptied. Are her kidneys not working?" He looked for the slightest reaction from the nurse. "I mean, you've been pumping all these fluids in her since she came in, and her urine bag has dark orange piss in it—and not much at that. Where is all that fluid going—to her lungs or heart?"

"These are questions a doctor needs to answer. The other doctors are called in for their opinion. Dr. Rosenman wants to be certain that all areas of Ms. Hollingworth's care have not been overlooked. Consults with other doctors are quite normal."

Her answers told him nothing and created more questions. "When will Dr. Rosenman be here?"

She checked the clock on the wall. "Around mid-morning or so. Maybe around his lunch break."

"That long?" *He should be here now to see her.*

Her voice softened. "Dr. Rosenman called twice during the night and again this morning. He's keeping a close eye on her." She walked to him. "I think you need some rest. Why not relax in the visitors' lounge? I can give you a blanket and a pillow."

He looked at Amelia, hoping her eyes would open. "I'll stay here."

"I'll bring you a blanket, pillow, and a cup of coffee." She started to leave.

"Thanks. Black on the coffee is fine." He held Amelia's hand, stroking it with his thumb, and looking at her puffy fingers.

If she had accepted my ring, it would've been cut off by now.

He studied the tips of her fingers. They seemed a bit thinner just past her cuticle.

Maybe this is a good sign. I could've sworn they were just as bloated as the rest of her.

Minutes ticked away like hours. He had called the studio after the night nurse left and told them that he wouldn't be in for the day, giving the excuse of the flu. The last thing he wanted was any nosey news hound storming the hospital, and Krantz trying to figure out how Amelia's illness could be turned into a sensational news item to benefit future profits.

The thought of the spiders being planted to harm her kept playing in his mind—trying to determine how someone had climbed the fence and gotten away. Alex had told him earlier that there was no video footage. Then an idea struck.

What if the camera angle was changed? Moved by a broom or a stick?

He knew what he had to do next.

Believing that unconscious people might still be able to hear voices and sounds around them, he walked out in the hall, found a corner, and faced a wall while grabbing his phone. He tapped his contacts list and found the number.

A female voice answered on the third ring, "Malibu police. Deputy Campbell speaking. How may I direct your call?"

"This is Trenton, Trenton Lowe. I need to speak to a detective. My fiancée is in the hospital. Someone tried to kill her."

"In what way?" Background voices and ringing phones chimed in the receiver at his ear.

"She's severely allergic to spiders—keeps an allergy injector pen with her at all times." He started to pace. "Someone dropped off a plant with spiders. I have it in a plastic bag at home for the police as evidence."

Her muffled chuckle didn't go unnoticed by him and stirred his anger. "I'm not joking. Are you going to send a detective to Malibu Memorial or not? Her name is Amelia Hollingsworth. I don't know if she will live or not."

"Mr. Lowe, are you *the* Trenton Lowe of movie fame?"

"Yes. Yes, I am." *What type of asshole am I speaking with?* "That should make no difference. I am reporting a *crime*."

"I'll pass your information to our detectives. Someone should be there by the end of the day." Her tone was nonplussed and left him feeling that his complaint would end up in a circular file.

"She could be dead by then." He banged his head against the wall. "Or is that what you want—to make for a juicier case?"

She raised her voice a decimal. "As I *said*, Mr. Lowe, someone will be *there*. You can give your statement *then*."

He proceeded to give her his full name, address, and Amelia's room number. He believed that she was going through the motions to appease him. He had met types like her before.

Over two hours passed as he sat by Amelia's bedside. The only positive sign was that her urine hadn't decreased any further in output. Two nurses remained at her bedside monitoring all the data that the electronic screens displayed in bright green on a black background. They rubbed her back, turned her every two hours, propped up her back with pillows, and reapplied an ointment to her lips and eyelids.

He stared out the window and turned when he heard a masculine sound, that of someone clearing his throat.

A medium height man dressed in a rumpled navy suit that had seen better days and a shirt open at the collar with a loose hanging tie approached him with an extended hand.

"Lieutenant Mike O'Connor. Malibu PD kicked your report up to me in LAPD. You're Mr. Trenton Lowe?" He flashed his badge, then angling his head, looked at her. "And this is Amelia Hollingsworth?"

Trenton nodded, then rose from his chair and shook O'Connor's hand. "I'm very pleased to meet you, Lieutenant. There has been an attempted murder."

Both men looked at her. The nurses appeared to ignore them and continued giving care.

The lieutenant leaned toward Trenton. "If I may, we need to go

somewhere more private. I wouldn't want to upset Ms. Hollingsworth. She might be able to hear."

"Yes. Of course." He ran his hand through his hair, then bent over
and kissed her swollen hand.

Pat suggested they talk in the quiet room, not far from the nurses'
station, used by families and clergy members.

At last! O'Connor will get to the bottom of this!

Naomi will get what she deserves! I'm certain of it ...

Fifty

"MR. LOWE, WHAT makes you think that there was an attempt on Ms. Hollingsworth's life?" They sat in the ICU's quiet room with a small table between them. "Does she have any enemies? Any threats before?" O'Connor patted several pockets before taking out a small notepad and pen from his inside jacket pocket. He let out an embarrassed laugh. "I'm always looking for something to write with. Can't seem to remember where I place things. Drives the wife nuts." He posed his pen on the paper. "As I said, does Ms. Hollingsworth have any enemies?"

"The first person who comes to mind is my ex—Naomi Lowe. She has never accepted our divorce." Seeing the pamphlets on death and dying on the few tables in the lounge unnerved Trenton. Somehow clutching her purse brought him comfort. It smelled of her.

"Would you mind writing down your former wife's name, address, and phone number on this pad?" The detective handed the small notebook to him. "I don't want to miswrite that information myself. Got to get all the facts correct. Where were you when Ms. Hollingsworth was bitten by the spider?"

"I was at the studio in a meeting discussing possible media coverage for the film—TV interviews that might boost sales and keep the movie on top for a few weeks longer." Trenton talked as he wrote as if he couldn't get the information out quick enough. "There have been questionable happenings surrounding Amelia." He handed the pad to Mike O'Connor.

"What exactly?" The lieutenant's eyes narrowed as he stroked his chin.

"Well, first there was this young guy—a jerk pestering her in public—blatantly flirting on more than one occasion." He let out a labored sigh. "I tried to keep her out of the limelight—her private life at any rate. No one but her immediate family and myself knew of her allergies—wait—I take that back. Alex, my houseman, and Jane, her maid knew, of course—no one else—I'm certain of it."

"How many times did this unknown man pester you?" O'Connor's brows drew together.

Trenton watched him scribble. "Twice ... maybe three times. Then flowers—roses arrived with no ID of the florist, and cards inserted with suggestive messages."

The detective looked up. "Do you still have those cards? Might be able to get an ID as to the perp based on the handwriting or a fingerprint. Even a trace of DNA might be discovered if the person licked their fingers before touching the card. Those evidence guys in the department can find the most incredible things from a scrap of paper to a piece of lint."

He shook his head. "No. I threw them out along with the flowers. Then there were the brakes of my car failing, and the seatbelt latches didn't work properly—came unhooked. We—Amelia and I—nearly went to our deaths over a cliff on PCH."

"How does that tie into this?" He inclined his head with a knitted brow. "Brakes failing aren't unusual."

"My car was in the shop a day or two before." *He thinks I'm overreacting. I can feel it.* "The mechanic later said he saw some young punk sniffing around my car in the lot, but he was unable to say for sure that the vehicle was tampered with. There is a police report about the accident, but I don't think the Malibu PD detectives believed it was sabotage."

O'Connor passed the notebook back to him. "Please write down the mechanic and garage's name, address, and phone number."

Trenton continued his story as he jotted down the information. "Then my ex-wife appeared in the ladies' room at the premiere party, and knocked over Amelia's purse. They were both in the ladies' room at the time. The contents fell out, and Naomi insisted on placing the items back in Amelia's bag. Next thing Amelia knows, she's missing the medication she had in her bag. She has it with her constantly. I *know* Naomi stole it." His eyes widened, emphasizing his last statement before returning the pad back to O'Connor.

He related events the best he could to the lieutenant, feeling that his words would be chalked up as coming from a person quick to make fanciful assumptions. "The last occurrence was with a plant that appeared on my doorstep without any note or explanation of any sort. Jane—Amelia's lady's maid, brought it into the house, thinking it was some sort of gift, and placed it in the bedroom— right next to Amelia's side of the bed, on the nightstand. As you can see, she's deadly allergic to spiders. The plant was crawling with spiders—black widows. I told Jane to place the plant in a zipped food bag for police evidence. That plant with those spiders was the weapon to murder Amelia!"

"We don't know that for certain." O'Connor leaned in closer. "Mr. Lowe, have you taken any steps to increase security?"

Why is he asking this? "I hired a PI, and increased the camera surveillance at my home. The cameras showed nothing."

"What's the name of the PI you contacted?" O'Connor's eyes pierced into Trenton—a feeling he began to detest.

Trenton scribbled the PI's name and number on the pad. "The cameras didn't record anyone climbing the fence to deliver that deadly plant. I've been in contact with my houseman Alex, and he checked."

O'Connor's brows rose. He looked reflective and impervious to Trenton's concerns. "Could be someone who knows your home and how to avoid them, maybe used a pole to change the angle so they wouldn't be seen."

Was that pity or disbelief in his eyes?

O'Connor continued as he scratched his knitted brow. "This might be nothing at all. Spiders are not unknown to Malibu, L.A., or the entire country, for that matter. Anything else you can think of?"

"Well, she has a cousin she loathes, Clive in London—Clive Bradford, the Duke of Bryningmead." He took a deep breath. "I doubt he'd be able to cause problems from the UK."

"Yes. That's unlikely." O'Connor rose, took a business card from his pocket, and handed it to Trenton. "Call me if you think of anything—anything at all." He started to leave, then turned before opening the door. "This is most likely a case of horrible coincidence. But we'll check out all the facts."

"If she dies, it will be murder." Trenton stood to follow him out.

"Let's hope that doesn't happen, Mr. Lowe." He stepped into the hallway, then paused in thought. "Just how deep do these bad feelings go between you and your ex? If she was locked up somewhere, your life would be easier, wouldn't it?"

"We don't get along—but nothing would make me want to frame her for a crime and certainly not enough for me to cause harm to Amelia. I know Naomi's at fault." Trenton dug his hand in his pocket, fingering his keys. *He thinks I set this all up?* "Lieutenant O'Connor, have you always worked out of LAPD?"

"I transferred from Tampa PD." He chuckled lightly. "Wife got tired of dealing with hurricane threats, and the humidity. Been out here for a few months learning my way around." He must have seen the concern on Trenton's face. "Don't worry. If there was a murder attempt, I'll get to the bottom of it. Been snooping for most of my life." He started to leave, taking a few steps, then turned around. "I love your movies. Wife sees them all the time." He rubbed his thumb against his furrowed brow. "Since the duchess endorsed the film your studio just released, this *accident* will without doubt make the film more popular—more profit for the studio." He tilted his head and arched an eyebrow. "Let's face it ... studios are in the business to make money. I'm not saying that is what happened, you understand ... still it is a thought ...." He turned back one more time. "We'll be in touch, Mr. Lowe. Don't worry about that—we'll definitely be in touch."

What exactly is he getting at? This was a put-up job? He's an old rookie type—probably was kicked out of Tampa PD and is out here starting over. I bet he doesn't even know where PCH is located!

~~***~~

Before returning to Amelia's bedside, Trenton thought of notifying Alistair of her grave condition. It would be the decent thing to do. Yet he inwardly cringed at the idea of speaking with the soon-to-be ex in her life.

He took her cell from her purse and swiped the contacts list, found the number he wanted, and dialed. It rang several times before there was an answer.

"Duchess Amelia. What can I do for you?" He slurped something. "I needed a break from reading the sports' stats."

"Is this Joe? Joe Winton?" He started to pace two or three steps in each direction.

"Yeah. Who's callin'?" His voice was gruff, but not unpleasant.

"I'm Trenton Lowe. We met at the premiere party." He shifted his weight and leaned against the wall, his chin nearly on his chest. "Amelia had a terrible reaction to a spider bite. She's in Malibu Memorial—I'm calling from the hospital. I don't know if she'll pull through."

There was a moment of silence before Joe said, "That's tough, man. I must tell Tay and Larry." It sounded like Joe turned off a radio or something. "How can I help y'?"

"She's divorcing Alistair—should be final in a week or two. Even so, he should still know about her condition." *If Alistair knows, will he contest the divorce at the last moment?* "I don't want to call him directly because of my relationship with her. Would you call him for me? If you're not comfortable with that—don't sweat it."

"Tell y' what ... I'll call Stuart, you were at their weddin'." He coughed into the phone. "It will go down better from him."

"I just finished talking with Lieutenant O'Connor." He stared down at the floor.

"Mike O'Connor?" Joe's voice held alarm.

"Yes. That's his name." *What's wrong with O'Connor?*

"What the hell did y' talk to him for? He's out in Tampa." Joe's shrill voice sent a chill through him, bristling the hairs on his neck. "How is he connected to this?"

"Lieutenant O'Connor showed up at the hospital. Said he transferred from there to L.A." Exasperation rose in him. "I think spiders were planted to kill Amelia. I reported this to the police and they put O'Connor on the case."

"He's a snoop, all right—a fuckin' dog on a bone. Nothin' gets past him. O'Connor likes to keep y' off balance—his friendly style. He must've got promoted since Tampa." Joe's voice lowered. "You think someone did this deliberately to her?"

Trenton explained about the plant and the spiders. "Whoever is responsible knew she didn't have her second epinephrine pen and there wouldn't be a high enough dose in one."

His strident voice hammered Trenton's ears. "The duchess been talkin' to me 'bout some things that've been goin' on, but you're talkin' murder, man. That's a bad load of shit."

"It is definitely an attempt on her life. I'm sure of that." So far, talking with Joe did next to nothing to ease his fear.

"Who y' think the killer is? Clive?" Joe took a breath. "Just so y' know, I'm writin' all this down."

"Not Clive—he's too far away. I'm certain it's Naomi, my ex. She's always been half crazy. Now, she's a full-blown nut—a dangerous nut." He took a deep breath. "I didn't appreciate O'Connor intimating this was a studio stunt gone wrong or that I was trying to frame Naomi."

Joe remained silent as if thinking before answering. "That's him, all right. Sniffin' 'round—checkin' everythin' out. Don't worry 'bout him thinkin' you did somethin' wrong. He's just tryin' to keep y' off your pins—messin' with your head."

"How did you meet him?" *Was Joe in trouble with the law?*

"Rather not say. Gotta go. I'm prayin' for y' and Amelia. Hope she feels better fast. She's a good person and don't need this hell."

Knowing that Joe knew the lieutenant, and described him as if he was a force to be reckoned with, reassured Trenton and lessened his fears—but not by much. Her life still hung in the balance.

A DAY HAD passed since O'Connor's fact-finding mission. Sitting at her bedside, Trenton believed Amelia looked better. Did he dare hope she was on the mend and not rallying before her death? He had heard of seriously ill patients seeming to recover and then the next day they were gasping their last.

She had been off the ventilator for hours with no indication of complications reversing her recovery. Her generalized swelling had subsided. Most importantly, she was conscious, although the breathing tube had left her complaining of a sore throat, wincing whenever she tried to speak.

"Don't try to talk yet, if it hurts. The nurse said that tube would make your throat feel raw." He pulled his chair closer, taking her hand in his. "Sorry about forgetting your toiletries. I was too concerned about you. I haven't been home yet to get them."

"Yes. I remember the nurse telling me that about my throat." Amelia made a face as she swallowed. "I don't need brushes and combs. You're here and that's what's important." She lifted her free hand, moving it from back to front slowly. "My fingers look normal."

"All of you looks normal to me ... and it's wonderful from where I'm sitting." He stroked her lower arm. "You had me scared. Terrified." His eyes watered, fighting the tears back. "I thought you might be out of my life forever."

"Not me." Her voice was raspy and she swallowed hard, scrunching her face as if in pain. "We have too much history yet to write."

Dr. Rosenman entered the room, holding a chart. He opened it up, flipping through the pages. "I have good news." His lips tugged at a smile. "All your lab results are back to normal range. I see no reason why you can't be released tomorrow."

Trenton's heart raced. "Why can't she come home now?"

"I want to be certain her vital signs remain stable. I don't anticipate any complications." He turned his attention to Amelia. "You may not recall all the details that brought you to the hospital. That's normal. Some of those facts might never return. It's the brain's way to safeguard you against the psychological effects of trauma. In a

way, that can be good. You don't need to be plagued by nightmares."
He glanced at the overhead monitors for a moment. "The soreness
in your throat should subside in a day or two. Over-the-counter
lozenges ought to help." He scribbled on a pad as he talked, then
handed the piece of paper to her. "This is a new prescription for
epinephrine pens. You should definitely have more than two pens
with you. Never go anywhere without three—not with your severe
allergy. As before, if you use your epi pen, call 911 and get to a
hospital. Call me with any concerns—no matter how minor. You
both have my card."

Amelia nodded. "I understand."

"I'll be certain she's never without them." Trenton patted her
hand. "I don't ever want Amelia to go through this again."

The doctor said something to the two nurses in the room then left.
At that moment, Trenton's phone rang.

"What is it? I told you I'm sick—at home with the flu. I can't think
of everything." He winked at Amelia. "No. Get the AP to handle it
... What? ... I'll be back when I'm back. If you have to, kick it up to
Krantz."

He put his cell back in his pocket.

"I don't, don't," she made a face as if in pain again, "want to keep
you from the studio. You have work responsibilities."

"Stop it right there." His jaw set. "No responsibility is more
important than caring for you—keeping you safe. There will always
be other jobs—there is only one *you*." He chuckled. "In case you
haven't noticed, you're special to me—very special."

"I know." She swallowed and motioned for the water at her
bedside. He handed her the glass and watched her take a couple of
painful gulps. "That's better. Back to what you said, I feel the same,
too."

"Then accept my ring." He started to reach in his pocket. Her
hand on his arm stopped him.

"Not yet. Not here." She took a labored breath. "I still don't know
if Alistair will contest the Decree Nisi. We should know in a few
days. Then you can place that ring on my finger, properly."

I wish she wasn't so damn difficult. "As you wish. But sooner or later,"
his finger playfully touched the tip of her nose, "you *will* be Mrs.
Trenton Lowe. As far as I'm concerned, that day can't come soon
enough."

"Patience." She squeezed his hand. "All good things come to
those—"

He finished her sentence, "... who wait. Waiting has never been my forte."

Trenton stood and gently kissed her lips. A gruff cough caught their attention, breaking the tender moment.

"I'm sorry to intrude." Lieutenant Mike O'Connor stepped to the foot of her bed. He flashed a polite smile to the nurses, then looked at Amelia and Trenton. He showed his badge as before, then handed his card to Amelia. "I'm Lieutenant Mike O'Connor, Ms. Hollingsworth. I need to ask you some questions. We can speak alone, if you prefer."

Her raspy voice pierced the air. "I'll do my best. I can whisper. I want Trent to remain." She looked up at him. "I warn you, lieutenant, my memory is not what it was."

The two nurses quietly left.

Trenton inched forward in his seat. "Can't this wait, lieutenant? She only recently had her breathing tube removed and her throat hurts when she talks."

"Trent," she touched his arm. "I can speak for myself. Let Lieutenant O'Connor get on with his duties. He has a protocol to follow—heaven knows—I'm an expert on protocol and how to break the rules."

"Fine." He glanced at Trenton, and then back to Amelia. Patting his pockets, he finally took out his trusty notepad and pen. "Do you know of anyone who would want to harm you? Anyone at all?"

"My cousin, Clive in London," she whispered. "His name is Clive Bradford, master of self-importance and blatant rudeness." She managed a smile. "I highly doubt he would travel out here to cause trouble for me—not when he's doing important research and working on some hush-hush project for MI6."

"So there is no one else?" He continued to write while firing out questions. "Someone who you might have slighted in some way?"

"There was this young man, in his early twenties, who pestered me on three separate occasions." She patted Trenton's hand, looking at him with pride. "My lord and savior took care of that."

"Please tell me what happened, to the best of your recollection." He glanced at Trenton as she spoke.

"A rude man came up to me while we were at a restaurant, sitting at an outdoor table, and made a comment that Trent was an old man and I could do better by being with him." A broad smile triggered her lips. "Trent took him by the shirt collar and escorted him away."

"What was the name of the restaurant?" O'Connor's pen flew along his notepad.

Trenton answered for her, "The Blvd restaurant of the Beverly

Wilshire Hotel."

"And the other two instances?" He looked directly at her.

"Once when I was clothes shopping by myself on Rodeo Drive. Another time, when I was out with Trent on Santa Monica Pier." She chuckled and looked at Trenton with smugness. "Trent gave him a right pop on the nose. I took a picture of him on my mobile."

"Which I happen to have right here," Trenton interjected. He handed the purse to her. She pulled out the phone and scrolled to the photos. "Here he is—that lout."

O'Connor took the phone.

"Ma'am, would you please send that picture to my phone?" He handed her a piece of paper with his information on it. "This will help me a great deal. We can run this through the facial recognition software." He glanced at Trenton and then back to her. "Computers are wonderful things. I've never been able to really figure them out—my grandkids are still teaching me."

Trenton didn't appreciate his disarming approach.

What is this guy getting at? Talking about computers when there is someone out there who wants Amelia dead? Ridiculous!

"Flowers were delivered, roses, with suggestive messages. There was no identification on the card or the box as to who sent them, nor the florist." She reached for the water glass and took a large swallow. "There was a spider plant that arrived. I thought that was Clive's sick joke. He knows my allergy to spiders. After Mum died, when I was little, he would chase me around, pretending he had a spider in his hands. He can be quite diabolical."

"Do you remember the moment you were bitten or when you noticed a reaction?" The detective kept jotting down notes.

"I recall that I lay down to take a nap. Jane, my lady's maid, had placed a gift from a neighbor, a plant on the night table next to my side of the bed. I fell asleep. Then I woke finding it extremely difficult to breathe. I went to the bathroom for my medication, returned to the bed, injected my thigh, and the next thing I remember is waking up in the hospital with this horrid sore throat. I vaguely thought of calling someone, but must have passed out shortly after giving myself the injection."

Trenton interrupted, "Lieutenant O'Connor, that was the plant I told you about—the one in the plastic zipped bag—evidence that someone is trying to murder Amelia."

"Murder is a strong word, Mr. Lowe." He furrowed his brow. "Let's see where the evidence leads. As I mentioned, coincidence can account for a lot of this." He turned back to Amelia. "Are there any bad feelings between you and the movie studio that produced *Duchess in Love,* the movie you endorsed? Anything that they wanted you to do? Something that you refused?"

"Not in the least." She sat up straighter in bed. "I don't like what you're intimating. I'm on excellent terms with the studio and so is Trent. I have given them no cause to dislike me."

O'Connor rubbed his forehead with his thumb. "I don't mean to upset you, Ms. Hollingsworth. But ... I need to cover all possible angles—even the ones that seem out from left field." He looked down at the floor and then back up to them. A sheepish smile formed. "If I may, the wife's a collector of autographs." He tore off a piece of paper from his pad. "May I have both of your signatures? It would make her so happy and get me out of the doghouse for forgetting our anniversary a few days ago. Please make it out to Karen O'Connor."

Trenton signed first, then passed the pen and paper to Amelia. She scribbled her name with a flourish and handed the autographs to the detective.

"Thanks. She'll be very pleased. Will probably tell me we should've moved out to L.A. a long time ago." He scratched his head. "Funny, I obtained Larry Davis' autograph a while back. Got me out of a scrape with her birthday." He tilted his head and narrowed his eyes, which didn't set well with Trenton. "Did he ever mention that to you, Mr. Lowe?"

Amelia and he exchanged glances, then looked at the lieutenant.

He shifted in his seat at the bedside. "No. He never did."

"What an odd thing to bring up, lieutenant." Amelia looked serious and not forthcoming.

"Just making small talk, you understand." O'Connor's casual smile didn't ease Trenton's apprehension. "Sometimes, small talk can reveal valuable facts." He started to leave, then turned at the doorway. "Ms. Amelia, if you remember anything else, please call me. You have my card."

"Certainly, lieutenant." She watched him leave as the nurses re-entered.

Trenton held her hand. "Larry and Taylor called. They hope you recover quickly and send their love—Joe, too."

"They're dear friends—the best friends I have outside of Elizabeth." She looked to the ceiling and then back to Trenton. "I hope Mike O'Connor will unearth the facts."

"His investigation runs deep." Trenton rubbed his brow. "I have a feeling it's in the wrong direction."

"It could be as he said, or more correctly, as Shakespeare wrote, '... full of sound and fury signifying nothing ...'. He strikes me as having a bit of *Sherlock Holmes* in his veins," Amelia said, squeezing his hand.

"I hope you're right." He kissed her cheek. "As long as he gets to the bottom of whatever it is, he can dig as deep as he wants."

Why did he investigate my relationship with Larry? How does he even know that I've met him? Joe's right—he's a force to be reckoned with.

Fifty~Two

JANE PACED IN her room. Everything that had happened since her arrival weighed heavily on her, and each passing day made her feel less secure with fear blooming deep within. She didn't know what to make of the mysterious happenings to Amelia and was terrified that if there was someone who wanted her mistress dead, she would be caught in the crossfire and become a target. Hair on her arms rose. She made a decision and knew it was correct.

She fished the phone from her bag and dialed the number. A moment passed before the ring-ring tone sounded in her ear.

"Jane Denton speaking. I'd like to speak to the head of assignments." She continued to walk around her room, clicking a pen in her hand.

"Thank you for holding. This is Mrs. Branson. How might I assist you, Miss Denton?" The voice was friendly and yet professional.

"I need to return to London." *I hope she won't be difficult.*

"Is there a problem with your assignment? Are they not happy with your service?" The tone changed to a near reprimand.

"No, no. Nothing like that." *I don't want a negative mark on my record.* "It is family concerns. I need to return promptly." *Can she tell I'm lying?*

"Have you given two weeks' notice?" She heard the clicking of computer keys. "That is what all our employees are required to give their employers. It's printed in your contract when you joined this agency."

"No. But they are fine with it." Her throat tightened. Lying was not her strong suit. "I don't do much for the duchess, other than lay out her clothes, light mending, and serve tea. She really doesn't need me. As I mentioned, I need to return to England for family issues."

"Well, her anonymous benefactor thought you would be of some service." Her firm tone grated on Jane's nerves. "Otherwise you would have never been sent on this assignment. Truthfully, many young women would jump at this plum situation, living in Malibu near Hollywood and caring for a duchess."

"I'm more than happy to have one of them replace me." Jane took a deep breath.

I shouldn't have said that. She might take me off the agency's roster.

"It is not that easy." She sounded exasperated. "I will need to contact the person paying for your service first—that takes time. Your replacement must have the proper credentials to attend to a duchess."

"I am very sorry. I have already booked my flight for tomorrow." She bit her lip and screwed up her face. "I'm returning to London. This can't be helped."

"May I ask what this particular situation is that has forced you to leave your assignment so abruptly and place a mark against this agency?"

"No, you may not." Her agonized breath escaped. "It is personal and not something I wish to share."

"Is the duchess agreeable to you leaving your post—leaving her to fend for herself?"

She's putting me through the bloody meat grinder.

"Her grace is completely agreeable," she lied. Jane took her suitcase from the back of the closet as she held the phone.

"There will be no further remuneration, as I don't expect your employer to provide any." Her steely voice sent a chill through her, but not enough for Jane to change her decision.

"That is fine with me." She pulled open the dresser drawers, the phone pressed to her ear, placing the folded clothes on the bed with her free hand.

She wouldn't be reacting like this if she knew my fear. Still, it's not my secret to tell. The first rule of service is to never disclose a confidence.

"Since you're so firm about this ..." Mrs. Branson's tone was just short of rude.

"I am." *At last! She's ending this call.*

"I will call your employer tomorrow and notify him you have a family emergency." There was more clicking of keys over the phone.

"Thank you so much for understanding." Jane placed items in the suitcase. She didn't want to stay another night here, but had no-where else to go.

With the dreaded call ended, she swiftly finished packing, then scribbled a message to Lady Amelia on the notepaper in her room. She was sorry that there was no envelope to keep her comments more private.

Jane walked to the kitchen. No one was there. She crept down the hall and turned into the media room. She found Alex sitting on the sofa watching a movie and stuffing handfuls of popcorn into his mouth as the images traveled across the screen.

He patted the cushion. "Join me. This one is a classic. *Ben Hur—*

got it from Mr. Lowe's library."

She eased onto the cushion beside him. "Alex, I'm leaving tomorrow."

"Going on vacation for a few days? When will you be back?" His eyes remained fixed on the screen.

"No. Not exactly," she shuddered. "I need to go home to London. My family needs me."

Alex straightened up and looked at her. "I'm sorry. Is it serious?"

She couldn't look at him. Alex had been kind to her. She had always hated lying to anyone, especially to those who were nice. "It's serious enough for me to leave." She swallowed hard. "I'm using the return ticket the agency gave me when I first accepted this assignment. I need to go first thing, around six in the morning." She looked at him. "Can you drive me to the airport then? If not, I can get an Uber. I'd rather have you drive me instead of Tom."

"Sure thing. I'll drive you." He adjusted his position, angling to see more of her face. "I hope whatever it is, that your family will be okay."

She handed him a note. "Please give this to her grace when she returns. Tell the duchess and Mr. Lowe that I'm very sorry. I've enjoyed being in service to her—I have no choice. I must leave."

"For what it's worth, I've enjoyed having you around." He patted her shoulder.

"Thank you, Alex." She smiled. "You're a nice person. I'll miss you."

Jane had never felt any love toward Alex in a romantic sense. He was more like the big brother she never had.

~~***~~

"Are you ready to leave?" Trenton started gathering Amelia's clothes from the hospital room closet.

"I'm more than eager." Amelia eyed the nurse. "When are you going to remove that IV tube in my arm? I'm fit and ready to raise some bloody hell." She flashed a suggestive glance to him.

"All in good time." Pat typed on the computer keyboard. "The doctor is just finishing up your discharge orders. Then you'll need to sign a few papers which contain your instructions for after-care and any follow-up appointments with Dr. Rosenman."

Amelia looked at the clock on the wall. "Half the day will be gone before I'm free of this ruddy hospital gown."

Trenton handed her a brush from the bath and personal supplies the hospital had provided her. "Brush your hair and don't worry. It won't be long."

"Every moment here is one less moment at our home." Her eyes pleaded. "I want to smell the sea air, feel the breeze, and have your arms around me as we both enjoy our little paradise."

"My very thoughts." He winked. "Look, Duchess. I have all your clothes laid out. Jane couldn't have done any better."

She arched an eyebrow. "Well, it's not bad for a novice." A devilish smile curled at her lips. "Speaking of Jane, we might have to send her back to London."

"Why? Did she displease you?" He paused with her shoes in his hands.

"Elizabeth is arriving tomorrow. I sent her tickets." She grimaced, hoping he wouldn't object. "She's bringing Rodney, too."

"Well, you are one for surprises, aren't you? Who's Rodney? Her boyfriend or husband?" He straightened out her dress at the foot of the bed.

"A loveable King Charles spaniel." She pouted, hoping to soften any refusal. "He is so sweet and won't be a problem."

"He's a dog. Dogs have fleas and God knows what in the line of bacteria." He put his hands on his hips. "Have you forgotten most of my—no *our* home is decorated in white?"

"I can top that one. Most of my décor in the London townhouse consists of antiques and satins." She pouted again. "He's very good. He even stands by the door waiting for his hands and feet to be wiped before walking into the house." She took her phone from the over bed table and scrolled to her pictures. "Here," she handed the mobile to him. "How can you resist such a loveable face? Look at those big brown eyes."

"Yes. He does look sweet." Trenton furrowed his brow and grimaced. "Trouble is, you fall in love with this cute little being, and then they die on you."

"Yes. That's difficult." She gently touched his arm. "Think of all those years of love and memories they give you. It's the way of life—we all have to say goodbye at some point .... Did you have a pet die that you never recovered from? A childhood pet?"

"Yes. A horse named Maggie—when I was a teen. I knew she was ill. There wasn't anything that could be done." He wiped a tear before it fell. "I stayed with her all night to the end ... stroking her brow and talking gently. I like to think I helped her pass in a good way."

Amelia felt her own tears form. She pressed his arm. "You did. You gave her a precious gift. I've lost pets, too."

"My father told me to buck up and be a man." He sniffled. "I tried and put on a good face to shut him up." He sighed. "But, I never did. I still miss her and hope she's at Rainbow Bridge, enjoying green pastures." He wiped another tear away.

"That's a lovely thought." She kissed his cheek. "Hang onto that and remember Maggie as being happy."

He let out a labored sigh. "Yes. Rodney is welcome to join our family. I was just a little surprised at first, but I couldn't resist such an adorable furry face."

Trent is so sensitive. I had no idea.

Amelia looked at the nurse and noticed she was wiping a tear with her fingers.

Another nurse came into the room with papers secured on a clipboard resting on the seat of a wheelchair. "Ms. Hollingsworth. If you will sign these papers, you can get dressed and be on your way." She handed the forms to her.

"Gladly." Amelia signed and initialed in the appropriate places on the forms.

Pat reviewed her discharge instructions with the duchess, then took the IV catheter out of her arm, swabbed it, placed a large band-aid, and left the room. The other nurse assisted her with dressing while Trenton made certain Amelia had all of her personal items. She sat in the wheelchair and the nurse rolled her down the hall.

She looked up to him. "I feel free as a bird. When we get home, fix me up a smashing G and T."

"You got it." He hummed a tune she didn't recognize.

~~***~~

Amelia declined Trenton's suggestion that she rest on the bed, and sank into the big living room sofa.

"Welcome home," Alex said with his hands on his hips and a broad smile on his face. "I'm very happy to see you are okay, Milady." His grin faded when he handed her a note. "This is from Jane."

By his look, it must be serious.

She opened the folded paper and read Jane's message, then looked up at Trenton, who was standing in front of her with a raised eyebrow. "She left and went home to England. Said she had some sort of family emergency. Well, I hope all turns out properly for her. She was nice—but nothing like Elizabeth. It will be splendid to see her again."

"Did you know she had left permanently?" she asked Alex.

"Yes, she told me." His posture stiffened. "Did I do anything wrong? I couldn't keep her here."

"Of course, you couldn't. You did perfectly fine." She handed Alex an envelope from her purse. Please give this to Tom, the driver. As it happens, my trusted maid, Elizabeth is on her way and needs picking up at the airport tomorrow. All the details are in that packet."

Alex and Trenton exchanged looks. The houseman nodded, then left.

"As you requested ..." Trenton came from the bar, and handed her a gin and tonic. He smiled proudly. "See, I didn't forget."

She took a swallow and closed her eyes. "Perfect! A right proper G and T."

"I aim to please, Duchess." He sipped his own drink.

"After what recently happened with those beastly spiders, I think I'll forgo napping out on the balcony in the wee hours." She picked up a copy of *Variety* on the coffee table and leafed through the pages, not fully understanding the headlines written in Hollywood lingo.

"When did you do that?" His eyes widened. "Was I a bed hog? I'd never want to chase you from my side."

"I'd go out there to listen to the waves and clear my thoughts. It has nothing to do with you. I'd prowl the townhouse at two or three in the morning, too." She looked at him beneath her long lashes. "I won't be a duchess much longer." Amelia ran her tongue along the top edge of her teeth, her smile broadening. "If you want to ask me a question, I suggest you do it in the bedroom."

His eyes brightened. "Definitely. Are you certain?"

"Yes. Very certain. But you must ask me properly." She stood up and headed to the bedroom, then coyly looked back at him over her shoulder. "Coming?"

"Do you feel well enough for sex? Holding you would be just as good for me." His eyes darted back and forth.

"I have never felt better." Her small laugh escaped. "Ask me that question I've been avoiding, and let's celebrate in a way I enjoy the most—with our bodies—all hot and sweaty."

In their bedroom, Trenton fumbled with the box from his pants' pocket. "I wanted the presentation to be special—a fancy dinner or something."

Amelia removed her wedding band, and dropped it in the wastepaper basket by her bed. She held out her hand with a slight tremble. "The place or the ring doesn't matter—the man does—the one who is giving me his heart."

"Will you do me the extreme honor of being my wife?" He motioned his hand for her not to speak. "Are you certain? You still want to relinquish your title and live an ordinary life with me out here in Malibu?" He swallowed and licked his lips before continuing. "There will be no royal events, no garden parties to go to."

"None of that has been important to me. And, yes, I will marry you." She watched him slide the diamond onto her finger. "I didn't know until this moment—I've been waiting all my life to find a man to love me—and to love."

He kissed her softly and then more firmly. His hands unbuttoned her dress as his lips trailed kisses along her neck to the sensual hollow at the base of her throat. Eagerly, she unzipped his pants and reached inside—his arousal growing firm in her hands. The heat of his grip on her flesh, the fragrance he wore, his body drove her increasing need—an urgency to have him, and have him now without the teasing foreplay. The fabric of clothing between them became a shackle she seized.

Frantically, they undressed, tearing back the covers and tumbled onto the bed. His kisses were tender as his fingers caressed her and increased her desire. His knee parted her thighs. She gasped at the feeling of his erection against her leg. He was so near to being one with her and it drove her craving to near screaming heights. She decided not to allow him to prolong the lovemaking. She wanted him now.

He started to lower his body as if to kiss her stomach. "No," she cried. "I want you in me. I want you fucking me." Without a word, she felt him easing inside of her, bit by bit then, pulling back. Again a bit further, sliding to his hilt. She let out a heavy satisfied sigh. "Yes. That's it." She kissed his neck. Delicious sweat slipped between them. "Faster, Trent." He picked up his rhythm as her hips ground against his. "I can't hold back." Her hands grabbed his buttocks, driving him to her ultimate pleasure. She was one with him. Their hearts beat in unison as her climax rose to meet his.

He gasped into the pillow between muffled words. "I hope you are pleased. Sorry about the quickie." He lifted his head and looked in her eyes, tracing her ear with his finger.

"You always satisfy me. Quickies are great fun, too." She toyed with the damp hair at his temple. "Sex is beautiful when it's shared with love."

He gently kissed her fingertips. "*Everything* is beautiful when it's shared with love."

My life will never be the same. And, thank God for that ...

ELIZABETH HELD LITTLE Rodney in her arms as she rode in the backseat of the car that had come to collect her. He looked up at her with large brown eyes. She kissed the top of his head. *Dare I hope this new adventure might bring someone into my life who would be as loyal as little Rodney?*

Arriving at LAX and now heading to Malibu was beyond anything she had hoped would happen in her life. Even though it had been less than six months since she last saw Amelia, it seemed an eternity to her. Her mistress leaving London had made her existence boring at best with little to do.

Trenton's driver hadn't said more after his initial greeting with a tip of his hat at the airport. She forgot his name as soon as it escaped his lips. She stared out at the new and exciting scenery, thankful she had slept during most of the flight. She wondered what amazing things would happen in her new life.

They pulled up at an elaborate wrought iron gate. *This looks like a small mansion. It's no wonder why Milady wanted to stay here.*

She spoke softly into Rodney's ear, "This is your new home—*our* new home." Wagging his tail, the pup looked up at her with loving eyes. She kissed the top of his head again, enjoying the warmth of his fur and his soft breath against her chest.

The driver rolled down his window and tapped the buttons. Seconds later, the gates opened. He parked close to the house and assisted her out of the car, walking her to the front entry, where he pressed the doorbell.

Trenton opened the door, but Amelia rushed past him to give her a big hug, which nearly crushed Rodney. The driver mentioned something about unloading the bags promptly to a man who stood to the side in the foyer.

"Did you have a good flight?" The duchess took Elizabeth by the arm and led the way to the living room, opening her free arm, showcasing the floor-to-ceiling windows with their expansive view of the Pacific Ocean. "Have you ever seen a more splendid sight? Beyond the horizon, miles and miles away, is Asia."

"Never, Milady." She still held a small case in one hand and clasped Rodney with the other. He squirmed to reach Amelia. "Rodney wants to say hello." She let him down onto the carpet.

"Rodney, good boy." Her mistress bent down, petting his head and stroked his ears, and gave him a gentle kiss.

"I'm so remiss. Everyone, may I introduce Miss Elizabeth, the finest lady's maid and … my dearest friend." Smiles from the others greeted her. Amelia walked over to Trenton. "Of course you already know the most wonderful man in the world, Trenton Lowe. You've met Tom, our driver, and this is Alex, houseman extraordinaire and a fantastic chef." Elizabeth and Alex shook hands briefly. "He will show you to your room. It has a view of the Pacific, too." She shook their hands and gave a small curtsey to Amelia.

Alex said softly, "Welcome to California. It's very nice to meet you."

Elizabeth nodded with a smile. His warm handshake gave her an immediate sense of belonging.

The driver had piled the enormous amount of luggage onto the foyer floor. Elizabeth glanced at them.

"Milady, the luggage with blue ribbons is yours." She handed over the small leather case to her. "Your important jewels are packed in this one. It never left my sight. A few other bags are being shipped via FedEx and should arrive by tomorrow. I used the extra money you wired me." She bit her lip. "I hope that is all right?"

"Perfectly fine. That money was for *you*. I'll give you back what you spent on my behalf." She lifted Rodney and handed him to Trenton. "It's high time you meet the other man in my life."

Rodney planted doggy kisses on his fingers and looked lovingly up to him. "I can tell he and I will be best buds—I have a feeling about these things." He placed him on the sofa, then looked at Elizabeth. "Does he need a walk?"

"No. He had a proper stroll outside the airport." She beamed. "I can tell you and Rodney are getting on straight away."

"How old is he?" Trenton looked serious.

I hope his age won't be a problem. "He's four, Mr. Lowe. He's good, truly he is—never been a problem."

Standing behind her, Trenton placed his hands on Amelia's shoulders and gave a squeeze. "Four years is good. Rodney has many years to enjoy his home. Hard goodbyes are a long way off."

"You shouldn't feel obligated to curtsey before me much longer." Amelia flashed an enormous diamond engagement ring radiating a rainbow of lights. "Jolly soon, I'll be Mrs. Lowe. The duchess will be a mere history of boring indulgences—traded for a life of love and caring."

"Milady." Elizabeth's eyes grew wide. "I have never seen anything so beautiful—truly, I haven't." Her gaze went to her mistress' face. "You will always be a duchess to me—more like the bloody queen in my eyes."

Alex interjected, "I'll get the dog a bowl of water and then shop for the best dog food Malibu has to offer." He turned to Elizabeth. "I can show you to your room." He took her luggage, veins budging in both arms.

"Certainly, Mr. Alex." She started following him to her quarters. Rodney jumped off the sofa and trod close to her heels.

"Please, call me 'Alex'. We have no class system in this house. You're part of the family." He opened the door to her room and led the way. "If you need anything, my room is next to yours." He lifted the suitcases onto the bed. "All the bedrooms have private baths. So, set up your things any way you like."

Rodney jumped on the bed and settled onto the pillow, his tail wagging with approval. They both looked at the pup.

She laughed. "Rodney thinks his new home is right fine. He's my best mate."

Alex touched her shoulder. "We're all your friends under this roof." He smiled, then left, closing the door.

I've a good feeling about him. He's about the same age as Mr. Lowe and could be a good friend, like an older brother or uncle.

~~***~~

As she answered the front door, Naomi wondered why this strange man wearing a worn, old rumpled navy suit and a kind face would be standing at her entry.

"I'm not buying anything." She started to close the door.

He stopped her with his foot on the threshold. "I'm not selling anything." He flashed his badge. "If I may, ma'am, I'm Lieutenant Mike O'Connor investigating an occurrence involving Ms. Hollingsworth."

She gave a brief cold smile while fully opening the door. "By all means, please come in, Lieutenant. There is nothing more I would like to discuss than that whoring shrew."

He patted his jacket as if searching for something, then clumsily retrieved his pad and pen from his inside jacket pocket as she led him into the living room. "I'm always forgetting where I place these things."

She pointed to a chair. He adjusted his jacket before sitting down.

"Your name is Naomi Lowe? Do you know Ms. Hollingsworth?" He glanced around the room. "Have you ever met her?"

Naomi arched an eyebrow. "Yes to your first question. I only know what I've read in the papers and seen on TV. Never had the unfortunate experience of meeting her." She strolled over to the bar and lifted a glass. "Drink?"

"No thank you, ma'am." He tapped the face of his watch. "I'm on duty." He scribbled on the pad balanced on his knee as she poured a drink. "Other than yourself, do you know of anyone who would want to cause her harm?"

Naomi spun on her heels. Alarm beamed from her eyes. "Who said I'd want to harm her?" She took a large swallow of scotch. "She irritates me because of her association with my ex, Trenton Lowe, but nothing more beyond that." She sank onto the sofa.

"No one has said you wanted to harm her. I'm merely here gathering the facts, ma'am." His eyes narrowed. "You still love your husband?"

"I'd have him back in a heartbeat if he wasn't so pigheaded and enthralled with that damn British empty-headed crumpet." She swirled the contents of her glass. "Lieutenant, you never mentioned what has happened to that lovely example of English saintliness. Was she ill?"

Wouldn't it be wonderful if she had to return to the UK for special treatment of some kind.

"I never mentioned any illness." He leaned forward, his elbows on his knees. "What made you think Ms. Hollingsworth was sick?"

"I must have read it somewhere or heard it on the news." Alarm flashed through her like a live wire jumping on the pavement. She crossed her legs and straightened her back.

"Nothing has been publicized." He chuckled. "As I said, I'm merely trying to gather the facts, ma'am."

"I don't know more about her than what is on the Internet." Watching him jot down her comments, she took another swallow. "I did contact her cousin, Clive Bradford."

"Why would you do that?" He rocked his head and raised his brows. "I mean, if you don't like the woman, then why call her cousin?"

"I was curious." A disguised sigh escaped. "Seems there's no love lost between them. He's glad she's gone and hopes Amelia will never return. He mentioned that she needs a good spider bite to set her straight."

The lieutenant sat forward. "Why would he mention spiders? Do you have a record of contact with him?" His eyes bored into her and she didn't like it. "Phone calls? Emails?"

"Just emails." *He's getting too damn close.* "I deleted them. I guess he was making a joke about the spiders. You'd have to ask him."

"Who's your email server?" He inched closer as if trying to read her thoughts.

"It doesn't matter." Naomi huffed. "I did nothing wrong. If there's any wrongdoing—check out the duchess' past—tomes of juicy reading there."

"No problem." His face showed no opinion. "Email information is easily obtained." He stood, then turned and looked out to Manhattan Beach. "Documentation of phone calls can be found."

She joined him. "It's a beautiful view, isn't it? Too bad I have to pay a mortgage."

"Yes, ma'am. Very beautiful." He scraped his thumb along his furrowed brow. "I could be wrong on this, and please, ma'am, correct me if I am. But wasn't your home here free and clear as part of your divorce settlement from Mr. Lowe?"

"I have a son who is very expensive, lieutenant. I took out the mortgage in my name *after* the divorce." Her eyes narrowed as she tried to read his cat and mouse game. "Of course, you already knew that, didn't you?"

With raised brows, O'Connor appeared sheepish for a moment as if caught. His chuckle escaped. "Yes, ma'am, I did. A quirk of mine—digging the facts."

"I think it's more than a 'quirk'." Eager to change the subject, Naomi nodded to the view. "I never take this for granted—ocean waves, taste of salt air, all of it."

"The wife and I can't afford such a lovely home as this." He scratched his head. "Do you take walks along the beach?"

"Often." She hunched her shoulders and rubbed her upper arms as if feeling a chill. "It's very relaxing. Helps me think."

"Yes. I imagine a lot of thinking goes on when walking—a lot of thinking in this house." He looked to the right, watching the waves. "Does this beach extend all the way up to Malibu, meaning if someone wanted, they could walk from here to there?"

She laughed heartedly. "Malibu is over twenty-eight miles away. I seriously doubt anyone would take that on."

"A boat would make it faster." He looked directly at her. "Wouldn't be difficult to motor a boat up to Malibu and then walk the rest of the way on the beach. A person could enter someone's home if the doors facing the ocean weren't locked."

"What are you getting at, Lieutenant?" *I don't like the sound of this.*

"I'm clearing my thoughts ... letting my mind wander, you understand." She felt his scrutinizing gaze before he returned his pad and pen to his pocket.

"If that's all, Lieutenant O'Connor, I'm meeting a girlfriend for drinks—Jessica." *I've got to get him out of here.*

"Yes, of course." He chuckled. "You wouldn't want to keep Miss Black waiting."

He's a mind reader! "How did you know her last name?"

O'Connor shot her a snide smile. "Well, like you said, 'I must have read it somewhere or heard it on the news'." He tapped his temple. "I have a knack for details." He continued walking on to the door. "No need to see me out. I'll be speaking to you again."

He's trying to connect me to Amelia and the spiders. What if he finds out Jason helped me? Oh, my God ...

~~***~~

Amelia sat on the balcony gazing out to the night sky. Trenton was at a club having drinks with Krantz, and she enjoyed this brief solitude. The sound of the surf soothed her. She savored the times she sat in a chair or lounge at three in the morning while Trenton slept. That was her private time to gather up the new pieces of herself and glue them to the whole.

Her life seemed more perfect than she could have ever imagined. Without looking, she had found a man who loved her for who she was and she didn't have to bend to his expectations. She had been pleasantly surprised when Alistair hadn't posed any objections about the divorce. Even Clive had stayed out of the picture. Life was good and she was ready to enjoy all of it. She leaned forward when seeing a boat out on the waves.

What fool is boating at this hour with hardly any moonlight? Wait. There aren't any lights on that boat at all. What are they doing? Trying to commit suicide?

Fifty~Four

DRESSED IN A black wetsuit with black gloves, the man wasn't visible to a casual onlooker. Ebony camouflage covered his face. He stood under the pier. The case concealing his weapon was wedged under the wet wooden planks. He reached up and pulled out the binoculars from the same hiding spot. The sliver of moonlight was his friend—just enough light for his mission. Soothing waves from the black ocean induced a calm that would soon be history for one.

There she was. He was in luck. She was backlit by the house's bright interior and sat on the balcony with her eyes shut.

Maybe she's napping? All the better. I like the challenge of a moving target, but this will be better. He licked his lips and his mouth watered.

His days of surveillance had paid dividends. He knew her habits as well as he knew his own. She seldom went to bed before midnight and if she did, her habit of being restless and sitting outside on a lounge at two or three in the morning made his quest easier.

Nothing got past him. He was good at what he did and he knew it. Tailing a victim was part of the fun, as a lion stalks its prey. He'd spend days, planning, visualizing the moment was what he savored.

He listened for footsteps and held his breath. He could still hear the murmur of voices from the neighboring residences. A woman's high-pitched laugh. Footsteps on the pier. He checked his watch. Two o'clock.

Don't these fuckin' people ever sleep?

Another hour passed. He grew anxious, hoping she wouldn't rise and go into the house, making his job more difficult.

If I'm lucky, she'll sleep out there as she often does on a warm night like this.

At last, all sounds of life had subsided. He peered through the binoculars again. She was still there. He rarely allowed emotion to interfere with his task. This was different. He didn't like her.

He sighed, his breath blowing out of his mouth as if he had just taken a drag from a cigarette. He took the case from its hiding place and opened it up. The foam rubber interior kept all the parts in good working order. With smooth movements, he assembled the rifle, attaching a silencer on the end. He loaded the magazine, and chambered a round, pulled it into his shoulder and lifted it, zooming in on his target through the rifle's scope, the cold trigger warming against his finger.

He aimed at her chest. No, that was no good. Her wrist was over her heart. He edged the crosshairs of the sight to her forehead. Perfect. He leaned against the pier's piling to steady his aim. He peered through the scope again. She hadn't moved. He could make out her chest rising and falling with each breath.

The hair bristled at the back of his neck. His heart raced and his mouth again watered. A small and growing electric sensation started in his gut and spread to consume him. This was a feeling he knew well and cherished—power coiling within, ready for the ultimate release.

His finger caressed the trigger again. He swallowed his increasing saliva, then took a deep breath and held it. This was the moment he enjoyed best—when the choice of life and death was in his control. That power belonged to him and no one else.

With one slow squeeze, the bullet shot forth, barely creasing the night air with sound. A fine mist of red violently sprayed outward from the entry, flesh yielding to the perfectly placed bullet. Her head fell to the side. Blood gushed from her forehead and splattered backward as the shot passed clear though the bony target. He could barely detect human tissue behind her on the balcony and against the glass doors. He swallowed the golf ball in his throat. Satisfaction filled him, as sweet as any whore he had ever screwed. For a heartbeat, he admired the artistic purity of his creation, its divine precision.

Then, like a fine-tuned machine, he dismantled his rifle, removing the magazine, and placed them both in the case. He unzipped the wetsuit, tore it from his body, and then hurriedly wiped his face clean with a towel from a plain duffel bag, into which he stuffed the rifle and zipped it shut. Carrying it in one hand, he climbed the timbers at the end of the pier as nimbly as any lumberjack logger.

Peeking over, he saw he was alone, lifted his sack, and hoisted himself onto the platform. Within moments, he was just another beach bum with a duffle bag slung over his shoulder as he shuffled into the black night, leaving no trace of his existence.

Fifty~Five

JESSICA RANG THE doorbell repeatedly. Her fists pounded the wood panel as she screeched, "Naomi! Are you there? Is anything wrong?" She had received no answer from her numerous voicemail and email messages.

Her fearful fingers searched the bag for the keys her friend had given her. Trembling, she unlocked the door, then opened it. Jessica looked around. Nothing seemed out of place. She moved carefully up the stairs to the bedroom. Nothing wrong there. The bed was made. Coming back down, entering the living room, she searched for a note from Naomi and stopped, hardly daring to breathe. Naomi's purse lay on the coffee table. That was odd.

She must be here. She'd never leave without her pocketbook, always within her reach—especially with Jason's sticky fingers.

Jessica moved toward the patio. "What the …?" She gasped. The glass patio doors were strewn with fragments of what looked like fatty hamburger and blood splatters.

Did someone play a cruel joke and dismember an animal?

She walked closer. "There you are." Naomi appeared to be resting on a chaise lounge, but when she saw her face, she knew something was seriously wrong. *Oh my God! She's been shot!*

She flung the door open and ran to her friend, her heart thumping and kicking into a gallop, threatening to burst from her chest. It was almost too much to comprehend. Naomi's forehead had a black hole in the middle, surrounded by dark, crusted red matter. Dried blood matted her hair. She looked down and realized what she had seen on the doors were bits of bone and pink-stained brain tissue, which was also sprayed across the wooden floor. Naomi's skin had a pale yellowish waxy hue—eyes open, pupils dilated with a vacant stare. There was no mistaking the look of death. Her friend was long beyond help.

Jessica's mouth dried and she found it difficult to think clearly. That's when she saw the hole in the door. The hair at the base of her neck pricked up as it might in a cartoon Halloween cat. She couldn't bring herself to touch her dead friend's body.

After a half dozen deep breaths, she pulled the phone from her pocket, tears streaming down her cheeks. She looked at it, trying to realize she needed to call someone. With trembling fingers, she dialed 911.

Am I alone? What if the killer is still in the house!

~~***~~

Jessica sat on the step outside Naomi's front door as the forensic team went about their duties, gathering evidence. The reality was difficult for her to digest. Just yesterday, they were chatting and exchanging gossip about one celebrity or another, their laughter piercing the air. Today, her friend and closest confidant would remain as a memory with no tomorrows.

Why did this happen? Naomi wasn't a bad person—not really.

The zipped bag on a stretcher holding Naomi's body was wheeled out the front door past her. Searing tears flowed down her cheeks at the sight. Yellow tape with a notice of "Police Line Do Not Cross" in black letters isolated the area, as if all that belonged to her friend was vile, and a taped-off quarantine was needed to protect others.

She didn't want to talk to anyone, especially not to the man in a worn blue suit who had just sat down beside her.

He took out his notepad, a pen posed in his hand, ready to take down every word she spoke. She opened her swollen and red tear-rimmed eyes to see his kind, yet professional expression.

"The officer told me to wait out here—something about me not contaminating the crime scene." She clutched a damp rumpled tissue. "I guess you want to ask me questions."

"Yes, ma'am. I do. I'm Lieutenant Mike O'Connor." He flashed his badge, then took a deep breath. "The police officer who responded said that you're Jessica Black and that you found Naomi Lowe around eleven this morning. Is that correct?" His soft voice didn't ease her immense pain.

"Yes. That's correct." *Why must I go through this?* "Who would do such a thing to her?"

"That's what I'm trying to find out, ma'am." He appeared concerned and compassionate. "Do you know of anyone who would want her dead—no matter how remote?"

"Trenton Lowe comes to mind—her ex. They weren't on the best of terms, especially since him taking up with that duchess with the infamous reputation—Amelia Hollingsworth." She pulled a fresh tissue from her purse and wiped her eyes.

"Did they recently have any arguments?" He jotted on his pad, looking at her between notes.

"Oh, yeah. He came over here twice since that bitch moved in with him. Yelling and telling her to lay off Amelia." She blew her nose.

"But she didn't back down. Naomi, Naomi," she started crying once more, "told me what she did."

"What was that, ma'am?" The lieutenant touched her arm as if to encourage her.

"It was all innocent—high school pranks." Jessica blew her nose again. "She had some young guy flirt with that bitch, and send flowers with racy messages. She even researched the Net and discovered Amelia didn't like spiders—some allergy or another." Jessica took a deep breath as her lips trembled. "When I heard about Trenton's car accident, at first I thought that was her doing—but she would never do that. She only wanted to pester them—nothing more." Her voice pleaded Naomi's case. "Whatever she did—it was for the right reasons. He broke her heart. She always hoped that someday they would get back together."

"Ma'am, did you know that Amelia Hollingsworth recently almost died from a spider bite? What you told me could mean Naomi Lowe had the intent of murder—but that's a moot point at this time." He scratched his head and wrinkled his brow as if a thought came to him. "Would anyone help her with these plans? Someone else I could talk with?"

"None that I can think of. Certainly not her son, Jason." *Why did I say that? Jason wouldn't ever do anything to get himself in trouble—not this much trouble. Starring in skin flicks is a far cry from murder.* "I didn't know a thing about any spider bites."

"What is her son's name? Jason who?" O'Connor leaned a bit closer to her.

"Jason Banner—a son from her first marriage." *I wish he would go and let me go home and grieve.* "It's not in him to do anything wrong."

"So you said, ma'am. So you said." He scribbled notes that she couldn't make out. "Do you know his address or phone number?"

"No. I don't." She dabbed her eyes. Her lips quivered. "He comes and goes on his own schedule."

"Well, if you do speak with Jason Banner, we need to take a statement from him. A statement and fingerprints from you, too—all routine, you understand." He rose to his feet as he spoke, "Thank you for your time, ma'am. I understand this isn't easy for you."

"I already gave my statement to the detective inside Naomi's home before you arrived. Someone took my prints, too." Jessica brought her hands upwards, showing him her inked fingertips."

"I've got good men on the job." He glanced at the car in the driveway and then returned to her with a warm smile. "If you need, leave your car here. An officer can drive you home."

"Thank you, Lieutenant." Jessica inhaled deeply. "I'll be all right. I can drive myself."

I hope Trenton is charged with murder! No one else could've done this!

~~***~~

"Trent!" Amelia called out while sitting on the sofa in the media room. "Come here. You've got to see this."

"Be right there." She heard his footsteps growing nearer. He stood in the doorway, hands on hips. "What is it?"

"On the TV. It's about Naomi." She patted the cushion next to her.

He grabbed the remote, boosted the volume, and sat on the sofa, leaning forward. "What happened?"

"Shish, the police are talking." She listened intently to the local news announcement. His muscles tensed as if they had a mind of their own.

The officer made a statement. "The body of Naomi Lowe, former wife of famous movie producer, Trenton Lowe, was found dead this morning, killed by a single gunshot wound to the head. She is survived by an only child, Jason Banner, from a previous marriage."

A news reporter called out, "Are there any murder suspects?"

"All avenues are being explored." The officer cleared his throat. "This is an ongoing case. For the sake of this investigation, no further details will be shared at this time."

Trenton's jaw dropped and his eyes glazed over as if in a state of disbelief. His mouth opened ready to speak. Amelia clutched his hand and stroked his shoulder. His muscles tensed under her fingers in rippled cords. All the color had drained from his face.

"Trent, I'm terribly sorry." She kissed his cheek. "This is just ghastly, too ghastly for words."

"It wasn't that long that we were arguing." He rubbed his brow. His eyes froze on flashing images of his ex wife on the television screen.

"Arguing about me?" *I wish he never went to see her.*

"Yes. Twice." He looked at her with terror as if he realized something.

"Were there any witnesses?" *I pray he was alone with that woman.*

"I don't think so. I never went past the foyer." His bottom lip trembled. "Anyone could've been within earshot in another room."

"Well, hold onto that thought—that you both were alone." *How will his boss react?*

"The police might see me as a suspect." He rubbed the stubble on his chin. "It's no secret that we couldn't stand each other." He looked at her as his eyes widened larger than she could remember. "My God! I'm the logical first choice."

"Never think that!" Amelia squeezed his shoulder. "You're letting your imagination run away with you." *He's right. Any detective would think of my dear Trent, first.*

"Don't you see?" He held his hands out, palms upturned as if his reasoning should be evident. "*I* called the police about your harassment—telling them that I thought Naomi was behind all of this. They are going to say I had the motive. In their mind there will be no one else."

"There is no *proof.*" She kissed his cheek. "Besides, you were with your boss last night, having drinks and talking business."

"I wasn't with him *all* night." He rubbed his hands as if this action might help him sort out the facts.

"No. You were with me all night." Amelia grabbed his forearm. "I will tell them that. There is no way you could have killed her." She bit her lip. "Do you think you should call her son?" Twinges of foreboding twirled up her spine as if transmitted from Trenton's fear.

"No. I better stay clear of him." He released a huge breath. Beads of perspiration dotted his brow "The police can deal with Jason." His voice held more fear than hope. "Maybe my surveillance video will be proof that I was here most of the night."

Naomi is causing hell ... even from the grave.

If I hadn't come here, would she still be alive?

O'CONNOR POURED OVER Trenton Lowe's telephone records. All looked typical until he came upon one brief incoming call from the Cambridge area of Massachusetts. It was less than a minute in length. He rifled though his notes. There it was. Naomi had relatives in Boston.

The plant that arrived to the Lowe household came from this same phone, but no records for any flower deliveries. The ex could've had her relatives do this deed for her. They might've thought it was a playful prank played on a very deserving ex family member.

The anonymous flowers? Who sent them and from where? Who wanted Naomi dead? Did one of the toy boy types pestering Amelia turn on her— one of Jason's friends? Asking him for more money and he refused? A threat—"Give me more money or your mother is dead"? Nah, those guys are all too worried about getting into the movies—if anything, those pretty boys would want Naomi alive to use her influence with Trenton to further their careers.

He bit off a hangnail and thought out loud. "Jason Banner? No motive there. He'd want his mother to live as long as possible to suck down her monthly alimony. Her ten million dollar home was in debt. Naomi's life insurance would keep him afloat for a while if he didn't use it to pay down the hefty mortgage. He could rent it out for income. Either way, she was worth more to him living than dead."

He shifted in his chair and knitted his brows. *Then there is Clive Bradford in the mix. He disliked his cousin, Amelia. Could he be the one behind the harassment? Naomi admitted to contacting him and finding out about her allergy to spiders. It's too far a reach for him to commit murder.*

Trenton Lowe? Maybe. Yet, not likely. He has money for a hired gun, but it's not his style.

He stroked his brow with one hand and scrolled the computer screen with the other.

That PI Trenton Lowe hired is straight up. Came to the station as soon as he heard about the murder—spilled everything he knew. He didn't tell us anything we didn't already know.

On a hunch, he picked up his phone and pressed the contact he wanted. It rang a few times before there was an answer.

"Joe Winton, here." The gruff voice rang in his ear.

"I don't know if you remember me, this is Lieutenant O'Connor, Mike O'Connor. We first met in Tampa." *Maybe Trenton called Joe or Larry Davis.*

"Yeah, sure." He cleared his throat. "What you want? I've kept my nose clean."

"That's not why I'm calling." *He's on the defense.* "The wife and I moved out here—California. I'm not a tourist—been working for the L.A.P.D. I'm investigating the murder of Naomi Lowe—ex wife of Trenton Lowe."

There was a pause. "I had no idea." He could hear Joe's breathing and assumed the news shocked him. "How? When?"

"Early in the morning between two-thirty and three-thirty a couple of days ago." He took a sip of his tepid coffee that had been sitting on his desk since he came to the precinct that day. "A single bullet took her out—very professional."

"I know nothin' 'bout no murder." His tone seemed pressured. "Been here in Bel-Air for years—livin' with Larry and Taylor."

"Did Mr. or Mrs. Davis say anything to you about Naomi Lowe?" He grabbed a pen, ready to jot down any notes. "Maybe something about Naomi being harassed in some way?"

"Like I said, they mentioned nothin'." His voice tightened. "Wish I could help you, Lieutenant O'Connor. But, truth is, this is the first I'm hearin' of such a horrible thing. Don't see TV much. Read the sports' stats most of the time. I feel sorry for all concerned."

"Yeah. Do you think a friend of a friend would want to help Amelia or Trenton out in some way—put a PI on her tail? Someone not from this area—maybe out of New York?"

"Lieutenant, what are you gettin' at?" Joe's voice lowered with a slight tremor.

I've got him thinking now. "I'm just exploring all possibilities, you understand. What if this PI became a loose cannon type—wasn't satisfied with just tailing someone, but got trigger-happy? Maybe this PI found out something he didn't like about the person he was watching? In some way felt he was doing everyone a favor by hitting this same person?"

He heard Joe swallow. "I hope you find answers to all you highfalutin questions. Can't help you here." He sighed. "My answer barrel is dry. Look, I gotta go and run an errand. Good talkin' to you, O'Connor. Congrats on the promotion."

"Thanks for your time, Joe. Contact me if you know of anything." He chuckled. "I stick to a detail until I can figure it out. Don't worry. I'll get to the bottom of it."

Mike continued to think of anyone who would fit the profile of the murderer. This case had him stumped—a feeling he never liked.

~~***~~

Joe purchased a throwaway phone from the local food-mart. He didn't trust O'Connor and figured that phone records weren't beyond his reach. He had turned off his GPS before driving to a shopping mall parking lot to make identifying his location more difficult—if that's what the cops were set out to do.

He held the phone to his ear waiting for the answer. Early shoppers arrived for the big sale advertised by banners in the lot, waving in the breeze. The morning sun was already beating down. He pulled out a handkerchief from his pants and wiped his beaded brow. His perspiration was more from the fear consuming him, growing stronger each minute, than from the rising temperature. Finally, the person picked up.

"Sal, what type of fuckin' hell did you unleash here in L.A.?" he nearly yelled.

"What are you talkin' about, man?" The sound of puffing from a cigarette or cigar came over the phone. "My friend got back a day ago, and said all was good. Only spoke on the phone. Didn't learn nothin' new. He ain't set a meet yet."

"I can smell the horseshit through the phone. I got a disturbin' call from Mike O'Connor—that gumshoe outta Tampa, and now in L.A. Seems Trenton's ex got herself murdered—Naomi Lowe." Joe adjusted his seat. He glanced side to side, checking if anyone was spying on him.

"I don't have nothin' to do with that." His voice rose. "I sent my friend out there to snoop around. He promised he wouldn't do nothin' more than that—keepin' an eye on whoever was mixin' things up for Amelia and Trenton."

"I wouldn't take his word as gospel." *Everything is so laid-back with Sal.* "What if he went off the deep end? Already, O'Connor is askin' if I had anythin' to do with this. Askin' if I had a friend of a friend to do the killin'—someone out of New York."

"He's just snoopin' ... tryin' to get a rise out of y'. Playin' y'— hopin' you'll slip up." Sal's voice faded a moment from the city noise in the background. "Y' didn't tell him nothin'?"

"Hell, no!" *Does he think I'm a jerk?* "No info came from me." He gripped the steering wheel, ready to drive off if needed.

"Good." He took another puff. "Don't show that bastard your hand ... Hey, you want me to call my friend and talk to him again? Tell him what happened?"

"Yeah. Maybe you'll learn somethin'." Joe watched a pretty, middle- aged woman walk to her car, her tight jeans made her butt look good. "Maybe he saw someone sniffin' around Naomi's place. Don't give him any ideas of retunin' out here. I don't need any more shit in my lap."

"Okay." He chuckled. "He won't visit L.A. Likes New York too much—has roots here." An uneasy silence. "Man, you got the rest of the money to give my guy?"

"That's payback for your friend puttin' O'Connor on my tail. You eat the balance due." A lady strode by with a seductive sway and winked at him. He flashed her a smile and ran his hand through his white hair. Sal's voice jolted him back.

"He did no shit." Joe envisioned Sal's angry expression. "Only had eyes on her! If my friend doesn't get paid—I get hit."

"Not my prob." *Sal is all bullshit.* "Gotta go. A lady on my radar." Joe put his keys in the ignition. "Call me if you learn anythin'."

~~***~~

Trenton felt more than uneasy with Lieutenant O'Connor sitting on his balcony. He didn't like the idea of him wanting to have Amelia present either. Possibilities humored his inner thoughts.

If I were a true suspect, he'd want to question me and Amelia separately.

Alex had served them all iced tea. O'Connor's manner was overly relaxed. He noticed that he wore the same navy suit and wondered if he had more than one in the same color.

Why is my mind wandering—thinking about his suit? A defense mechanism?

"You have a nice pool, Mr. Lowe." He looked at the water and then to Trenton, his hand shading his eyes. "You get to use it much?"

"No." He took a swallow of his drink. "I'm too busy at the studio."

"And you, Ms. Hollingsworth—you swim much?" O'Connor looked out to the Pacific for a moment.

"I've only been in it once." She adjusted her seat. "My skin is too fair to tolerate much sun. Such is the fate of a redhead."

"Me? I tan up pretty quick—always have." His eyes darted from Amelia to Trenton.

What fucking game is he playing?

Trenton leaned on the table toward O'Connor, who sat opposite him. "Exactly why are you here, Lieutenant? You're surely not interested in our swim habits. Have you learned anything new involving my ex's murder?"

"Still putting all the pieces together on that score—they have to fit to make a case." He tilted his head and looked at Trenton as if he expected a reaction. "You must get a lot of breeze here—being up high. You have a boat, Mr. Lowe?"

"No, I don't." *What is he getting at? I paddled down to Manhattan Beach and shot Naomi?* "Have you considered a random shooting or a terrorist?"

"Not a terrorist." His eyes narrowed, running up one side of Trenton and down the other. "A terrorist targets large crowds. This was a well-planned murder by someone who knows the late Mrs. Lowe's movements—someone who would know her habits very well, as if studying her, or had lived with her." He paused a torturous moment. "You know of anyone who fits that description?"

"No, no one comes to mind." *He's trying to pin this on me.* "Maybe her son? Jason?"

"Yes, sir. He did cross my mind." He took a deep breath. "But that doesn't ring right. What would be his motive? He was living off her money." His chuckle grated on Trenton. "If Jason was the murderer, then he's killing the goose laying the monthly golden egg—the golden egg you provide." His eyes bored through him. "Are you a bit fed up with supplying that monthly income for your dead ex wife?"

"Ridiculous!" *He's trying to break me—make me react.* "Her support was nothing more than another monthly expense out of my pocket." He took a large gulp of tea. "What about the random shooter idea? It's not unheard of these days."

"Well." O'Connor rubbed has hands together. "That conclusion would be the last resort." He shook his head. "A sad one, really—the killer might get away. I never like that—loose ends—never a good thing. Loose ends keep me up at night until I can—"

"Yes. Until you can make all the pieces fit," Trenton finished his sentence with an irritated tone. "Look, I'll just come out with it. I was having drinks with Aaron Krantz that night, and came home to Amelia. We were awake most of the night making love if you must know, and didn't fall asleep until four or five in the morning. I have witnesses who saw me with Krantz." He leaned back in his chair. "Hell, we even woke Alex with our playful noise."

Amelia's snide smile appeared. He hoped O'Connor would notice that her expression was validation of his last comments.

His eyes froze on Trenton. "I didn't mean to upset you, Mr. Lowe. I was merely talking off the top of my head—seeing what would stick to the wall."

The hell you didn't. "Well, you certainly sound as if you were making a case for me being Naomi's killer." He set his jaw and clenched his teeth. He found it difficult to control his breathing and not alert the annoying lieutenant.

Don't lose your cool—that's what he wants.

"No, not in the least." He rose from his seat and checked his watch. "I need to get back to the precinct. Don't get up. I can see my way out." O'Connor walked to the balcony's doorway, paused, turned back to them and said, "You're probably right, Mr. Lowe—about the random shooter." He rubbed his forehead with his thumb. "I'll keep digging. Never fear. I'll get to the bottom of this."

They watched the detective leave. Trenton put his finger to his lips as a gesture for Amelia not to speak. He listened intently for the sound of returning footsteps. There was none.

He opened his mouth, ready to tell his thoughts. A raspy voice came from behind them.

"One more thing."

Trenton twisted his face and turned to see the lieutenant standing in the living room on the patio's threshold. "What is it, Lieutenant O'Connor? You forget something?" *He sleuths around like a ghost.*

"Just wanted to remind you not to leave the city until this case is closed." He started back to the door.

"Is that all?" *When in hell will he go?*

"Yes." O'Connor stepped farther into the living room, as if to leave.

Trenton followed. "I'll see you to the door. I wouldn't want you to lose your way out."

"That's kind of you." He paused in the foyer. "Nice place you got here."

"So you've said." Trenton opened the door. "Goodbye, Lieutenant O'Connor. Thanks for the chat."

Trenton promptly locked the door and returned to Amelia, still on the balcony. He was glad that at the beginning of O'Connor's visit Alex had run out on an errand and Elizabeth was busy with duties and out of sight. The last thing he wanted was giving O'Connor a reason to extend his stay.

"Well, that was being put on the bloody rack." She took a swallow of tea.

"Why can't he be looking for the killer instead of trying to frame me?" He took two large gulps, then sneered. "Framing me would make for an easy case. I didn't appreciate his nonchalance and disarming talk." He drew in air from his gritted teeth. "If he's looking for a pile of shit—he won't find it here."

She squeezed his hand. "Do you think you need a solicitor?"

"Not yet." He peered out to the blue horizon. "It's ludicrous that an innocent man would need a lawyer."

I hope to God I'm wrong about O'Connor. Has he talked to Krantz yet? Would he ask him if I was capable of murder? That could mean my job.

"IS THIS MISS Jane Denton? The Jane Denton who arrogantly and with disregard left her post?" Clive was more than irritated as he spoke on a mobile phone in his room—the room at the club. Amelia had forced him to be relegated to this two-room domicile and give up his family's London townhouse. That never sat well with him—another cog welded to his hate of her.

"This is she. Whom am I speaking with? Your voice sounds vaguely familiar." Her sweet tone had no effect on him.

"This is Clayton Smythe. I'm calling to discover the reason for your abrupt leaving the care of Her Grace, Amelia Hollingsworth, the Duchess of Steffenfordshire. Would you care to explain yourself?" He doodled a hangman stick figure on a pad and wrote Amelia's name under it in bold angry letters.

Did Amelia dismiss her or worse, discern that I had the agency send someone to keep a watch on her?

"I told my agency that I had personal family issues that required my immediate attention." He heard a kettle whistle in the background. "I know for a fact that you are *not* Clayton Smythe."

She's smart. Who would have thought it from someone in service—especially from a female.

"I have no idea what you are talking about. Ms. Denton, you are treading perilously close to the window with this agency." *How near is she to my truth?*

"I left because a lot of dreadful things were happening to her grace, Amelia—mysterious flower deliveries, spiders everywhere despite the poison we sprayed all the time, and a horrendous car accident. I had no idea what I was walking into and that people could possibly die. The times you called me when I was out in Malibu, the country code never appeared, and the area number was for that of Cambridge, Massachusetts. Now, to my way of thinking, you are an imposter calling from the States. For all I know, the police in the States are investigating the matter and might be extending that investigation to the UK. Scotland Yard could already be involved."

Clive immediately hung up. Disbelief filled him with a tinge of outrage that an impertinent girl should call him out in such a manner—she had more than crossed the mark.

He looked at the phone in his hands. With quiet resolve, he proceeded to dismantle it with a small screwdriver from his desk. Gathering all the components in his hands, he went to the bathroom and drowned the only record of his devious deeds in a sink full of water. He wasn't taking any chances that a burner mobile might be traceable to the authorities. *Scotland Yard? It's ludicrous to think they'd end up investigating me—not with my title and medical accolades. Would they?*

~~***~~

Mike O'Connor kept staring at his notes. A half-finished cup of room temperature coffee sat on his desk at the police precinct. Dried coffee drips marked his notepad. His mind churned like a high-speed blender.

He couldn't make the pieces fit. Something was missing. Trenton Lowe had an airtight alibi for his whereabouts when Naomi was murdered if Amelia Hollingsworth wasn't covering for him. Even Alex backed up Lowe's story. Elizabeth was of no help as she arrived after the fact. True, he had a motive, but no means. There was no record of him ever having owned a gun of any sort, so it was unlikely he would be able to shoot as accurately as that.

Who else would like to see her dead? Jason Banner? Nope. After interviewing him, he'd want her to live forever for the money she gave him. Now his meal ticket was gone. Yet, he didn't seem broken up by his mother's death—a real cold character. By all accounts, they had a screwy relationship.

A police colleague stood at his desk. He tossed a report in front of him. "Here's the ballistics on the Naomi Lowe case." The other detective left.

Without looking up, O'Connor replied, "Thanks."

Taking the report in his hands, he sighed deeply.

This had better hold a shitload of information I can use.

He read the findings slowly and couldn't believe his eyes. He scanned the report a second time, flipped the paper over in hopes of discovering more information. There was none.

The trajectory came from the direction of the nearby pier. The locals had been questioned. All denied hearing and seeing anyone suspicious at the time of the murder. No evidence on the bullet shell casing found at the scene either. Whoever it was, this perp was an expert sniper and looked like a professional.

Mike had harbored the thought that a friend or family member might be behind all of this. Yet, he couldn't find a friend or family member with any record of shooting skills—hobby or otherwise.

There were no fingerprints obtained that couldn't be accounted for. No footprints either. Being stumped in a case grated on him.

What now? Send out an alert that a sniper is on the loose? That would send panic running through the streets of L.A. What if this was a contract? A hit of some kind? The background search on Trenton Lowe showed no dealings with the underworld or mob connections. Clive Bradford wouldn't risk his royal standing to devise such a scheme. Besides, Bradford was in England. Alistair Hollingsworth wasn't a choice either—not with his gay record. He was probably glad his wife was thousands of miles away with his history of not caring who her lovers were.

Was there some snot getting his kicks, trying out a black-market sniper rifle? A test of some kind for acceptance in a local gang? Again, Jason. He had shady dealings and lived on the fringe of the drug world. Porn wasn't beyond him. Did a drug goon have his mother killed to send a message for an unpaid debt? Nah, Jason didn't snort more than he could pay for.

He couldn't go to the DA with a pile of theories—not when he had no evidence to substantiate a charge.

Reluctantly, he took the report and placed it in the Naomi Lowe folder. An expansive and labored sigh escaped from his lips. He hated dead ends.

~~***~~

At a corner table of a dingy east end saloon, Sal fidgeted with the napkin under his beer bottle. Through the dim light he watched Elliott come through the back door. He gestured with his hand, showing him where he sat.

Elliott stopped at the bar, spoke a few words to the bartender, grabbed his beer, then swaggered to Sal. He pulled up the chair in one swift movement and sat down. Others eyed him with awe. His zippered black leather jacket, metal chains from his waist, heavy black jackboots, and slicked black hair induced respect from Sal, too. He knew his friend was someone who would be loyal, yet he never wanted to get on his wrong side. To do that could mean a bullet. Elliott had told Sal he was a freelancer, and not connected to any one "family"—it was better to be his own boss, not takin' any shit from nobody.

Sal glanced at him and waited for his friend to start the conversation. If it was one thing he knew, it was not to pressure his friend when he didn't want to talk.

Elliott nudged Sal's arm. "You had that new whore standin' by Jimmy? She any good?"

"Nah. Doesn't give longer than a three minute blow job." *He looks relaxed.*

"What does she do?" He laughed. "Set a fuckin' timer? Bing! You're done whether you shoot your wad or not? If she did that to me, she wouldn't be suckin' no more cocks—no more nothin'.'"

"Somethin' like that." Sal inched closer, elbows on the table. "You have somethin' to tell me?"

"Yeah." Elliott continued to look at the shapely prostitute, lips partly open as if his mouth watered.

"Well?" *He's gonna play this one out for as long as possible—teasing me like a cheap whore.*

"Simmer down." Elliott took a gulp of beer. "Gotta be certain no ears are listenin'." He lowered his head and looked up, his black eyes darting about the room.

Sal fingered a coaster. "This is your territory. No problem." He decided not to let his friend know he knew about Naomi's death—at least not right away. *Sometimes it's better to play dumb and see what the other guy knows.*

"Well, Trenton Lowe's ex was the bitch—causin' a shit-bag of trouble for him. Hirin' young guys to flirt with his woman, Amelia. Havin' someone tamper with his car which caused an accident—nearly took them both out in the crash." He let out a half-hearted laugh. "Amelia was a fuckin' pawn in the game she hadn't known she was playin'. Then that bitch had spiders planted in Lowe's house."

"Spiders?" *He was tailin' a nut.* "What the hell for? She scared of 'em?"

"Fuckin' no." Elliott took another swallow. "She's allergic. One bite and it's a final whack—no more Amelia, except for plantin' her in the grave."

"The L.A. cops know all this?" Sal asked. *She's worse than a viper.*

"Nope." He took a swig of beer from the bottle, his eyes on Sal. "Too stupid to know."

"What do you mean 'nope'?" He struggled to stifle his reaction to what he already knew.

Elliott motioned for him to lower his voice, his hand moving sideways.

Sal spoke softer. "That bitch could be killin' Amelia right now—might have already done it."

"Won't happen." Elliott finished half of his beer.

"How you know? I ain't gettin' a good feelin'," Sal said.

"All is good in California. You don't need to know more than that."

He hunched over with his elbows on the table. He watched Sal tense. "You're holdin' onto that table like it was stripper's tits."

"My buddy in California said Naomi is dead." Sal looked for a reaction from Elliott.

"Yeah. Took a bullet—clear through the head." Elliott smiled, showing white teeth. "Was on the news."

Sal hung his head. "That wasn't part of the contract. You were only supposed to tail her and get intel—not blow her fuckin' brains out."

"Don't go sayin' crap that'll lead to trouble." Elliott popped a nut from the bowl on the table. "All is good in California. I didn't say *I* did the job. It is what it is."

"Did you?" *If he did, I can't trust him. He's gettin' fuckin' emotional— losin' his edge.*

"Like I said, 'It is what it is.' Shut up about it—don't go shootin' off your mouth." He leaned forward and pushed his chair away, ready to get up. "I'd hate to lose you as a friend 'cause of your loose lips—it'd be tough to do—but I'd get it done." Elliott patted his cheek giving an unspoken warning, then turned his palm up. "You got somethin' for me?"

Sal took out the final payment sealed in an envelope and slipped it to him. Fear gripped him—fear he had never known before from a trusted friend. His chest tightened and sweat glistened his brow. He watched Elliott place the packet in his jacket and then leave.

I can't ask Joe again for more money—not after this. He already said the balance was on me.

His heart beat fast and his mouth grew desert dry.

My God! Elliott's serious. He'll kill me if I say anything.

I knew he was cold—just never knew how much before.

Fifty~Eight

ALISTAIR'S HAND TREMBLED slightly, waiting for her to answer the phone. The comfort of his library didn't sway his nerves. He hadn't confronted Amelia since the beginning. This was a new position for him and he wasn't certain he could pull it off. True, he could take charge when he needed to do so with his subordinates involving a research project. But this was different. This was the force who had put him in his place from the second day of their marriage.

"Yes, Alistair," she sounded irritated. "What do you want?"

"I thought the only decent thing to do was to tell you that I posed no objections to the divorce—didn't even attend the court hearing, you see." *This is my last hope.* "Since I've been upstanding about this matter, the only honorable thing for you to do is allow me the funds awarded to me upon our marriage—your dowry."

"You're bloody daft!" Her shrillness made his gut churn, bile climbing up to his throat. "After you ruining my life for years due to your deceitful ways, I'm supposed to roll over and say 'Thank you very much, Guv'ner'? I think not. My twisted sense of duty to my dead father kept me in that marriage—certainly nothing on your part."

"Won't you please reconsider? The manor will need to be opened to the public to support itself." *I must make her understand I'm in dire straits.* "Or worse, I might be forced to turn it over to the National Trust."

"To put it bluntly in American terms, 'ain't no skin off my ass!'" Her tone turned vicious, her words clawing his ears. "You have no regard to my safety. Not once did you mention what your cousin has done to me while I'm here. He sent me a spider plant as a sinister joke, then sent flowers, and had some man pester me, not to mention having a minion tamper with Trent's car."

"What?" *What in hell is she talking about?* "Do you have proof? Conjecture means nothing."

"I don't need proof." She scoffed. "I know him. He put Trent's ex up to carry off his dirty deeds. Only this time, it backfired."

Alistair visualized her expression—blazing eyes and thin angry lips. "Your imagination is getting the better of you. Backfired? How?"

"Naomi Lowe was shot dead—bullet through the head." *Amelia is beyond reason.* "You can tell dearest Clive that Naomi paid the price for his diabolical dealings."

"Who killed her?" *Was Trenton the murderer?*

"That hasn't been ascertained yet." She sighed. "Before you say anything—it wasn't Trent. He was with me when she was murdered."

"I wasn't about to suggest he was at fault." *Is there any way to soften her?* "Elizabeth left me. Her note said she was on holiday to visit you—even took Rodney with her. When is she returning?"

"She's not as far as I'm concerned." Amelia clipped her words.

He imagined his housemaid being enthralled and wooed by Hollywood's glamour.

She exhaled a labored breath. "Of course she'd bring Rodney. He's her pet—fusses over him as if he were her child. And, for what it's worth, I missed him, too. He has an honest love that has been missing in my life all these years until ... until Trent."

"That cuts to the bone." *Why is she so cruel. I can't help the way I am. It's not like I chose to be gay.* "I have loved you in my own way. I've been discreet, not flaunting my boys in public—not as you have done to me. I can't change my true nature. It wasn't a choice. I was born this way."

"I'm not condemning you for your lifestyle. As I told you in many conversations before, I want more than the love from a brother." Her frustration grated in his head. "I want the love from a man who loves me as a woman on all levels and not as a sister. I was obvious with my liaisons to give you reasons for divorce all those years. Unfortunately for me, you never found our marriage nor my actions to be less than satisfactory."

"How am I supposed to get on after all this?" *She'll never understand.* "All is lost to me. I might even lose the Mayfair townhouse."

"Do like Clive—live at the club. Hire a room. You make enough for that standard of living."

The phone went dead. His spirits sank as his future as a penniless duke flashed before him.

Forever, I'll be known as the failed duke who let it all fade away—the one who let the legacy fall to dust.

~~***~~

Trenton walked along Highland Avenue, only a few blocks from Ocean Drive, and then another block to Naomi's home feeling oddly drawn there. A detective or mystery writer might say he was returning to the scene of the crime. Nothing could be further from the truth. It was time for closure—closure from all those horrendous years spent with her, enduring her bickering and backbiting ways. He had long stuffed those feelings down deep, out of sight and mind. Now it was time to face them and put everything she had tainted in his life to rest for once and for all. He had to let go of and bury his ill-fated memories. Amelia deserved it.

He stopped a moment to stand on the sidewalk, watching others go about their lives. It all looked so commonplace—eating, drinking, shopping, and sharing memories. Did they have worries they couldn't escape? That bitch who had plagued him was finally at her rest. A strange sense of freedom swept over him—more freedom than he felt when his divorce was final. He never wished her dead. Yet, that was a gift. All that she had done would never happen again.

He felt a firm poke at his back.

"Lowe, who did you hire to murder my mother?" He turned around slowly. The flaming hatred in Jason's eyes burned bright.

"You're overwhelmed with grief, and I am sorry for your loss, but you don't know what you're saying." He tried to walk past him. Naomi's son took a sideways step, blocking the way.

Jason was yelling now, wagging his finger in Trenton's face. "I know exactly what I'm saying. You came back here—back to the scene of the crime, like the murderer you are!" A crowd started to form around them.

Trenton was aware of the camera hounds among the spectators. This was the last thing he needed. He pushed through them and ducked into an alley with Jason hot on his heels.

"You can't run away from the truth, Trenton Lowe! Not this time." His voice pierced above the crowd.

Leaning against an exposed brick foundation, Trenton panted while catching his breath.

Jason caught up to him and lolled against a garbage bin. He sneered as if holding a royal flush at a poker table. "You didn't like that publicity, did you?"

His snicker made Trenton's skin crawl. "Who would? Your anger is misplaced. I had nothing to do with your mother's shooting and you know it. I don't own any weapons and I don't know how to hire anyone to shoot her—unlike you, I don't associate with those types." He took a few more deep breaths. "You're only pissed because she won't be receiving any more alimony checks from me—meaning you can't grab money from her anymore—your money-well has dried up."

"I won't go to the cops if you make it worth my while." Jason sunk his hands deep into his pockets and jutted his jaw, a cocky grin on his face.

"Go to the cops, for all I care. You're talking out of your ass. I can point out that one of your friends was sniffing around my car in the mechanic's lot. You forget about security cameras—every business has them." His determination met Jason's head on. "Hell, it might've even been you. Now, who is the *real* murderer here?"

"I wouldn't put in the effort to knock you off." Jason took a step closer. "When can I expect the first payment into my checking account?"

"Never!" Trenton took a step closer. He steeled his courage, ready to defend himself if needed. "I don't yield to blackmailers. Keep it up and I'll give a shitload of details about you to Lieutenant O'Connor."

"It will be my word against yours, Lowe." Jason's jaw set, teeth clenched. The muscles in his cheek twitched as the veins in his neck grew hard and sharp. He pulled his hands free from his pockets and formed fists.

Trenton widened his stance, sizing up his adversary. "I'll risk it." His eyes narrowed. "Besides, you have all the assets from Naomi— her beachfront home on The Strand, bank accounts, furnishings, jewels—all of it. That should be enough to feed your various sick habits for awhile."

"Not long enough—she put a fucking mortgage on the place." He angled his chin out further, showing his growing cockiness. "I'm not about to give up my lifestyle because of her death—not because you're too cheap to give me what I deserve—dear father."

"*Step*father. You're no blood of mine—thank God." *He's as crazy as Naomi!*

"I was at the funeral—you weren't." Jason sucked air in through his gritted teeth.

"Unlike you, I'm not a hypocrite." He thinned his lips. "No—wait. You were mourning the loss of your income—not your dead mother."

Trenton didn't see it coming. Jason landed an upper jab to his jaw and lower lip. He swayed backwards, caught his balance and righted himself. He tasted blood in his mouth. He wiped his split lip with the back of his hand before taking his handkerchief from his pants and holding it to the fleshy wound. Drops of blood had fallen onto his yellow shirt.

"That was classy." He dabbed the sore, and applied pressure hoping it would stop the bleeding. "Being a thug must run in your genes—from your dead father."

Jason raised his fist again.

"I won't fight you—that's what you want. You're not worth the effort." Trenton wrestled with the fiery urge to flatten him. Oh how he wanted to beat Jason to a pulp and wipe that arrogant sneer off his face. He stiffened his posture and shoved past him onto the sidewalk, never looking back at the spoiled brat Naomi had spawned. He half expected his stepson to tackle him as he left. He glanced over his shoulder. There was no sign of him following. Jason was long overdue for a good beating, but someone else would have to deliver it.

IN HIS STUDY, Amelia sat a Trenton's computer, reading as her search took on a life of its own. Her eyes scanned the pages, clicking one link and then another as she delved and uncovered more information. O'Connor wasn't the only one with a bone in his teeth. She had one hell of bone clenched in her teeth, and its name was Clive Bradford.

She ignored the sound of the front door opening and closing, as well as the footsteps coming up behind her. These facts were too critical for distractions.

Trenton rubbed her shoulder. "What is so important that you can't give me a hello kiss?"

"I've found out what I always knew." She clicked another link and read the text. Trenton looked over her shoulder. "See that! Clive was in Cambridge, Massachusetts the *same time* I started receiving those flowers. It wasn't Naomi after all. It was Clive!"

He appeared bewildered. "You already knew he gave a presentation at Harvard. What is so new? I don't get it."

"It's the dates!" Her eyes widened. "The dates don't lie." She noticed his red and swollen lower lip. "What happened?"

She touched his wound gently with her fingertips causing him to wince. "Ouch. It's still a bit tender."

"Did you fall?" Her brow furrowed. "Are you all right? Do you need to see a doctor?"

"Not a fall." He lightly touched his lip. "I met up with a piece of scum who wanted something for nothing. It's of no consequence."

She stared at him for a few seconds. "You should go and wash it and put something on it. Do you need stitches?"

"It'll be fine." He touched the wound again.

She turned back to the computer screen. "Do you think I should contact Lieutenant O'Connor with these dates? Maybe he could reopen the case. I'd love to see Clive get what he deserves."

"There is absolutely no point in it." He cupped Amelia's cheeks, forcing her to look at him. "O'Connor is interested in who killed Naomi—not who tried to murder you or us." He leaned across and closed down the computer screen. "Let sleeping dogs lie. Digging up old shit just makes it stink more."

He kissed the top of her head and caressed her shoulders.

Maybe Trent is correct. Still, I hope someday Clive pays.

~~***~~

Clive sipped his brandy at the club's social room. He sank deeper in the leather chair as Alistair approached.

What in bloody hell does he want now?

He did his best to be unobtrusive, and angled his body away from his friend, but he knew it was futile. Alistair had armed himself with a drink, and he deduced that he was in for one of his long torturing dissertations on all his mishaps with that wench, Amelia.

Alistair eased down in the chair opposite. He didn't wait for Clive to speak. "She's ruddy done it. Truly did."

"Did what?" Clive took a swallow of his drink. "I put nothing past her."

"Divorced me." He placed his drink on the side table. "She won't give me a penny. I've been chucked out with the trash in the dustbin."

"You're in good company." He sneered. "Because of your now ex-wife, I lost my family home and half of my bank accounts."

"It's not the same, ol' man." His fingers tapped his knee. "The manor house and the estate will most likely end up in the National Trust if I can't rent it out to tourists, open it to tours and social events. Most of the land will need to be sold. I have no idea what else she's done."

"I do." Clive leaned forward, clasped his hands, and lowered his voice to a near whisper laced with loathing. "The bank account of hers that I oversee has been closed out. Nothing left. All monies transferred to a bank in California—I couldn't get any information from any bank official—here or in Malibu. True it was her money, but her father had me watch over it. Lord only knows what she has planned. Had she not done this, I could continue to tap any interest that accrued."

Alistair glanced over his shoulder, then cleared his throat. "Ex wife of her new lover, Trenton Lowe, was murdered. Her name was Naomi. A clean shot through the head." His voice lowered and he leaned closer to Clive. "Was Amelia the one who was supposed to be killed? Was it you? Did you plan all the events that went awry?"

"Bosh!" A slow smile crept from his lips. "I'm a doctor. Doctors don't do those things ... do they?"

Alistair is sharper than I thought.

I'm too clever to get caught, and they're too stupid to find me. She's out of my hair. Too bad Amelia survived. Not all endings go as planned. There's always next time. She must pay for ruining my life—eventually.

Father never thought much of my accomplishments, never thought a doctor was a proper profession for a royal—too middle-class. What would he think now from the grave? Pat me on the back with his skeletal fingers and say "Well done"? I'm far from the weakling he always accused me of—far from it!

~~***~~

In an effort to distract Amelia from what was becoming her Clive obsession, Trenton drove her to a private Pacific cove—the same one as before. He could think of no other beach more beautiful and romantic.

The setting red sun kissed the ocean's horizon. Pink and orange light sparkled across the waves in dazzling patterns. Seagulls sang their songs. Even the gentle breeze behaved. It could have turned into a blustering wind, but it didn't.

Amelia carried the blanket while Trenton toted the cooler with champagne and glasses. He had something to tell her, and hoped his decision wouldn't upset her.

Having found the perfect patch of sand, she spread out the plaid blanket. Trenton placed the cooler near them. She sat down and extended her legs, and watched him pop the cork and pour the effervescent liquid, its bubbles streaming over the top and oozing down the side of the stem. Amelia giggled when first taking a sip. "It tickles my nose."

Trenton sat beside her. A long moment passed as he looked in her eyes.

A breeze blew her hair across her face. She reached into her pocket and pulled out a clip. In one swift movement, she had secured her hair in a loose bun. Amelia drew up her knees to her chest and hugged them with her arms. "I feel bad about how the divorce affects Alistair—putting his future in grave jeopardy."

He stroked her cheek with a finger. "Do you feel bad enough to want to return to your life in London?" He held his breath and his heart pounded.

"What a daft question." She laughed and touched the wound on his lip, her finger stroking it lightly. "That was my past—a wretched past. You're my stunning future."

Trenton kissed her lips gently while his fingers tangled in her hair. It was a kiss of innocent love.

A wayward curl played in the breeze at the curve of her neck. In that curl Trenton saw the face of the child they would have together someday. He visualized their future in beautiful vignettes that played over and over in his mind.

She tilted her head and smiled. "Why so serious? What are you thinking?"

"Well, I've been busy—and not just with movie business." He tilted his head, trying to read her face.

Amelia playfully punched his arm. "Do tell. Don't be a tease."

"You are either going to be very pleased," he took an enormous breath, "or won't speak to me for at least a week, and tell me the whole thing is off."

"Never!" Amelia feigned a pout.

"Remember when we were discussing, if we did marry, what type of wedding you would like?" He reached for her hand.

"Go on." She nudged him. "Get on with it."

"The invitations have been mailed." His fingers ran up and down her arm. "Our wedding date is eight weeks from today. Everything is set, just the way you described, an old Hollywood theme from the 1930s—even the invitation's typography is of that time. The studio's social secretary took care of the details with Elizabeth's help." His eyebrows rose and drew together as if pleading.

Will she hate the idea?

"Elizabeth was in on this? She never said a peep—not once." Amelia faced him directly. "You didn't pick out the wedding gown, too?" She scowled.

"No. Of course, not." *She's upset with me. I can feel it.*

"You are a wonderful, marvelous man." Amelia kissed him.

"Then it's okay? You'll still marry me?" He had to hear her say it again to make it real for him.

"Yes, yes, yes! I will marry you." She kissed him again.

He wiped a tear from her cheek. "André will have whatever gown you want ready for the day."

"I'll have Taylor and Elizabeth as maids." Her eyes darted about his face. "The absolute best is—you'll be my husband."

She kissed him softly as he embraced her. Her love filled him, glowing from every pore. His whole life's mission was to make her happy. Nothing was beyond his reach with Amelia by his side.

Sixty

AMELIA TOTED HER Jean Harlow styled off-white wedding
gown in an enormous garment bag slung over her arm as she entered
the living room with Elizabeth. She always thought that satin was the
best fabric for her shapely form. A bag containing her shoes,
decorative hair clip, and underpinnings for the big day occupied her
other hand. On the coffee table, three stacks of wedding responses
sat with her journal containing the details to the countdown.

She sashayed into the bedroom while Elizabeth went to her own
room. Propped against the headboard with a couple of enormous
pillows, Trenton read a script, apparently in deep thought, jotting
notes with a red pen.

He looked up at her. His brows rose in question. "All neat and tidy
in your world? André had your gown ready I see. How about a
peek?" His impish ways charmed her and she found them utterly
irresistible.

"Nooo, you may not." Amelia feigned control as she pursed her
lips. "It's bad luck for the groom to see the dress before the
wedding. We've bloody well had our fair share of bad luck. I'm not
taking any chances." She hung up the garment bag in the closet.

"You were gone most of the afternoon." He checked the bedside
clock. "A final fitting takes hours?"

"You missed me?" She shot him a coy look.

"Always." He patted her side of the bed. "Come, Duchess. Make
me happy."

"Let me put my other things away." She carefully placed her
shoebox in the closet under her gown. "As to why I've been gone
for hours—Taylor and Elizabeth were with me—picking up their
gowns, then we enjoyed a fabulous lunch—discussing all things
feminine, the wedding and such—nothing that a man would be
interested in." She pointed to the script. "What's that you're reading?
Another smash hit in the works?"

Trenton picked up the brad-bound pages. "Yes. It's *Dark Wizard*
by John B. Rosenman, based on his novel by the same name. It's
quite good with all the right elements—it's solid and has everything
the moviegoer would want, sex, sci-fi, intrigue. The studio will add
CGI for the bells and whistles. This was a real coup for the studio

seizing on this property before the competition. *MuseItUp Publishing* has a hot author on their hands." He tilted his head. "You think that Dr. Rosenman—the specialist who treated you in the hospital, is related to this author?"

"Maybe. Isn't Rosenman a somewhat common name?" She handed him a book from her nightstand. "I recently read a book that has movie potential—*Redneck PI* by Trish Jackson." Knowing she could contribute something that involved his world pleased her. "Crime, romance, action, intrigue—all the qualities for a runaway success, plus she's a bloody good talented author. The best part—the heroine is a jolly right strong woman—like yours truly."

"I'll have to check it out." He studied the cover, then read the back text. "If you liked the story—I'm pretty certain this is a property the studio needs to option. I'll run it by Krantz in the morning."

Amelia sat on the bed, kicking off her shoes, then slung her legs over as her toes played with his.

She plucked at the buttons on his shirt. "Are you so absorbed that you have no time to pay any attention to your future bride?"

"Never." Trenton placed the script on the bedside table, then rolled to his side, facing her. "No one and nothing will supersede you." He glanced at his watch. "Alex should be coming in."

"What for? This is our bedroom." Her eyes widened. "What have you commenced?"

"I told him to bring in a surprise after you arrived home." The glint in his eyes intrigued her.

Minutes later, Alex knocked, then opened the door and carried a large tray filled with cheeses, fruits, and two champagne flutes. He placed the delicious-looking repast on the satin dressing bench at the foot of the bed.

"I'll be right back with the rest, sir." He quickly left and less than a minute later returned with an ice bucket holding a bottle of opened Moët. Alex nodded as he shut the door.

"You constantly amaze me." Amelia scooted to the foot of the bed and plopped a ripe strawberry in her mouth. She chewed with relish.

"Keeping you off balance can be a good thing—keeps the interest alive." Trenton poured the bubbly in the glasses, then moved to the foot of the bed, his fingers trailing up the back of her leg and lingering behind her knee before moving farther to her buttocks.

A small sigh of pleasure escaped as she shut her eyes. "If this is your definition of 'off balance', you can keep me off balance as much as you wish."

Trenton rolled her over onto her back. He stared into her eyes. She saw his unending love in them. He kissed her lightly, brushing his lips against hers, teasing her for more, his tongue lightly touching hers. Then another kiss, more firm. His mouth opened, his tongue searching for hers. Smoldering embers of passion stirred deep in her center. He unbuttoned her blouse while she opened his shirt and enjoyed the feel of his hard chest. She broke off their kiss and removed her bra, inviting his hands to cup her breasts and give gentle squeezes, and then she shimmied out of her skirt and panties while he removed the rest of his clothing.

Trenton's kisses followed the curve of her neck to her rosy nipples, which became firm with his lingering tongue. She reached for him, thrilling at the throbbing, heated erection in her hand. He teased her with slow kisses as his tongue made lazy patterns on her midriff, traveling farther and farther to her sex. She raised her hips, begging for more, begging for his mouth to tantalize her where she enjoyed it most. He fondled her soft folds with deft fingers, slowly entering her and driving her desire higher.

When she felt his tongue caressing her to near screaming, she grabbed the back of his head so he couldn't stop. "I can't hold back much longer," she nearly screamed as her back arched. "Fuck me now!"

She raised her hips, begging for him. He eased into her, then stopped midway. Her hands grabbed his buttocks, forcing him into her hard and fast. She felt his heat as her rhythm dictated his pace, her sole attention centered on the pleasure he gave her. There was no other sensation but this—his driving passion bringing her ever higher. His panting enhanced her pleasure as she knew he was one with her in achieving the ultimate—the ultimate expression of love and ecstasy. Her movements quickened as she dug her fingers into his flesh. "Oh, God!" she yelled. Her spasms met his in one beautiful moment of prolonged bliss.

He lifted his head and stroked her dampened hair. Her limbs fell to her side in complete exhaustion. She caressed his face and traced his jaw with her finger. "I think I loved you from the beginning and was too scared to admit it to myself." She chuckled. "The ol' 'love at first sight' scenario."

"There's a lot of truth in that—for the right people—like us." He kissed her forehead and then her fingertips. He rolled off Amelia and handed her a filled flute from his nightstand. "To my duchess, who will forever be my always."

Her finger glided along his lips. "You have eternally been my destiny."

~ End of *Dangerous Reach* ~

The passion and intrigue continues in *Twisted Intent*, book 5 in the *Forbidden Series*. Read on for chapter 1.

"Intent turns ...
            perilous consequences..."
                        ~ CB Ainsworthe

TWISTED INTENT

One

"I DON'T KNOW anyone here." Elizabeth shifted her weight from one foot to another as she chatted with her American friend, Beverly Mitchell.

"Well, if you continue to hide in the corner, you won't get to know anyone." She sipped her colorful cocktail from a martini glass. "This is one of the best clubs in Hollywood and a private party at that. If I didn't work at the studio and know someone, we would've never gotten on the list."

Elizabeth scanned the room. The throbbing music, exotic fragrance of incense and low lights created a sense of the unknown—something exciting—and she gave a little shiver.

"You've got eyes on you." Beverly discreetly pointed with her pinky finger. "Three tall dark and handsome types right over there."

"Bev, you're ruddy daft." She took a swallow of soda from her glass and glanced across the tables. "You're the one they fancy. Your dark hair and red lips lure them in."

"Once they hear your English accent, I'll be a thing of the past." She slowly licked her lips as if sending an invitation. "Thank God the music isn't so loud that we can't talk."

A tall good-looking man approached with a warm and easy smile. His clothing was casual, but not the designer style of most milling around. "What are you two lovelies doing over here, secluded away?" He offered his hand, his voice low and warm. "I'm Kyle— Kyle Henson of all famous drinks." Elizabeth shook his hand. "Seriously, I'm a hardworking bartender by night and a student at UCLA—screenwriting major."

Beverly took the lead. "I'm Bev. This is Elizabeth, Elizabeth York— not long from London."

Kyle looked at Elizabeth a bit too long. "It's a pleasure. Let me tear you away from this dark corner and bring you into the light."

She stood still for a few seconds, waiting for Beverly to react.

Her friend winked and nodded. Elizabeth clutched her purse. Kyle slipped his hand on the small of her back and guided her to an undersized circular table with chairs. A battery-operated candle flickered in the center.

Elizabeth smiled meekly, then looked over her shoulder and saw Beverly giving her the thumbs up sign.

He pulled a chair out and assisted her to sit. The table forced their knees to touch. "It's certainly cozy." *I don't know him well enough for knee play.* "Are you the barkeep ... I mean bartender at this club?"

He threw his head back slightly, then let out a chuckle. "I should be so lucky to haul in those tips. Nah, I got into this party by a friend of a friend. Most of the big media types are here."

"You're networking?" Elizabeth noticed another extremely handsome man, his hand in his pocket, leaning on the bar as if he owned the world, gazing at her intently, his eyes so brown they looked almost black and smoldering, peeling her clothes off layer of layer. His dark hair cut short, and styled in a way that only comes with a three-figure price. His expensive clothes made her want to know what he looked like when naked. She drifted into wondering about this mysterious man who had such power over her, and they hadn't even met.

Her cheeks warmed and she hoped that Kyle hadn't noticed the brief moment she shared with Mr. Tall-dark-and-handsome. She turned her attention back to Kyle. "I'm sorry. I was checking on my friend."

"That's all right." He shrugged. "I'm used to being overlooked because there is a handsome hunk nearby." He took a slug of his drink, then flashed an insincere smile. "Blond, blue-eyed men don't have much of a chance with the ladies when 'dangerous and dark' is around."

Elizabeth touched his forearm. Hurting his feelings bothered her, and they had only just met. "I'm sorry. Truly, I am." She cleared her throat. "I asked if you were networking."

"In a way, yes." He folded his hands on the table and looked at her. "It's a tough gig in Hollywood. I'm hoping to write the next great blockbuster. But, with my luck," he finished his drink, "I won't get beyond the Indie status—that's not bad. The importance is that I'm expressing myself and creating original work."

"This is my first Hollywood party. I'm thrilled to be in the company of such important people." She twirled a stand of blond hair. "I feel an element of danger—something I should be careful of. Maybe I'm being silly. Yet, it's so appealing, isn't it? The idea of forbidden fruit."

"Be careful. Lots of forbidden fruit in this town." His expression turned deadly serious. "The old 'wolf in sheep's clothing' applies to everyone—just about everyone in the biz."

"That's rather cynical, don't you think?" She finished her soda. "I work for Mr. and Mrs. Trenton Lowe, and they couldn't be more nice and genuine. He's always looking for a new script from an unknown." She fingered a napkin on the table. "I'm a lady's maid to Amelia, the former Duchess of Steffenfordshire—a right proper lady, she is."

"Yeah, I heard about that divorce and her marriage to him— Hollywood is still talking about it. I pay no attention to that type of gossip." His eyes narrowed as his chin rose. "How long have you been out here—from London? I love your accent."

"Not long ... about three months give or take a few days." Her back straightened. "Understanding people is not a matter of location. And if you don't listen to gossip, how do you know so much about my master and mistress?"

"Guilty as charged. By the way, how old are you?" He looked kindly at Elizabeth as if wanting to know everything that made her tick.

"I'm twenty-one, just." Pride rang from her voice. "A very *old* twenty-one, thank you very much."

"I see your drink is empty." He stood and took her glass. "What are you drinking? Care for something more festive? A Cosmo?"

"I doubt they have a proper Guinness. Diet cola is fine with only a few ice cubes." She chuckled. "You Yanks have lots of ice in everything."

"Only in drinks that are supposed to be cold." He took a step from the table. "We like our cold drinks to be cold and not tepid."

Elizabeth watched him weave through the throngs of partygoers until he was out of sight. His American charm was appealing, but not the kind of appeal that would have her ripping off her knickers by night's end. A shadow fell over the table. She looked up.

"Since your friend has left you all alone, and someone as beautiful as you should never be alone, I thought I'd introduce myself. I'm Neville Dench—please call me Ned for short. I have no idea why my parents tied the Neville anchor to me." He boldly sat down in Kyle's seat.

He's rather cheeky. "Kyle should be back any minute with our drinks." She swallowed her nerves and quickly ran her eyes over him, enjoying every inch.

"You fancy him, then?" He made no effort to move.

"Are you from England?" *He is absolutely gorgeous. Those eyes!* "You don't sound like you're from home, but your sentences seem almost like you were brought up there."

He's the same one who was at the bar, undressing me with his gaze.

"My dead mum was. I picked up a lot of her lingo—way of speaking." He put his hand on the back of her chair and drew lazy patters on her back with his thumb. The heat of his proximity sent shivers down her spine. He scooted closer with barely a breath of air between them. His woodsy-mixed-with-spice aftershave hit her and she knew in that moment that she wanted him—wanted his hands and mouth all over her.

"I'm an orphan. Have been most of my life." She looked down at the table, then forced a smile. "But I'm as right as rain now, I am." She brought her head back up in an effort to prevent a tear from falling. "I have traveled from London to the most exciting city in the world—a city where make-believe is possible. I have a good post with Lady Amelia and Mr. Lowe." She bit her bottom lip to stop the quivering. "I'm really quite lucky—very lucky, in fact." *Crickey, now I appear pitiful to him. Why did I ramble on so?*

"Sounds like you had rough beginnings." He stroked the top of her hand with long fingers.

"Yes." She flicked back her hair off her shoulder. "What about you? How did you get a nickname of Ned from Neville?" She watched his lips move and wondered what they would feel like on hers.

A warm smile graced his face. "That was my mum. She always called me Ned. I've been Ned ever since."

Kyle walked up to the table, a drink in each hand and a less than happy expression on his face. "Thanks for saving my chair. But, I'm here now." His voice held a bit of assumed authority to it.

Ned looked up, but didn't move. "No problem." He nodded his head toward the other side of the room. "There are plenty single ladies over there. Why not busy yourself with one of them, mate?"

"The lady and I were chatting first." Kyle placed the drinks down on the table. "Be a gentleman and leave."

"I could say the same to you." The steel of Ned's tone cut the air. "Don't be difficult."

Two burly security bouncers approached. Ned glanced at them. "To avoid an upset that I would obviously win and to spare you the humiliation of losing, I'll leave." He reached in his pocket and handed Elizabeth his card. "Elizabeth, if you ever tire of sewing and such, you could be a beautiful and famous model—I'm certain of it." He left with a wink.

Elizabeth placed the card in her small purse.

"I hope he didn't say anything to upset you." Kyle sat down and watched him as he disappeared into the crowd. "He has a way of conning women—of all ages. Don't listen to his modeling line. He uses that on all the ladies he meets."

"So you know him?" Elizabeth straightened in her chair. "Well, I have a mind of my own." She huffed. "It takes more than the likes of him to turn my head." *I wouldn't mind Ned's slippers next to mine.*

"Glad to hear it." He pointed to her drink. "Take a sip. See if you like it."

After a brief taste, Elizabeth took a larger swallow. "Oh, Kyle, it's Guinness! You're a dear. You remembered what I said about wanting a proper drink and it's not too cold either."

"I aim to please." He took a sip of what smelled like whiskey or some other strong spirit and ginger ale. "There are a lot of Neds in this town. The main thing is avoiding them."

"So you've said." *I never had two men after me before. This is fun.* "And what sort of man should I take up with? Someone ... such as yourself?"

The vein in his neck budged as he turned various colors of red. "Kitty has claws." He took another sip. "I didn't mean to sound self-serving."

"Aren't most men?" She arched an eyebrow. "I may not be a woman of the world, but I haven't recently crawled out from underneath a rock, either."

He smiled weakly. "Look. Can we start over? I'm only trying to be nice. You look like a kind girl with a gentleness about you—a fragile quality."

"Go on." *Maybe he's worth a go.* "And for the record, I'm a woman, I am."

"Of course." He leaned closer to her. His clean soap fragrance just didn't do it for her. It reminded her of a boring bloke she once dated, and projected a sense of safe predictability. "What occupies your time, besides caring for Lady Amelia?"

"Lately, I've been interested in photography." She made a face. "All I have is my mobile phone and that makes my creativity quite limited."

"Why not buy a regular camera—nothing fancy, just something to get you started?" He grabbed a handful of mixed nuts from the bowl on the center of the table. "Let me see what you've taken so far."

Flattered, she blushed and bit her lip as her hand reached into her purse. "They aren't proper pictures, you understand. I was just mucking about." She handed him the phone after locating her photo file.

He studied each one for a moment then passed the phone back to her. "You have promise. Really, quite good."

"Go on, will ya." *He's only being kind, wanting to get in me knickers.* "Which one did you like and why?" She arched a brow, scrutinizing his reaction.

"The solitary adult gull with the chick on the beach, guarding the dead fish." He chewed on a few more nuts. "It spoke volumes of a mother watching over her baby and giving it food—the primal instinct of a mother's love and protection for her young. It's so poignant. It transcends all words."

He's sensitive. I had no idea. "You saw all that in one picture? Amazing!"

"Ah," he playfully touched the tip of her nose with his finger, "it was you, the photographer who saw it first ... capturing that one moment in time, forever preserved for others to enjoy."

Kyle's a good person. "You do the same—with your writing—creating people and situations that will live on the screen." Ned caught her eye from across the room. "I wonder what it would be like to be in front of the camera and not behind it."

"In front of the camera is a meat market." He tapped his finger on the table. "*Behind* the camera will keep you fed and a roof over your head." He scoffed. "Modeling, acting, and the rest of it is a blessing for very few. The shine of glamour soon wanes with the onslaught of time."

From the periphery, Ned's glare bore into her, beckoning her to his world. Elizabeth tried to avoid his eyes but something like an invisible string pulled her to him. She hoped Kyle hadn't noticed.

"Either way, I'm happy where I'm at. I know where I'm at, caring for Lady Amelia." She laughed. "I was just daydreaming about something more."

She looked at Ned and for a brief moment, wished he were talking to her and not Kyle.

"Daydreams can become tomorrow's reality." He stroked her hand with his thumb.

"Maybe, someday." Elizabeth pulled her hand away. She glanced at her watch. "I need to be going. I have to find my friend, Beverly."

"I can take you home." Hope dwelled in his eyes.

"I live in Malibu and so does she." Elizabeth rose from the table.

He grabbed her hand. "Won't you reconsider? Your friend knows the ropes. She can fend for herself."

"No, it wouldn't be right." She glanced over her shoulder. Ned was still staring. His eyes gave her a thrill, and her stomach tightened as he studied her every move. The tip of his tongue peeked between his lips. Her breath caught in her throat.

Elizabeth pulled away and walked toward the bar, searching for Beverly. She was relieved that Kyle hadn't follow her and pressed his cause.

As she passed, Ned nearly whispered, "Don't forget. You have my card."

My, my, Ned and Kyle. America is certainly a bounty of riches. Which bloke do I fancy? Hmm, Kyle is nice ... but Ned is so hot. He puts a bag of fiery coals in me knickers.

~ END *Twisted Intent* Excerpt ~
Release date yet to be determined.

MEET CYNTHIA

Cynthia B. Ainsworthe and Barry Manilow

Cynthia has longed to become a writer. Life's circumstances put her dream on hold for most of her life. In 2008 she ventured to write her first novel, *Front Row Center*, which won the prestigious IPPY (Independent Publisher) Award. This novel is now being adapted to screen. A script is in development by her and notable Hollywood screenwriter, producer, and director, Scott C. Brown. Cynthia has been a guest on several talk radio shows. As a retired cardiac RN turned author, Cynthia enjoys her retirement in Florida, caring for her husband and their five poodle-children.

Author Awards

2008 Prestigious IPPY Award in romance, *Front Row Center*
2013 Reader's Favorite International Award in fiction anthology, *The Speed of Dark* for two contributing sories: When Midnight Comes and Characters.
2013 Excellence in Writing Award, It Matters Radio, short story It Ain't Fittin'

Dear Reader Friend,

Thank you for reading my book. I hope you have enjoyed my story. I had a few laughs and some tears while writing this novel.

Please visit my website and sign the contact form so that we might keep in touch through my newsletter.

If you enjoyed it, won't you please take a moment to leave me a review at your favorite retailer? Don't hesitate to reach out to me on social media. My links are on the following page.

Thanks!

Cynthia

Visit Cynthia at:

Check out my website and sign up for my newsletter:
https://www.cynthiabainsworthe.com/

Please follow my Amazon Author Page:
https://www.amazon.com/Cynthia-B.-Ainsworthe/e/B00KYRE1Q8

View my book trailer/s:
https://www.youtube.com/watch?v=qhK7prWYxhk

Friend me on Facebook at:
https://www.facebook.com/cynthia.b.ainswortheauthor

Please like my Facebook Fan Page:
https://www.facebook.com/CynBAinswortheAuthor/

Follow my Blogs: http://ainsworthe1.wordpress.com/ And:
http://cynthiaswordsandpassion.blogspot.com/

Follow me on Twitter:
https://twitter.com/CynB_Ainsworthe

Follow me on Google+:
https://plus.google.com/+CynthiaBAinsworthe/posts/p/pub

Be my friend on Goodreads:
https://www.goodreads.com/CynthiaBAinsworthe

Let's connect on LinkedIn:
https://www.linkedin.com/in/cynthiabainsworthe/